Rough Terrain

Rough Terrain

◆

Hadley Hoover

Writers Club Press
San Jose New York Lincoln Shanghai

Rough Terrain

All Rights Reserved © 2001 by Hadley Hoover

No part of this book may be reproduced or transmitted in any form or by any means, graphic, electronic, or mechanical, including photocopying, recording, taping, or by any information storage retrieval system, without the permission in writing from the publisher.

Writers Club Press
an imprint of iUniverse, Inc.

For information address:
iUniverse, Inc.
5220 S. 16th St., Suite 200
Lincoln, NE 68512
www.iuniverse.com

Rough Terrain is a work of fiction. Names, characters or their conversations, places, and incidents are the product of the author's imagination or are used fictitiously. Any resemblance to actual events, locales, or persons living or dead is entirely coincidental.

ISBN: 0-595-20408-2

Printed in the United States of America

To my bearded guy: thanks for the years gone by, the promise of those still to come, and all the dreams and memories that form a solid foundation beneath our love.

Acknowledgements

◆

"In Ourselves Our Future Lies"
Thanks for the memories.
To my MOCHS Classmates

Linda Aalberts
Jan Bolluyt
Mary Bonnecroy
Sheryl Calsbeek
Jane Casey
Arthur De Goei
Gary De Haan
Lyla Dekker
Jane De Koster
Elaine De Koter
Muriel De Vries
Bonnie Doppenberg
Donna Duven
Kent Eknes
Kary Gesink
Henrietta Hibma
Alan Hofland
Carol Hulsart
Barbara Jacobs
Ruth Jahn
Ronald Jasper
Jane Jonker
Lynnette Keith
Beverly Kleinhesselink
Cheryl Kleinhesselink
Linda Korver
Mark Kraai
Rodney Kreykes
Arlin Kuiken

Paul Lubbers
Alan Menning
Sherlynn Menning
Willa Meylink
Donald Mouw
Conrad Muilenburg
Franklin Noteboom
Loren Olson
Helen Oolman
Jacob Oolman
Larry Oolman
Frank Osdoba
Audrey Pennings
Harlan Peuse
Lynn Peuse
Arlin Schalekamp
Linda Sybesma
Ronald Vander Weerd
Jay Vander Wilt
Marcia Van Gorp
Willliam Van Horssen
Cheryl Van Regenmorter
Judith Van Steenwyk
Judith Van Zanten
Rodger Ver Hoeven
Sandra Vlieger
Ivan Wiersema
Mary Viersema
Deceased indicated by italics

Contents

◆

October 1907—February 1908	1
June 1912	19
Summer 1916	39
1917	64
1918	107
January—August 1919	139
September 1919	171
October 1919	236
November 1919—February 1920	256
March—May 1920	273
May 1924—May 1927	306
June 1927—August 1940	323

October 1907—February 1908

♦

With windows closed tightly against night chills, Hans and Rebecca de Boer hovered over beds on opposite sides of their sons' room. The light from the single lamp was low, but shadows against the walls loomed as large as the couple's fears. Hans stood at the foot of one bed, his work-worn hands alternately clutching the bedpost and checking his pocket watch. Helpless and silent, he watched their youngest child, Cornelis, toss beneath the patchwork quilts.

Eyes swollen to mere slits, the eight-year-old boy's face appeared flushed in the dim light. His body seemed even smaller beneath his puffy face. His eyelashes, long and curling russet wisps against his cheeks, matched the mop of auburn hair that clung to his damp brow. Cornelis needed to sleep—as did his parents, now ragged with exhaustion after many unsettled nights and restless days—but sleep was elusive.

Across the room, Rebecca exhibited none of her husband's control and sobbed quietly. Kneeling beside the other bed, she caressed Bram's hand. Their eldest son had grown increasingly uneasy beneath his tousled bedclothes as the night progressed. While both boys shared symptoms of aches, sore throats, and malaise, Bram also complained of chest pains and fatigue unrelieved even by rest. He often flung off the covers, drenched with his perspiration—all the more worrisome for the persistent cough that left him short of breath.

Tonight was the worst. Hours ago, Hans had sent word to the doctor through a neighbor, but still no help came. When Bram opened his eyes and looked into hers with wordless anguish, it pierced Rebecca's mother-heart. "Can you hear anything, Hans?" she asked as she brushed strands of black hair back from Bram's feverish face.

"No, 'Becca. Not yet. But he'll come. Doc Draayer's word is good." In his heart he, too, wondered at the delay. *Two boys. Our hopes and dreams.* "He's on his way. We're not the only household around Dutchville with illness and *strubbeling* tonight."

The whinny of the doctor's horse offered the night's first spark of hope. Rebecca rushed to meet Doc Draayer on the porch and escort him to where three who formed the circle of her life awaited his skills.

Moving a lantern closer to each bed, Doc Draayer examined first Cornelis, then Bram. His face masked the thoughts behind his calming murmurs. Each boy rested easier after his ministrations. Finally, the doctor smoothed the quilts beneath Bram's chin and, with a final pat, nodded at the waiting parents. The three adults filed out to the kitchen where Rebecca hastened to pour cups of strong Dutch coffee from the pot that simmered on the wood-burning stove.

Saturated with the pleasant reminders of Rebecca's cooking, the kitchen provided a safe harbor in which to hear the doctor's verdict. "Your boys have had a siege of it, Hans, Rebecca. They are far from well yet, as you know, but the worst will be over soon. Continue with the medicine I left with you before and feed them broth and tea even if they ask for food. You have done a fine job of caring for them."

Though the doctor's manner was comforting, Hans and Rebecca sensed he had more to say. Instinctively, they reached for each other beneath the table; Rebecca shot a quick glance at her husband when his strong hand shook within her grasp. She had often teased him that he resembled *Sinterklaas* with his portly build, long beard, and twinkling eyes, but there was nothing jovial about her husband tonight. Dread lurched in their hearts as they waited.

"Young Cornelis will be fine. Eight years is a good age to have mumps. Soon you will have both boys out in the fields with you, Hans."

"But Bram…what about Bram, *Dokter*?" In his distress, Hans lapsed into the familiar Dutch. "You said Cornelis would be fine. But how long before Bram recovers from this *ziekte*? He'll be in the barn and fields with me, too, right?" The pitch of Hans' usually steady voice rose until the final question in his native tongue was almost shrill.

Gerrit Draayer tugged at his beard and shifted his eyeglasses to rub red-rimmed eyes. With the surge of mumps cases in the past month and rumors of tuberculosis in nearby communities, his days and nights had melted into one seemingly endless muddle. But this visit tonight required more than his medical skills—for this news, he longed for Solomon's wisdom. "You noticed how Bram cried out when I examined him?"

Rebecca nodded and flushed. The blankets had formed a shield for the doctor's scrutiny, but from having cared for her son's most personal needs over the past days, she knew exactly where his hands had probed. Giving Bram a bed-bath earlier today, she, too, had elicited sharp outcries from him.

Doc Draayer turned to Hans. "Bram is twelve now?"

"Soon to be thirteen. He's grown strong and tall for his age."

"I remember when I delivered Abraham. A fine young man from the start, your Bram. When I swatted him, he cried so loudly even I was startled!"

Rebecca took a deep breath. "What is wrong with Bram?"

Knowing she was now ready to hear, the doctor responded with a soothing voice, "No one wants to be sick, but some illnesses should come when we are young like Cornelis. When those same diseases strike us at an older age, we can have problems. Hans, recall when I asked if you'd had mumps as a child?"

"Yes. It was almost your first question when we called you."

The doctor nodded. "I was worried about you being near him if you had not had mumps. With Bram's rapid growth, he is more a young man than a child. I believe my earlier suspicions have played out. Because of the effects of this disease on his young body, I fear Bram may not be able to father children."

Rebecca's coffee sloshed in her cup. Hans' rapid intake of air hung around them like a sob.

"Mind you, I am not fully certain, but I would be remiss if I did not speak honestly. It may be the swelling and pain and tenderness so evident tonight will pass without damage. But there is also the chance his genitals have been affected, rendering him sterile. I am sorry to speak so plainly, Rebecca, but I do not want to cloud your understanding."

Rebecca stared numbly at the doctor's face until her vision blurred.

"How soon...?" Hans could not form a question to give shape to his despair.

"It may be years. Medicine in 1907 has come a long way from the last century, but there is still much to discover. We learn more every day. Typhoid Mary's arrest in New York last March was possible only because of what we now know about infections."

"*Ja*, 1907 is a good time to be *levend*," murmured Hans, half-listening, half-floundering in fearful contemplation.

"You need not say anything at all to Bram now. His recovery in all other areas appears to be sure. When he begins to court one of the pretty Dutch girls who swarm to him like bees around honey, speak to him then about his possible condition. Or have him come talk to me. Now is not the time to burden a young fellow with something outside the realm of his experience."

"Is there a chance you are mistaken?" Hans' trusting gaze robbed his words of any accusation.

"Yes. His symptoms are not limited to mumps, so it is possible that he contracted something else in his weakened condition. I will watch him closely, especially since he has developed such a cough since I last saw him."

"And it could be that he will be fine?" Rebecca leaned forward hopefully.

"Yes, it could be he will recover fully. Only our Heavenly Father knows, and good Dutchmen like ourselves know to trust Him."

Hans sank back in his chair, his ramrod posture abandoned momentarily. "This is not something others need to know, is it? Especially if it all turns out to be nothing."

"My records on his case will relate only the known facts, no suspicions. Now I must go." The two men shook hands as the doctor gathered his cap and bag.

"Are you heading home, at last?" Hans asked.

"Yes. I'm sorry to have been so late coming to you, but there is sadness at *Dominie* Ter Hoorn's home. Gustave and Hanna's infant was stillborn tonight."

Rebecca's fingers pressed against her lips as tears clouded her vision. "The *Dominie* and Hanna have waited so long, and now this. What can we do? I know Lena is there, but I want to do something."

"With illness at your house, it is best you do nothing now. Hanna will appreciate a visit later, and perhaps one of your special cakes would lighten Lena's load." Rebecca nodded and twisted a corner of her apron absentmindedly.

Beneath clouds that flirted with the moon, Hans and Rebecca watched their friend and physician climb wearily into his waiting buggy. With heavy feet and hearts, they headed back to the house.

An owl hooted eerily as they leaned numbly against a porch post; Rebecca shivered and Hans pulled her into an embrace. "Our problems, though hard to bear, seem small compared to our *Dominie's* tonight. He carries a heavy burden," Hans murmured, rubbing his chin against her hair.

As the doctor's horse took him along the bumpy road back to town, Hans waited for Rebecca to reach the boys' bedroom before he extinguished the kitchen lamp and joined her beside Bram's bed. They joined hands; each knew the other was raising the same prayer of desperate petition for their first-born son and the other lives devastated this night at the Ter Hoorn house.

Gerrit Draayer slowed his horse as he neared the corner the Dutchville Reformed Church dominated. One light still burned in an upstairs room of the house in the shadow of the church: the home of *Dominie* Gustave Ter Hoorn and his family. A sad, fragile family it was tonight.

Inside that room, the lamp cast a shadow across Gustave's open Bible as he sat beside Hanna's bed. Their only daughter, Brigetta, slept alone in a bedroom large enough for several more children to share.

One afternoon early in Hanna's pregnancy, Brigetta had overheard a conversation not intended for young ears. Since then, she had prayed regularly for a little sister. But tonight's events slammed shut that window of hope. Doc Draayer had said firmly, but compassionately, there could be no more children born to Gustave and Hanna.

After the doctor left, Gustave returned to the bedroom and leaned against the doorframe for a long time. The woman in the bed was his completeness—his first and only love. *And now the act of our shared passions must be monitored?* His sorrow overwhelmed him like waves of a stormy sea battering the frail vessel of his soul.

He helped his sister-in-law change the soiled linens. Offering his thanks, he then sent her off to bed. Though saddened by her sister's stillborn child, Lena needed to rest before the next day's responsibilities rose with the sun. Lena was a good woman, willingly taking on many duties that should have been borne by the minister's wife. In return, she received both Brigetta's unrestrained love and Gustave's heartfelt gratitude to counterbalance Hanna's silence.

Setting aside her own goals to be a teacher, Lena had stayed with them for nearly seven years—it was that long since Brigetta's birth and Hanna's retreat into an unreachable world. Seven years since his frantic telegram to his sister-in-law: *Come immediately? Hanna ill, baby healthy. Gustave.* Not only had she journeyed cross-country on the next westbound train, Lena had stayed with them. Without Lena in their lives…Gustave allowed an almost forbidden thought: without Lena, he wondered how his faith in God would have weathered the years. She was daily evidence of God's love and care for his family.

Gustave stared, unseeing, at the pages of the Dutch Bible in his hands. He found no comfort there tonight. Since Brigetta's birth, he had seen his beloved Hanna sink into a depression so profound she no longer reached out to him. He often wondered if she prayed.

Before Brigetta's birth, he had often halted his studies when he heard Hanna's lilting voice lifted in praise as she sang, with the Psalter perched above the dishpan and opened to Number 150, her favorite of all Dutch *Psalmen: Hallelujah! Looft God in Zijn heiligdom; looft Hem in het uitspansel Zijner sterkte…*Those bright days had faded long ago. Hanna's Bible often lay untouched for weeks, her Psalter tucked beneath it.

But Doc Draayer had rejoiced with him when they finally dared to hope that Hanna could carry this child to full term. For several months, Gustave believed the sun would shine again in their marriage.

There was nothing in the quiet vigil beside his wife's bed tonight to mute the echo of the doctor's words that day three months ago: "*Gustave, even though Hanna's sadness has deepened with each miscarriage, once she holds this child, she will see beyond the valley of despair where she has lived so long.*"

Gustave remembered the gist of his reply: "Perhaps. I still see how she was when Brigetta was born. At a time when most mothers rejoice, she began the weeping that continues almost daily. She became so distant…sometimes, I would come into a room and see her watching Brigetta with such detachment it chilled me. Through the years, she has steadily withdrawn. Part of me hopes it will be different with this child, but part of me fears…"

There had been no need to name his fear to Gerrit Draayer. The doctor had weighed each word as carefully as he measured medicine: "You and Lena have never faltered in your love for Hanna. Brigetta's unquestioning acceptance and devotion for her mother is like a balm. When someone has a visible physical condition, we know they are unable to do the same work as others without that problem. We must allow those who have an invisible condition—Hanna—the same respect and concessions. You and Lena have done that, and you have raised Brigetta to love and honor her mother even though Hanna is not like other mothers."

Gustave now looked at Hanna, her face as white as the pillow beneath her head. He had told the doctor: *"Lena once lived in her sister's shadow— Hanna shone like the sun, and Lena merely reflected all her brightness. When you look at Lena now, you see a spark of what Hanna was like."*

The doctor's reply had brought comfort then: *"Brigetta brings that same sunlight to all who meet her—she, too, is like the old Hanna. Perhaps the Hanna you see only in your mind will return."* But the trauma of this night had snatched that modicum of comfort and thrown it like feathers to the far winds.

The long-awaited day of birthing had come and gone, and with it any expectations for a transformed Hanna had fled. Gustave watched his wife's still form in the four-poster bed they had shared for nearly a decade. Doc Draayer had given her a sleeping potion, but in the morning—*in the morning*…Gustave buried his face in his hands. A chill brushed over his spirit as doubt did battle with faith.

Helplessly, he had watched Hanna flounder in the seas of depression through several miscarriages. Any lifelines he had thrown—whether compassion, loving acceptance, or attempted understanding—had been rejected. He now feared she would sink beneath the surface, out of his grasp, beyond the reach of human help.

As pastor of the Dutchville Reformed Church that loomed beside the parsonage, Gustave had often stood at other bedsides with equal sadness. Tonight, he cried out alone to his God for solace.

Beneath a hazy Iowa sky, Doc Draayer passed along the street and, seeing the single light still flickering in the window, offered his petitions for peace in the midst of such trials.

One doctor. Two families. And on this 1907 autumn night, the silence from heaven tested their faith.

*   *   *

One brisk February Saturday morning, Brigetta tiptoed between the church pews. Each week, she dusted the long wooden benches and straightened Psalters in the racks in preparation for services on the Lord's Day. For completing these tasks, she received three pennies from Papa: one for the collection basket, one for the pretty jar on her dresser, and one to spend as she wished. Usually she was alone in the sanctuary, but today Mister De Haan worked with the boys' catechism class as they recited the Nicene Creed and Heidelberg Catechism's questions and answers.

Tomorrow, these gangly disheveled boys would look quite different than the ones who now shifted from foot-to-foot, responding when called upon, but otherwise itching to get away. Sunday, they would graduate from catechism class. Today, the boys fidgeted and poked each other and generally behaved as if Mister De Haan were blind to their antics.

Brigetta, who was learning a shortened version of the catechism in the younger children's classes, whispered scattered sections along with the boys' singsong responses. Mister De Haan finally closed his book and enumerated his expectations for their demeanor the following day, stressing the importance of speaking up so the people in the last row could hear them.

The power of suggestion was strong; all eyes sought out the last pew where Brigetta sat quietly, having finished her tasks. "Hello, Brigetta! What do you think? Has my class performed well enough to be excused?"

Brigetta bobbed her head in response. Within seconds, the boys whooped their way past her in a mad dash to the coat racks in the narthex, the rhythmic brush of *klompen* along the aisle carpet-runner drowning out Mister De Haan's futile pleas of "No running in church, *knaaps!*"

Their excited voices mingled as they grabbed coats and hats and mittens. "Last one to the river is a rotten egg!" Brigetta heard the church door open and close; she hugged herself with delight. *The boys are going skating!*

Papa had strict rules about Brigetta ever skating alone, and since her friend, Mary, was housebound with a cold, she had nearly despaired of skating any time soon. But now, she could skate to her heart's content and still obey Papa's rules. There was no more delightful way to spend a cold, crisp Saturday morning.

"I'm going to the river with the catechism class!" she shouted through the kitchen door. Grabbing her skating boots and blades from the hook behind the kitchen door, she soon pounded along the foot-packed trail.

The section of the river designated as the skating rink was bordered with waist-high mounds of snow. Within those boundaries was a winter wonderland of invigorating air, abundant exercise, and friendly games and competitions.

Since it was still quite early in the morning, only the catechism class populated the ice. Later, with Saturday chores completed, families, groups of children, and couples who skated hand-over-hand, their bodies swaying in perfect rhythm would answer the call of the frozen river.

Throughout the day, grandparents—those who walked slowly from pillar-to-post on land—glided with grace and renewed vigor along the ice. Their eyes glistening with memories of Holland's frozen canals on wintry days gone by, they nodded to others with gray hair and silver skates, as all dipped and swept across the ribbon of river, with hands clasped behind their backs.

Brigetta hastened to buckle the blades onto her skating shoes and soon joined the boys who fanned out across the slick surface. The air hummed with the sounds of crackling ice and merry voices. Wrapping her long scarf around her neck and flinging both ends over her shoulders, she pulled the matching woolen hat a little lower over her ears.

She felt like singing and shouting and spinning—so she did all three. When the frosty air rushed into her lungs, she quickly switched from singing to humming and, after startling the boys with her gleeful shouts, decided to concentrate on spinning.

The boys chased each other and raced from side to side, often crossing in front of Brigetta at break-neck speeds. She ignored them, staying out of their way as they played rough-and-tumble games. She tried to remember all that Papa had taught her about executing a perfect figure-eight and attempted to imitate *Tante* Lena and Mama with their graceful swan-like movements.

Abruptly, a blur took shape as it skidded to a stop in front of her. Red-cheeked and panting, Bram de Boer towered over her. "Hey! Do you want to play crack the whip with us? You can be the tail."

"Me?"

"Yeah, thanks to you, Mister De Haan let us out a little early. Come on!"

The tail! The most exhilarating position on a crack-the-whip chain! Mindful of her father's concerns and aware an accounting would be expected, she asked gravely, "Are you grown-up yet, Bram?"

"Huh? I'm half-way between thirteen and fourteen—just today I've finished my last recitations of the Heidelberg Catechism, don't you know!" he boasted. "That means I'm accountable for my own self now. But, what's that got to do with you skating?" He filled an invisible circle on the ice with intricate designs in a flurry of swoops and dramatic spins as he waited for her answer.

Almost fourteen—that's ancient! "Let's go!"

Bram grabbed her hand and pulled her along with him back to the boys clustered on the opposite side of the river. "Brigetta gets to be the tail. Whoever is next to her, hang on tight; she's just a little kid." The natural leader of the group, Bram skated to the front of the line that quickly formed, mittened hand grasping mittened hand.

Like a schooner at sea, Bram cut through the wind and propelled his followers on a wild adventure. They moved in a straight line until he dipped to one side and it became an "S" and then he cut back and the line jerked from a "U" to an "L" with Brigetta's delighted squeals marking each shift.

She clung to the hand that linked her to the others and scarcely breathed. Her scarf whipped the air behind her, sometimes obscuring her view until another gust blew it away. *Skating has never been such fun!* Only the tip of her other skate connected her to reality. *I feel like a bird! Ooooh! Did my hand slip?* Before she could reinforce her connection, she truly was flying, clutching a boy's empty mitten in her hand.

Even when she finally landed, she didn't come to a complete stop. She continued to skim along the ice, the secrets of the river screeching wildly in her left ear, until she crashed, face-first, into the boundary wall of crusty snow. At last she lay still, knocked breathless and nearly unconscious.

A thundering herd of scared boys reached her side, but she was only dimly aware of them. Through a cold and distant fog she could hear accusations, scared speculations, and Bram's shaky voice above the din: "It's all my fault!"

No! It's my fault—I let go! Her protests went unheard and unspoken, trapped in her mind.

"Move back. I'll carry her home and tell the *Dominie* what happened," Bram said, taking charge. His skates hit the ice with a thud, their buckles tinkling upon impact. Brigetta felt herself being lifted off the ice.

Voices mingled: "She's bleeding a lot!" and "Take off her skate—her foot is twisted!" and "Here's her hat!"

These ministrations complete, Bram shuffled to the edge of the river, his body trembling both from the weight of his burden and fear. He clutched Brigetta against his chest and struggled up the slope. With each jerky step Bram took, Brigetta's seeping wounds rubbed against his rough-weave coat. She stirred; his grip tightened and pinned her nose against a button. Everything inside her seemed jarred, and the cold air hurt with each breath.

She moaned as they bumped along and a responding sob rose from Bram's chest. "Don't-die-don't-die-don't-die! Please-God-please-please-don't-let-her-die!" His pace increased until his breathing echoed like a tugboat's note: tuneless and haunting.

By the time he reached the corner of the churchyard, Bram's breathing was ragged. Brigetta was lighter than the hay bales he hefted from haymow to feeding troughs, but he didn't usually carry hay up from the river, along three streets, and across the churchyard to the parsonage. His muscles burned, but he dared not stop.

For the first time, he looked intently at the load he was carrying and felt something inside him tilt like the arms of the Dutch windmill in the town square. Brigetta was just a kid, but her eyelashes fluttered like the wings of a soaring bird and her skin—where it wasn't bruised and broken—was the creamy pink of his mother's favorite summer flowers. White-blonde curls created an exquisite frame for the heart-shaped face that was swelling to lopsided proportions.

It was this thirteen-year-old boy's first occasion to closely observe a girl. What he saw took hold of his senses and shook them up like soil from a newly plowed field in a windstorm. He swallowed hard and lengthened his stride along the foot-stomped path to the back door of the parsonage.

Tante Lena was cleaning the parlor when she noticed a most unusual sight through the lacy curtain. A staggering boy carried some sort of a cumbersome package across the lawn. Her curiosity hooked, she pulled back the curtain to watch his slow progress. When he got closer, she recognized a red tasseled scarf and cap and flung her feather duster aside with a scream, "Brigetta's hurt!" Hanna and Gustave pounded down the stairs and all met at the back door.

Bram stumbled across the kitchen and relinquished his precious load to the tabletop. Lena quickly wet a dishtowel and gently pressed it against Brigetta's nose and face to stem the bleeding. Hanna carefully loosened Brigetta's clothing. Gustave searched for broken bones.

All three voices became a cacophony of sound soon joined by Bram's quavering words behind them. He offered up the full story in a frightened jumble of facts and emotions. "*Dominie*-this-is-all-my-fault-I-asked-Brigetta-to-be-the-tail-for-crack-the-whip-and-I-was-the-lead-and-didn't-stop-to-think-that-she-was-too-little-and-couldn't-keep-up-I-am-terribly-sorry-and-if-you-don't-want-me-to-take-communion-tomorrow-I-understand."

Gustave had paid scant attention to Bram in his overriding concern for his daughter, but the confession nested in Bram's rush of words snagged him. "Bram, thank you for bringing Brigetta home. Perhaps inviting her to skate with older, stronger boys didn't show the greatest wisdom, but your honesty and courage outweigh that lack of judgment. I will gladly serve you communion tomorrow." Gustave pulled his eyes away from his daughter to look at the young fellow. Heart-wrenching agony was evident in every inch of the lad's posture.

"I am so sorry," Bram's voice trembled

Gustave said soothingly, "Son, perhaps you could find Doc Draayer on your way home and ask him to come by?" Bram nodded and, after one sorrowful look at the kitchen table, fled from the parsonage.

Bram raced to the doctor's house. *What if she dies all because of some stupid game? She's such a funny little kid—always using big words and singing the Psalmens so loud that the old men smile.*

He could not imagine anyone in his family possessing even a fistful of the zest for living that Brigetta exuded. *And now I have maimed her for life.* He sobbed and ran all the harder, crossing through back yards, ducking behind buildings.

Within a short time, the doctor knocked on the parsonage's kitchen door and held out a pair of *klompen* to Lena. "You might want to bring these in or someone's feet will be quite cold."

A surprised Lena accepted them and stepped aside so the doctor could enter. "Bram must have gone back to the river to get them—they are Brigetta's. She was still wearing her skating shoes when he carried her home."

Doc Draayer conducted a thorough examination and finally turned to assure the anxious family that her injuries were surprisingly limited, given the circumstances. A broken nose, the potential for quite a few colorful bruises, and a twisted ankle that would mend itself in a couple of weeks were all he noted.

"When can I go skating again?" Brigetta asked faintly from the sofa.

"Let's not set any specific time just yet. Let your Papa carry you up to bed tonight—no heroics from you!" the doctor cautioned with a smile before following Lena and Hanna to the kitchen to give more detailed nursing instructions.

Brigetta insisted on going to church on the next day. "I want to hear the catechism class recite," she pleaded. "Papa can carry me and I'll sit as quiet as can be in the back pew with my ankle on a pillow. Please!"

"You will hear the girls' class next week," Gustave promised.

"If I don't go tomorrow, the boys will think they killed me. They *must* see that I'm still alive." Gustave and Hanna offered futile arguments and Lena snorted her opinion of such folly, but Sunday found all four in church.

After services, Brigetta held court at the back of the sanctuary for each member of the boys' class, all of whom were impressed with the array of black, blue, purple, and hints of orange that had spread across

16 Rough Terrain

her face overnight. She regally shook each boy's hand, assuring him she bore no hard feelings.

Bram had hovered at the end of the line of solicitous well-wishers. When the last boy had moved out of view, Bram shyly pulled his fisted hand from his pocket. "Here. I carved this for you. I only had time to do one, but someday I'll make you another one if you'd like."

Brigetta opened the tissue-papered lump, damp from being clutched in Bram's hand for the whole morning. Sheer bliss transformed her bruised face and produced new and wondrous sensations inside Bram. "Oh, a little skate—tiny enough for a doll! It's beautiful, Bram. Thank you! No one ever gave me anything like this before."

Bram blushed furiously and jammed his hands back into his pockets. "I know you like to skate—and you're good, for a girl. I'm sorry you got hurt."

"I had lots of fun—until the end, I mean. I can hardly wait to get back on the ice!"

Bram turned and fled, leaving Brigetta unaware that she had snared his affection as surely as the traps he set in the woods captured unsuspecting game.

Several guests joined the Ter Hoorn family for Sunday dinner. Tucked in among the conversational gambits around the table came Brigetta's question, "Papa, how old are you?" She fingered the small carving hidden in the pocket of her Sunday dress.

"Thirty-three." Seeing Brigetta's glance rest next on her mother, Gustave added with a chuckle, "Before you ask your Mama, I'll give you her answer, but you will need to use arithmetic to solve it! Here it is: I met your Mama when she was a pretty sixteen-year-old. Now, a decade plus one year later, she's even more beautiful."

The adults smiled and resumed their tableside conversation while Brigetta performed mental calculations to determine the answer to her ultimate unasked question: *Can a girl marry a boy who is five years older?*

At the de Boer farm just outside Dutchville, a festive meal was nearly ready. Hans' parents had walked across the farmyard to join their son and his family in the big house. Celebrating the spiritual milestone of Bram's completed catechism was a long-awaited family event.

Bram excused himself from visiting with his beloved grandparents in the parlor where they waited to be called to the table. *Cornelis can talk to them without me—I have something important to do before dinner.*

The night before, with moonlight streaming through the window and Cornelis sleeping soundly across the room, Bram had worked long past his bedtime. Each twist of his pocketknife had quietly shaped a chunk of soft wood into the boy's first gift to a girl.

Alone in the now sunlit bedroom, he hurriedly scooped up the pile of wood scraps he had brushed under the rug in his rush to get ready for church this morning. He hastened to clean up his mess before Cornelis would find it and ask questions. Carefully, he sought out every sliver lest Mother would discover some stray shaving and wonder why he had been carving in the bedroom rather than his usual spot over the wood-bin in the kitchen.

The memory of Brigetta's pleasure over his gift made him straighten his shoulders. His knees had jiggled like his mother's custard when Brigetta said all those nice things about the carved skate; but now he stood a little taller and felt more grown up. For a girl, Brigetta was really quite pleasant. He was glad he had made the carving for her—it was the gentlemanly thing to do. *Mother always says she wants Cornelis and me to be kind and gracious gentlemen.*

He wrapped the leftover hunk of wood in a bandana and tucked it in the back of his dresser drawer. Since he had promised to carve another skate, he was glad that the remaining piece allowed the two skates to match perfectly.

Twisting the newspaper containing the shavings into a rope-like casing, he made a surreptitious detour past the wood box and then joined his family for the best meal of the week: Sunday dinner. He inhaled the fragrant roasted chicken that had baked all morning. When he spotted the dish Rebecca always used for sweet-sour cabbage, all other musings fled.

This is my big day! Bram knew that, after dessert, Grandfather de Boer would sift through his coin purse and pull out something silver to commemorate today's special event. Then, Grandfather would probably tell how, long ago in Holland, he had learned not only the full Heidelberg Catechism with its one-hundred-and twenty-nine questions and answers, but the Belgic Confession, too.

Bram's seventy-nine memorized catechism questions and answers were just the beginning if he were to hold his Dutch heritage in high regard. But today was an important start—his family recognized that. It was obvious his mother had been thinking proud thoughts when she baked the almond-filled butter cake he saw on the buffet. As he circled the table to reach his chair, he wrapped his arms around Rebecca in a quick hug that made her smile.

Today, in the eyes of the Dutch Reformed Church, Bram became accountable—a man, in many respects. He realized this, having heard it repeatedly from Mister De Haan throughout the months of catechism classes. But here in the presence of his family, he was glad to still be a *knapp* whose mother fixed his favorites in honor of special occasions. She firmly believed that certain events in life deserved distinct recognition, and this was his day.

The image of the carved skate in Brigetta's hands flitted across Bram's mind. Making a present for her had been like Grandfather opening his coin purse and Mother baking butter cake to mark this day. At first, he had considered it the right thing to do; now he wondered, *Will she think I'm silly?* He accepted a second helping of potatoes and stuffed all thoughts of Brigetta and her shining eyes into the back corner of his memories just like the piece of wood hidden in his drawer.

June 1912

◆

Brigetta rested beneath the coverlet on her bed and pulled the quilted spread up to her chin as a finger of fear scratched its way across her thoughts. For six hours she had been harboring a shattering secret; she needed to ponder all ramifications before she told anyone.

She knew Papa was in his study with books and papers spread all around as he hunched over the big roll-top desk. From time to time the clatter of his big old typewriter with Remington in fancy gold letters echoed down the hall. It was a most familiar sound to Brigetta: Papa was fine-tuning his next sermon. Usually, she would never interrupt him.

Poor, sweet Papa. Her news would devastate him. *Devastate: a word from last week's vocabulary test.* It was as if Miss Wiersma had known that at least one of her pupils would require such a perfect word. Brigetta had certainly never had occasion before this calamity.

Her life had been a series of joys: crisp lace-trimmed blouses; *vet and stroop* with lots of syrup for special breakfasts; colorful hair ribbons in her *klompen* from *Sinterklaas;* spelling bees—which she adored; a best friend who was like a sister; and the affection of three adults. When she offered the thanksgiving prayer to end each meal, it was impossible to squeeze everything on her list into one prayer. Hardly a storm cloud had blotted the skies of her life. Until now.

It will be so hard on Papa when he learns of my tragedy. She was astute enough to realize he carried a heavy burden about Mama. *And now I add this terrible trauma to his life.* Her lower lip trembled and she reached blindly for a dry handkerchief from the diminishing pile to stem her renewed flood of tears.

She knew children at school wondered about Mama, though no one dared to ask specific questions. Other mothers came to school events and bought supplies from Vander Molen's store and talked over back fences. Not Mama. As long as Brigetta could remember, *Tante* Lena had done those things. *Tante* Lena filled the motherly void.

Mama seemed to float through the house, occasionally landing in a chair, willing to listen, but rarely asking about activities or opinions. If it was not a day when she cried quietly in the parlor chair, she welcomed Brigetta to climb up the little wooden bed-steps to cuddle beneath an afghan after school.

Mama knitted and quilted, made cornbread and worked with *Tante* Lena putting up jams and jellies in crocks, and sometimes weeded the section of the garden where her special flowers grew in profusion. But she never inquired about the things going on around her, and she was often sad and tired—even though she napped frequently. Mama was rather like an imaginary friend, at times.

Papa had talked to Brigetta, years ago, about Mama. From her vague memories of that conversation, she carried two impressions: Mama had "a depression," and there would be no baby brothers or sisters. She was quite unclear just what "a depression" was, imagining it to be large, dark, and silent like the covered well in the back yard. She fantasized herself as a squeaky pump, bringing up gushes of Mama to catch in her hands, treasures from the unseen depths of the earth. Sometimes she covertly watched her mother, hoping to catch a glimpse of this puzzling and invisible depression. She saw only a beautiful, dark-haired, subdued and familiar figure—nothing frightening, nothing mysterious, just Mama.

Papa held the whole family together like flour paste and Brigetta knew he loved her fiercely. Other fathers rarely asked their children questions; they just told them things. Her Papa sat with her at breakfast, asked about her plans for a summer day, or helped her practice riddles to tell at recess, or listened to her latest adventures with Mary. In winter while she ate porridge before heading off to school, Papa included made-up words when he quizzed her for a spelling test and she would giggle until her sides ached. Papa was a larger-than-life friend.

And *Tante* Lena: she was the stemmed cherry atop an ice cream sundae, the perfect bow on the end of a braid, a wrapped *liquorice* drop if church services dragged on and on, the wiper-of-tears when Trixie died. *Tante* Lena was happy, inquisitive, and adventurous. She laughed heartily at Brigetta's stories from school, and sighed loudly over any injustices life served up to her niece. *Tante* Lena was love with skin on. Just thinking of her made Brigetta feel safe and happy at the same time.

A realization that the awkward precautions she had made for her current disaster were proving inadequate interrupted Brigetta's musings. Perching on the edge of the bed briefly, she inched her way along until she could grasp a bedpost and rest her head against it. *It is time to talk with Papa.*

She stood unnoticed in the study doorway, soaking up the sight of her father hard at work. "Papa?" she said in a voice suddenly tremulous.

"Yes, Brigetta?" He tipped his head to look over the rim of his spectacles. "Oh, you've been crying!" He held out his arms and she ran across the room to fling her head against his chest. Her tears soon drenched his collar.

Gustave patted her back and waited out her tears. He knew of no other Dutch girl like his Brigetta when it came to displaying emotions—one rarely had to wonder how she felt. Her heart was tender, and while impetuosity caused her to snitch a cookie or otherwise disobey, time alone with her conscience brought her around to full remorse.

When a hiccup told him her sobs had run their course, he asked, "Can you tell me what is troubling you?" wondering idly what sin she would confess today.

"Oh, Papa! I hate to weigh you down when I know you carry so many other burdens," she rushed on, oblivious to his twitching mustache, "but I am dying."

That startled Gustave out of his ruminations. *I was prepared for repentance, but dying?*

Brigetta burst into a fresh round of tears, partly because a burden shared truly is halved. But she sobbed uncontrollably also because the announcement to her father had brushed aside a curtain obscuring a haunting image—that of herself as a lifeless form.

Brigetta had little to go on, Trixie's demise being her sole encounter with the Grim Reaper. Thus, what she imagined came from Papa's telling of funerals he conducted, and on overheard tidbits about deaths in Dutchville. But her primary source of information about reaching the afterlife was her borderless imagination.

Even burrowed into the safe place of Papa's arms, she revisited the mirage of herself in a small satin-lined polished casket. She could see black-clothed Mama in the shadows, a veil hiding her tears from curious eyes. Close at hand would be *Tante* Lena sobbing uncontrollably, *She was too young to die!* and Papa bravely standing alone, often unable to speak during the graveside service he conducted.

Mary Huitink will be there, too, with terribly red eyes and a pocketful of sodden handkerchiefs. Mary will make other friends but always warn them: "I cherish you all, but Brigetta Ter Hoorn was my best friend from the time we were babies until she was taken to heaven at age twelve. No one can ever replace her in my affections."

Unaware of the melodramatic scenarios running rampant beneath the jumble of ringlets pressed against his chest, Gustave murmured wordless sounds and let the next wave of sorrow pound against unseen shores in his child's heart. "Tell me why you believe you are dying, Brigetta," he said gently, wiping away her last gush of tears with his own handkerchief. "Have you pain somewhere?"

Hadley Hoover 23

"I have been ravaged with aches and pains for nearly two days, but at noon today something awful began and hasn't stopped yet!" She flushed and looked away briefly, "I *know* it is not ladylike to talk about this, but I must tell you: I am bleeding most frighteningly, Papa. From my inner parts."

"Oh, my." Gustave had offered solace when that wicked little fellow, Johan Muilenberg, had pushed Brigetta into an ash heap. And he had found adequate words when *everyone* but the *Dominie's* daughter was given money to go to the silent picture show. But this was new territory. He envied Hanna asleep in her bed, and wished he had mental powers sufficient to signal Lena and bring her running full-tilt from her Sewing Circle.

"Yes, my very life is seeping out of my most private place and I cannot stop it!" Gustave bit back a smile. Brigetta's bookshelf held dozens of storybooks and schoolbooks and stacks of *St. Nicholas* periodicals— all of which put a great many words at her disposal, words she employed regularly with great abandon.

After a quivering breath, she continued, "I remembered how you put a tourniquet on Trixie when the horse kicked her, so I made one out of an old petticoat and put it around my middle and down and under and across. But even though I pinned it as tight as I could stand, it hasn't helped. Trixie stopped bleeding right away, but I have not ceased for over seven hours!"

Gustave hugged her closely before the renewed wails could rouse Hanna. He managed to capture the loudest of her sobs against his shoulder. "Sit on my lap, Sweet Pea."

"Oh, Papa, there's nothing I want more, but I just know I would bleed on your trousers. I would hate for Mama or *Tante* Lena to ask about your stained trousers before we decide how best to tell them about this sorrow."

Gustave smiled above Brigetta's tousled head. "Let me worry about my trousers." He shifted in his chair to accommodate her and they sat in companionable silence for several moments. He was startled to realize her feet now nearly reached the floor.

Gustave often pictured his wife and daughter as being on opposite ends of a teeter-totter. Somehow, Brigetta managed to keep Hanna and herself balanced and give both of them pleasure. Gustave saw himself as the fulcrum in that imagined scene.

But, when Hanna disappeared without warning—as she was wont to do—from her end of the board opposite an unprepared Brigetta, Lena was the one who flew to take Hanna's place. Until now, Lena always arrived just in time to prevent Brigetta from being jarred by the brutal reality of hard ground.

Tonight, Gustave recognized Brigetta's very real vulnerability—she was growing up; there would not always be someone at the other end. Their little girl with a big vocabulary was becoming a young lady with a big world waiting just beyond the horizon. He hugged her a little tighter and blinked quickly to trap the tears misting his eyes.

"Papa, you are such a comfort to me," Brigetta sighed, snuggling into the familiar embrace. "You'll help Mama and *Tante* Lena bear their loss when I'm gone, but I wonder who will console you?"

"I'm not ready to say good-bye to my daughter just yet; I believe God will let you live a bit longer. I suggest you will talk with *Tante* Lena when she returns from her Sewing Circle and tell her exactly what you have told me. She will know better than I how to help you. I will talk to your Mama in the morning."

"But I must talk to *Tante* Lena alone?"

"Yes, she will appreciate that." Gustave enjoyed a moment imagining Lena's utter mortification if he shared in such a conversation. Brigetta planted a string of kisses across Gustave's face and shifted off his lap, sneaking a peek for damages.

"See? No problems with the trousers."

"Thank you for all the loving you have given me through my whole life. You have been the best Papa God ever created."

"Let's not say farewell just yet. Will you wait for *Tante* Lena in your room?"

"Yes. I'll put a note on her door in case I don't hear her come in."

"That's good. I'll see you in the morning, Brigetta. Don't forget to say your prayers."

"Don't worry, Papa. I have never prayed more than I have today. I know it's selfish, but I have asked God over and over to spare my life."

Gustave nodded with full solemnity. "I will do the same."

At her desk, Brigetta wrote a note and made her way down the stairs to slide it beneath her aunt's bedroom door. *Dear* Tante *Lena. Please come to my bedroom no matter how late it is when you get home. It is urgent that I talk with you. Your loving niece, Brigetta Ter Hoorn.*

An hour later, Lena peeked into Brigetta's room and smiled at the sleeping form stretched out—inexplicably on top of Trixie's old blanket rather than beneath the covers. *Ah, she's missing her dog and wants my help to persuade Gustave to get another one.* She entered the room and pulled an afghan off a chair to drape across Brigetta. Before extinguishing the bedside lamp, she planted a light kiss on one pink-tinged cheek, marked the place in the over-turned book, and left the room.

Lena knocked lightly on the study door when she saw the light still burning beneath it. "I'm home, Gustave. Brigetta left me a note saying she wanted to see me, but she has fallen asleep. I know what it's about and it can wait until morning. She and I will talk with you about it later."

Gustave's eyebrows arched. "It can? You will? Well, I trust your judgment," he said in a voice that sounded less than certain. "Thank you, Lena. I am so glad you're part of this family—especially at times like this."

Lena shrugged with fleeting wonder over these incongruous remarks and waved goodnight.

The next morning after their typical laundry-day breakfast of bread with *hagelslag* and coffee, Gustave stood beside his wife's favorite over-stuffed chair by the parlor window. She held needlework in her still hands as she stared out across the lawn. "Hanna, would you care to join me for a walk this morning?"

He could almost see her mind at work, testing several demurrals to find one that would prompt him to ask Brigetta instead. "Brigetta is helping Lena with laundry. The day is especially fine—when the snows blow next winter, we'll remember sunny mornings like this." He tipped her chin up until she met his smiling eyes. "I will spend much of my day inside studying and would enjoy some morning air with my lovely wife."

Hanna stuck her needle in a pincushion and set aside the piecework and rose from the chair. Gustave tucked her hand beneath his arm and held it in place against his side. As they passed Brigetta helping Lena with breakfast dishes, he said, "We're off to enjoy God's wonderful world!" and plucked his cap and Hanna's bonnet off hooks behind the door.

The *Dominie* and his wife—they were a familiar sight to all as they walked past neighbors' homes, waving to one man fixing a loose shingle on the roof, stopping to admire a particularly heavy-laden bridal wreath bush, and moving toward the edge of town. Following a favorite country road, they strolled companionably beside grassy fields where cows lifted their heads in contemplation of the couple. Hanna commented on wild flowers, and Gustave offered a silent prayer of thanksgiving that today appeared to be a good day.

Long ago—but still remembered—a well-meaning parishioner had suggested that Hanna might fare better if Gustave admitted her to an institution. True, there had been days when she had exhibited excessive anxiety over Brigetta's health, alternately with days when she scarcely went near the infant. Other times when he knew she harbored recurrent, though infrequent, contemplation of her own death, and he knew she repeatedly had difficulty concentrating or making decisions. But to commit his precious Hanna to a place with inebriates, or criminally insane?

He and Lena had an unspoken, unbroken vow to form a human chain of love around Hanna—with Brigetta as a crucial link when she grew old enough to augment their efforts. He would never separate his wife from their love.

"Brigetta is growing like a weed, isn't she?" Gustave chose this opening from the myriad he had weighed as a means to broach the subject that necessitated this walk.

"Lena says all Brigetta's dress hems will need to be lengthened even before the summer is over."

"Did Lena mention she will have a talk this morning with Brigetta?"

Hanna looked at him with mild curiosity. "They talk constantly! A particular talk, I gather, is what you mean?"

Gustave breathed an inner sigh of relief. An innocent remark for anyone else, for Hanna it was almost as if she told a joke. That bode well for the difficult topic he must introduce into this pleasant morning. Conversations with Hanna were frequently quite one-sided. She could turn even open-ended questions into one-word answers. Today, it was important not only that he talk to her, but that she respond to him.

"Lena is like a big sister to Brigetta." No sooner did the words leave his mouth, than he regretted them. *To speak of siblings for our child— what was I thinking?* Each miscarriage had sent Hanna plummeting into a despair that equaled or exceeded her depression after Brigetta's birth. Hardly the topic for today.

But the morning sunshine worked its magic on Hanna. She seemed unaffected by something that would have usually pulled her back into the cave of mental hibernation. "To hear the two of them laughing in the kitchen, or see them chasing each other with a frog—sometimes I wonder if Lena ever grew up. But what is special about their conversation this morning? Are we to feign surprise over something they are planning?"

Gustave launched his words to his wife from an altar of silent petition to his God. "Last evening after you had retired, Brigetta came to see me in the study. She was quite worried about some changes in her body—to the point where she believed she was dying. When she mentioned bleeding, I was quite sure what was occurring. I comforted her as best I could and told her to speak with Lena. But she fell asleep before Lena returned home, so they will talk this morning." *There. It is all said.*

Hanna pulled Gustave to a stop and sucked in her breath as if hit in the stomach. "Brigetta has begun her monthlies?"

"Yes. She plans to talk with you later today." Gustave felt no guilt for this necessary white lie. "I just wanted you to…"

"Oh, no, Gustave!" There was sheer terror in Hanna's eyes. "Oh, *goode* God in *hemel*. If only she had been a boy and thus could be spared from what I have become."

"Hanna…"

"Please, don't say another word just now."

He honored her request, and they continued to walk, each buffeted by a tumult of emotions. Hanna alternately sagged against Gustave's arm or seemed to race—though still beside him—as if seeking to escape an unseen pursuer. Gustave alternately beseeched God for wisdom and berated himself for clumsily handling this critical event.

At last Hanna broke the silence. "May we sit for a moment? I feel faint."

Gustave quickly spotted a fallen tree and helped Hanna cross the ditch. Once seated, she spoke. It had been many years since Gustave had heard the quantity of words that spilled out. He knew he would listen as long as she would talk, for each word wiped another speck of dirt from the window to her soul and allowed him a glimpse into the darkened cavern it had become.

"Do you know what I think of most often? I remember the last time I felt truly happy. It was the day I knew Brigetta would be born by nightfall."

Gustave allowed his mind to wander back down that same path. He, too, had often mused about Hanna—rosy-cheeked, heavy-with-child, and affectionate that long-ago morning. When he had first opened his eyes, he had seen the smile that now he rarely saw repeated anywhere but on Brigetta's face.

In that dawn-streaked moment, Hanna had turned to him with all the joy of heaven shining through her eyes. *"Dearest, today you'll be a Papa."* They had lingered beneath the covers longer than usual and Gustave still cherished the memories—and hoped for a revival—of that time whenever he reached out to an unresponsive Hanna.

Hanna's low flat voice interrupted their reveries. "That day you became a Papa, but I never did become a Mama. I gave birth to our daughter, but something inside me changed that day. Do you know how often I have seen you with Brigetta and wondered how it is you were transformed into a parent and I was not? Isn't it odd that giving birth killed something within me? With each child lost since then, a little more of me dies until I scarcely feel alive." Gustave put his arm around her, a boulder-sized lump constricting his throat.

Both sat and watched a curious bird on a nearby fence post. Hanna idly flicked an ant off her skirt; Gustave plucked a blade of grass and chewed it. Minutes passed before she resumed. "I long to be a better wife to you, even if I seem unable to be a mother to Brigetta. Your love sustains me, Gustave, though I do not know why you continue to give it. You are a good man. I have often thought you would be better off if I were gone."

"Hanna, no!"

She continued, pensively, "You somehow always know when such ideas overwhelm me. Sometimes when I wish my life would end, I find you there reaching out to me. I have never understood how you can continue to love me, day after day, year after year—your love is like a rock beneath me when all else is shifting sand."

"Ah, Hanna, it is not I who is the rock beneath you. Remember how the Heidelberg Catechism begins?"

Hanna sagged against Gustave; he looked into her face. Slowly, she nodded; her lips shaped themselves around the whispered words she had known from childhood. *What is thy only comfort in life and death? That I...belong unto my faithful Savior Jesus Christ; who...so preserves me that without the will of my heavenly Father, not a hair can fall from my head...*

Gustave pushed himself off the log and turned to lift Hanna up. He grasped her shoulders tightly until she met his eyes. "I love you more than all God has made, Hanna." His kiss quickly moved from gentle to intense. Lips sought lips, banishing the world around them to a place outside the circle of their love. His passion flashed like a blacksmith's torch and ignited something within her.

But Hanna's reflections intruded on the moment and extinguished the brief blaze as effectively as the sudden downpour of a summer rain. She pushed away from his embrace. "And now it begins for Brigetta." Tears welled up in her eyes until her whole world blurred. "Someday she will marry and bear a child. And her poor husband will face a life like yours, one without a true wife."

The moan that escaped Gustave's lips dredged emotion from the bottom of his soul. "Oh, Hanna, do you think I hate my life? As God is my witness, nothing could be farther from the truth! You are a gift from God to me. Sometimes He gives gifts we do not comprehend, but He also offers an ability to trust Him for what we cannot grasp. I vowed at the altar to love, honor, and cherish you—and it has never been a burden to do so."

"Your vow of 'in sickness and in health' has been tested more than even God should expect."

He shook his head resolutely. "I cannot pick and choose which vows to keep: it was a package of vows, not each one separate to be weighed and then honored or discarded at will."

"I love you, Gustave. Do you know that?"

How long has it been since I heard those words? "Yes, Hanna, I know it well. Even when you endure turmoil I have never known, you bravely face another day. Each time you make the choice to go on living, it speaks of your great love for me more clearly than words. You keep holding on—for your family—even when it means denying yourself release from sorrow."

"It is because I have tasted the bitterness of depression that I weep for Brigetta. She is so much like I was—full of life, each day a new joy to behold, seeing only the best in every situation. Someday, she will have the love of a good man—someone who will be drawn to her like a moth to a candle—and their love will create a child. And then…"

"And then," Gustave interrupted gently, "with God's help, they will begin to make a home filled with love. A safe place for that child to grow."

Hanna looked up into Gustave's eyes as tears streamed down her face. "Brigetta has had that, hasn't she? A safe place?"

He nodded and wiped her cheek with his thumb, unwilling to relinquish his hold on her even long enough to reach for his handkerchief. "She wishes for nothing more than what she has. Her love for you and me and Lena is boundless."

Hanna stood silently within his arms. At last she spoke, "Perhaps she will be spared my condition."

"Perhaps. But if not, then God will provide for her. He does not leave us alone, Hanna." Hand-in-hand, they walked slowly back to town—to their home and to their changing daughter and the brink of a new unknown precipice.

Lena blew a wayward curl out of her eyes and took a moment to stretch and yawn in the morning sunshine filtering through the trees. It had been an unusually quiet breakfast. Brigetta, the instigator of most mealtime conversations, had dunked her buttered rusks in milk until they became a most unappetizing muddle of floating crumbs. *No stimulating discussion from her this morning. Nothing.*

32

Rough Terrain

Tuesdays were long days—Lena started pumping water for the wash-tubs when the moon was still in the sky. Today, the wringer jammed once on the first load; water had sloshed out of the tub, leaving her with a wet left foot; she was sure she was getting a toothache—and then Brigetta had lost her usual sunny disposition. It reinforced Lena's belief that laundry days were a curse. Even if the parsonage budget could afford a washing machine that churned clothes clean, she doubted the miserable task would be any more tolerable.

Other households in Dutchville claimed Monday as washday, but thankfully the Ter Hoorn calendar assigned the chore to Tuesdays. Instead of waking up on Mondays to face tubs of rapidly cooling soapy water, washboards, and sagging clotheslines, Lena greeted each new week by producing the delightful smells of baking that would feed her household. She loved Mondays.

Gustave frequently took the family for a buggy ride in the country on Monday afternoons to enjoy a relative calm after each Sunday's furor. Lena often packed a late *tiffin* in a basket, including some of the morning's fresh-baked sweets. As they bumped along dusty roads in the buggy with the fringed top folded back for these Monday adventures, Lena would smile blissfully at each loaded clothesline in someone else's yard. Unlike these women bending over their washtubs, she had one day's reprieve between every Sunday's full agenda and the backbreaking chores of laundry.

Sundays were hectic, no denying that, she thought as she scrubbed a stubborn stain. Always, they began with a special breakfast, then much tying of bows and fluffing of curls, morning services and Bible classes, and finally home to place the fruits of her Saturday labors on a table laden with food. Extra leaves added to the dining room table for Sunday dinners accommodated the inevitable guests. But dinner wasn't the end—oh, no! Sunday afternoon stollers-by became porch visitors whom Gustave predictably urged to stay for supper. Then the evening service closed the day. *Oh day of rest and gladness, indeed!* Even Gabriel with his trumpet would find it difficult to roust the sleeping Ter Hoorn household on Sunday nights.

Lena hefted a mound of heavy sheets from beneath the wringer into the waiting basket and headed for the clothesline. Birds chirped from their nests in the towering Dutch elm that raised leafy limbs toward heaven. Midst the heady scent of marigolds fringing the garden, Brigetta held a pillowcase on the clothesline with one hand, staring at the wooden pin in the other hand as if seeing such a peg for the first time. Lena teased pointedly, "If you stick that clothespin over the line, it will hold the pillowcase right there—and you can move along to the rest of those clothes drying in the basket instead of on the line!"

Brigetta turned and stared as Lena expertly shook wrinkles from a sheet and positioned it like a ship's sail to dry in the breeze. Finally securing the pillowcase in place, Brigetta ambled over and leaned against the clothesline pole. Staring at the dewy grass at her feet, she said softly, "*Tante* Lena, I…"

The ensuing pause halted Lena's teasing like no rush of words could. *Brigetta speechless? My, my.* From dawn to setting sun, Brigetta talked of happenings and curiosities and calamities and thrills. And now, the cat had her tongue. "Yes, Brigetta? Your note said you have something to talk to me about?" Three towels flapped on the line before another word was exchanged.

Brigetta squared her shoulders. "*Tante* Lena, I am dying. I talked with Papa last night. He is telling Mama this morning. We must all be brave because Dutchville will be watching us."

Toothache and wet *klompen* forgotten, Lena looked shrewdly into the girl's serious face. "Dying, you say? Have you been feeling ill?"

Brigetta moved a few feet closer and lowered her voice. "I have had unceasing pains and aches for over two days, and then yesterday I began to bleed. There's no stopping it. Since I probably don't have much longer with you, I want to get my affairs in order and dispose of my possessions. Like Mister VanderWater did."

The man was eighty-five when a horse kicked him, and he owned three farms! Lena bit her tongue and folded a tablecloth in half before hanging it. "Brigetta, quickly help me empty this basket and before we bring out the next load, we'll sit down for a glass of milk and a good talk."

Brigetta rose to the occasion and, like a departing soldier seeing home and hearth for the last time, heroically finished the task at hand. *Here is dear Papa's shirt—he'll miss me so.* She brushed the back of her hand across her eyes. *The piano cloth with the velvety fringe—they'll think of me playing in the twilight each time they see it.* She sniffed and choked on a sob. *And this is my sweet Mama's crinoline—I wish I didn't have to cause her any more pain.* She blew her nose loudly. *So many aprons for* Tante Lena—*she has selflessly cared for me since I was born. Every year on the anniversary of my death she'll retell the story of my life.* Blinded by free-flowing tears, Brigetta valiantly labored on.

Lena picked up the empty basket and prodded her troubled niece back to the porch. Brigetta gravitated to the swing, mentally revisiting several deathbed scenes she had polished to a high sheen since her shattering discovery. Lena disappeared into the kitchen, returning with the promised milk.

"Now, Sweet Pea, let me set your mind at ease." She pulled a fresh handkerchief from her pocket and thrust it into Brigetta's hand. "You are not dying. I guess your Mama and I each assumed the other would talk to you about changes like this."

"You *knew* I would bleed to death? Is it hereditary?" Alarm widened Brigetta's eyes.

Lena bit her cheek until it hurt. "In a way, yes! Girls grow into women, and this is part of being a woman. Let me tell you a few things, and then if you still have questions, I will try to answer them." Lena, single for the nearly three decades of her life, attempted to assuage a young girl's fears and misconceptions. Since her source was the shallow box of an unmarried lady's knowledge of unmentionable things, her information was riddled with gaps.

Though well intentioned, this talk missed several key points. While Lena did an adequate job of explaining a woman's monthly functions and how to handle them, she skipped over pregnancy altogether. Despite her multitudinous skills in running a household and even assisting in Hanna's care after miscarriages, she knew little more than the basics of procreation—none of which she felt appropriate to share with a young girl. And that youngest member of the *Dominie's* family in 1912 knew even less to ask. This pivotal conversation ended with Lena's words, "That's all there is to know. See? You're not dying."

"Oh no, Papa still thinks I am! Mama will worry needlessly—I am so distraught!" Lena had long ceased thinking she had seen the heights of drama Brigetta could achieve; there were continual surprises living with a hummingbird in the midst of a flock of Dutch crows.

"He suspects the truth," Lena said dryly. "He has been married to your Mama for quite a few years and he knows what happens to her—and other women—each month."

Brigetta's cheeks burned. Oh, how she wished she could pull back last evening's conversation with her father and bury it in the back yard like Trixie would do with favorite bones. *Tante* Lena had said the bleeding would happen every month for many years, so she had to believe she would not die from it any time soon.

She suddenly looked at her aunt with new respect: to think her own Mama and *Tante* Lena had harbored this undiscovered mystery! *Every month, they nearly die and yet go about their daily tasks without faltering.* Tears threatened again, but this time Brigetta staunchly blinked them back. It was time for her, too, to fearlessly face the world.

She wondered if Mary would be able to discern her new secret, or if with the bleeding she had also gained the skills of subterfuge women obviously possessed. Seeing Mary immediately became the most important activity of the day.

In record time, the remaining wash was scrubbed clean and hung to dry. The laundry tubs were emptied over the back porch for Brigetta to broom-scrub and rinse clean. At last, lunchtime was over and Brigetta asked, "May I go see Mary?"

"Why, yes, of course," Lena said, relieved to grant a normal request after the drama of the morning.

Soon, the two friends lolled on a blanket beneath the huge cottonwood tree at the far corner of the church. Mary had brought both the scrapbook and autograph book that usually prompted countless topics for discussion. This afternoon, however, Brigetta scarcely gave the books a glance. She seemed more interested in lying flat on her back, staring at the sky, every so often allowing her hand to creep up and press against her abdomen.

Eventually, Mary gave up trying to hold Brigetta's attention. She closed the book with a sigh. "What's wrong with you?" she asked peevishly. "Did you eat a sour apple? Why do you keep rubbing your stomach?"

Brigetta murmured faintly, "It's much worse than a stomach ache." She sneaked a peek at Mary, but Mary's education in such things was woefully inadequate and she failed to pick up cues. "It's in my private parts."

Fully aware of what proper young ladies do and do not discuss, Mary gasped at her friend's indiscretion and looked around guiltily. She fully expected their blanket to be pelted with rocks from heaven. "Brigetta!" she reprimanded primly.

Brigetta felt a twinge of proper remorse for she, too, had received similar lectures over the years. But this was such a tempting morsel surely God would understand if, just once, she and Mary skipped lightly across this forbidden ground. "Someday you'll know what I've suffered these past two days. I have had fierce pains and unending aches for two days. And then the bleeding began," she fluttered her eyelashes just enough to allow her the tiniest glimpse of Mary's spellbound face, "and it hasn't stopped. Don't be filled with sorrow. I won't die, but I must bear this sickness every month because I am a woman now."

Accustomed as Mary was to Brigetta's dramatic flair, the words captivated her. She tipped her head to peer into Brigetta's face. "Is the pain unbearable? Is it like getting hit in the head with a ball?" Mary asked.

"Much worse. You'll know someday."

"Oh." One word seldom bears the weight of such envy and fear and wonderment.

"If your mother doesn't tell you all about it, *Tante* Lena can talk privately with you. She knows *everything*."

"Mama did tell me I would soon have a monthly discharge." This being the sum total of her mother's euphemistic information, Mary's contributions to this conversation began and ended with that weak offering. "I wonder if the discharge comes before or after the bleeding?"

"It comes afterwards," Brigetta said confidently, "never at the same time." Brigetta marveled at her new heightened ability to grasp and connect and interpret details. *And this is just my first womanly episode!* "Women would surely die if their monthly discharge came at the same time as their bleeding."

This sobering concept effectively stamped *Done* on the afternoon and two quiet girls gathered up the blanket and books. It took them quite a while to actually reach their homes; Brigetta walked Mary half-way home, and then Mary walked Brigetta half-way back, and that distance was split again and again until they were basically at a stand-still and neither girl was home.

Hearing her mother's exasperated voice calling her name, Mary threw her arms around Brigetta in a rare display of affection and whispered, "Your secret's safe with me."

"I knew I could trust you. I'll say special prayers that your bleeding will start soon. You must let me know the *instant* my prayers are answered."

Mary ran toward home, looking back only once to observe Brigetta making her way with suddenly transformed posture and demeanor and a lady-like, measured pace. Life was changing rapidly, and unless it balanced out to include Mary, she wasn't sure she liked that fact one bit. But soon she would be a woman, too. God had to listen to Brigetta's prayers: she was the *Dominie's* daughter!

Summer 1916

◆

"Father, I would like to try something different next autumn with the tulips," Bram said, pushing back his chair from the supper table as Hans marked his place in the Dutch Bible. "Last year when I trimmed the bulbs before planting them, I know they rooted more quickly. I suspect if I can keep the bulbs at a more consistent temperature this fall and winter, it will slow their growth and give us even bigger blooms. I'm going to need extra hay."

Hans nodded. "It sounds like something worth trying. Since you somehow managed to increase the yield on our seed potatoes by almost a third, I have no doubt your plan for the tulips could work. We won't starve if it doesn't work—tulips feed the soul, potatoes feed the body." He looked at his son with evident pride.

Rebecca frowned as she carefully put her folded napkin back in place for the next meal. "I would hate to starve my soul next spring if the tulips didn't come up. You won't disturb the bulbs already producing, will you, Bram?"

"They'll always come up, Mother. I would never risk that. I know even with violets and buttercups and daisies, spring means tulips to you! I might be able to get some earlier than before, and have some bloom even later than ever—so you'll have tulips for an even longer season next year."

"You have a way, Bram, of coaxing life out of the soil like no other farmer along the Floyd River," Hans admitted willingly.

Bram shrugged self-consciously. "I just love the idea that I can bury something that looks dead and soon it comes up a living, growing plant."

Cornelis had been listening in silence until now. "I'm just glad *you* love farming, Bram, because I intend to live in town—or better yet, a big city. I'll marry someone who can garden while I drive my automobile!"

Though he helped with all aspects of farm life, Cornelis' heart wasn't in farming. He loved automobiles. If it was a mode of transportation with four wheels and didn't require a horse that added hay in one end and subtracted fertilizer out the other, he wanted to know all about it. On winter evenings when Bram had spread seed catalogs out across the dining room table, Cornelis scoured newspapers and magazines and soaked up details about all the models, sketching endless drawings of their inner workings.

Almost every evening meal at the de Boer's table included a recitation by Cornelis of the merits of some automobile. Once their heads lifted after Grace and Rebecca signaled the beginning of the meal with her traditional *"Eet smakelijk,"* Cornelis attempted to educate his pathetically disinterested family about his obsession. "I heard about the 1913 Model 69T Overland today from Mister De Zeeuw. I would sure like to see one—it's a self-starter, has a 110-inch wheel base, and comes with features you'd have to pay extra to get on other automobiles, Father."

"We don't need an automobile, Cornelis—with features or without. Farmers need farm equipment—that's a necessity. An automobile is a luxury we can't afford and don't need."

But tonight Cornelis was ready for this argument. He reached under his chair and pulled out the August 1912 issue of the *Farm, Stock and Home* magazine. "Look what I found in a stack of magazines at the feed store! If farmers don't need cars, then why is this in a farmer's magazine?" He held up a full-page advertisement and slowly turned it for all to see.

Hans, Rebecca, and Bram burst out laughing. Hans finally recovered enough to say, "If you can't make a living selling automobiles, Cornelis, you would make a good lawyer with your abilities to dig out facts and present a case in pursuit of seemingly lost causes."

Rebecca smiled at her youngest son. "Go ahead, read it to us."

Needing no further encouragement, Cornelis read, "I will skip some of it. Let's see; okay: *This is the car—a big, powerful, beautiful, spacious, comfortable, self-starting, thirty horsepower, five-passenger touring car— fully equipped—all ready for night or day, rain or shine service. Made of the best materials on the market, by the most skilled men known to the trade, and in the most efficient automobile shop in America. And the price is but $985.* There's much more about the motor, and ignition, and crankshaft, but I'll skip that. Oh, Mother, this will interest you: it says the Model 69T is Overland blue with gray wheels. Doesn't that sound pretty?"

Catching his parents' shared amusement, Cornelis finally offered a crooked grin and admitted, "A fellow has to try, doesn't he?" Undaunted by his family's weak attention, he continued with a new burst of enthusiasm. "You know, I might like to work for Mister Henry Ford someday. Did you know he pays his employees five dollars a day—five dollars! That's so they can all own the cars they make. If I worked for him, I could own a Ford in no time."

"If you work hard enough on the farm and save the money Father pays us during harvest—and hire yourself out to other farmers like I do from time-to-time—you will be able to afford your own automobile without leaving home." Bram couldn't comprehend why his brother wanted to escape the farm. "And you could earn money even more quickly if you were willing to help me sell flowers and vegetables on Thursdays in town."

42 Rough Terrain

"Not interested, big brother; sorry. Besides, I don't know why your tomatoes are red and solid all the way through—and all that other stuff people always ask." He raised a hand to stem the words ready to spill from Bram's open mouth. "I know I could learn, but I'd rather use my time in town to hang around people who own automobiles and learn about them, not crops. Say, instead of working for Henry Ford, maybe someday I'll join the Thomas B. Jeffery Company," he let the name roll off his tongue, "out in San Francisco and then I'll get to drive their finest: a Cross Country. There was a full-page advertisement in…"

"…*The Farmer*…" chorused all three members of his family, effectively halting his discourse.

"You've mentioned it before," Rebecca said gently.

"Several times," muttered Bram.

"I just wanted to say it has ten-inch upholstery and I know Mother hates a bumpy buggy ride." Cornelis was interrupted with whoops of laughter from around the table a second time as he fell back on his most common ploy: to enlist his mother's endorsement.

Undaunted, he finished in a rush, "…and a gasoline and an electric motor which means the driver doesn't have to get out of the car to start it or light the lamps."

"Yes, we recall those details," said Hans dryly. "Rebecca, wouldn't this be a good time to tell the boys your idea for the *Sinterklaas* parade?" That dragged even Cornelis' attention away from automobiles and got the family talking excitedly about something that would require months of preparation.

But later that evening when only moonlight filtered through the windows, Hans and Rebecca lay beneath the covers and talked softly of topics that find their best expression in the dark. It was an established fact the farm would go to Bram when Hans and Rebecca could no longer manage. Established, because it seemed certain Cornelis would be only an infrequent visitor, if his words held true, not a contributing partner.

His passion was the horseless carriage—and a farmer without a passion for the soil makes a poor farmer.

"A fine meal tonight, 'Becca. You take good care of your menfolk," Hans brushed his hand across his wife's arm in a private display of the deep affection between them. The look of sadness on her face as she had listened to Cornelis' chatter at the table tonight had pierced his heart. Cornelis was practically counting the remaining harvests until he could climb aboard a train to Chicago—or any place far enough away from farms so he could kick the clods of dirt off his feet and forget about crops and the worries of whether rains would be well-timed.

The farm would flourish under Bram's care and keeping. To the uninformed, this seemed a good thing—hardly a concern, at all. But to the two lying wide-eyed in the darkness, it was what hid in the shadows of unspoken truth that draped a poignant silence across each discussion of the topic. Neither Hans nor Rebecca could forget the night in 1907 when Doc Draayer sat at their kitchen table. As he had predicted, Bram and Cornelis rejoined Hans in the fields and, with youth's capacity for recovery, regained their strength and stamina. All their memories of the mumps receded, surfacing only from time-to-time in stray comments. *"Remember how you made custard every day for us when we had mumps, Mother?"* At such times, a cold hand would wrap itself around Rebecca's heart and squeeze it until she felt faint.

The haunting question neither Hans nor Rebecca put into words lurked in the shadows: *Had Bram's recovery been complete?* He, no doubt, would marry. And the farm would flourish under his care and wisdom. But what then? If there were no children for Bram, what became of the family farm? As good Dutchmen, they believed passionately in passing a family's possessions along to future generations. And a farm—that was a Dutchman's dream. To be entrusted with a piece of God's green earth was a responsibility not taken lightly.

Even more worrisome was the fact that Hans and Rebecca had not—despite nine years' passing—found opportunity to discuss Bram's potential problem of sterility with him. With full visible recovery from all symptoms, no occasion had arisen that demanded such a dialogue.

Growing up with livestock in their care, procreation was no mystery to either son. Now, with Bram towering above his father and the constant bevy of young ladies waiting on the church steps every Sunday to catch his attention, Hans and Rebecca both knew it was long past time to speak of difficult things with Bram. To delay further could mean catastrophe. Questions they whispered in the night had no answers: *How will Bram react to the news? What will he say about our delaying to tell him something potentially so important? Will our family be torn asunder?*

Though both boys shared equally in Hans and Rebecca's love, it was the eldest with his consuming interest in all things green and growing who held their hopes and dreams—the promise of the future—in his hands. Where Bram was hope personified, Cornelis was a mystery to them.

Summer's exit allowed for autumn's entrance. Rebecca kept busy feeding her family and canning food for the winter months. One evening at the supper table she teased, "For each stroke of the scythe in the wheat fields you require another piece of bread! I have baked nine loaves of bread this week—of which only two remain. Even after consuming pancakes, cornbread, biscuits with ham and cheese, cookies and doughnuts today, you eat like starving men at supper! Look how little sausage stew remains tonight. I should hire a kitchen helper during harvest."

"That's a good idea, 'Becca. Bram has us planting twice as much wheat and alfalfa, which means we'll need to hire harvest help. Cornelis, you may actually see a threshing machine in our fields rather than our horse-drawn reaper," Hans teased and turned back to Rebecca. "With a half dozen men to feed, you should hire help, too. Bram, do you know of any girl to help your mother?"

Bram swallowed a mouthful of cherry pie before answering, "There's Brigetta Ter Hoorn. The *Dominie's* daughter," he added unnecessarily. "She's still young, but she might be willing to come help."

Hans and Rebecca's eyes met across the table. *Brigetta. My, it didn't take long for him to come up with that name.*

✶   ✶   ✶

Standing beneath the welcome shade of a sprawling oak tree, Brigetta and Mary stood with arms linked as they watched the bustle of activity across the road. "Let's go over before all the berries are gone," said Mary.

"No, Silly. There are too many people. We have to wait until there's hardly anyone around so he'll have time to talk with us." The shoppers filling their baskets beside the farm-wagon were impressed both with quality of the young man's produce and his knowledge of all he grew.

The duet of sixteen-year-old girls, however, scarcely gave a thought to the new potatoes, the season's first asparagus, or the early berries Bram had picked in the coolness before dawn that were the result of his special grafting last autumn.

Like most Dutchville girls, they swooned over Bram de Boer. It would be hard to find a girl around those parts who hadn't let her eyes roam from the well-worn straw hat perched atop his stick-straight coal-black hair on down to his shoulder and arm muscles rolling beneath the clean, but faded, shirt. The same young ladies often sidled up next to Bram, positioning themselves near enough to measure their own height in comparison to the six-feet-one-inch that his long legs elevated him above the earth he loved.

Two of those smitten young ladies sighed in unison across the road as Bram hefted two crates to his shoulders and strode toward a waiting automobile. While Cornelis would have stroked the hood of the 1915 Buick Roadster with its fold-down top, Bram merely gave great care to placing the boxes where his produce would be less likely to be bruised on the trip home.

In a whisper that could have passed for a prayer, Brigetta said, "Someday, I will marry him."

That remark snatched Mary's attention back to their side of the road. Her amazed reply bordered on a stage whisper. "*What?*" Brigetta always had the most interesting plans for ways to spend a summer day, and the juiciest gossip—and now this: a truly startling announcement.

"In my heart, I just know someday I will be Mrs. Abraham de Boer," Brigetta declared theatrically and twisted a curl around her finger.

"Is *he* the one you've been wishing for on the evening star? I can't believe it! He's too old. He already has a beard."

"Papa is six whole years older than Mama, and Bram is only five years older than we are." Brigetta replied so promptly it was obvious she had thought through all potential arguments.

Mary protested further, "Still, you don't really know him. He's been out of school for ages! Sure, he carried you home from the river when you got hurt, but that was years ago. He certainly doesn't know you."

"That, my dear Mary, is about to change." Brigetta's chin jutted out with a determination all too familiar to her friend. "We're about to buy berries. I have money right here." She patted her pocket. "And when we get over there, please don't just stand there like a fence post. Talk to him so it doesn't look like I'm a chatterbox. Come."

Mary scurried after Brigetta, both gathering their skirts above the swirls of dust as they crossed the road. One housewife remained, claiming Bram's attention while she sorted through the herbs. She finally offered up the posted price and moved away with her purchase. Boldly, Brigetta stepped up to the wagon and stared intently at the crates of berries.

Bram announced, "These berries grew in the best soil in Iowa—and I grafted two kinds to get the juiciest, plumpest berries you'll ever taste."

"They look beautiful."

"Taste them. Go ahead, both of you." Needing no further encouragement, each girl popped a perfect strawberry in her mouth and reveled in the burst of flavor. "Didn't I tell you?" the young farmer prompted.

"Wonderful." Mary responded, and poked Brigetta who was now staring at Bram's sun-browned forearms and long-fingered hands as he shifted crates to fill in empty spaces on the wagon.

"The best I've ever tasted," Brigetta agreed belatedly and then added in a rush, "My Papa says you're a remarkable farmer for someone so young."

Mary blushed for her friend, knowing Brigetta's boldness indicated just how firmly she anchored her dreams on the wild prediction she had made just minutes earlier.

"Thank your father for me. I'm sure *Dominie* Ter Hoorn would not tell tales!"

Brigetta beamed back at him and announced, "We will take a crate of these berries."

"How will you get them home? I don't see your buggy."

Brigetta's laughter filled the air and hooked a permanent place in Bram's memory. "We forgot to bring the buggy!" *What was I thinking? I remembered money, but didn't think beyond that.*

Oblivious to their schoolgirl blushes, Bram offered, "No problem. I will be happy to drop them by the parsonage on my way home."

"That's fine," Brigetta said calmly, though her heart threatened to beat right out of her bosom and dance a jig beside the wagon. *Fine? It's superb! It's beyond my wildest dreams!* "Thank you. Let me pay you now, but I'll be there when you deliver them."

Out of Bram's earshot, Brigetta erupted with joy. "Oh, *Mary!* Can you believe it? Bram will come to my house and I'll have a second chance to talk with him!"

"Your family will be eating an awful lot of fruits and vegetables this summer—what with all your family grows in your own garden and what I just *know* you'll want to buy each week from Bram!" Mary said, practically.

Brigetta knew better than to contradict Mary as they headed home. Emboldened by her success, she had every intention of doing what her friend had said: she would become Bram's most loyal customer.

Now, she must move quickly; she had some fast-talking to do with *Tante* Lena before Bram de Boer showed up, unanticipated, at the kitchen door with a crate of berries. She hugged herself with delight over how well her long-planned *chance* encounter had worked out. *This is going to be a most delightful summer!*

Leaving Mary at the corner, she galloped across the lawn to her own back porch and slowed to a stop just shy of the steps. Two voices filtered through the open window: that meant Mama was helping in the kitchen. She strained to make sense of the low rumble of their sporadic conversation. If her Mama were having a good day, *Tante* Lena would be more open to Brigetta's announcement. If Hanna were in a dark mood, *Tante* Lena would be putting all her energy toward her sister and would have no patience left over for a young girl's schemes.

At the exact moment she was about to sink down on the top step in frustration, Brigetta heard her mother's rare chuckle. She bounded to her feet and reached the door in two steps.

Flinging her arms first around her startled mother and then racing across the room to capture *Tante* Lena in a frenzied whirl, she sang out, "Mama, *Tante* Lena! I have the most wonderful news! Bram de Boer is coming to deliver a crate of berries to us! *Bram de Boer! Coming here!* I've already paid for them out of my own spending money and they are beautiful and I want to be the one to open the door for him!" She flopped inelegantly onto a kitchen chair, looking up at last into the astonished faces of the two women.

Hanna and Lena exchanged an inscrutable glance before Lena said calmly, "They must be uncommonly good berries."

"They are, but did you hear me? *Bram is bringing them!* To our house! Soon!" Unable to sit still a minute longer, she reached across the table to grasp her mother's hand. "I'm so glad you'll be here, Mama, when he comes! You are so beautiful and sedate and…oh, *Tante* Lena, could you please take off your apron?"

Lena smiled wryly, "I imagine that would be quite upsetting for Bram if he were to see me in my apron—especially when I'm peeling carrots. Perhaps I should change into my Sunday dress?"

Brigetta was oblivious to the gentle teasing. She smoothed her mother's hair and blew an impetuous kiss in the general direction of Hanna's curls. "Oh, Mama, I love you so much!"

Hanna smiled and captured her daughter's hand in both her own. Lena breathed a silent prayer of thanks when Hanna did not leave the kitchen despite this advance notice of an impending guest. Usually, she fled to the bedroom when anyone came; Brigetta's infectious ways had won this small victory.

In all fairness, Lena had to admit Hanna was taking more of an interest—silent though it was—in Brigetta these past months. She often wondered what was going through her sister's mind as she listened to her daughter's endless observations about friends, other households in Dutchville, school events, changing dress styles, and activities at church. While not offering a mother's advice or inviting further confidences, Hanna had begun to listen more intently, and, Lena thanked God nightly for this blessing.

Brigetta stiffened as all three heard the unmistakable sounds of a wagon pulling into the back yard. "He's here. He's really here!" she whispered, wide-eyed.

"That's not a surprise, now is it, since he said he would come? Go let him in, Sweet Pea," said Lena, and smiled as Brigetta's look of determination swallowed up a sudden flash of uncertainty.

Brigetta waited in the doorway, memorizing Bram's every move as he hopped down from the wagon and reached over the side for the crate of berries. His long strides brought him quickly to the porch. Brigetta's trembling knees were the only external clue to her inner turmoil.

Lena moved into position behind Hanna's chair and dropped a light hand on her sister's shoulder as Bram's shadow fell across the kitchen floor. "Come in, Bram," Brigetta's voice was hardly recognizable to the two women behind her. "I've told Mama and *Tante* Lena about your beautiful berries."

Bram nodded politely and greeted first Hanna, then Lena. "I hope you'll eat some today—they were picked fresh this morning and are at their best." He looked at Lena's pile of carrots on the kitchen table and recalled a long-ago winter's day when that same table had held the girl now beaming before him.

"They're very good," bubbled Brigetta, "I had a taste. Isn't it a grand idea Bram has to allow customers to have a taste?"

Even Hanna's cheeks twitched with hidden merriment as the two women watched the young girl glow and wiggle with pure pleasure.

"Brigetta paid me earlier, so I'll be on my way. Thank you for your business," Bram stole a shy look at the elusive Hanna and quickly included Brigetta and Lena in his glance.

"You're welcome. I have rusks and buttermilk on hand so we'll have our favorite summer dessert tonight," Lena promised. "Your mother tells me you are becoming quite competent with cross-breeding tulips, Bram. Do you also have bulbs for sale?"

"Not this year. I am still testing them. I bring fresh-cut flowers in each week, but they are gone in early morning. People like the longer stems on this year's tulips."

"I'll have to send Brigetta next week to get some. We dearly love tulips, don't we, Hanna?"

Hanna nodded, Brigetta beamed, and Lena followed Bram to the door.

He was scarcely seated in his wagon before Brigetta spun around the kitchen, pausing only to gather her mother and aunt into a stifling embrace. "Thank you, thank you, thank you, *Tante* Lena! I will be first in line next week to buy tulips! And if there's *anything* else you want, Mama, he has a wonderful variety of vegetables. Isn't he wonderful? I just wish Papa had been here, too!"

"Your Papa rarely finds it necessary to be on hand for fruits and vegetable deliveries!" *Tante* Lena teased dryly, knowing Brigetta was lost in a field of new joys just beginning to bloom.

At supper, Gustave looked up into his daughter's dancing eyes as she carefully positioned a heaping dessert bowl before him. "Just wait until you taste these berries, Papa! I just know you'll agree they are the freshest, plumpest, juiciest we've ever had." She reached for his spoon, slid it into his hand, and stood back expectantly. "Go ahead, taste them!"

Dipping his head to hide twinkling eyes, he obliged. Brigetta spun around the table to her chair where her own dessert waited, her gaze never leaving her father's face. She waited impatiently until he swallowed the first bite. "Well?" she prompted.

Gustave carefully took another spoonful and savored it slowly before replying. "I am quite delighted anytime *hangop* appears on this table. It's a true harbinger of summer." His eyes twinkled as he looked at Lena. "Did the berries come from the Rowenhorsts? They are usually your source for such delicious early berries."

Brigetta wailed, "Oh, Papa, no! Bram de Boer grows a much better garden than the Rowenhorsts. These are his berries—he grafted them and everything. You've said yourself he is remarkable."

"I would never disparage the Rowenhorst berries, but yes, he is becoming an excellent farmer." Gustave grinned to himself, wondering if his daughter had the slightest clue what grafting entailed. He had to admit, though: these were exceptionally fine berries.

Mollified, Brigetta settled back to concentrate on eating every morsel. Around her, three adults shared amused glances and enjoyed this family favorite. When the table was cleared and Gustave had completed the Scripture reading, he queried, "Brigetta, will you offer our prayer of thanksgiving?"

God has rarely received such profuse gratitude from one of His creatures for simple joys as Bram's berries elicited from the sixteen-year-old daughter of *Dominie* and Hanna Ter Hoorn.

The parsonage garden produced mightily throughout the summer under Hanna's persistent weeding, Lena's careful monitoring of pests, and Brigetta's absent-minded assistance. More often than not, Lena had to follow behind her niece—who weeded, watered, and picked in random fashion—to pull a few more carrots from a row, or to banish a thistle Brigetta had overlooked in her efforts, or to water a row completely missed—while the one next to it appeared flooded.

This morning, Lena had sent Brigetta out early before the heat of the day descended. When she joined her, Lena found Brigetta staring into a cloud-laced sky as water dripped from the pour-spout of the watering can and splashed off her feet. "If you're trying to grow bigger shoes by watering them, it's a lost cause, Sweet Pea. The way to get larger *klompen* is to tell the wooden shoemaker you need a new pair!"

Brigetta grinned sheepishly as she looked down at her soaked feet and sloshing shoes and shrugged her shoulders. "I guess I was thinking about something and didn't notice."

"More like *someone*," Lena muttered and shifted a stake to give better support to a heavily laden tomato plant.

Still happy, always friendly, but somehow different, Brigetta was spreading her wings in new and sundry ways this summer. The two worked in companionable silence in the morning air.

"Those beets are lovely! Knock the dirt off before putting them in the basket, though, Brigetta."

"Hmmm?" Dreamy blue eyes turned slowly toward Lena as Brigetta held a fistful of greens with dangling vivid beets and absent-mindedly dropped the lot on top of a half-basket of string beans.

Lena watched the dirt fall off to filter through the nest of beans to the bottom of the basket. *And now it will be all over my nice clean kitchen floor.* She sighed.

Hearing the sigh, Brigetta asked, "Did you say something, *Tante* Lena?"

"I said, 'The beets are lovely.'"

Brigetta looked into the basket between them as if surprised to see beets in it—and certainly unaware *she* had just picked and placed them there—and agreed, "You pulled the best ones."

Lena shook her head with a rueful grin and stepped over a row of spinach. For a girl who loved words, Brigetta had used surprisingly few of them lately to share her inner thoughts. Their closest moments came when Brigetta worked with Lena in the kitchen and seemed to absorb Lena's secrets for coaxing bread to rise, and peeling onions with fewer tears, and flavoring stews without overpowering the senses. Standing together paring apples, or buttering iron gem pans for stove-top *broedertjes*, or rolling out *stroop koekjes*, or measuring out the meat for *saucijzenbroodjes*—these times had provided hours of uninterrupted conversations and seemed to loosen Brigetta's tongue.

One evening, with supper dishes dried and back in the cupboard, Brigetta lingered in the kitchen after Lena had gone to join Gustave and Hanna in the parlor. Several minutes later when Gustave had suggested that a glass of buttermilk would taste good, Lena returned to the kitchen and found Brigetta bent over the table, whatever she was doing hidden by her curls. "What's that, Sweet Pea?"

Startled, Brigetta quickly jumped to her feet, grabbed something off the table and stuffed her hand into her pocket, turning toward Lena with guilt etched on her face.

"Are you hiding something?" There was more astonishment than accusation in Lena's words.

"Nothing, I mean, only a piece of paper." Brigetta shifted her eyes from Lena's face to the icebox behind her. Right now she wanted nothing more than to jump behind its carved doors and stay in the porcelain-lined ice compartment until the iceman brought the next load of ice.

"May I see what's in your pocket?" Brigetta looked so ashamed that Lena knew she must assume the uncomfortable and relatively unfamiliar role of disciplinarian.

Brigetta snagged an uneven breath as she slowly pulled a crinkled paper from her pocket and handed it to her aunt. *Tante* Lena opened it and read silently, her eyes darting from line to line:

Soak two cups of dried peas overnight in rainwater. Put two pounds of meat (or a soup bone with sufficient meat remaining) and the soaked peas in four quarts of water (can add to same water the peas soaked in). Boil for two hours, and then cut up into fine pieces four potatoes, three medium-sized onions, and one stalk of celery. Add vegetables with salt and pepper to pot. Cook until peas begin to soften and lose their shape.

Lena looked up, her jaw sagging. "Would you like to tell me why you felt it necessary to hide my own recipe for *erwten soep* from me?" she asked as a twinkle softened her eyes like the peas in the recipe. Relief flooded her heart; she had not had sufficient time to conjure any idea of what trouble could be unveiled when Brigetta emptied her pocket—but a recipe? *Goede God in Hemel!* She fanned herself with the paper.

Brigetta offered her reluctant confession in a near-whisper. "I have been writing down everything you've taught me for weeks now. My *Tante* Lena Book is almost full."

"Your *what*?"

"Would you like to see it?" Brigetta asked shyly.

Speechless, Lena responded with a dramatic bow and a sweep of her hands pointing to the kitchen door. Upstairs in Brigetta's room, Lena dropped into the rocking chair and stared in bewilderment at the book Brigetta carefully removed from beneath a quilt in her hope chest.

It was a scrapbook about two inches thick—as full as the rawhide string that bound it would allow—with sections marked "Recipes," and "Housekeeping Hints" and "Sewing, Et cetera." The smell of flour-paste rose from each butcher-paper page where trimmed cards of carefully penned recipes—representing Lena's Dutch cooking in the parsonage kitchen—were carefully inscribed and secured in place.

"I had almost given up on ever getting your recipe for pea soup—it's been ages since you made it."

Hadley Hoover

Lena turned page after page containing the last months' menus: *ingemaaakte roode kool, spinazie, peulen, Hollandsche snijbonen, vlaai, kroket, frikandel, stamppot, karnemelksche pap, bonen soep, hutspot, haring salade, rollade, gehakt, brentenbrood, flensjes, suiker koekjes, appel beignets*—it was like a diary of her life. She sank back against the chair and let the book fall shut.

"Are you terribly upset with me, *Tante* Lena?"

"Upset? No, Sweet Pea. Just confused. Why on earth would you go to such trouble to write down all these things—and in such a furtive manner? You could ask me at any time for my recipes, you know."

Brigetta blushed furiously. "You know so much, and someday I will be a wife…"

It was as if lightning illuminated Lena's mind. "Oh, my." Her memory flashed back to the day by the clothesline when Brigetta had feared her own death. A more realistic jolt awaited this household: Brigetta *would* soon leave, though for the happier reason of starting her own home. Sadness nibbled at the edges of Lena's heart.

"*Ja.* For tonight's recipe, you might want to add that if the rain barrel is empty and I'm using water from the pump, I put in a pinch of soda when soaking the peas." She handed the paper back to her flushed niece.

"Thank you, *Tante* Lena." replied a subdued Brigetta.

The parade of young men who frequented the front porch on summer evenings and consumed gallons of buttermilk and iced tea, dozens of cookies, and pans of apple crisp now marched before Lena for a mental review of the troops: Dirk van Gorp, Henry Muilenberg, Conrad van Steenwyk, Bram de Boer…ah, yes. Bram of the river accident. Bram of the berries episode. Bram with the endless supply of tulips. Bram with ice-skates dangling over his shoulder as he waited on a cold winter day for Brigetta to join him on the river. Bram, Bram, Bram.

Lena pushed herself out of the chair—feeling the weight of every one of her thirty-four years—and placed the scrapbook carefully back under the linens in the chest before pulling Brigetta into her arms with a crushing hug. Surreptitiously wiping away a tear, she led the way back downstairs to join Gustave and Hanna for a game of dominoes and the almost forgotten buttermilk.

One Monday morning that promised a warm day ahead, Mary appeared at the Ter Hoorn kitchen door searching for her friend. "I hoped Brigetta might like to ride with me along the river, but her bicycle is already gone."

Lena stopped kneading rye bread to puzzle through where Brigetta might have disappeared without Mary, her usual shadow, knowing her whereabouts—and having taken her bicycle with her. *Odd, indeed.* Lena always assumed the two girls were together, often eating *tiffin* at either the Huitink or Ter Hoorn kitchen table or sitting out in the *zomerhuis* where they talked and embroidered. Apparently, that assumption required another look-see.

She learned nothing from Brigetta who catnapped on the porch swing midafternoon, but she gained a wealth of information from Rebecca de Boer at Vander Molen's store a few days later. As the two women waited while the clerk weighed coffee beans and sugar, Rebecca unwittingly filled in the gaps in Lena's information and contributed even more details as they pondered which buttons would best enhance a bolt of newly arrived satin dress goods.

It seemed Brigetta had been appearing on her bicycle at the de Boer farm on a fairly regular basis—usually twice a week, sometimes three times—throughout the season of tilling and planting and weeding and harvesting of some of the earlier garden produce. "She is such a good worker! She just tucks up her skirts and kneels on her *klompen* and works right beside Bram and Cornelis. I declare, the mornings she's there, even Cornelis seems to enjoy digging in the soil as much as his brother!"

"Did Bram *invite* her to help?" Lena asked, aghast.

Rebecca's melodious laugh rippled through the store. "The first time she came, she wanted to surprise you with a new variety of lettuce. So

Bram took her out to the garden and the next thing you know, they're both down on their knees, looking over the rows and laughing together, and chattering away like a couple of magpies. I always considered Bram my silent son until this summer!"

Lettuce? That was weeks ago!

"Bram says she seems to enjoy herself. He told her anytime she wants to help, she is welcome. Apparently, she is interested because several times each week I look out the window and there the three of them are."

And so the days had passed, with Bram and Brigetta and Cornelis transforming annoying gopher and prairie dog mounds into beds of lettuce, carrots, cabbage, and beans, and keeping pests away from the seed potatoes they had thrust between the plow's furrows. All this had transpired without the Ter Hoorn household taking notice. *Mercy!*

According to his mother, Bram was elated to have Brigetta take such an interest in his ideas for ways to coax tulips to grow taller, carrots to be sweeter, and tomatoes to be heavy with flavor. "Heaven knows his own brother is bored by it all—unless Brigetta is around!" Rebecca glowed as she recounted that this past week, Bram had convinced Brigetta to stay for lunch. It had been the day Mary appeared at the parsonage in search of her friend.

Assuring Lena Brigetta had been a most welcome addition to their table, Rebecca said, "Which reminds me, harvest is coming soon and Hans said I should hire a girl to come help me feed the threshing crew. If you don't mind, I'd like to ask Brigetta if she would work for me for a couple of weeks. Could you and Hanna spare her?"

Lena made wordless sounds and meaningless gestures while Rebecca chattered beside her for a few more minutes. Watching the clerk carefully weigh dried beans on the scale, Lena admitted to herself that on the one hand she felt great satisfaction Brigetta had represented the *Dominie's* family well. However, the other side of her mental scale was loaded with heartfelt dismay at the unladylike—and certainly non-Dutch—actions of her niece in unabashedly chasing after the de Boer boys.

And then there was her utter confusion as to how so many hours throughout the summer had passed unaccounted without raising an ounce of suspicion at the parsonage. All this shifted the scale when the fact she had learned of such goings-on in this manner was dropped on the opposite side. She sighed. *It is beyond the realm of my experience.*

Unaware of the wide swath of destruction cut by her words, Rebecca bid farewell to Lena, gathered up her packages and followed the clerk's helper out the door to where he swung a fifty-pound bag of flour off his shoulder on to the de Boer's wagon.

Within minutes, Lena settled her account and strode out to the Ter Hoorn buggy, mentally planning her discussion with Gustave. By the time she reached the church corner, she had a lengthy list of points to cover and marched directly to the study before she forgot a single one.

That evening at the supper table, Gustave took matters into his capable hands. "So, Brigetta, tell me—what have you learned about farming this summer? Do you want to live on a farm, or are you happiest in town?" As if these were the most casual of questions, he helped himself to a scoop of mashed rutabagas.

Brigetta's fork landed on her plate with a clatter; she slapped her hand across her lips. Slowly, she lowered her hand to her lap and clutched her napkin. "I have learned," the words came as slowly as molasses from the jug on the windowsill, "farming requires a great deal of hard physical labor and much planning."

"That's true, but are you basing your opinion only on one family, or have you investigated several farmers' lives?" His voice remained calm.

Carefully spreading a generous layer of raspberry jam on a slice of bread, Brigetta finally meet her father's eyes. "I chose the family I felt was the best example of good farmers: the de Boers. Everyone speaks highly of their crops and produce." A bright red circle popped up on each cheek—the only clue to the pandemonium within her.

"Perhaps your research is nearly done, then?" Gustave asked as he ladled rich gravy over potatoes and roast beef and passed the dish to Hanna.

Brigetta felt a wave of sadness sweep over her as she thought about the harvest she now would not see. "Yes, Papa," she said respectfully.

Lena swallowed hard and released a breath she had not realized she held. Nothing tasted good to her tonight. For as little as anyone's mind was on the meal, she could just as well have served a saddle blanket and saved the fine roast for Sunday.

At the close of the meal, Gustave offered the prayer of thanksgiving. Brigetta allowed herself a quick peek at his bowed head when he ended with words never before included in prayers at the *Dominie's* table, "Heavenly Father, I thank you for the wondrous gift of Brigetta. Keep her within Thy loving care. Amen."

That night, Brigetta gave and received extra loving pats along with the ritual bedtime hugs. Lena knew another time would be soon enough to mention the idea of Brigetta helping Rebecca during the harvest. *Sufficient unto the day are the troubles thereof*—that was Lena's guiding principle.

True to her word, Rebecca talked to Hanna and Lena after services on Sunday. "Our Brigetta?" asked a surprised Hanna. "You want Brigetta to help you cook?" She looked from Rebecca to Lena.

"She helps us quite often with kitchen work and has learned many things, Hanna, especially this summer," Lena said calmly, mindful of the *Tante* Lena book in the cedar chest.

"She will only assist, never taking on the full responsibility," Rebecca hastened to reassure them. "It would be such a delight to have a girl in my kitchen with me, especially one as full of life as Brigetta."

As they walked across the lawn toward the parsonage, Hanna said pensively, "It is startling to realize how others see Brigetta. But you have taught her well, Lena. You're right; she'll do fine."

Lena squeezed her sister's arm and nodded. "We see her in the nest; others see her stretching her wings in the sky." They slowed their pace, each lost in private reflections. "So, I will talk with Brigetta later today and then she can ride her bicycle out to the farm to talk with Rebecca tomorrow about what is expected and when to begin. If she is interested." Hanna's head jerked to the side and she caught her sister's dancing eyes. The two women clutched each other and sputtered with laughter. *If she is interested!*

At Sunday dinner, Lena brought up the subject and waves of smiles broke across Brigetta's face. "To be chosen like this! I will do my best." Her bright eyes swept the family circle until they reached Gustave and another conversation involving the de Boer family burst her bubble. "Oh, Papa!" Tears crested in her eyes.

Gustave quickly eased her distress. "This is different, Sweet Pea. You will be hired to help Rebecca—that is an honorable task."

Each adult at the table felt the slightest brush of a wing as their own hummingbird prepared to take her first peek over the edge of the nest they had shared with her since birth. A first flight is an adventure for the young bird, and a time of terror and sadness for those who know how far down the earth is and how hard that ground can be.

*   *   *

Within weeks, Brigetta began her first employment. She awoke just as the sun sent its first pink sprays above the horizon and headed out on her bicycle to help Rebecca begin the daily tasks of baking and cooking. Putting in long days like the harvesters, she returned to Papa, Mama, and *Tante* Lena who all subconsciously listened for the squeak of her bicycle amidst the melodies of the evening bird songs.

Each day, three subdued adults pulled up chairs to the table at the parsonage for breakfast, lunch, and supper. The first meal without Brigetta had seemed odd and quiet; the second meal dragged by with each person watching the door as if expecting her to burst in at any minute with apologies for being late; and by supper of the first day, Lena asked wistfully, "How long do you suppose harvest lasts?" The days of the 1916 harvest were odd and quiet times at the parsonage.

"I'm home! Is anyone around?" Brigetta would call out as she rode across the parsonage lawn and leaned her bicycle against the porch, ready for her ride the next morning. Reunited as a family again, they gathered on the porch to hear the news of Brigetta's day. Eventually, either the annoyance of mosquitoes or someone noticing Brigetta's muffled yawns would serve to pull the family indoors. With the sun setting over the buggy barn in purple splendor, Brigetta would head off to bed, falling asleep instantly.

Gustave asked one morning at breakfast, "Remember Brigetta's first day of school?" He needed say no more; that had been a milestone unmatched until now. Conversations at the *Dominie's* table on the Sundays surrounding harvest—with Brigetta spending a whole day at home—were speckled with wisdom and witticisms from the de Boer household. There seemed no end to the stories Brigetta could tell; her world had grown outside the scope of their shared experiences.

Brigetta's life was now entwined with another family in ways beyond even her vivid imagination. Her words flowed around bites of Lena's special Sunday dinners and continued throughout the evening until she floated upstairs to bed. She had tales about the whole de Boer family:

Stories about Cornelis.

"Cornelis has promised to give me a ride in his car!"

"Hans has an automobile?" Gustave's eyebrows arched.

"Not yet, but if they ever get one, and Cornelis learns how to drive it, I'll get a ride. Isn't that exciting? Someday, Cornelis is going to either sell or make automobiles."

Stories about Bram.

"Don't ask, because my lips are truly sealed, but Bram has shared his secrets with me for starting tulips from seeds!" This from the same girl who wrapped birthday presents and then promptly told the recipient the contents. "I greatly admire his abilities!"

Stories about Rebecca.

"Mrs. de Boer's secret for her famous roasted chicken is an iron kettle with a *rounded* bottom, not flat. When she plays their pump organ with the eleven stops, it sounds just like the carillon in the church tower!"

Stories about Grandfather de Boer.

"Did you know Bram's grandfather once skated forty miles on a canal in Holland? When we see him skating on the Floyd River next winter, we simply must look at his skates-—they are the very ones he used back then. He'll never give them up, he says. The day they wear out is the day he stops skating."

Stories about Grandmother de Boer.

"Bram's grandmother once made twelve dozen Dutch handkerchief *koekjes* with their four corners pinched around an almond filling that has been a secret family recipe for four generations. And she baked dozens of Dutch lace *koekjes* for a wedding in Holland that Royalty attended! She showed me the thank-you letter—the stationery has a crest on it!"

Stories about Hans.

"Mister de Boer has a pocket railway watch and when we bring food out to the men, he always pulls it out and says, 'Right on time!' Oh, the funniest thing happened yesterday. Mister de Boer was heading out to the field along with Bram and Cornelis. One minute he was walking, and the next he was turning cartwheels across the lawn! He could be in a circus."

These revelations were essentially a one-sided discourse since any stories Lena, Hanna, and Gustave could tell paled beside such wondrous accounts. Little did they realize Brigetta found much to tell about her own household at the de Boer's table—tales that left that family silent, feeling their lives were dull indeed compared to the truly astonishing adventures apparently occurring daily at the *Dominie's* house.

Brigetta loved to tease Cornelis, finding him someone with a ready retort. They joked with ease. With Bram, her tongue tangled and her words either collided or halted altogether, and she found she could hardly swallow if he looked at her.

When Brigetta wore a fluffy apron to protect her dress—though it did nothing to prevent dabs of flour from landing on her pert nose or dusting her pink cheeks—Bram couldn't keep his eyes off her. Or when she and his mother brought mid-day meals to the field and Brigetta's laugh spread like the fragrant odors beneath the covered trays she carried. Even with a stalk of wheat sticking straight up out of her hair and one braid coming undone, she was a creature of wonder to Bram. *Why can't I talk to her as readily as Cornelis does?*

At the oddest times, his body responded in embarrassing ways to thoughts of Brigetta. One such time, catching her curious glance at his rising color, he rushed to say the first safe thing that crossed his mind, interrupting a conversation about grain prices. "Your bicycle must know the way to our farm just like how our horses find the barn in a snow storm."

Cornelis stopped eating and stared at his brother with bewilderment stamped across his face. His "*Huh?*" was brushed aside by Brigetta's glorious laugh. "Tomorrow I'll close my eyes and keep on pedaling and hope I end up beside your back porch and not at the bottom of the Floyd River!"

In spite of his earlier embarrassment, Bram grinned. "More likely, you'll end up in the ditch with brambles in your hair!" *This is a wonderful girl! Too bad she is so young, not even Cornelis' age.*

1917

◆

The tantalizing smells of Lena's doughnuts brought the Ter Hoorn family from their beds to welcome the arrival of 1917. Doughnuts, symbolizing life's full circle, graced New Year's Day breakfast tables of Dutch homes around the world, including those in Dutchville. That custom, along with dozens of *nieuwjaarskoekjes* filling the cookie jars, ended the holiday season and commenced each new calendar year.

Crisp and shortened days brought February to Dutchville. Gustave stopped at the post office on Valentine's Day to collect an order of books, and the postmaster handed him the box along with a loose postcard. "What's this?"

"It appears Brigetta has a sweetheart."

Eyebrows arched and lips dipping in a frown, Gustave examined and then stuck the locally postmarked card in his pocket. Back home, Gustave handed Brigetta the exquisite card. Cupid sending an arrow straight into the heart of a young lady who looked much like Brigetta.

"Turn it over, Sweet Pea!" Hanna said, peering over her shoulder.

The block-letter message on the back read: "Hoping you'll be my Valentine. __ __ __ __"

Brigetta's hands shook. *Bram?* A two-cent stamp. *Why spend first-class postage to mail a postcard less than a mile?* She expelled enough air to flutter the hair that framed her blushing face.

"It is certainly romantic!" Lena pronounced. "Our Brigetta has a *vriendin*!" Suppertime was awash with teasing speculation.

Brigetta spent the night in a cloud of mystery. She had never seen Bram's handwriting—but that mattered little since the brief message required few skills in recognizing distinctions in how an *i* was dotted or the angle at which a *t* was crossed. Thoughts of Bram had never been far removed from her thoughts even though he had already graduated from Dutchville High School. She frequently saw him in town, still skated with him, always watched for his arrival at church, and thought of him each time she saw Cornelis at school.

Then came Easter. The postmaster handed Brigetta an envelope from the Ter Hoorn slot. She stared at the ivory paper: MISS BRIGETTA TER HOORN, DUTCHVILLE IOWA. Her face turned a vivid hue and she hurried to the town-square, clutching the envelope to her heart. Dropping to a bench behind the windmill, away from prying eyes, she carefully opened the sealed flap. Inside was an embossed card with lavender flowers decorating a white cross and a yellow chick looking up at a butterfly. Certainly not religious, despite its gold-gilt message: *A joyous Easter.* The other side was blank except for "YOUR SECRET ADMIRER" written in indistinguishable block letters.

∗   ∗   ∗

The war stretched out its grasp and reached into the hearts of Dutchville and other small towns, big cities, and farms along dusty roads throughout the country. Young men from east to west, north to south, lined up at Armed Services Induction Centers where physicians either pronounced them fit to go to war, or sent them home to face their families and neighbors who wondered *Why?* To serve ones country was the greatest honor, the deepest fear.

Bram de Boer meandered through such a line in the June sunshine, shuffling a few steps at a time, waiting and wondering, until it was his turn. His physical examination was both impersonal and extremely embarrassing. But to have endured all that for these results? A standard form with the shattering decision—*medical exemption.* His head spun and he lurched away from the table and out into the open air.

He had ridden into town this morning full of optimism and apprehension. Like others standing in line, the call to war interrupted his plans at the time he was truly beginning his life's work. But he came willingly—ready to give as deep a commitment to soldiering as he did to farming. *But my country doesn't want someone with weak lungs. My country has rejected me.*

He walked slowly over to his horse and swung his leg over the powerful back. The slight pressure of his heels got no response. In his haze, he heard an old schoolmate laugh as he loosened Bram's reins from the hitching post and tossed them up to him. "You won't get far unless you untie your horse, soldier!"

Soldier! He had come to town a farmer; his family expected a soldier to return. When he had been standing in line, part of him had been afraid of the unknown. Now, riding away from the Induction Center, part of him was inexpressibly glad he would not face enemy fire. To Bram's thinking, that gladness was almost as unacceptable as the fear. It was his duty to serve and his body was defeating him. Someone would have to answer for this.

Several hours later, having spent the morning in the company of anguished thoughts, Bram stood before Doc Draayer with the damning paper in his hand. "I am a strong and healthy man, Doc. How can I have weak lungs? They asked if I had ever had tuberculosis, and I told them that was ridiculous. Surely I would either know about it or be dead. Isn't there something you can do so I can serve my country?"

Gerrit Draayer examined the proffered paper. Recognizing a trusted colleague's signature, he had no doubt the examination had been conducted completely and correctly. As the family doctor for most young men standing in line with Bram, Doc Draayer had not been part of the

Dutchville process; he had spent the morning at a nearby county's Induction Center to avoid any accusations of partiality. He pulled a pouch from his pocket, tamped a scoop of loose tobacco into his curved pipe and stuck it in his mouth without lighting it. "Do you recall when you had mumps, Bram?"

"Yes; why?"

"At the time, I wondered at some of your symptoms. It is possible you also contracted a mild case of tuberculosis. That could account for lung problems now and how sick you were then. The initial symptoms of TB were present, but were distorted by those that define mumps, which you obviously had."

"So it's possibly I *have* had TB?" Bram asked, astonished.

Doc Draayer lifted the army's form from the desk again and sucked on his pipe as he scanned it. "Though you recovered outwardly, inwardly, there were troubles that still affect you. Obviously the doctors find those repercussions serious enough to keep you home."

"But I feel fine, Doc," Bram protested. "I have no trouble breathing. How could the rigors soldiers face be any more demanding than those of a farmer? I am capable of defending our country against all enemies!" His voice resonated with conviction.

"I'm not saying weak lungs would keep you from serving with valor and success, but their word is final."

Bram said bitterly, "My country doesn't want me, and if I'm not fit to serve my homeland, I doubt..." He stopped abruptly. A previously unexamined thought exploded to the surface of his thoughts and he gripped the edge of the doctor's desk as the unuttered completion to the sentence detonated in his head. *I doubt Brigetta will want me, either.*

Gerrit Draayer studied the young man with concern. "Are you feeling ill, Bram?"

Bram shook his head sharply—not in reply, but to jar loose the distress in his mind. "Are we finished here?" He clipped the words off sharply and stuffed the form into his pocket.

The doctor nodded and rose from his chair, rounding the desk to face Bram. The young man's strength stiffened every muscle into tight coils. "Work in your field, talking with God until you can safely go home and sit down with your family to plan the days ahead."

"I can't face them yet."

"You have had much success in life, Bram. Don't let this shock keep you from a rich, full life. With your skills in farming, you will be able to contribute much to the war effort, perhaps even more than wearing a uniform and carrying a gun would have allowed you."

Gerrit Draayer watched pensively from his office doorway as Bram left and approached his waiting horse and thrust his wooden shoes into the stirrups. Throughout the town, the youth turned to modern ways, becoming more like those in nearby towns without a common heritage and less like their Dutch forebears. Though most citizens still owned at least one pair of *klompen*, few younger than forty years of age wore them on a regular basis. Bram, however, kept the Dutch ways, realizing *klompen* served him well for farm work and daily living. He saved his leather shoes for church. *That says a lot about the young man. He'll come through this—he's made of good stuff.*

Bram let his horse take the lead and sat numbly astride the reliable steed. He felt inadequate. The trip home was a blur.

Rebecca had sent Bram off to the Induction Center with a good breakfast in his stomach, knowing real fear in her heart. Now, inside the farmhouse on that fine June morning, she turned to her kitchen seeking for a task to keep her hands busy. This could be the day the de Boer family crumbled.

This morning, Bram had finished the earliest chores and then gone off whistling to appear at the Armed Services Induction Center. Rebecca and Hans had stood shoulder-to-shoulder on the porch watching his lanky body until he turned the bend. Rebecca retied her apron; Hans tucked his thumbs beneath his suspenders and asked, "What will you do today?" She shrugged. Hans lightly touched her arm and headed out to the barn.

The kitchen was already spotless, and it was too early to begin lunch, so Rebecca scalded milk and sprinkled breadcrumbs in a buttered pan in preparation for the family's favorite rice pudding.

Hans stood in the quiet barn for a full minute. It was a busy time in the fields, but he had sent Cornelis out to get started. As a father whose oldest son could be heading off to war, he needed something to do to keep him close to the house and Rebecca. He selected tools and headed back to the porch steps where he soon began mending a harness, his hands were often still, but his mind raced.

He could hear Rebecca working in the kitchen, but they didn't speak. There was no need—each heard the other's questions as if shouted from the highest hill: *Will Bram go to war? Why did we wait so long to speak to Bram of hard things?*

Standing at the sink, Rebecca caught her breath as the familiar figure rode into view of her kitchen window. "He's back, Hans," she called out softly. Her forehead furrowed as she saw Bram dismount and fling the reins over the horse's back and slap his rump, sending him riderless toward the barn. Her eldest son turned toward the garden and snared a shovel and a hoe leaning against a post he passed. In the distance, Cornelis worked in the field alone, a cloud of dust marking his trail.

It was an odd moment—usually her menfolk were together, working as one. Even though she could see all three from where she stood, a chill floated around her as she realized the four members of this close family were, at this moment, each an island unto themselves. It was not right, but Rebecca was helpless to change it. *Will they uncover the secret Hans and I have harbored and reveal the brutal truth of his sterility in front of neighbors and friends?*

Rebecca looked out at Hans as he sat on the top step. His silence was weighty—usually he whistled or talked to the cats or spoke with her through the screened door. "Bram's gone to work in the garden," she said softly.

Hans lifted his head, but did not turn. He nodded and bent over his harness. "That's good."

Bram attacked clods of dirt and let his mind roam free. He worked the earth—allowing the familiar physical labor to break down the clumps both in the soil of his mind and in the fields he loved. Time passed unheeded. With each jab of the shovel, his frustration dissipated a little more. Each stroke of the hoe helped diffuse the shock. He had never been disqualified for anything before.

Each rock he loosened cleared the path in his mind for a fresh review of the startling idea of Brigetta as someone more than a pretty little lass who loved to skate. The thought she might not want him if he were unfit to serve his country had erupted to the surface like a volcano, as startling as any such force of nature. He was amazed at the raw spot such a thought left inside him on its first journey through his mind.

With hoe in hand, Bram was now subdued. The simple, steady, familiar activity helped him sift through the rubble of his thoughts and examine newly revealed feelings. Brigetta had been part of the fabric of his life forever. He had felt like her protector on the river. He had heard her clear voice ring out in recitations at church programs. He had sought her approval in the garden. Mesmerized, he had watched her in the kitchen during the harvest.

He admitted amusement at seeing her standing back shyly when other girls fluttered around him like so many butterflies—she had been different than the rest all along. He acknowledged that, in any crowd, he sought out the cloud-colored curls brushing her trim straight shoulders and framing the heart-shaped face. The truth: he felt more alive near Brigetta and he craved her presence even though there had never been a moment for just the two of them.

With Brigetta a willing skating partner, the river had become a sanctuary for him. Each winter he waited for the ice to freeze solid, and now admitted that most important about that event was the realization he could hold out his hand and find heaven in her response. Each time, the ice became a secret arbor for two skaters who moved to the majestic music of wind across the frozen river.

Standing in the garden on this warm June day, Bram could swear he felt the trusting grip of her mittened hand in his, the weight of her body against him as they leaned into dips and curves, the purr of her steady breath in his ear when he tilted his head to catch the words she tossed into the wind. He swallowed hard and looked down to where the ice imagined in his mind melted into the tangible rich black soil.

While Rebecca and Hans occupied their hands with mindless tasks and Bram worked through his emotions in his garden, Gustave Ter Hoorn was heading home along the road beside the de Boer farm. The horse pulled the buggy down the well-known route without much human intervention because the *Dominie* was distracted. After visiting an ailing elderly parishioner, he attempted to ease his troubled spirit before returning home.

Gustave was weary. It was not a tiredness sleep could cure, nor a physical exhaustion after hard labor. It was an inner, spiritual fatigue. He longed for a wife with whom he could share such feelings. He loved Hanna intensely; he lost himself in the wonder of her, yet sometimes felt lost beside her. He talked to her—keeping her abreast of his thoughts and experiences, and Brigetta's life, the concerns of the church, the goings-on about town, but expected little conversation in return. He swayed with the movements of the buggy, lost in a muddle of contemplation.

The words of a hymn reached into his darkness. Like Brigetta collecting fireflies in summer and Lena constantly seeking new recipes, Gustave collected hymns, incorporating truths from them into his sermons. Absentmindedly, he began to sing a song that had found its way across his desk and now niggled at his memory.

The first time he had read the words he had asked Hanna to play it on the piano, over and over, until he knew it well. Today, those words soothed his troubled heart: *There's a wideness in God's mercy like the wideness of the sea; there's a kindness in His justice, which is more than liberty…*His horse stepped a little lighter as Gustave's voice rang out confidently: *There is no place where earth's sorrows are more felt than up in heaven; there is no place where earth's failings have such kindly judgment given…*

"Hello, *Dominie!*" Gustave straightened up and followed the sound of the voice. He was surprised to find himself by the de Boer farm. Bram waved his straw hat in greeting, a welcoming smile as wide as Iowa's horizon on his face.

Gustave frowned at the intrusion. And then it was as if God whispered the last verse of the song in his ear: *For the love of God is broader than the measure of the mind; and the heart of the Eternal is most wonderfully kind…*Gustave silently acknowledged the gentle divine rebuke.

"I've a bunch of beets I'd like to send home with you."

Tugging on the reins, Gustave complied, stretching his legs to the ground, and ambled toward Bram. "Hello, Bram. My, you could easily sell those! Let me pay you for them."

"No, no. You have saved me a trip—I was planning to bring them in to town to you later today." Inexplicably, Bram's face reddened. "I have something of great importance I wish to discuss with you. If you don't mind, could I talk to you now?"

Banishing his earlier introspective thoughts, Gustave nodded.

"As you know, I work with my father and live with my parents in their house. I have a great love for the farm. With the United States entering the war now, there will be a great need for farmers to feed the troops and all who stay at home. So that is how I will be serving my country. Here, on the farm."

Gustave had seen the long line of young men forming that morning outside the Armed Services Induction Center and remembered seeing

Bram among them. Gustave said, "And doing so very well, Bram. You can be proud of your contributions."

Bram wasn't finished. "My grandparents lived in the small house," he nodded to the dwelling set back from the road, "for many years."

Gustave nodded, suddenly wondering where this conversation was headed, and allowed his eyes to follow Bram's glance to the well-preserved cottage.

"Since my grandfather died, my grandmother's health has worsened. She will be moving into my parents' house where my mother can care for her more easily. Then, I will move out to the small house."

"It will be good for you to have a place of your own. How old are you, Bram?"

"Twenty-two, Sir. Yes, it will be nice—but I do not want it to be only my own." He gulped a great chunk of air and twisted his hat in his hands as he rushed on, "I would like permission, *Dominie,* to court your daughter. It is my hope someday soon Brigetta will consider me worthy to be her husband."

In a flash, Gustave knew he would always remember this surprising conversation had taken place midst rows of beets with their colorful tops waving like flags. He looked with fresh eyes at the small house in the distance and was startled how easy it was to imagine a laughing Brigetta standing on the steps with a basket of tulips on her arm. *Brigetta! Bram! Married!* He closed his eyes and rocked back on his heels, feeling very old.

"Sir?" Concern clothed Bram's single word.

He opened his eyes slowly and looked into the face of the first man to declare intentions for the hand of the only Ter Hoorn daughter. "You are a fine young man, Bram. A hard worker, a good Christian Dutchman. All that a father could ever want for his daughter." He suddenly felt giddy. "Yes!" The word rang with joy. "You have my permission to court Brigetta. Tell me, does she know of your intent?"

"I have not spoken to her. In fact, just today I realized I have truly loved her for many years," stating this glorious fact aloud sent blood rushing to his face again, "and would like to marry her one day if she'll have me. I wanted your blessing before I speak with her."

"You have my blessing, son." Gustave had often used the word in speaking with young men, but for the first time it caught him up short: *Bram will be my son. I will have a son!*

"I have not even mentioned my intentions to my parents. I have been doing a lot of thinking out here in the garden today, and when you came by, it was as if God had sent you. I took advantage of the opportunity for a private conversation. When I speak to my parents, I will be able to say you have given your blessing. I know they already love Brigetta from when she helped us during harvest and will welcome her to our family." The words tumbled from his lips.

"Perhaps you can call on my family tomorrow evening."

Bram's grin rivaled Thomas Edison's electric lights. "Yes, Sir! Thank you, *Dominie!*"

"Why don't you have supper with us? Come at six o'clock."

That settled, Bram set his hat back on his head at a jaunty angle, carried the beets to the buggy where he dropped them on the floorboard, and clapped the dirt off his hands before extending his right hand to Gustave. Bram stood ramrod straight, at full attention like the soldier he would never be, on the edge of the road as Gustave moved toward town. The whirlwind of unfamiliar events that had enveloped this day suddenly left Bram drained.

It was days like this a man needed a wife beside him, sharing in his joys and sorrows. He had high hopes Brigetta would soon be his—to love, honor, and cherish. *When I speak to my family, there will be happy news to offset the hard news.*

He was suddenly hungry and hurried to care for his horse and his tools before heading to the house. Throughout his childhood, Bram had read the adage *Na regen komt zonneschijn* on a china plate hanging over his mother's kitchen stove. Today he believed it: *After rain, comes sunshine.*

As he bumped along the road, Gustave marveled. It was as if the cares of his life had been discarded in Bram's garden like the pile of weeds. There would always be new burdens to bear, but there was always a fresh start. *Why do I forget that and let myself become so weighed down with hidden cares?* He whistled cheerfully as he headed home to his houseful of three women who had a big surprise awaiting them.

One would be kept in the dark—it was only fair for a young man to be allowed to do his own proposing.

One would be delighted, having kept a soft spot in her heart for young Bram ever since she saw him carrying Brigetta across the church lawn.

And the other—the one dearest to Gustave's heart...*How will Hanna respond?* This was yet another slippery precipice, but for once Gustave faced it with confidence because it is true: *There's a wideness in God's mercy.*

His joy left no room for worry about how Hanna would handle the news. She would walk a rocky path for a few days, but he knew Brigetta's exuberance could conquer Hanna's despair. With Brigetta growing into a fine young woman, Hanna's worry over her maturing process was subsiding. Brigetta's enthusiasm for life banished discouragement and decreased the frequency of Hanna's withdrawals.

Gustave was determined not to fret away his joy: If all things hoped for came to be, he would someday soon be the father of the *meisje!* For seventeen years, he and Hanna had held and loved and housed Brigetta Ter Hoorn. Now Bram could soon hold, love, and house Brigetta de Boer. It was a good thing the act of unhooking the horse from the buggy was second nature, because Gustave's eyes were misty when he performed the task hardly able to see past his nose.

He stood unnoticed in the kitchen doorway for a moment. Lena cubed potatoes, Hanna measured ingredients for cornbread, and Brigetta sliced carrots and celery into a bowl on the table. Love welled up inside him until he feared his chest would burst. His sharp intake of air pulled three sets of eyes to where he stood.

"Hello, Papa! We wondered when you would arrive. Now we can add the vegetables to the stew. We will have the most delicious supper you can imagine. Just smell it!"

He latched on to the proffered topic and moved toward the stove to lift the lid off the simmering pot. A wonderful aroma wafted into the room. He dropped his arm around Brigetta, facing Hanna and Lena. "It smells so good I almost wish you could serve it tomorrow instead of tonight. I've invited Bram de Boer for supper tomorrow evening, and I'm sure he would love a good bowl of stew—which everyone knows is always better the second day. But then, I'd have to wait a full day to taste it myself. Such a dilemma!" An abrupt silence and cessation of activity, then three voices and six questions:

"Bram? Coming *here*?"

"*Tomorrow?* For supper?"

"*Stew?* For company?"

Gustave gave no answers, but merely tweaked Brigetta's cheek and pulled Lena's apron string on his way around the table to bend over Hanna's shoulder and kiss her cheek. "Yes, I saw him working in his garden—oh, he gave us beets which I have left out in the buggy. I'll go get them now. Anyhow, in the course of our conversation, I invited him." He turned toward the door.

Brigetta reached out and caught the corner of his jacket. "Forget about the beets, Papa! Tell me, I mean, tell us everything!" Gustave quickly noted that his daughter's cheeks were the same hue as Bram's had been less than an hour before and wondered if he had been oblivious to something so important right under his nose.

'Will the whole family come?" asked Lena, immediately beginning to plan a menu in her head.

"Only Bram. Now, I'm going to wash off his gift at the pump and then I will be up in my study while the stew simmers. Whatever you decide to fix tomorrow night will be fine—just don't feed the man his own beets!"

As the household quieted after supper and all headed off to their own bedrooms, Gustave quietly filled Hanna in on the highlights of his earlier talk with Bram. "I gave him my blessing, Hanna, and invited him for supper to allow him an opportunity to talk with you and Brigetta."

Hanna was quiet as she sat at her vanity and ran a hairbrush through her curls. He watched her from the rocker, fascinated as always by this simple and altogether feminine task. Catching his eye in the mirror, she spoke softly, "He has all the potential to be a good man, Gustave. Just like you. Even at his young age he has a reputation as trustworthy and a diligent worker. I have no doubt he could keep Brigetta as happy as she has always been. I hope tomorrow night goes well."

It was a long twenty-four hours for the four residents of the parsonage. No one could have imagined one guest would spawn four avenues of contemplation as diverse as this young man's impending visit created. Brigetta's heart leaped and hoped. Lena planned and smiled. Hanna was a picture of pondering and *angst*. And Gustave prayed and dreamed.

Rebecca had come back to her kitchen window throughout the day, seeing Bram still at work in the garden each time. When Hans took lunch out to Cornelis in the field, he had stayed to work with their younger son for a while, but he now lingered close at hand again, tightening Rebecca's clotheslines, pounding in loose nails in the porch railing, pumping water to fill the kitchen stove's water well. They had eaten herring with mustard on rye bread for their own lunch without tasting a thing, thinking of nothing but Bram hoeing out in the garden.

Now Rebecca passed by the window again; her surprise at seeing *Dominie* Ter Hoorn stopped along the road kept her there. She could see Bram's back straighten, and watched curiously as the two men talked intently at length, then smiled broadly, shook hands, and the buggy rolled down the road with a cluster of Bram's beets in it. *Bram is coming to the house!* Rebecca pressed her hands against her cheeks and flew to the icebox to bring out a covered plate.

She heard Bram's voice rumble in greeting to his father, and then the two men filled the doorway in rapid succession as they moved to the kitchen table. "Hello, Mother! How did you know I'm starved?" Bram asked as he pulled out the chair and took his usual place. Rebecca shot a questioning glance at Hans who shrugged almost imperceptibly.

"'Becca, Bram says he has something to tell us. Can you sit a minute?" Hans asked in an even tone as he, too, found a chair.

Rebecca sank down to the familiar safety of her four-spindle bow-back kitchen chair. Her body was shaking enough that she worried whether the chair could hold together.

Bram ate several bites of his lunch before stopping to take a long draught of milk. Then he realized his parents were staring intently at him. He smiled, and wiped his mouth on the back of his hand. "I got back from the Induction Center quite a while ago, but I needed some time to think, so I worked in the garden. Thank you for keeping lunch for me, Mother."

Rebecca nodded and pleated her apron into accordion folds beneath the table. "I saw you out there. You got a lot hoed."

"Yes, I also got a lot of thinking done. When I came home, I was quite upset. The doctors there told me I have weak lungs, which keeps me from joining the service. My status is *medical exemption.* I still can't believe it." He paused to take another bite.

"Weak lungs?" Rebecca and Hans' words echoed in the kitchen and they exchanged a look of disbelief.

Bram nodded. "After I left there, I wandered around for a while, trying to sort things out. Finally, I stopped by Doc Draayer's office and talked with him. When I had the mumps, it is possible I also had a mild case of tuberculosis. That would account for the cough I've had through the years, and the problem the doctors found today. And that's what keeps me home. It was a shock to hear."

Rebecca's heart pounded so hard it hurt in her ears. "I'm a proud citizen, but I am also your mother. While I understand your disappointment, I am not sorry you will still be home."

Hans' voice was low and expressionless. "Did Doc Draayer mention anything else?"

Bram looked puzzled. "Not really. He said I could contribute as much being a farmer as I would being a soldier—there will be a great demand for food and we will undoubtedly be called on to help supply it."

"That's true," Hans said evenly.

"So, that's a piece of news that is a mixed blessing. But I have something else to tell you!"

Rebecca's eyes widened. Hans' head jerked up from his distracted contemplation of the tablecloth to search Bram's face.

"*Dominie* Ter Hoorn passed by when I was working in the garden— and his timing couldn't have been better. He has given me his blessing to court Brigetta! I will go to the parsonage tomorrow night—he invited me to join them for supper. Imagine—someday Brigetta may be my wife."

A breeze coming through the kitchen window shaped the curtain into several undulating waves and, just as quickly, receded and left it limp once again against the frame until the next gust. Bram's words did the same to Hans and Rebecca: puffing up their hopes and instantly sucking them slack and lifeless.

"You approve of Brigetta, don't you?" Bram asked, curious in the face of his parents' silence.

"Oh, yes, Bram! Yes. It's just that you've given us quite a bit to think about in such a short time," Hans hastened to assure his son. He tipped his head toward Rebecca. "Your mother and I already love Brigetta like a daughter."

"A delightful girl—so full of life and energy," Rebecca pulled herself up straighter in her chair. "She will bring much joy to your life."

"Let's not put the cart before the horse! She does not know of my intentions yet!"

Hans mentally shook off all plaguing thoughts, reached across the table, and grasped Bram's shoulder. "I have to agree with Gerrit Draayer. Your contributions to the war effort will be significant—those soldiers will tell stories in their letters back home about the wonderful food coming from Iowa" he teased and then added, "and you have given us delightful news besides that, son."

"I was wondering if your grandparents' small house wouldn't seem large and lonely to you, even with Cornelis sharing it with you for the next few months, but now you can look forward to the day Brigetta joins you!" Rebecca's eyes lit up and the two men laughed.

"Your mother has jumped right past your courtship, Bram!"

Their laughter was punctuated by the creaks of the screen door opening. Cornelis stepped out of his mud-stained *klompen* and stood stocking-footed in the doorway. "What's happening? Bram, where have you been? I thought you were going to help me plow when you got home?"

There was a jumble of words as all three tried to sooth, inform, and include Cornelis. Rebecca quickly poured him a glass of buttermilk and brought the cookie jar to the table. Hans pulled out a chair and motioned Cornelis to sit. Bram sat grinning from his place at the table. "Little brother, I'll tell you what's happening! There's some problem with my lungs, so I won't be going off to fight the enemy. And after tomorrow night, I hope to begin courting Brigetta Ter Hoorn in hopes of giving you the prettiest and sweetest sister-in-law you could ever have!"

Cornelis licked his lips clean of their milky mustache and stared at his brother with an unreadable gaze.

Hans said, "Quite the news, eh, Cornelis? Little did any of us realize when Bram rode off this morning just how the day would end." The family talked for some time. Finally, Hans said, "We must thank God for His goodness and ask His blessing on our family."

Four heads bowed around the table, but while Hans lifted words of thanks and petition to heaven, unspoken prayers joined them on their upward journey to the heavenly Father.

Rebecca wiped a tear from her eye. *Spare him, Lord, from disappointment. May Brigetta love and accept him as he is.*

Cornelis folded his hands in an attitude of prayer, but he alone knew how tightly they were clenched. *Why are you letting this happen, God? How can I spend the rest of my life seeing them together?*

Behind the sincere words his lips formed, Hans' silent supplications came from deep within. *Give me the strength, Father, to do the right thing. Prepare Bram to hear what I must say to him.*

Bram's heart soared above the sadness and bitterness of the morning and filled with the brightness of the Heavenly Father's love. *Thank you, God, for helping me see beyond my anger and resentment.*

Hans' "Amen" echoed like the final peal of the mantle clock at the top of the hour, resonating on a cloud of all the chimes before. Four chairs emptied as the occupants moved to accomplish late afternoon chores. Hans brushed a lock of hair out of Rebecca's face when she passed him and tipped her chin up for his kiss. The dishes rattled in her hands. Bram slung an arm across his brother's shoulders as they headed to the barn.

Hans and Rebecca stood alone in the quiet kitchen. She put the dishes into the metal dishpan and turned, bumping into Hans who gathered her into his arms and whispered, "It will all work out, 'Becca."

"I can't see how, but I hope you're right."

"I'll talk to him. Tomorrow."

But that evening as the family was finishing supper, a neighbor rode up to inquire if the de Boer men could spare time the next day to help rebuild another neighbor's barn that had burned the week before.

And so it was the next morning Rebecca sent Hans, Bram, and Cornelis off with bottles of cold tea wrapped in rags and ham-filled biscuits for mid-morning, and began her day—like the neighboring farm wives—baking her contribution for the workers' noon meal.

While Bram was pounding nails several miles outside of town, Brigetta stood in her bedroom dressed only in her muslin drawers, her favorite underskirt with the cambric ruffle and delicate embroidery, and her new four-hook summer corset. Mary perched on the cedar chest at the end of the bed and offered a mixture of advice and opinion. Brigetta frowned as she held up first one and then another of the three dresses on the bed.

"That's your favorite school dress, and the ribbon trim is new."

"It makes me look like a schoolgirl. This is my best chance to impress Bram with how mature I am! How about this one?" She tucked the billowy blouse with twenty covered buttons and a lace collar with matching cuffs under her chin, and then held the skirt of whispery taffeta silk against her waist.

"Very elegant—almost too fancy, especially since you don't know why he's coming. What if all he wants to do is talk with your Papa about taking on church responsibilities? He could not even look at you, or he might wonder why you're so dressed up for supper!"

The third frock was a Dutch dress that made her look like every other girl in town—but it was such a pretty periwinkle. "This makes your eyes look even brighter blue, Brigetta!" Mary exclaimed.

It couldn't hurt to have Bram notice my eyes. Brigetta took a closer look at the white-yoked dress.

And then there was the matter of her hair. "What am I going to do, Mary?" she wailed as she saw herself once again in the mirror. "*Tante* Lena even rinsed it with vinegar this morning, but now it's flying everywhere!"

"Bows would hold it in place," Mary suggested helpfully.

Brigetta rolled her eyes. "Yes, and make me look like a mere child."

She pulled her curls back into a dignified chignon with her hands, and looked questioningly in the mirror back at Mary who wrinkled her nose. "Now you look as old as our Mamas!"

Here she was one hour before Bram was expected to arrive, and she was still brushing and combing and trying to tame her white-blonde curls into submission. "Oh, how I wish my hair had some color—any color—to it. Yours is such a lovely brown, Mary. Distraction: that's what I need. Something to pull his eyes away from my hair and down to my face."

Mary looked furtively at the closed bedroom door and pulled Brigetta over to a spot by the window. She thrust back the drapery hiding a section of wallpaper roses now distinctly more pale red than those throughout the rest of the room. Licking her index finger, she rubbed it along a rose and carefully smudged several dots of color on Brigetta's cheeks, repeating the lick-rub-smudge routine several times until she was satisfied with the results.

"Remember: do *not* touch your face tonight and no one will be the wiser." She pulled Brigetta into a quick hug. "Remember *every* detail to tell me!"

Alone in her room, Brigetta breathed in the wonderful smells coming up through the grate in her bedroom floor. Pork chops and gravy, roasted potatoes, spinach with nutmeg, applesauce with triangles of Gouda cheese, biscuits and honey, and cream puffs. She knew the menu well, having assisted with each stage of the preparations so Bram would realize, if anyone volunteered the information, she was quite able to set a table to suit a man's fancy.

"*What delicious gravy!*" Bram would say as he savored the first bite and closed his eyes, letting it slide slowly down his throat.

"*Thank you, but no one can beat the lumps out quite like Brigetta!*" The image of her hunched over a frying pan smacking gravy into submission certainly didn't spark the romanticism she desired. Maybe he would be so caught up in the vision of her across the table he would barely be aware of what he was eating.

"*What did you have for supper at the parsonage, Bram?*" his mother would ask.

84   Rough Terrain

"I can't remember a thing—all I can see is Brigetta's beautiful blue eyes and her pretty pink cheeks. She wore a simple Dutch dress, but her waist is so slender and…"

"Brigetta? I could use your help, please!" *Tante* Lena's voice crept around the smells of supper coming through the grate. Brigetta hurriedly buttoned her dress.

She had almost given up on *ever* being able to be the only girl in Bram's view—and tonight dear, sweet Papa plopped the opportunity right in her lap! He was frustratingly closed-mouth about this whole occasion. Each time she asked for more details, his eyes twinkled and his moustache twitched, but his lips stayed closed when she tried to coax him to say more than "We talked, I invited him to supper, and he accepted." And then he would whistle and walk away.

Brigetta smoothed the skirt of her Dutch-smocked dress with its broad white collar and crisp embroidered apron as she walked down the steps. She paused midway and looked at the door where Bram would enter. *There are decisions at every point of this adventure!*

Should I be standing right here on the landing, my hand resting ever so lightly on the banister? She looked at the fading sunlight filtering through the oval stained glass window. *The light could dance around my head like a halo. When he senses my presence, he will watch me move my hand, just so, to lift my skirt. But what if I trip on the stair-runner or catch my heel on the hem of my skirt? Better to be downstairs when he arrives!*

She bypassed the dining room, having already analyzed the cutlery, each napkin in its silver ring, and every stick of furniture. She had even sat at the place assigned to Bram and looked across the spotless linen and sparkling china at her own chair. Her mission throughout supper was to become unforgettable.

She moved along to the parlor. What if she were sitting on the piano bench, as if just finishing a song—or actually playing a song to filter out across the lawn and coincide with his approach? That would certainly set a mood. *Oh, phooey! In all the years Mama has taught me, why haven't I practiced something romantic? What if I make dozens of mistakes? What if he assumes it is Mama playing! No, no, no—there will be no music tonight.*

"Brigetta!" There was a new urgency to *Tante* Lena's voice that jerked Brigetta into motion.

The kitchen: the precise place to fit the occasion! At the exact moment he would step into the hallway, she would drift out of the kitchen carrying…what? The bowl of honey—perfect! He would see the bowl in her hands and think *Sweet!* and subconsciously remember her each time he ate honey for the rest of his life. *What a marvelous plan!*

Things were in an equal tizzy on the farm. Bram arrived home late in the afternoon with just enough time to bathe beside the pump and change clothes. Three solemn de Boers were preparing to eat Rebecca's onion soup and meat rolls as Bram pointed his horse toward Dutchville.

The first chime signaling the three-quarter hour sounded and Brigetta giggled excitedly in the kitchen and spun *Tante* Lena around in an impromptu jig. "It's nearly six o'clock!" she caroled, "He'll be here soon!"

"Sweet Pea, you're going to make me spill this lemonade, and then what will we drink?" Lena asked with a grin she made little effort to hide. "Now get ready to greet our guest like a proper young lady. Enough of this dancing with your *Tante* Lena—oh, no! The gravy!" She placed the pitcher on the table and raced to the stove. "Please check the oven for me, and then get the buttermilk from the ice box."

The firm knock on the front door followed the echo of the final tolling of the hour and Brigetta could hear her father cross the floor and open the door with a greeting. She swallowed hard as she placed the pitcher of buttermilk next to the lemonade, bit her lips to ensure their bright color, made herself count to ten, and slowly picked up the honey bowl that now played such a crucial role in the evening's success.

As entrances go, Brigetta's was timed perfectly; she floated into Bram's view at the split second he was in position to see her carrying the honey. Beyond that point, however, her strategy fizzled. If only she had included one more detail—like how she would move along, rather than stand frozen in place. Had she expanded the plan just one more level, she would have been out of the way when *Tante* Lena—carrying the twin pitchers of lemonade and buttermilk—charged through the swinging door a few steps behind Brigetta.

Whoop! The mighty first thrust of the six-panel oak door clipped Brigetta right in her posterior and she yelped indignantly. Lena stumbled against her and lurched to one side, sending half the lemonade cascading like an ocean wave down the back of Brigetta's dress.

Brigetta jumped, but unfortunately that move placed her in the direct path of a large portion of the buttermilk that made its journey out of the pitcher, up to her face and swiftly followed the lines of her collarbone down into the scooped neck leading to hidden recesses of her bosom.

The resounding *thump* of the door making its return journey narrowly missed the hem of Brigetta's dress, but instead caught one puffy sleeve on a splinter. A resounding *rip* separated that crucial part of the ensemble right at the seam in a six-inch split that gaped over her right shoulder. "Yow!" Brigetta howled in dismay.

The swinging door, usually such a marvelous feature, still had one final insult to fling at its hapless victims. It propelled *Tante* Lena—as she attempted to regain her balance—into a spin that launched the remaining buttermilk and lemonade down the front of Brigetta's dress in a *Whoosh!* running from bodice to hem.

With a startled shriek of her own, *Tante* Lena dropped the pitchers. She lunged futilely to grab them and, in the move that capped the fiasco, bumped Brigetta's hand holding the honey, adding that slow-moving nectar of the gods to the decoration of the *Dominie's* daughter on this, the most important night of her life.

The contents of two pitchers can go a long way, drenching much of a crisp blue Dutch dress, running in rivulets along a polished hallway floor to form a murky lake in a foot-worn spot. It can soak quite a few curls. And it can dislodge the bottom dose of sugary pulp of lemonade to land, like a well-aimed cannon ball, right on the left arc of a young girl's heaving chest.

Lena moaned and dashed for the kitchen. Gustave rescued the pitchers skidding along the floorboards, and Bram reached Brigetta's side in four steps. Through it all, she had managed to hold on to the bowl of honey even though losing its contents. But at some point in the debacle, one long curl by her left ear had dipped into the bowl and now released random golden drops across the intact sleeve of her dress.

The lemonade wash and buttermilk rinse had accomplished what hours of brushing had failed to do: Brigetta's hair now lay perfectly flat, except for the one curl set with honey.

Hanna stood in the parlor door, wide-eyed, wondering fleetingly if there were any dignified way to remove sticky pulp from her daughter's bodice.

Lena returned with rags and a dishpan of soapy water and thrust a wet mop into Gustave's hand, "Mop, or we'll have ants galore, to say nothing of sour-milk odors all summer," she ordered as she proceeded to wipe her way down and around Brigetta's skirt. "Stick your foot out and I'll wipe your *klompen* off, too, Sweet Pea, or you'll be tramping this mess all over the house."

Brigetta obliged and Lena rubbed vigorously, putting Brigetta off-balance. Bram reached out and caught her as she tottered. She need not have worried about pink cheeks; the touch of his hand on her arm gave her face a glow rubbing all the wallpaper roses in the world would never accomplish. She looked at him and sighed inwardly. *My whole life is ruined! All my plans are for naught!*

As if reading from her earlier script for the evening, Bram said softly, "You have the most beautiful eyes, Brigetta. So *very* blue." He spoke with the reverence of someone who has panned for gold and found the mother lode.

Brigetta's jaw went limp and the rest of her body followed suit. She promptly lost her grip on the bowl of honey. It bounced off Lena's head and sent the remaining contents meandering in a lazy stream down that woman's hair and back as she hunkered down in her ministrations. Only Lena's resulting "Oomph!" yanked Brigetta back from the depths of Bram's gaze.

That's when Hanna laughed. Her first sound was a chuckle, then a giggle, and then an outright laugh—a belly-shaking, teary-eyed, sidesplitting laugh. She leaned against the doorframe; Gustave was by her side in an instant. When he realized his wife was not hysterical, he looked back at the scene she pointed to in their hallway and added his own spontaneous laughter.

All the energy Lena had put into cleaning sputtered to a halt when the honey bowl hit her. She plopped her rump down on the sticky floor and rolled her head back on her shoulders. She stared at her sister and brother-in-law in amazement as they held each other, helpless with infectious laughter and soon joined in their merriment. Only Brigetta and Bram were silent, neither having a clue what to say, where to look, or what to do next.

Gustave wondered if the evening could be salvaged. He need not have worried. Hanna's giggles finally weakened and she collected herself long enough to ask, "So, Bram, are you enjoying your first invitation to the parsonage for supper?"

"Very much, Ma'am," he responded seriously, turning to face Gustave and Hanna all the while keeping a firm grip on Brigetta's arm. As realization dawned at how truly inappropriate such remark was, his face broke into a grin. "It's been quite exciting already, and I'm still in the hallway!"

"You might need some help to pry yourself loose from Brigetta's arm!" Gustave teased.

Bram blushed and dropped his hand immediately, unobtrusively rubbing sticky fingers across his trousers. He looked at Brigetta shyly, and then stared. Something odd was happening to her face.

Lena's eyes followed his and she leaned back against the wall and hooted with laughter once again. "Brigetta, I do believe your roses are running!"

Brigetta instantly reached for her face, adding honey to the mess. She moaned aloud as she remembered and realized her face was now a telltale confession of her toiletry secrets. Tante *Lena knows about the wallpaper?*

Hanna took charge, "We invited a guest for supper and we must feed him! I'm sure we won't see either Brigetta or Lena for the rest of the evening if we allow them sufficient time to clean up, so we will have to accept them as they are. We will have a picnic right here in the hallway!"

Four sets of amazed and curious eyes stared into Hanna's face. She didn't flinch.

"Gustave, will you get an old bed sheet from the bottom shelf in the linen closet and spread it out for our tablecloth? Bram, you may help me carry the dishes from the dining room table to the hallway. Lena and Brigetta, please bring our supper in as soon as you have cleaned up a bit."

"Where will we sit, Mama?" Brigetta asked, weak-kneed and interested in sitting *anywhere*—and soon.

"Why, on the floor, of course—it's a picnic! Besides, I'm not about to let you and Lena anywhere near my dining room rug and chairs!" she said merrily over her shoulder as Bram followed close on her heels.

Wide-eyed, Brigetta and Lena looked at Hanna and then each other and then Lena hissed, "Come!"

Out in the kitchen, Lena made short work of wiping Brigetta' face, neck and arms with a dishrag. Brigetta, in turn, cleaned the worst of the mess from her aunt's dress. Then, they quickly loaded trays with the same serving dishes and platters that were to have graced the dining room table. Brigetta filled a pitcher with water and poured more honey into another bowl.

They caught each other looking longingly at the kitchen sink, and then Lena's stare zeroed in on Brigetta's head. "Your Mama said we couldn't take much time to clean up, but dear me—you're dripping like a pump! We must do something about your hair." She pointed to a hook on the wall. "And put that shawl around your shoulders—at least the bare one!"

And so it was that for Brigetta's first supper with Bram, she sat like a queen enthroned on a pillowcase-covered cushion in the middle of a sticky hallway with splats of buttermilk and drizzles of lemonade adorning its wallpaper. Instead of royalty's crown on her head, however, her curls were tucked neatly beneath a dishtowel-turned-turban on which Hanna's embroidered wisdom read *Into each life some rain must fall* and a robin appeared to be plucking a worm right out of her skull.

It was a rowdy supper. Once they settled in on the cushions Gustave provided, a great many things prompted gales of laughter. Hanna passed out linen napkins and remarked, "Be sure to use these, Brigetta and Lena! I hate to have you spill anything on your lovely dresses!"

"We'll have to swear you to secrecy, Bram, or the whole town will wonder what went on here tonight!" Lena said.

"I'll just tell them I have never tasted such a wonderful supper and I didn't have to worry for a minute about my *table* manners!"

A lantern cast a cozy glow around the circle. The food was delicious, the conversation was well seasoned with humor, and each time the honey was requested, someone repeated yet another detail of the whole fiasco that set them all laughing again.

Over dessert and coffee, Gustave suggested casually, "This is a good time to tell my family about your plans, Bram."

Bram shifted on his cushion and leaned back against the wall. Brigetta watched his Adam's apple bob. "Yesterday," he cleared his throat nervously, "I learned I will not be going into the Armed Services because of a long-ago medical problem." He looked around the circle of intent listeners before he continued. "It's nothing that will keep me from doing what I love: farming. So I plan to keep working with my father, and someday the farm will be mine."

"That's good," Lena said encouragingly, shooting a quick glance at Brigetta who was surprisingly quiet. "It's a good farm and you're a good farmer."

Bram nodded with a shy smile. "My grandmother will move into the big house with my parents to make it easier for my mother to care for her and I will move into my grandparents' house."

"So you'll live in the small house with Cornelis?" Brigetta asked in a strained voice.

"Only for a few months. By next summer, Cornelis hopes to have saved enough money to move to a big city, which is perfect timing for my plans. My brother does not have the same love for the soil as I do, as Brigetta knows."

When he said her name, it was as if angels sang. Brigetta leaned back against the wall with thoughts pounding like drums that drowned out the angels' voices; the internal din sickened her.

Bram will soon have his own house, but he has plans—plans requiring perfect timing. He'll soon be finding a wife—Cornelis will leave and Bram will marry. Has he come to supper to talk to Papa about the wedding date? Oh, dear God, help me to be kind to his wife even though right now I despise her! Brigetta wished this whole wretched evening would end so she could sob into her pillow.

Gustave shifted on his cushion and leaned forward, elbows on his knees. "I had never really observed the cottage before, even though I have visited Bram's grandparents many times. It is a fine home—much like where you and I lived, Hanna, when we were first married."

Papa! Brigetta's eyes flashed blue lightning at her father but she was intensely curious to hear about the house Bram's bride would occupy.

The silence that rounded the circle of five pushed against Bram's chest until he thought he would burst with what he had yet to say. Then that looming hush bumped across to Brigetta and nudged another wave of heat from her toes to her nose. *This must stop! If I am to live without him, I cannot blush when someone says his name or I hear his voice.*

"Thank you for inviting me for supper, tonight, *Dominie*. It gives me an opportunity to tell the rest of your family what I asked you about yesterday."

"Yes, it does. You're most welcome at our…" Gustave swept his hand across the bed sheet and chuckled, "…table!"

"Brigetta," Bram's voice seemed to span an octave in just one word, "yesterday I asked your father for permission to court you." Brigetta sucked in her breath as Bram continued. "I know you still have one year of school left, but will you keep company with me?"

A drum roll began in Brigetta's stomach, rumbled through her rib cage, circled her heart, echoed through her lungs, and shot past her lips in a gasped "Oh!"

The hallway might have been a canyon for an echoing "Oh!" reverberated from Lena's throat.

The room spun until Brigetta was aware only of Bram sitting so close she could touch him.

She remembered the strength of his arms as they skated each winter; he recalled the precious weight of her wounded body in his arms.

He could still smell the sweet scent of her hair as they knelt together in his garden; she inhaled the pleasant earthy fragrance from the fields he exuded with much dignity.

She found pure goodness in his steady gaze; he saw a life of happiness in her sparkling eyes.

His question placed his vulnerable spirit in the palm of her hand. Her answer cleared her mind of plots and plans and wrapped herself up in the profound gift of a resounding and simple "Yes!" Her heart soared like the dulcimer stop on Rebecca's pump organ and she was swept up in excited laughter and talk.

Later at the front door, Bram thanked his host and hostesses. "I will never forget tonight as long as I live," he said fervently.

"I should think not!" Gustave looked down at his radiant daughter in her ripped and stained dress. "We rarely produce such entertainment for guests!"

As Bram disappeared into the night, Brigetta raced from Gustave to Hanna to Lena and back to Gustave, aiming kisses at their cheeks and receiving hugs all around. "There has never been a night as perfect as this in all of history!"

Divesting herself and her niece of their soiled supper attire, Lena pulled a laundry tub out on the porch to soak the two dresses, one dishtowel, a sticky bed sheet, five pillowcases and a pile of rags. She filled buckets of water at the pump and Gustave carried them to fill the tubs. No words were necessary to explain their levity.

Moonlight mingled with gentle lamplight as Hanna washed her daughter's hair at the kitchen sink. She hummed bars from *Psalmen 100* which were interrupted frequently with joyous laughter. At such points, she would say, "Oh, Brigetta!" and the two would lean helplessly against each other.

Brigetta alternately blushed and giggled as she revisited the whole day in her mind: the excitement of setting the table no one even sat at, the worries about hair only to have it hidden for most of the evening, the careful selection of the perfect dress which was soaked within minutes of donning it. But it all paled beside the wondrous fact Bram wanted to keep company with her—and every time she thought of *that* she got weak-kneed and breathless.

For the four parsonage residents and the young man heading home to the farm, the bliss of knowing tonight was the beginning of something beautiful and holy shrouded the evening with a gossamer veil. And the smile that flitted across the five faces—in town and on the farm—sealed the memories to last for a lifetime.

*   *   *

Rough Terrain

While nearly every encounter between Bram and Brigetta was chaperoned—either by dozens of other skaters, or a church full of fellow parishioners, or family in the next room—they always found opportunities, as lovers do, to sneak hugs and kisses.

Their secret ritual always made Bram smile as he thought about Brigetta during the hours they were apart. Bram would ask, "I wonder—do you love me?" knowing her response would always be: "Just a bushel and a peck—a hug around the neck!" which made little sense to anyone but them.

On the days leading up to the *Sinterklaas* parade, most lunchtime conversations at the schoolhouse revolved around speculations as to what information was contained in *Sinterklaas'* big red book. The sobering notion of nothing in their *klompen* in 1917 but sticks or stones or dull black coal—or worse, no visit at all from *Sinterklaas*—motivated good deeds from children otherwise unable to resist temptation.

This year Brigetta was lost in anticipation of a new dress that, to her, was as magnificent as *Sinterklaas'* raiment. In the secret corners of her mind, it was part of her fledgling trousseau if Bram were to propose marriage, though ostensibly it was her Christmas dress.

Brigetta and Lena spent hours pouring over the Sears, Roebuck catalog. "A store-bought dress!" she exclaimed. "I've always loved the clothes you make for me, *Tante* Lena—but no one will have a dress made out of velvet and lace like this one! No one in all of Dutchville will have touched the cloth on the bolt or seen the buttons before. Thank you, Mama, for such a wonderful present!"

Brigetta marked days off on the kitchen calendar as she worried about delivery of her new dress. She often just *happened* to be near the post office when the mail came in, and as long as she was there, why not wait around to see if anything had arrived for the Ter Hoorn family? Her head was filled with what-ifs: *What if it doesn't arrive on time? What if the dress doesn't fit? What if the train derails and the package burns to cinders?*

Finally, the much-anticipated box arrived—a much larger and heavier box than required for one dress! Brigetta not only had to run home and hook up the buggy in order to get the box home, but she needed help to lift it into the buggy.

Wrapped in her winter shawl, Lena waited on the porch as Brigetta pulled into the parsonage yard. "Just leave the box on the buggy—your Papa will bring it in for us." Lena called across the snow.

"The package is huge, *Tante* Lena!" Brigetta called back as the horse headed for his feedbag. "I guess there *are* surprises even in houses where the child is nearly eighteen years old!"

Throughout Dutchville, the holiday season began—as in the Old Country—with the mid-November arrival of *Sinterklaas* in his velvet-gowned splendor. Whereas in Holland he arrived by boat, *Sinterklaas* rode along Dutchville's Main Street in a sleigh—one not unlike that belonging to Hans de Boer. Brigetta recognized it instantly as being the one repainted and hidden in the de Boer barn. She took a closer look at the whitened beard of the man holding the reins, and smiled broadly.

This year, Hans de Boer was *Sinterklaas*, having donned an ornate and flowing bejeweled robe guaranteed to transport Dutchville children to heights of ecstasy. Just then, one of his helpers, traditionally all named Piet, rose from bending over a bag at his feet and tossed a rainbow of candies to the children lining the street.

Brigetta laughed outright when she recognized that, though the face was coal-blackened as folklore required, the eyes were Bram's. She didn't doubt for a minute Cornelis was the other fellow—his cap hiding what would be incongruous red hair for a black-skinned Piet. He, too, responded to children's cries of "Piet! Over here!" by tossing candy to those on the opposite side of the street.

All around her, children scrambled after the paper-wrapped goodies hurled from the sleigh. The festivities beginning today would build each day until they reached feverish proportions when *Sinterklaas* arrived at every child's home on the evening of the fifth of December. That was the night when the year's favorite visitor received children's gifts of carrots and hay for his horse and refilled good children's *klompen* with trinkets, candy, and toys.

Brigetta stuffed her hands deeper into her muff as the crowd jostled her. She shared in their excitement even though she doubted *Sinterklaas* would appear at any household where the youngest person kept company with a young man! Still, she was not immune to intoxicating holidays. Their culmination came with the celebration of the Christ Child's birth on the twenty-fifth of December—and then it would be *Nieuwjaars*!

From his place on the sleigh, Hans saw Brigetta standing in the crowd, and felt a stab of guilt. Months had gone by since Bram had returned from the *Dominie's* house. *Later* Hans had promised himself that night when Bram reported his joyous news. *He is so happy tonight, why squelch his joy?* But a better time had never come.

Now the whole town knew of the romance. From the first Sunday when Bram made his way from the de Boer pew to join the *Dominie's* family and stand straight and tall beside Brigetta during the Scripture readings, it was obvious someday banns would be read and *plechtig beloven* would be made before God and man, making Bram and Brigetta one flesh.

Hans had kept his silence and broken his promise to God, Rebecca, and himself—and done his eldest son a great injustice, and now he lived with the guilt.

✳   ✳   ✳

When Brigetta skimmed down the stairs for breakfast on the sixth of December, she sniffed the air. *Rusk pancakes!* She sped to the kitchen with all of the excitement of a child. "Good morning, *Tante* Lena! You always remember rusk pancakes today and *vet and stroop* for Christmas morning!"

Lena beamed and carefully moved the rusks from the skillet to the heated platter she covered with a dishtowel. "The coffee is already on the table, so you take the powdered sugar, I'll bring the platter, and we won't keep your Mama and Papa waiting another minute."

Brigetta led the way to the dining room and halted so abruptly in the doorway Lena had to quickly step sideways to save the pancakes. Speechless, Brigetta stared at the spot where her chair usually stood.

In its place this morning—pulled right up to the table as if awaiting her arrival—was a fully assembled, gleaming green-enamel lady's bicycle. The dish of powdered sugar tilted precariously in Brigetta's hand and Lena made a flying leap to rescue the bowl and save the carpet.

Brigetta and *Tante* Lena had read the catalog so often in the past months Brigetta knew instantly this bicycle boasted all the latest features: dress guard, combination pedals, tool bag—but it cost nearly sixteen dollars! "Papa, Mama! *Tante* Lena! Oh, my!"

"Hanna, I do believe our daughter has run out of words!"

"So it would appear. Maybe she wants to keep riding the bicycle she got when she was ten and has nearly worn out on a certain country road?" Hanna's smile played at her lips.

Lena added with a mock frown, "Maybe she liked having her skirts drag in the dust."

Brigetta skimmed across the room to run her hands along the curved frame, the handlebars, and the saddle seat. "I am so glad *Sinterklaas* still has me on his list!" Only the tempting smells of the breakfast cooling on the table induced her to roll the bicycle to one side and pull her chair back in its place. Throughout breakfast, her eyes returned to the shiny frame. "It's beautiful! I can hardly wait for summer!"

"We want you to have a good bicycle to ride back to see us if you live in a special small house on a certain big farm!" Gustave teased. The three sharing her table smiled when a blush covered Brigetta's shining face. "Papa, Bram is *courting* me, but you know that doesn't always mean marriage."

Lena rolled her eyes heavenward. "Of course, how silly of us! As foolish as to think just because the sun comes up, it's daytime! You'd better dress warmly today, Sweet Pea. That fellow who probably *isn't* planning to marry you will be here soon to take you out for a sleigh ride, and it's cold enough outside to frost your nose!"

Gustave checked his pocket watch. "Lena, my coffee has gotten cold. Do we have more in the kitchen?"

Lena jumped to her feet, "Why, you're right—yes! Yes, we do!" She was gone in a flash, but it was several moments before she returned, bringing back a fresh pot with a smile nearly splitting her face. "Won't you have a cup, too, Brigetta? It will warm you inside and out."

Brigetta looked at her aunt with amusement. "Even coffee is not nearly as enticing as a sleigh ride! May I be excused to go get ready?"

"Aren't you going to check your *klompen* first, Brigetta?" asked Gustave.

Brigetta jerked her head toward her father. "My *klompen*? I have the most beautiful bicycle in the world sitting right here. What could possibly be in my *klompen*?"

Lena teased, "It could be there's only coal in it."

Brigetta pushed back her chair. "Coal? I think not—I've been very good this year, *Tante* Lena!" she tossed back over her shoulder and headed straight for the parlor. During the night, someone had placed her *klompen* on the Delft tiles surrounding the stove as she had done throughout her childhood. She was right: no coal this year, but there was a shiny box!

She flew across the room, dropped to her knees and with a squeal of delight lifted the cover of the tiny square box. Resting on a velvet bed was a lady's locket watch with a diamond set in a raised gold star. Lifting it out by the chain, she opened the locket and gasped. Bram smiled back at her from the face of the watch. And on the inside of the case, in the most exquisite lettering, it read *Brigetta. Yours for all time. Bram.*

"Do you like it?"

Startled, she jerked and turned around. Bram sat in the chair by the window. "Bram! How did you get here? This is…from you?"

"Slow down! Lena came up with a ruse to get me into the house while your family was at the table. Yes, it's from me. Do you like it?"

"Oh, yes, but…" She blushed as red as the beets Bram had sent home with the *Dominie* that day in June. "It's such a…personal gift…and says such…"

In an instant, Bram crossed the room and pulled her up beside him. He tipped her chin until her eyes met his. "It would be much too personal if a man gave it to someone he didn't care about."

Brigetta trembled and clutched the watch in her hand. Bram looked down, took her hand and opened each finger one-by-one. When the watch was freed, he carefully slid the chain over Brigetta's curls. When the coolness touched her throat, she shivered and looked into his misted eyes.

"I wish there were a better word than *liefhebben* to express how I have felt about you since the day I carried you home from the river. I'd like to be able to know you're promised to me."

She whispered, "I will gladly promise. Remember? A bushel and a peck, a hug around the neck!"

Bram grasped her waist and met her lips in a kiss that moved from their dreams to the new sanctuary they now shared. "All I ask is your promise for now."

"Could you please do that once again?" Bram was only too happy to comply, several more times. Brigetta said breathlessly, "Perhaps we should see Papa and Mama and *Tante* Lena while I can still speak!"

Each person saw the locket gleaming around Brigetta's neck and the rosy glow on two faces and moved to encircle the couple with love and good wishes. "I know we won't marry until Brigetta is finished with school, *Dominie,* but since Brigetta has agreed, I want to declare my intentions."

The sleigh ride was postponed as they talked of plans, shared stories, and the young couple took the first steps of discovering a new level of love in the safe embrace of Brigetta's loving family.

Choirs practiced at the four churches in town, their carols mingling as they echoed across snow-packed fields with the bugled notes from the traditional daily blowing of horns to herald the birth of Christ. *"Vrolijk Kerstfeest!"* was on everyone's lips as they passed on the street.

More cars filled the streets this year than ever before, and those riding in horse-drawn buggies had to keep a grip on their reins when horn-tooted greetings scared the animals. Whether verbal or mechanical, cheer was in the air.

In town-and country-kitchens alike, oven-fires burned steadily as *Sint Nickolaas koekjes, klets koekjes, stroop koekjes,* and *nieuwjaarskoekjes* moved from floured boards to baking sheets to cookie jars in every pantry. Brigetta's favorite spice cookies had to be replaced twice before Lena finally hid a fresh batch away to last through the season.

One snowy day Brigetta came to the kitchen in response to *Tante* Lena's call. She found a grinning and red-cheeked Bram bearing a covered plate. "Eat all the *T*'s first, because the *D*'s are what I want you to remember!" Brigetta lifted the napkin and found a dish filled with Dutch letter-cookies: the traditional gift at Christmas, made all the more meaningful when a young man surnamed *de Boer* gave them to a young lady surnamed *Ter Hoorn*. Brigetta ate a half-dozen of Rebecca's *T* cookies in one sitting with a pot of milk tea, and doled out the dozen *D*'s one letter at a time.

Each year, Dutchville leaders planned a mid-December Friday night party traditionally held at the schoolhouse. The entertainment for this event was always secretive. The families in and around town *were* the program—and with the considerable talents of Dutchmen on display and tapped for this event, every year promised something new and exciting.

Meanwhile, everyone skated. Throughout December, with winter firmly in place, footprints of all sizes led to the river's section where the ice was thickest. As school ended each day and chores were completed, the ice filled with skaters—young and old—who skimmed along the frozen river with bent bodies and happy faces, snatching time from the sinking sun for their favorite sport. When numbers increased, there would be races or great bursts of applause when someone mastered an intricate cat's cradle or demonstrated a graceful pirouette.

Brigetta loved to watch her parents skate. They moved as one—graceful and swift. She followed behind them, matching their moves as she unconsciously mined the secrets of their marriage from their example of intimacy evident even in the simple activity of skating together. When they caught her watching them, they held out their hands and the three of them glided across the shimmering ice.

On many Saturday afternoons, someone would beg a fiddler to brave the cold and play for the skaters, warming his fingers over a barrel fire. Brigetta loved the skating music. Cold air rushed around her, trapping the notes she hummed behind her woolen scarf and keeping her ever mindful of the cool locket against her throat. When melodies from stringed instruments or brass horns braided themselves into the strands of the river's harmonic breezes, she believed it was the most beautiful symphony in the world.

Bram de Boer was usually on hand to help her tie on her skates and claim her hand when the skaters paired up. When she skated alone or with Mary or *Tante* Lena, she always sensed when Bram arrived. The sound of his voice wrapped around her name when he asked, "Skate with me, Brigetta?" heated her up from inside out even more than *Tante* Lena's hot chocolate.

Together, they moved like lightning on flashing blades, zigzagging between skaters, the bells on Brigetta's feet never quiet. They joined others to play crack-the-whip—each mindful of the role that game played in their new and tender love—and worked together to perfect their most intricate steps.

They would often rescue a sprawling young child and take her out for an exhilarating spin between them. Few words were spoken—few were needed in such a special place. And always as they parted, the ritual words: "I wonder..." with the fervent "a bushel and a peck!" response provided lingering smiles as they separated.

Everyone's mind was on the December fête. "What will your family perform at the party, Bram?" Brigetta asked feigning wide-eyed innocence as they rested on a makeshift bench beside the river.

"Ho! My family has practiced too long and hard for me to tell that secret! Wait and see."

She pouted prettily. "I thought, maybe, since we are keeping company, and I *do* have a special locket, you'd tell me!" she teased and then tugged at his hand. "Come; let's show those little girls how to do a figure-eight."

Based on what folks knew about friends and neighbors, the list of expected contributors to the much-anticipated party was all conjecture and shrouded with mystery. Children were tight-lipped and mysterious about what their families were preparing, and diligent in their attempts to tempt others into revealing family secrets.

Suspecting the bulk of the program would consist of seasonal songs, the Ter Hoorn family chose a musical number sure to surprise those who assumed the *Dominie's* family would present something religious. Hanna practiced faithfully until her fingers moved flawlessly across the piano keys. Lena and Brigetta and Gustave hummed snatches of the melody throughout the house.

Each night after supper, they gathered around the piano to practice their parts. Gustave's rich baritone formed a solid foundation for Lena's strong alto and Brigetta's true soprano. Their goal of learning both words and music well enough to sing without a song sheet before them was almost realized—and just in time, too. The party was just days away!

Brigetta felt a thrill run through her each time she looked at the sheet music on the piano: *My Farewell Don't Mean Good-bye*. It was so romantic! She could hardly believe her family would sing a song that announced "Sung with great success by Miss Grace Dean in Vaudeville" right on the cover. *Vaudeville!*

When he had gone to Chicago for a medical convention back in 1906, Doc Draayer had brought Hanna a piece of sheet music from a Sunday issue of the *Chicago American and Examiner*. All these years it had been tucked in the parsonage collection of piano music—virtually untouched.

Just in time for the program, Hanna not only remembered she had it, but actually suggested it would be a nice piece for them to perform. Each member of Hanna's family would have been hard-pressed to reject her proposal—just having her willing to participate was the best gift of the season. Such were the changes wrought in Hanna since the hallway picnic.

The night of the fête arrived with a dusting of snow—just enough to make it special. By the time everyone gathered, the level of excitement was intoxicating. Dutchville's mayor served as both Welcome Committee and Master of Ceremonies, which meant he alone knew what comprised the program.

Jan and Lizzie Mouw and their four stair-step boys sang "Two Little Sailor Boys" to start the festivities—a performance made all the more special by the boys' sailor suits and hats. Much to the audience's delight, the two youngest boys became puppets for the older boys who ducked down behind each smaller boy and moved their brothers' chubby little arms through hilarious gestures. Coupled with older voices appearing to come from little lips mouthing the words—often one or two syllables out of sync—and the fact the parents stared straight ahead throughout the entire song, seemingly unaware of their children's antics, made for much hilarity. It was the perfect opening act for the program.

A juggling act followed, performed by Antonie den Hartog whose wife, Katie, was too close to childbirth to do much more than sit in the corner and smile encouragingly at him as he tossed three items in the air. However, the bag at her feet was filled with objects. These she lobbed at him, forcing him to incorporate the fast and furiously arriving items into his routine. Their rhythm was flawless, evidencing much preparation when Antonie didn't drop a single piece and Katie's aim at her husband was perfect.

The crowd gasped as more and varied items joined the whirling frenzy around Antonie's head. Finally, he captured each piece and tossed them, one-by-one, back to Katie—keeping all the others in continuous motion as he did so—until he held just one red apple. This, he carefully polished to a high sheen with his bandana and walked over to his wife, presenting his gift on bended knee. It was such an intensely romantic ending Brigetta sighed and looked with new eyes at the swollen woman who inspired such love from her husband.

Next, the Maas family, swaddled in woolen scarves and muffs, glided across the stage as if on skates, whistling in four-part harmony one of the favorite songs the fiddlers played on the shores of the frozen Floyd River. As they dipped and whirled on invisible ice, stopping from time-to-time by the equally imaginary barrel to warm their hands, whistles from the audience joined in and soon the room was alive with skating music.

Next on the program was tall, dark, and somber Marten van den Berg. It was the first year this bachelor farmer was participating, and many in the audience exchanged curious glances when he took his place. *Would he sing? Hopefully not!* Many had sat near him in church services—the man was not blessed with musical gifts. In a loud, solemn voice, Marten intoned, "I will sing *My Wife's Gone to the Country*. It is the story of Mister and Mrs. Brown."

Marten anchored a black cap of indeterminate age on his head, folded his work-roughened hands primly before his gangly body, and positioned his scuffed *klompen* along a mark on the floor visible only to him. He stared off into a distant corner of the room. Apparently hearing a musical introduction in his head, he waited patiently and then his head began to bob, almost in time to a silent beat and then he lurched into his attempt to render—without accompaniment—the Irving Berlin song.

During all his nodding and through the first four words, enough worried looks were exchanged around him that a lesser man would have returned to his seat immediately. But Marten had signed up to perform, the mayor had called his name, and perform he would.

Abruptly, he reached Mrs. Brown's lament *"I just can't stand the heat"* at which point he switched to a jerky falsetto. After a split second, during which realization dawned that Marten was a funny man, whoops of laughter rolled up and down the aisles until it was difficult to hear a single word he sang.

"Start over, Marten! We want to hear the whole song," someone called out, interrupting the startled performer. The packed room fell silent. Though it hadn't moved a speck, he again secured his cap, folded his hands a second time, positioned his feet once more along the undetectable line, and stared off at unseen things. He barely said Mrs. Brown's words—once again in the startling falsetto—before his audience erupted with laughter.

This time Marten frowned sternly but kept on singing, changing from the high range to a deep bass each time Mister Brown told everyone he knew, *"My wife's gone to the country, Hurrah! Hurrah!"* By this time, Marten had the crowd clapping and stomping in rhythm while he sang, expressionless, staring off into the distant corner.

As the program neared the end, only the de Boer family had not performed. It was a well-known fact that Rebecca's voice was as pure as sunlight, and her two boys had inherited her gift. Hans' baritone was true and the resulting quartet guaranteed rapt attention when the Mayor called out, "And now the final presentation this evening comes from the de Boer family!" and that family made their way to the stage.

With the three menfolk clustered behind Rebecca at the piano, she played a short introduction and the words floated out in perfect harmony: *Shine on, shine on harvest moon up in the sky.* In the decade of its existence, few had sung this song with the ease and skill of the de Boer family, and it set feet tapping and bodies swaying all around the room.

Just seeing Bram in any setting was enough to get Brigetta's blood racing, but to have him *right here* where she was supposed to give him her full attention—no sneaking peeks required—and then have him looking *right at her* when he sang *"I ain't had no lovin' since January, February, June, or July"*—why, it was enough to make her dizzy!

She wasn't the only one held spellbound by this family's abilities—the crowd erupted in applause and someone called out "Encore!" and others picked up the cry. Rebecca conferred with her menfolk and stilled the room instantly with the opening notes to *Look for Me When the Lilacs Bloom.* The song expressed a soldier's promise to the girl he left behind, but Bram's eyes held Brigetta's and made her forget all but *"Look for me when the lilacs bloom...I'll come back...with a heart that's fond and true."*

When applause drowned out the last chord, Brigetta lifted her hands fully intending to join the clapping, but instead reached for her locket, pressing it against her burning cheeks. *Was there ever a night as blissful as this?*

Even though he would not go off to war, Bram sang of a vow transcending mere physical separation—he would always be there, in her heart, in her life. Tonight, his promise rang out for all to hear. As a child, she had wished upon a star. Most wondrous of all: tonight, the One who knew her heart and made the stars had created a desire for her in Bram's heart, too.

What a marvelous night! Brigetta looked around her and wondered if there could possibly be another person in this room so happy. Bram's message to her was as pure as the gold in her locket—he was hers, for all time.

1918

◆

Bram loved living in his grandparents' house. He had changed little by way of furnishings or decoration, but living on his own made him feel more like a man. However, like Adam of old, Bram grew lonely. Missing from his five-room Garden of Eden was the companionship of a woman. *Brigetta.*

In his mind, he saw her sparkling eyes across the table from him, or heard her humming as she hung dishtowels on the clothesline in the back yard. He ached to hold back her long locks of hair when she bent over the rain barrel with a pail, or lose himself in the softness of her skin as they burrowed beneath the covers on the bed each morning…

For any of that to happen, he must put feet beneath his thoughts. It was time. The waiting must end. "I'll do it tonight," he announced to the cat napping beneath the stove.

He rousted his surprised horse, saddled up, and headed for town. Outside the parsonage, he halted. Lights sent sparkling rays through the windows and out across the snow. Brigetta sat at the dining room table with a stack of schoolbooks beside her. Just then she arched her back, rolled her head as if to loosen kinks in her neck, and offered an unseen companion one of her glorious smiles. Bram swallowed hard. *This is the one I love!*

Gustave answered Bram's urgent knock. "Hello! Come in, Bram."

In an instant, Brigetta was there beside them. "Hello!" The brightness of her smile could have brought ships safely to shore in a storm; it certainly lit the way for Bram. All his mind could absorb was the unbridled joy in Brigetta's face at seeing him. He dropped to one knee. Gustave withdrew to the parlor, closing the door behind him.

Bram reached for Brigetta's willing hand. "Brigetta, my love, I am growing impatient: will you marry me when the tulips bloom?"

"Oh Bram! I have dreamed about this moment ever since you gave me the locket! Yes, yes, yes—a thousand times yes!"

The parlor door flew open as if blown by a northern wind and Brigetta danced into sight pulling a beaming Bram behind her. "Papa, Mama, *Tante* Lena! We have news—such wonderful news you cannot even begin to imagine!"

"They might suspect! I have asked Brigetta to marry me this spring and she said yes! Do we still have your blessing, *Dominie*?"

"More than my blessing, Bram; you have our love. Brigetta will be joining your home and family, but you are also becoming part of our family, too. Welcome!" Gustave's voice cracked.

"Your wedding will be in May?" Hanna asked, rising to meet Brigetta halfway across the room. "Oh, my! We must plan a betrothal dinner and the wedding, and prepare wedding clothes and Brigetta's trousseau..."

Gustave laughed. "Welcome to my world, son! I will be glad to have another man in our family circle."

"We would like to marry after Brigetta graduates in May. We haven't had time to talk through these things, but if we were to post our banns in April, perhaps a wedding on the third Saturday in May would be possible."

Lena sighed blissfully, "Ah, yes, the bride's basket can have tulips for Ter Hoorn and daffodils for de Boer! May is the perfect time for you two to marry!"

Brigetta teased, "How could we ever have satisfied that Dutch tradition if we married in February or November?"

"Don't even joke of such things," Lena said sternly.

"Have you spoken with your family, Bram?" Hanna asked. "Your mother and I will want to plan the festivities together."

"I would like to take Brigetta out to the farm tonight so we can tell them together, if I may borrow your daughter."

Gustave dropped down into an overstuffed chair, "I suppose we might as well get used to it. You'll be taking her home with you permanently in just a few months!"

Brigetta flew across the room and flung herself into her father's lap. Years of memories flooded Gustave's mind and he blinked quickly, but not before she caught the glistening of his unshed tears. "Oh, Papa, Bram is taking me only as far as the closest farm—not to foreign lands! You'll see me nearly every day."

Hanna headed for the coat closet, returning with Brigetta's muff and hooded cape. "If you hope to talk with Bram's parents before they go to bed, you had better leave now. It is important you share your joy with them, too."

After hugs and handshakes all around, the happy couple left the parsonage. Brigetta's laugh rang out through the night in accompaniment to the steady clip-clop of the horse's steps. They hurried to the back door of Bram's parents' house where light streamed out across the porch.

They cupped their hands around their faces and leaned against the kitchen window to peer in on the peaceful still-life scene where Rebecca scoured a pan at the sink, Hans' lips moved as he read sections aloud to his listeners from a newspaper, and Cornelis polished his leather shoes, the ragbag on the floor beside him. At the sound of the door opening and the rush of cold air, all looked up and Cornelis exclaimed, "Look who's here! Bram's been out with the ladies!"

"Not *ladies*, Cornelis, just one special *lady*! Drop your scouring pad, Mother, and put your paper aside, Father. We've got all the news you need tonight. Brigetta and I are going to be married!" Bram announced proudly and circled Brigetta with one arm. "I'm glad you're all together to hear the good news."

Rebecca emitted a happy cry, wiping her hands on her apron as she ran across the room. "And what wonderful news it is, even though we've suspected it would happen!" She reached up and kissed Brigetta on both cheeks and flung her arms around her tall son. "When will the wedding be?"

"Probably the third week of May, with banns in April," Bram replied.

Hans rose and, able at last to find his voice, said, "Congratulations, son! Welcome to the de Boer family, Brigetta!"

Rebecca said dreamily, "May is perfect for tulips and daffodils, Brigetta! What a pretty bride's basket they'll make!"

Brigetta's cheeks ached from constant smiling. "That's exactly what *Tante* Lena said! Which reminds me: Mama wants to meet with you soon."

Rebecca nodded excitedly. "I'll pour us some coffee and you tell us all about it."

"It was so romantic, Mrs. de Boer! Bram knelt beside me when he asked me to marry him!"

Bram winked at Brigetta, "And it happened in the same hallway as where I asked you to keep company with me!" The two young people broke into gales of laughter and the three other de Boers sat by, unenlightened and wondering what could be so humorous.

Brigetta caught their curious glances and looked at Hans. "You haven't told them?"

Bram shook his head, "I didn't want to tell tales out of school and ruin your family's opinion of me."

Brigetta stared at her newly minted fiancé with amazement and squeezed his hand. "There's much more to tell than the story of this evening! It all started with lemonade and buttermilk." So, Brigetta and Bram relived the events of the hallway supper culminating with Brigetta's "yes" tonight.

Even Cornelis, watching the faces around him, grinned throughout the story. But no one around the table dreamed how each word from

Brigetta's lips, each loving glance between his brother and this beautiful, vivacious young lady thrust spears of jealousy and loss into his heart.

"That's a story our children will love to hear—how their Mama won their Papa's heart wearing a dishtowel on her head."

Hans and Rebecca locked glances and then shifted away. Hans cleared his throat and pushed back his chair. "Tomorrow is another day. Come, Cornelis, we'll close up the barn while Bram takes Brigetta back to town." Without a backward glance, he grabbed his coat off the hook on the wall and disappeared into the cold night.

Rebecca's eyes darted from her sons to her future daughter-in-law, all of whom looked questioningly at her. "Yes, we're happy for you, but it's been a long day." She quickly untied her apron and hung it over the back of a chair. "Run along, Cornelis; your Father needs your help. Good night, my dears." She, too, fled the kitchen.

Brigetta waited until Cornelis was safely gone before asking, "Is anything wrong, Bram? One minute we were laughing, the next it was as if we had offended someone. Did I say something amiss?"

Bram shook his head slowly, lost in thought. "No, we must be imagining things. Come, I'll take you home." His forced smile was hardly reassuring.

Brigetta looked at the dishpan. "Wait a few minutes. Your mother will be unhappy if she comes down in the morning and finds that pan still soaking. Let me finish scouring it before we go." She quickly tied Rebecca's discarded apron around her waist, added hot water from the teakettle on the stove to the cooling soapy water in the dishpan, and finished the job their arrival had interrupted.

Bram watched her from the far end of the table. "My mother will love having a daughter as wonderful as you."

"Our marriage will make both families happy."

A week passed. Bram's parents moved through his life with the same regularity as always, but something was different. They smiled at him, but the smiles did not engage more than their lips. They waved at him across the yard, but it was no different than their greetings for mere acquaintances passing along the road. They laughed with him, but the sounds stopped short of resonating with joy. They talked, but it was as if they carefully skirted a sinkhole in each conversation.

Nearly two weeks after his proposal to Brigetta, Bram stopped by his parents' house at a time when he knew his grandmother was settled for the night. He found his parents in the parlor. "What's been wrong with our family these past few weeks?" he asked abruptly. Hans reached for a knob and silenced the radio program he and Rebecca had been listening to while she mended.

Rebecca set her jaw. "Tell him, Hans. Now."

Hans' hands shook as he pulled his tobacco pouch from his pocket. He moved to the pot-bellied stove where a small fire chased away the evening chills; he held a straw into the flames until a spark lit the tip. Rebecca and Bram watched in silence as he stuck the straw into the bulb of his pipe, puffed several times, and then tossed the red-tipped grain stalk into the flames.

"Please sit, Bram. There is something we should have talked of long ago."

Bram dropped to a chair like a rock plunging off a cliff.

Hans blew several smoke rings before he finally spoke. His voice was low, his words slow. "When you had mumps, Bram, you were very sick."

Bram nodded, looking from his mother's unreadable face to his father who avoided meeting his eyes.

"Doc Draayer warned us of something you were too young to hear at the time," Hans continued in a strained voice.

"I have already learned about the possibility I have tuberculosis, remember?" Residual bitterness sharpened his tone.

Hans nodded. "The problem concerning him then was that you were older than most children who get mumps. It is not a good thing for a boy who is almost a man. You know the meaning of sterility, don't you?"

"*Sterility*? Of course—we sold a bull several years ago because he was sterile. What are you saying?" Bram's voice grew so harsh Rebecca shivered.

"It was a long time ago, 1907. Doc Draayer said he saw signs then mumps could render you sterile. If you fail to father children, at least you will know why."

"And you are just *now* telling me this? Knowing I have been courting Brigetta for several months? Fully aware I have asked her to be my wife? *Now* you decide to tell me something you have known for over ten years—I could be sterile?" Bram pushed himself up and stormed to the doorway. "Families don't keep secrets like this from each other, or let one of their own make a fool of himself. What am I to tell Brigetta?"

The clock ticked. Neither Hans nor Rebecca answered.

Bram pounded his fist on the doorframe. "Once I was afraid Brigetta would not want me because of my lung condition!" He laughed harshly. "And now I must tell her the man she has agreed to marry is unable to father children? Maybe she'll wish I *had* gone to war rather than ruin her life."

"It may not be true—your sterility." Rebecca spoke at last. "We have prayed all these years…"

"Maybe you should have included me so I could pray, too," Bram said curtly and slammed the door behind him.

Before either Hans or Rebecca could speak, they heard a creak and turned expectantly toward the door. Cornelis strolled into the room, heading to the stove with hands extended toward the warmth. "I met Bram leaving the house at a full-clip. Hope he didn't eat all the onion soup you said you have left over! What's wrong?"

Rebecca slowly got to her feet and smiled weakly at her youngest son. "I'll fix you a bowl. Come."

Cornelis watched Rebecca putter around while he ate. Sopping up the last of the steaming liquid with a slice of bread, he attempted conversation. "Is everything all right? You haven't said a word the whole time I've been eating."

"Hmmm? Oh, I'm just tired. It has been a full day."

Cornelis stared at his mother. He had told the truth when he said he saw Bram, but Bram had stormed past him in the hallway—not outside the house as he had implied. Just as Bram was saying the words...*we sold a bull*...Cornelis had entered the house, unnoticed by anyone in the parlor. He had stood in the hallway, eavesdropping shamelessly. He knew he had missed part of the damning conversation, but he read something powerful between the lines: Brigetta might not want Bram!

If...*when* that happened, Cornelis would be around to help Brigetta grieve—taking full advantage of the chance to woo and win the young lady whom he had let slip through his fingers once, but never again. *At the first sign of shattered affections between Bram and Brigetta, I will be there!*

He pushed away the empty soup bowl and smiled broadly at his mother. Life was falling into place nicely for Cornelis de Boer. Bram would have the best farm in these parts of Iowa, but Cornelis would have the best girl.

For days, Bram kept up his end of the farm work, but whenever possible he fled to corners of the field, to tasks at the farthest end of the garden, to the dizzy heights of the hay loft in the barn—anywhere he could be alone, away from Cornelis' flippant conversation, his mother's sad eyes, his father's feeble attempts to make amends. Long ago, he had learned the therapeutic value of a good day's hard labor—sleep came when the body could no longer endure.

But experience also taught him the mind is rarely quiet; his taunted him: *Tell Brigetta, otherwise you're no different than your parents in keeping a secret of this magnitude from the one person most affected by it.* But instead of listening to his conscience, he tilled the fields, buried seeds like secrets in the fields and garden, and worked himself ragged until his body begged for mercy.

Hadley Hoover

Brigetta rode her bicycle out to the farm almost every day, helping in the garden, walking around the pretty house that would soon be her home, joining Rebecca in the kitchen to lend a hand.

"I have been thinking," she said one morning as the two women worked together, "may I call you 'Mother' once Bram and I are married? I know some brides do. Since I call my own mother 'Mama,' there would be no confusion."

Rebecca stared at Brigetta's smiling face. "Why, yes, dear. Would you call Hans 'Father' then, too?"

Brigetta nodded happily. "That way I'll have one Mama, one Mother, one Papa, and one Father. It will make life much simpler!"

Mid-afternoon, Rebecca looked out and saw Bram working in the garden; she filled a glass with chilled cider to take out to him. She got to the point immediately. "Brigetta visited me this morning. She wants to call me 'Mother' and Hans 'Father,' once you're married." She handed him the cool drink.

Bram nodded and stood up straight beside his hoe as he took a long draught of cider, "Thank you. Yes, she calls her parents 'Mama' and 'Papa' so that would work out well." He tipped his head back and emptied the glass, handed it back to his mother, and returned to his labors.

Rebecca watched her eldest son work the soil he loved. "You haven't said anything to her yet, have you?"

Bram stiffened, but did not stop his labors. "No." He knelt beside a furrow and pushed seeds into holes the depth of his finger. "But I will. I won't wait for years, years during which she's wondering why there are no children."

"There are not many days remaining until your wedding, Bram."

"You're a fine one to talk about timing, Mother," Bram snapped. Rebecca heard the voice of a man in pain, not a disrespectful son.

"Do you now see how difficult it has been for your father and me all these years? To look at you every day of every year, seeing you grow strong and healthy and showing no signs of anything wrong. And to know learning something like this could lay waste to your confidence. I am not excusing our silence, but I hope you understand how hard these years have been for us."

Bram's eyes narrowed as he watched his mother leave. He thrust his hand into the bag of seeds and resumed his task. Late in the afternoon, he cleaned off his tools, saddled his horse and headed to town. He followed side streets to reach Doc Draayer's office with the fewest possible human encounters along the way. He waited under a tree, whittling a fallen twig to a fine sharp point, until he was quite sure the last patient had left the small building. Then he flung the stick aside and strode across the yard. He stepped over the threshold. "Doc Draayer?"

"Bram!" The doctor capped a bottle of ink and smiled in welcome. "What brings you here? Come in—sit down." He blew lightly across the page before setting it aside.

Bram nodded and sat stiffly in the proffered chair. After only the slightest hesitation, he spoke. "Several days ago, my parents told me I might be sterile. As you know, Brigetta Ter Hoorn and I will soon marry, so this is quite a shock. Now I must tell her something that..." He dropped his head until his chin brushed his collar. When he spoke at last, his words were muffled. "She will likely want to be released from her promise to marry me." Slowly he lifted his head; the earlier defiance in his eyes had changed to disconsolation.

Doc Draayer nodded thoughtfully. "Possibly, or she could surprise you."

"Actually, I have thought of that—she may say it doesn't matter, but her innocence could change into resentment over time when other couples in Dutchville are having children and we are not. I am torn between giving her the opportunity to choose what happens to us or making the decision myself and releasing her from her promise. If I did that, I would not need even to tell her why—and my condition could remain a private thing, known only to you and my parents."

"You would be doing Brigetta a great disservice. She is entitled to hear of the potential situation and then make an intelligent choice. Brigetta is a remarkable young lady who is capable of doing just that." Gerrit Draayer said with resolve. "It is not in your character to be deceptive, Bram. Such an action against someone you love could torment you for years to come. And she would always wonder what she had done to fall out of your favor."

"If she turns me away when she hears of the problem, then each time I see her in town, or in church, or with another man will wrench the life out of me anew." His voice faded and he closed his eyes.

"I had hoped your parents would have told you long ago, but they, too, have had a difficult time with this, Bram. No doubt, they worried how you would take the news. Ask yourself, when *would* have been a good time for them to tell you?"

Bram shrugged and stretched his long legs, staring intently at the floor.

"Remember—it was not a sure thing in 1907 any more than it is a sure thing in 1918."

"They had no right to withhold this from me, especially knowing Brigetta and I are keeping company. Brigetta must have the opportunity before our wedding day to make the decision as to whether or not she wants to marry someone who is…inadequate. Even thinking of telling her is ripping me apart."

"Life has dealt you a hard lot right now, but you have faced difficult times before and come through them a stronger person; that can happen again if you face up to your troubles. Go to Brigetta—but first talk with your parents. Do not start a new family when relationships in your own family are strained. When two people marry, they become a family upon saying their vows—not only when children are added. A family is not based on the number of people, but on love and caring."

Bram sat quietly, his shoulders sagging and his face drawn. "It seems every time I come to see you, the answer is the same: talk to my family."

He expelled a puff of air. "I could save us both some time and trouble and just do that before coming to see you, right?" He managed a weak, humorless smile.

"I have always found it helps to talk—sometimes to myself, sometimes to my wife and family, and often only to God. Your problem is primarily what we all deny: we're not only human, we're Dutchmen! Being human makes us independent and willful; being Dutch makes us proud. That's a fine combination except when it gets in the way of doing the right thing."

"I will talk to my parents. I am not sure what I will say to Brigetta, or when, but I will talk to her, too. Thank you."

"I have great confidence you will do the right thing, Bram."

Bram raised an eyebrow and walked out to his horse.

At the parsonage, Gustave talked with Hanna in her flower garden. "I saw Hans de Boer at the blacksmith's shop today. He asked if he and Rebecca and Bram could drop by this evening. I said to come at seven o'clock."

"Lena will be gone to the Sewing Circle then. If they wish to talk about plans for the wedding, she is involved."

"He only asked that Brigetta be here with us."

After supper, Lena made a fresh pot of coffee and left it on the stove to keep warm over the embers as she hurried off to her evening with the Sewing Circle.

Soon, three de Boers faced three Ter Hoorns in the parsonage parlor. "Thank you for allowing us to come, *Dominie*," Hans said.

"It is always our pleasure. We see much more of your son these days, for some reason," Gustave winked at Bram, "but it is wonderful to have you all here."

"A troublesome situation brings us here tonight. In fact, it is a subject going back to 1907, and I bear full responsibility for any problems arising from speaking of it tonight. It most closely concerns Bram, but I am at fault."

Brigetta sat rigidly on the sofa beside Bram. She wanted nothing more than to steal a look at him, but his silence was like a wall blocking her view. *What is it Bram cannot tell us?* Panic rose like bile in her throat. *Does he wish to be released from marrying me? Is there someone else?* She choked back a sob.

Hans and Rebecca stared at the floor. Gustave and Hanna looked around the room at the others, and then locked questioning gazes on each other. Hans sighed deeply and cracked his knuckles. "When our boys had mumps back in 1907, Doc Draayer told us there was a possibility of problems later on for Bram."

Gustave nodded. "Yes, Bram has told us of his weakened lungs."

"It was a different problem we learned of back then, *Dominie.* The problem with his lungs is something we learned only when he visited the Armed Services Induction Center last June. Because of Bram's age—he was nearly thirteen years old—when he had the mumps, the effects of the illness indicate he may be sterile."

Someone's chair creaked, but no other sound broke through the ensuing silence.

The pain on Hans' face mirrored the misery in his voice as he continued; "Doc Draayer said we should tell him when he was older. No time has ever seemed right, and we never did talk with him about it—until a few days ago. By that time, as we all know, he and Brigetta had already planned for marriage. I am so sorry I failed in my responsibilities as Bram's father to speak to him. So sorry for the destruction of all our hopes and dreams."

The stillness in the room was palpable.

With the sure and steady tone of a silver bell, Brigetta spoke, startling everyone. "You have come tonight to tell us that when Bram and I marry, we might not be able to have children?"

Rebecca looked across the room through a mist of tears. "Yes, dear. When you came to tell us the news of your engagement the other night, Bram commented about how your children would enjoy hearing the story of their Mama and Papa's courtship. That's when we realized how great a sin we have committed."

"Oh, Rebecca, I don't believe it is a sin. You and Hans have carried a great sadness—often, it must have seemed more than you could bear. By not talking of it, you were able to continue to hope it wasn't true, or it would go away. This is not an easy burden for anyone, no matter how long you have known of it, but you have done the right thing in coming to us tonight," Gustave said.

Bram shifted on the sofa, turning to face Brigetta for the first time since his arrival. "I want you to know I asked for your hand in good faith. I was honest with you about the problem with my lungs—I would never hide something of this magnitude from the woman I had hoped would be my wife. I am so sorry. Naturally, you are released from your promise to marry me."

Brigetta sprung off the couch and all heads tipped up to look at her as she towered over them, arms akimbo. "Did you come thinking I would say, 'It's over—I could not *possibly* love a man who may not be able to father children!'? If so, Mister and Mrs. de Boer, you don't realize I love Bram for what he is—and if that means no children, that's part of what he is. I love him."

She let that simple truth hang in the air and looked into Bram's eyes with a tenderness that caused five hearts to beat erratically.

"I love you, Bram. A bushel and a peck! The best thing you can give me in return is your love—babies aren't necessary, mere possessions aren't necessary, just your deepest love. That's what will make our marriage thrive."

Gustave stared at his daughter with pride. *Dear child, I have prayed for you your whole life—even before you were born—that you would be a woman of integrity, of compassion, of substance. God has answered my prayers in abundance!*

Brigetta still had more to say. "He gave me a locket, you know." Her bright gaze swept the room. "What is inscribed on it, Bram?"

"It says *'Yours for all time'* because that's what I meant before I knew how little I could offer you," Bram whispered. Tears burned like coals behind his eyes, turning his fears to ashes.

"You forgot two important words: our names. You promised me—*Brigetta*—your love forever, and then added your name—*Bram*. That locket seals our lives together as much as the vows we will offer at the altar. It doesn't say anything at all about children—just the two of us."

Hans looked at his son and saw the power of Brigetta's pure love healing him instantly. *He is a good man, our son. And with Brigetta bringing out the best in him, he will be a strong and tender man.*

Brigetta's voice rang out unwaveringly. "I have learned from my parents that love endures through hard times and good times. My love for Bram is not shallow like the roots of some delicate little flower poking its head out of the soil that dies if it doesn't get perfect care. Our love grows deeper every day!"

Hanna let the mental curtain roll back in review of the years of her marriage to Gustave. *Even when I saw only the darkness, Brigetta was learning what marriage and love is all about by seeing her father's steadfast love for me. Oh, the goodness of the Lord to take the dross and leave the gold!*

Brigetta dropped to her knees beside Bram and grasped his hands. "Our love is like the roots of two trees starting out close to the surface. As the roots grow, they get tangled up in each other. When the winds blow hard, our marriage won't topple—it will be all the stronger because our roots are supporting each other down deep where no one can see. Like the tree that holds my swing in the back yard. When it was a sapling, it would have cracked beneath the weight of even an empty swing—but now even Papa can swing on it and the branches don't bend."

Rebecca wiped tears away and swallowed a hiccup. *Bram is getting a good wife—someone whose understanding of what really matters transcends my own.*

Brigetta jumped to her feet, tugged Bram off the sofa and stood so close to him he had no choice but to enfold her in his arms. They shared a precious moment, an island of intimacy in the ocean of their families' love.

Peering over Bram's shoulder, Brigetta asked with a smile rivaling the sun, "Is anyone else as hungry as I am for some of *Tante* Lena's apple pudding? Come on, Bram, help me get it ready."

Two sets of parents stared at the door. Rebecca sank back against her chair. "*Dominie* and Hanna, you have a remarkable daughter."

"Thank you," Hanna said, "but your son is the perfect partner for her—they will complement each other well. He is a fine young man, exactly what we wish for our daughter."

Gustave smiled. "We have lived with Brigetta for many years—your time of discovery is just beginning! As you have seen tonight, she is not afraid to speak up."

Hans replied, "Our family could have been spared much heartache if I had that gift."

"Let's put the episode behind us after this evening. When you reach home later tonight, talk with Bram to ask and receive forgiveness, and then start afresh without looking back." Gustave advised. "Now, let's enjoy some apple pudding."

In bed that night, Hanna murmured, "Gustave, remember my concerns the day Brigetta got her first monthly?"

Gustave nuzzled his wife's hair and murmured assent.

"What we learned tonight brings that day back to me. Bram and Brigetta will not have children—and while that removes my fears for Brigetta suffering dark times like mine, I can't help but wonder, why would God allow such a thing to cloud their relationship? The very thing that removes my fears brings heartache to others I love. I do not understand the ways of the Lord."

"Nor do I, Hanna. But we have learned to trust Him in the past—and we can trust Him with the future."

*   *   *

The weeks before the wedding were a flurry of baking, sewing, packing, laughter and tears. Hanna tended her garden with care—determined to keep the blooms bug-free, strong-stemmed, and vividly hued. Three flowers would come from her garden: daffodils, daisies and delphiniums to fulfill the *D* for de Boer. Bram would supply tulips in abundance to satisfy the *T* for Ter Hoorn. Since the names *Bram* and *Brigetta* brought a *B* to the mix, Hanna added bridal wreath knowing savvy Dutch would enjoy the floral humor.

Lena took her basket-decorating responsibility seriously. Daily, she fluctuated between choices of a lace liner or tissue paper beneath the flowers. She also experimented with ribbons or garland of flowers on the handle and fussed with it until Hanna laughingly suggested, "It would be simpler for Brigetta to float down the aisle with a tulip tucked behind one ear and a daffodil behind the other."

"I am ashamed to hear such heresy from my sister!" Lena sputtered and Hanna winked at her daughter who swallowed a giggle.

The morning of the wedding broke clear and cool. Lena drove the buggy out to the de Boer farm when sunlight was just peeking over the trees. Bram was already in the garden, marking the best tulips with stones beside the rows. He waved when he heard the Ter Hoorn buggy coming up the driveway and met Lena in time to help her down.

"Did you sleep last night?" Lena teased.

"Not much. I heard the wind come up and got worried about the tulips. I came out to see if I could protect them in any way. I wanted to wait until the last minute to pick them so they will be perfect this afternoon."

"I wanted to catch you before you would bring the tulips to the house. I had hoped you could pick them now and send them home with me. I know Brigetta doesn't want to take a chance on you seeing her before the wedding!"

Bram looked at the sky. "It will be getting warm soon; perhaps picking them now is a good idea."

They walked down the rows together. Bram carefully cut the voluptuous beauties he had tended for the long months of their journey from bulbs to blooms. He handed them, one by one, to Lena who cradled them like a baby. If a tulip's bloom, stem and leaves were not perfect in every way, Bram passed it by. When he had picked three times as many bell-shaped flowers as Lena could possibly need to fill the basket, he stood up and nodded. "There. A selection worthy of my bride."

The reverence in his voice made Lena shiver with awe. *This man will treat my Brigetta well.* She carefully put the last vibrant flowers in the bucket of water and then stood on tiptoes and aimed a loud kiss at Bram's cheek.

He recovered quickly and grabbed her by both arms to return the peck twice—once on each of Lena's ruddy cheeks. "I'll take good care of our girl, *Tante* Lena."

Embarrassed at how closely he had read her mind, and pleased with his gesture of affection, Lena picked up one laden bucket and headed for the buggy. Bram followed at her heels with two more buckets filled with fragrant blooms.

Lena hummed all the way home. It was time for her to meet Mary and get the two of them dressed and ready for the day ahead. As bridesmaids, they had much to do!

Brigetta's closet contained her white silk dress, a delicate lace-edged veil, soft kid gloves and matching slippers. Lena had pushed back all the clothes in her own closet to one side to accommodate the two Dutch dresses with satiny bodices and full skirts and lace aprons the bridesmaids would wear. Hanna's mother-of-the *meisje* dress was of a similar pattern with elaborate embroidery.

The last covered button on the four dresses had been sewed in place yesterday while Lena also tended the kitchen stove and oven. Hanna, Brigetta, and Lena had worked late into the night for weeks and, finally, every stitch was in place, each tuck pressed, and every inch of lace starched and ready—and the pantry bulged with food prepared for the happy day.

At last, the bells in the high tower of the Dutchville Reformed Church rang out across the countryside, announcing the marriage of the *Dominie's* daughter to one of the finest young men Dutchville could offer.

Outside the church, Bram's buggy shone from its morning cleaning and his horse pranced in place—seemingly aware he, too, looked mighty fine after his master's ministrations with the curry brush and comb.

Dressed in a new black suit, Bram sat in silent reverence, swallowing hard as he saw Brigetta beside her father. He felt faint as he realized what angels must look like—and this vision in white before him would soon be linked to him for life. Though he knew their families talked together off to one side, Bram saw only shadows where all but Brigetta were concerned.

Sensing Bram's presence, Brigetta turned. When their glances met, Bram stumbled off the buggy and headed toward her. The closer he got, the slower his pace—it was almost as if he believed she were merely a mirage; he didn't want to hasten her disappearance. When he reached her side, he murmured, "I'm almost afraid to touch you—you're so beautiful!"

Brigetta's laugh skipped across the church lawn, turning heads with its unfettered pleasure. "It's as if I'm dreaming!"

Watching his brother from a short distance away Cornelis shook his head ruefully and went to care for the horse and buggy Bram had deserted. Tying the horse's reins to a tree in a shady spot, Cornelis looked back at the wedding party and wished fervently he were not his brother's groomsman. Jealousy nibbled steadily at his love for his brother and made it increasingly difficult to wish him well. Slowly, Cornelis walked back to the church steps, his face inscrutable to all.

The church bells continued to ring. Gustave smiled down at his daughter as she clutched his arm. "It's time, Sweet Pea." He bent and kissed her forehead.

Hanna moved quickly to Brigetta's other side and whispered, "You are the most beautiful bride I have ever seen."

The groom was in the center of his own family circle. Rebecca flicked invisible lint from his jacket; Hans beamed with pride, one hand on Bram's shoulder. Cornelis looked handsome in his suit and crisp shirt— and had a smile only the most observant would notice did not change. He felt more like a daguerreotype of a young man at his brother's wedding than the flesh-and-blood sibling of this groom.

Brigetta could not contain herself a minute longer. She lifted her bride's basket high and called from the Ter Hoorn cluster across to the de Boer family, "Bram, I've got tulips and daffodils galore in this basket—I think we're supposed to get married!"

Startled, Bram looked up and when he saw the familiar impish grin creep around the lace and puffery that had seemed so untouchable and foreign, he relaxed and smiled broadly. "*T*'s and *D*'s—that's us! Let's go!"

A church Elder read from the Epistles and, as the wedding party waited in the church narthex, several hundred voices lifted up the familiar melody of a *Psalmen*. That was the signal for the parents of the bride and groom to escort their children down the aisle. The families entered the sanctuary and walked along an aisle filled with song. It was a solemn, holy transition in life.

As her father, Gustave tucked Brigetta's hand under his arm for their journey down the aisle. As her *Dominie*, he released her to Hanna's care and entered the pulpit. There, he read the formulas of marriage, prompted the couple through their solemn *plechtig belovens* and pronounced Bram and Brigetta *echtgenoot* and *echtgenote*. A ripple of amusement passed through the crowded church when Brigetta sighed with pleasure at hearing her father say proudly, "I present to you, Mister and Mrs. Bram de Boer!"

Back at the parsonage, *Tante* Lena and Mary took their bridesmaids' duties seriously. They showed guests to appropriate seats, initiated conversations to keep everyone entertained, and presented the beaming groom with the traditionally decorated bridegroom's pipe with ribbons and garlands matching those on the bride's basket.

As they took their places, the wedding guests quieted. Gustave waited until Brigetta and Bram were seated and then he spoke. "As frugal as we Dutch are in our daily lives, a wedding dinner is always an extravagant occasion. As you know, I have been part of many such events for your families, which gives me the right to say you are in for a royal treat once you pull up your chairs to our table! My wife, daughter, and sister-in-law have prepared a feast for us."

Even though the past month was a blur of dinners that had begun soon after the banns were read and had continued right up until the wedding, this meal was an important tradition. The menu would take its rightful place in the lore of Dutch weddings: sugar cake, marchpane, sugared almonds, and sweet cordials filled the side-board and tempted the palates of guests who also eyed the heavily-laden tables with the platters and bowls of fish and fowl, meats and cheeses, fruits and vegetables—all reminiscent of customs harkening back to old Holland.

As host, Gustave announced in a voice heard by all scattered at tables inside and across the lawn, "Come! There is food for all. Let no one leave hungry!" Everyone eagerly began the celebration that would continue as the newlyweds made their way from the parsonage to their new abode. There, all would be welcomed once again with even more food and drink at Bram and Brigetta's first open house.

Hostess in her own home for the first time later that evening, Brigetta whispered happily to her mother as they heard their guests exclaiming over first one tasty dish and then another, "*Tante* Lena was right: you cannot have too much food for a wedding!"

"I've put a little aside for you and Bram to enjoy later. I know neither of you has eaten much for days, even though you have sat down to meal after meal! So when we're gone, look in the covered basket in your new pantry and you'll find enough there to satisfy you. You'll be hungry later on, even though now you can't imagine it."

"I love you, Mama! Please hug Papa extra hard for me tonight." Her eyes shone bright with tears—knowing she would always be Gustave and Hanna's daughter, but never in quite the same way again. *I am now Mrs. Bram de Boer!* That thought dried up all her unshed tears in an instant.

When the last guest had left, Bram and Brigetta waved farewells from the end of the driveway and walked slowly beneath the evening sky back to their home. A cloud flirted with the moon, its actions mirrored by two lovers on the moonlit path below.

Stars danced in the sky and Brigetta's eyes when Bram slid his hands along her shoulders and arms, found her waist and dropped without hesitation to pull her closer than she had ever been to any man. Close enough to feel new and tantalizing changes in her husband. Close enough to take her breath away. Close enough to make her want to strip away every piece of wedding finery keeping this bride any distance at all from this groom.

"Are you hungry?" she asked in a voice that sounded strange even to her ear.

"Not for food," Bram murmured in her ear. "Come, my little bride; let's see how well the two of us fit in my bed."

Brigetta blushed furiously and released a ragged breath. She wanted nothing more than to do that very thing. And that very thing scared her to death. She nodded, not willing to trust her voice again. Bram bent quickly to carry her the rest of the way to the bedroom.

The last time he had carried her, he was a boy with a burden of guilt. Tonight, he was a husband with a bride who showered his face with kisses—no burden at all.

*   *   *

One morning, Brigetta was making room for Bram's winter clothes in the cedar chest next to her own when she noticed one pair of his woolen underwear appeared dingy compared to the others. Had Brigetta not been so caught up in the bliss and glory of her new life, she would have waited until the end of the summer to whiten winter woolens—such advice was even written down in her *Tante* Lena Book. But, being an eager new wife, she added them to the tub on the third laundry day of her marriage.

Just shaking out the intimate garment with its suggestive openings turned Brigetta's face pink. She hurriedly pinned the waistband to the line and bent to pick up a towel. *For all that they cover of a man's body, long johns sure do have all the slits and tucks necessary for a man to wear them!*

She hastened to finish hanging up the wash before her friend Mary arrived for her first visit to the de Boer home. Mary had just completed a week's training and soon would begin work as a bank teller, so this morning's visit offered the last opportunity for a private daytime chat.

It would be such fun to show Mary around her kitchen, and bring out all the wedding gifts for the two of them to *oooh* and *ahhh* over. Brigetta had cleaned the house until it squeaked in preparation for supper guests tonight, so Mary was coming on the perfect day to see everything at its best.

Soon Mary arrived and the expected tour of the small house was completed and all of Mary's compliments had been made and received graciously. Feeling mature, Brigetta made great show of preparing a pitcher of milk and a plate of cookies to carry out to the back porch. They settled in for a long talk.

Mary was properly impressed, not only with all she had seen—but how very *married* her friend had become in such a short time. Perhaps it was because Mary had so little to share compared to the life Brigetta now lived, but she found it difficult to pay attention. There was no Bram in Mary's life, only debits and credits and less than titillating conversations with the musty old banker.

During one detailed story of yet another incident in which Bram had proven to be the perfect husband, Mary allowed her eyes to roam the back yard. She continued to respond with appropriate murmurs of agreement and encouragement, but it was as if Brigetta's voice came from far away.

Mary watched a bird swoop from tree to fence to pump as Brigetta talked about canning jars. She focused briefly on a spider spinning a web between two porch-railing posts while Brigetta elaborated on the differences between several types of squash.

Her eyes followed a butterfly until it got lost against a flowered apron hanging on the clothesline. An apron right next to a very short pair of long johns. So short, in fact, it crossed Mary's mind they were hardly worthy the name *long* johns.

She dragged her attention back to Brigetta who, by now, was listing Bram's favorite meals she had prepared thus far. Just as she took the deep breath necessary to enumerate her plans for new curtains, Mary jumped in with, "Whose long johns are those on the line?"

Truly disconcerted by Mary's proffered conversational tidbit, Brigetta stared at her and finally followed Mary's perplexed gaze out to the clothesline. "Why, those are Bram's, of course. I found them in the box of his winter clothes and thought they looked dingy, so I washed them. I know I should have waited until the end of the summer, but I hated to put them in the cedar chest looking so gray."

Mary stared, perplexed, at the clothesline. "They're rather short, aren't they?" she asked bluntly, hesitant to scrutinize her best friend's husband's underclothes—but also quite curious. "I mean, my brothers and father wear woolen long johns, but I'm quite sure theirs come down to their ankles."

That got Brigetta's attention; she took a closer look. The pair hanging there did seem a bit short. Recalling how her thoughts had roamed the various parts of Bram's anatomy as she had hung clothes, Brigetta blushed. *Oh my—when my thoughts run along those tracks, I wouldn't notice much of anything! But to not notice something this dramatic? Mercy!* Like sleepwalkers, the two young women left the porch and headed for the clothesline.

Mary helpfully unpinned a pair of Bram's trousers from another line and held them up behind the pair of woolen long johns under their scrutiny. The ankles of the undergarment ended right at the knees of the trousers.

The width of the clothing was unchanged—but the length had shrunk to half its original size. Brigetta gasped and clutched at her friend. "Oh, Mary! I just realized—I washed them in the hottest water possible—in fact, I put them in first with the water fresh from the stove. And when they didn't look white enough still, I washed them again with the next load and added bleach. Oh, whatever will I tell Bram? Do you think we could stretch them?"

Mary doubted much would help; it was expecting a lot for them to double in length. But she wanted to be an encouragement to her obviously distraught friend. "We could try."

Having hung for several hours in warm sunshine, the long johns were nearly dry. Mary held the waistband and Brigetta grabbed one leg in each hand and they performed great feats of strength, pulling valiantly and tugging endlessly, all with Brigetta's frantic instructions, "Pull—harder! Good—now, again! Stand firm and I'll yank them!"

"We should get them wet—they were wet when they shrunk, so maybe they need to be wet to unshrink them."

"Of course!" Brigetta flew across the lawn. She lifted the handle on the creaking pump and propelled it up and down, up and down, wildly splashing great spurts of cool well-water across Mary's hands and over the child-sized long johns—child-sized, if a very short boy were quite wide in the beam.

When both Mary and the woolens were drenched and Brigetta was exhausted from pumping, the two girls repeated the tugging and pulling and straining. Any progress made disappeared when they released their hold. All they had to show for their efforts was a pair of already short and now terribly misshapen woolen underwear.

Mary suggested, "We could use something heavy to keep them stretched until they dry again."

"What a marvelous idea! I declare, Mary, you are the best friend a silly new wife could ever have!"

Doubtful Brigetta intended the insult beneath the surface of this sincere compliment, Mary followed Brigetta to the porch where they rested a few minutes and contemplated the next step.

"The heaviest things are in the barn. Come!" Sure enough, they found an abundance of heavy things—most of which neither girl could lift on her own—a significant detail since Mary would be long gone when Brigetta returned the items.

They settled on a cobwebbed anvil, several horseshoes they wrapped inside a burlap sack, and the loose head from a sledge hammer. All these they loaded into a wheelbarrow they pushed to a flat place in the sun behind the house.

Meanwhile, the woolens had dried somewhat, so a repeated session at the pump was required—with wet shoes the reward this time for the patient Mary—and finally they were ready to secure the pair of oddly stretched, soaking-wet long johns in place. The anvil anchored the ankle of one leg, the hammerhead on the opposite leg—the two legs forming a wide V. "A *V for Victory*," Brigetta proclaimed. "It's an omen."

With Brigetta holding the two legs and their anchors firmly in place, Mary gave a mighty tug, pulling the waistband as tight as possible, jumped on to hold it in place with her body weight and then dropped the bag of horseshoes smack-dab in the center.

"There." Exhausted, Brigetta flopped back on the grass and Mary followed suit. "Do you think it will work?" Brigetta asked in a voice strained with worry, her earlier confidence weakening.

"Oh, yes, I'm quite sure of it," Mary offered boldly.

Brigetta smiled weakly. At that point, neither girl could think of much more to talk about—and each was so tired, she could hardly move. Without their usual lingering farewell, Mary waved goodbye and Brigetta barely waited until the buggy was out of sight before she headed for the sofa and fell promptly asleep.

She woke with a start. *Whistling! Bram! Long johns!* She flew to the window and saw her beloved husband striding toward the house, a look of bewilderment noticeable the closer he came. She dropped the curtain as if burned and twisted her apron into a twisted knot.

"Brigetta?" Silence. "Brigetta! Where are you?"

"In the parlor." *Oh dear. Oh–dear-oh-dear-oh-dear!*

"Come with me—I want to show you something most unusual!" Bram entered the parlor and guided a reluctant Brigetta out the door, across the lawn, past the pump with a great puddle still evident, and right to the perfect spot from which to view a pair of long johns drying spread-eagle in the sun.

"The last time I saw these woolens, I'm *sure* they were put away with my winter clothes. Imagine my surprise to come in for lunch today and find them pinned to the ground as if they—and they alone—know of an approaching tornado! Do you think we ought to bring out milk cans and pitchforks and nail kegs and hold down the rest of the laundry, too?

134   Rough Terrain

I doubt those puny wooden clothespins stand a chance against the formidable wind that must be coming!"

Brigetta traced a pattern in the grass with her toe. Bram hadn't even mentioned her biggest concern—the undeniable shrinkage. *What to say? What to do?*

Bram kicked the anvil aside and the woolen leg beneath it sprang back like a stone from a slingshot; Brigetta jumped as if hit by the same. Bram stared at the now off-kilter clothing.

He moved the hammerhead next, releasing a leg that seemed to withdraw in fear. Brigetta winced.

Bram stepped up to the waistband and opened the gunnysack curiously. "Horseshoes?" he inquired. She nodded.

He lifted the bag and the two of them stared at the mangled pair of grass-and rust-stained woolens. Bram picked them up and held them aloft like a deformed flag. Brigetta's face burned and she wished fervently for that tornado to whisk her out of Iowa.

Without a word, Bram slung the underwear over one shoulder and headed for the house. Brigetta sank down in the center of the imprints made by three heavy objects in the grass and let her head sag down on her bosom.

"Hey, Brigetta! What do you think?"

Startled, she looked up and her jaw dropped. There stood her husband on the back steps in his shrunken long johns—fully covered from waist to kneecap, but naked as a jaybird above and below.

A laugh gurgled in her throat and pushed past her lips and shot out into the sunshine.

"I'm thinking if you can knit me a pair of extra-long knee socks with buttonholes along the top, and then sew a couple buttons under the ankle part of these, right here" he ran a finger inside the ankle band stretched around his knees, "I'll have a real versatile pair of long johns—if I get too hot, I'll just pull off the sock parts! What do you think? We could call 'em short-johns!"

Brigetta pushed herself up off the lawn and ran as fast as she could, laughing hysterically all the way and fearing she would not reach the outhouse in time. Her voice echoed around the spider-webbed structure, bouncing back at her as she wiped tears on her sleeves and succumbed to another siege of hilarity.

When she finally pushed open the door, Bram was kneeling beside the path—still clad only in his all-too-brief winter undergarments. He clutched at her skirts and pleaded, "Please, lady—have pity on me! My wife washed my woolens and I'm afraid to think what she's done to my trousers! Please won't you rescue me from her laundry-day wrath?"

Brigetta threw her arms around Bram's neck and leaned against his head, weak with laughter. "I'm so sorry, Bram!" she hiccoughed and giggled through her heart-felt apology.

Bram rose to his feet and pulled Brigetta into his arms and kissed her soundly on the lips.

"Do you know how scared I was to have to tell you about my mistake?" she asked huskily.

"Do you know how truly astonishing it is to find one's underwear pinned to the grass?" he asked.

"Do you know how much I love you?" she whispered.

"A bushel and a peck, if I'm not mistaken!" In the throes of the subsequent hug-around-the-neck, he added, "Do you know how little shrunken underwear matters?"

"At least I'll have some good material to make into potholders."

"Oh, no, not out of these! I plan to save them to wear every year on our anniversary! It's just the beginning of the folklore of our marriage," Bram declared and kissed her on the nose.

By suppertime, the kitchen was scented with the fragrant herbs and spices from the meal Brigetta had planned. It would begin with *Tante* Lena's recipe for onion soup, followed by Rebecca's shared recipe for roasted chicken and end with Brigetta's favorite spice cake. *To have Papa and Mama and* Tante *Lena as guests along with Bram's family—what a thrilling way to begin a life-time of entertaining!*

Brigetta's face glistened with perspiration springing as much from the excitement of entertaining both families as from the heat radiating from the cook stove on the warm summer day. She hummed while she frosted the cake, and whistled while she steeped teabags for iced tea, and sang outright while she set the table with bright and shining new dishes and crisp linens.

Throughout the afternoon, she thought how humorous she and Mary must have looked as they struggled to remedy the dilemma. She giggled each time she thought of Bram posing on the steps in his short-johns.

As he changed clothes for supper, with Brigetta's giggles reaching his ears with clarity, Bram smiled and tucked a crisply ironed shirt into clean trousers. They smelled of the bright sunshine and he knew Brigetta had ironed them especially for him to wear tonight. He grinned broadly as he folded his sparkling clean pint-sized long johns into a corner of the cedar chest and closed the lid. *I wouldn't trade this day for all the tulips in Holland!*

Bram stood in the dining room doorway and watched his wife of three wonderful weeks shift the creamer and sugar bowl ever so little to the left, then back to the right, finally placing them exactly where they had been originally. "Let's see…should I roll my sleeves up one turn or two? Or should I carefully fold them up so as not to muss the cuffs?" He studied his shirtsleeves with great seriousness. "Roll? Or fold? These details are *so* important—after all, my *mother* is coming to see me!"

Brigetta giggled and flew across the room to capture him in her arms. "Oh, Bram, you can tease me all you want, but I want everything to be just *perfect.* I want your parents to observe what a good wife I am, and I want my family to see they raised me well, and I want you to be ever so proud of me, and I want Cornelis to realize automobiles aren't enough—he needs a wife, too!"

"Whew, that's a lot to ask from just one supper," Bram teased and smoothed Brigetta's curls. That touch led to kissing and caressing; finally Brigetta unwillingly pulled away.

"My goodness, I wonder if every new bride is as wobbly in the knees as I am!"

"And I wonder if every husband has trouble keeping his thoughts and hands off his bride like I do."

Brigetta blushed. Her hands slide down Bram's arms, across his wrists, along the palms of his hands, and lingered just a second on the tips of his fingers before she disappeared into the kitchen.

Bram swayed and stifled a moan. *It isn't only the bride who is weak-kneed in our house. It's a good thing we've got company coming in just a few minutes or...*Bram headed for the front porch to watch for their company. *I never dreamed marriage would be like this!*

Eight chairs circled the oval table. Eight forks clattered against china, lifting bite after bite to hungry mouths. Eight napkins showed traces of chicken, lip-shaped shadows of gravy, a dab of potatoes, perhaps a stain or two from berry jam. Seven of those around the table ate heartily while the cook beamed from her end of the table and barely touched her plate.

Nearly every sentence Brigetta uttered began "Bram and I..." or "Bram says..."

Most segments of the conversation Bram contributed began "Brigetta is..." or "We think..."

Five of the guests noted this and shared smiles around the table. The sixth guest watched his brother and new sister-in-law with a sullen gaze not lost on Gustave. *Father God—help this young man to handle the disappointments of his life with wisdom beyond his years.*

Following the meal, nothing would suffice but a full tour of the newly-weds' home. No shelf in the pantry went unexamined. No drawer in the buffet remained closed. No item in the china hutch escaped notice. No corner of the bedroom, porch, or kitchen was unexplored.

Back in the parlor, the host and hostess grinned across the room at each other and felt truly married as their families talked and slipped easily into the life-long process of becoming joined together, just like the newly-weds.

January—August 1919

◆

Preparations for the holiday season had consumed Brigetta. Even harvest had not occupied her mind like the anticipation of this, her first Christmas as Mrs. Bram de Boer. While Bram studied seed catalogs and wrote letters to companies in Holland reputed to have exceptional tulip bulbs and seeds, Brigetta stitched sequins to red felt, trimmed green velvet with white lace, measured and remeasured every inch of the places she would decorate with garlands and ribbons.

At last the festivities came to an end. Brigetta woke early one morning mid-January and admitted glumly as she looked at the wilting greenery hanging around the doorframe that Christmas was over. "Bram, wake up. Can you hear me? I want to have our families over for supper tonight—just one last party before I put away all the pretty decorations. It's so terribly long until we have another holiday—I just want to make it all last longer. What do you think—shall I invite them?"

She took his sleepy mumbling for assent and jumped out of bed. Even before beginning breakfast, she checked the cookie jar: plenty of *nieuwjaarskoekjes* left. *I'll cut the fruitcake into little pieces, and make a custard...* She hummed bits of songs remembered from the Christmas Festival, and then picked up steam and volume, belting out "Shine On, Harvest Moon" while sausage sizzled.

Bram's voice echoed from the bedroom, joining her on the last verse. Breakfast was a rollicking affair. "I'll make the best supper you can imagine, Bram. In fact, this after-the-holidays dinner could become a regular event for our family—we could invite friends next year, and become famous for it! Don't you just love regular events? They make life so interesting!"

Swallowing a mouthful of eggs, Bram winked at his wife. "I just love you—you're the regular event that makes my life interesting!"

Brigetta set the table with her prized wedding-gift linens, sparkling china and silver, and then carefully lettered each name on little cards she decorated with bits of ribbon. Bram howled. "Thank goodness we'll have place cards—I'd hate to think Cornelis would just sit any-old-place instead of next to *Tante* Lena like he always does!"

"It's a touch of class, Bram. This is a big event."

He kissed her and tweaked her nose. "If I may, Mrs. de Boer, I'd be delighted to extend the invitations to our guests. That can become my main contribution to this first-of-many annual events."

"Oh, would you? That is just perfect—and when you invite them, make it sound special!"

When she opened the door for their guests, Brigetta's eyes widened. Even Cornelis was dressed in his Sunday best! Everyone stomped snow off their shoes and swept into the warmth. "Bram advised us to consider this as special as your wedding, so we thought we ought to dress the part!" Gustave said. Brigetta's infectious laugh rang out and the evening was off to a fine start.

Eventually, even the men refused Brigetta's repeated offers of plates loaded with sweets. "One more cup of coffee, Sweet Pea," *Tante* Lena said. "You've become a good cook in the months of your marriage!"

"Thank you. I've also become quite a good quilter, thanks to Grandmother. Come, I want you to see the wedding-ring pattern we've been working on. I've got it on our bed even though it isn't done because I just love to look at it! Every night I take it off and fold it up, but every morning I just can't resist putting it back on." All eight trooped into the bedroom to admire what was truly a beautiful work in-progress.

Hanna helped Brigetta refold the quilt after they had turned it over to see the tiny stitches she had painstakingly achieved. When she opened the closet door to put it away for the night, Lena pointed out the closet shelf loaded with clothing and bedding.

Hanna said, "I can see you would benefit from having a dresser in addition to your cedar chest. The one in your old bedroom is still sitting empty. Lena and I had planned to use it for our quilting supplies, but we can make do without it."

"We surely can," agreed Lena. "I have just stripped the old varnish off it. I'll want to have the doors wide open for fresh air when I varnish it again, but come spring, it will be ready and waiting."

"It will be wonderful. Thank you!"

They moved chairs from the dining room to the parlor to accommodate their guests and settled in for a companionable evening. Had Bram and Brigetta eavesdropped on their parents' bedtime conversations, they would have heard a common theme: Bram and Brigetta were as happy together as either set of parents had ever seen their respective child. It was, indeed, a perfect match—and one that brought a breath of heaven to each person who crossed their paths.

*   *   *

From the first Thursday morning after their marriage, Brigetta helped Bram at the vegetable stand on their designated corner in town. She loved seeing their lush, ripe produce move from the wagon to housewives' baskets at an astounding pace. Every week she looked across the road at the tree beneath which she and Mary had stood that long-ago summer and breathed a silent prayer of thanks for God's goodness in making her dreams come true.

Bram kept careful records over the years, filling notebook pages with planting schedules, expenses and matching income reports, weather charts, and fertilizing methods. Evenings, they studied the papers, dreaming of days ahead when their steadily growing nest egg would allow them to rent or buy more land, expand their crops, and through it all work together.

Early mornings, Brigetta worked in the garden with Bram pruning, weeding, watering, and shepherding their crops through the crucial early days of growth. "To get more outstanding results from fertilizing tomatoes, I cut the amount of compost I would normally use in half—but then I apply it twice as often," he explained with a shy grin. "And from the looks of things, by next week, I'll have to ask you to step aside so you don't get overtaken by a giant cabbage!"

"I know we must grow food, but the tulip beds are my favorite sections of the garden, Bram, with the rows and rows of swaying stems and leaves protecting the cupped blossoms. I sure glad we make enough money selling them to justify growing them!"

As someone who loved the earth, Bram was a good teacher, and Brigetta was a motivated learner—the team they made was thus ensured of success. Whereas Cornelis rolled his eyes and tried to cut corners and accomplish the same results Bram achieved only with painstaking labor, Brigetta listened wide-eyed, following Bram's instructions to the letter. She marveled each time his predictions came true and their beets grew firmer, their corn stood taller, and the raspberries bushes sagged beneath their exceptionally plumb and juicy fruit.

"Let's sing!" Brigetta usually begged, even before the hoe touched the soil. And sing they did, their voices rolling across the yard and into the big house where Grandmother smiled in her rocking chair, and Rebecca hummed along in the kitchen. "We could sing quite a fine number at the Winter Festival next December!" Brigetta beamed. "Our voices blend so well, don't you agree?"

"How could they not—we're *one* now!" Bram knew full well the innuendo would make Brigetta blush. Grinning wickedly, he planted a lingering kiss firmly on her lips and headed off to begin his fieldwork, whistling love songs as he left—melodies that hitched a ride in her memories.

Even though short-lived and unable to sustain life like the sensible produce otherwise filling the garden, the cheerful tulips satisfied something innately Dutch in their hearts. Perhaps it was the steadfastness of the fragile-looking petals, withstanding spring winds. Perhaps it was the flowers' persistence in pushing through the ground when sturdier plants held back until the soil warmed. Perhaps it was the beautiful memory of the bride's basket filled with tulips grown with her groom's pure love.

Whatever the reason, Bram persevered in learning the mysteries and mastering the intricacies of raising tulips from bulbs and seeds alike. Grafting hearty breeds to create new and interesting shades of familiar colors, some with delicately tinted tips, Bram created quite a stir in Dutchville and at the Sioux County Fair. New varieties of tulips set Brigetta's imagination whirling. Bram let her name them all—something she deemed necessary. Bram agreed special names added a certain charm.

One woman said wistfully, "I wish you were selling the bulbs this year for the Morning Dawn tulips!"

"If you can wait one year, that will be possible. But when I've grown something from seeds, I cannot let the bulbs go until a second crop has proven successful," When the woman was out of range of hearing, Bram chuckled. "I doubt if she would have even thought twice about something I would have just called 'the tallest yellow tulip in row seven'! See the success your whimsical names bring us?"

"Excuse me; will you ever interbreed the Sunset Rainbow with the Velvet Lace?" While Bram moved to answer the woman who called across the wagon, Brigetta noted her carefully lettered signs bearing romantic names for the peach-tipped pink blooms and the deep red, white-tipped flowers had snared another customer.

*   *   *

Brigetta loved waking before Bram to watch him sleep beside her, his hair tousled, an arm flung across her. Early-morning cuddling was the sweetest, but today she must rise quickly because she had promised Rebecca she would be over at the big house in time to help Grandmother de Boer dress. Hans and Rebecca were well on their way to Le Mars for the day to purchase a new horse, and Brigetta knew Bram's grandmother would be worried if she called out and no one answered.

Brigetta carefully lifted back the covers and slid out of bed. Bram deserved a few more minutes of rest. He had worked later than usual last night, hoping to beat the rain falling in torrents as dusk crossed the horizon. Brigetta and Rebecca had worked beside Bram in the garden at the end of the day, letting Cornelis and Hans work in the field. Knowing how exhausted she and Bram had been, Brigetta wondered how Rebecca and Hans had managed to awaken long before the roosters crowed.

Once she was dressed, she woke Bram with a tantalizing kiss and he roused himself, resigned to beginning morning chores when she skittered away from his grasp, thus removing any other activities from his wish list. Brigetta headed out across the dewy lawn to the big house. From the size of the puddles on the road, she knew they had gotten a good rain that would keep the brothers out of the fields today. This would give them a much-needed opportunity to work at other tasks that filled farmers' days until they bulged at both ends.

Today, they would breakfast together with Cornelis and Grandmother in Rebecca's kitchen. Since Grandmother was still asleep and she assumed Cornelis was out in the barn with Bram, Brigetta quickly began cracking eggs, mixing up pancake batter, and frying sausage. Remembering similar activities during harvest time, she smiled. "It's a good thing I know my way around Rebecca's kitchen, isn't it?" she asked the cat rubbing against her ankles.

She headed down the hall to Grandmother's room and soon both were back in the kitchen. "If you will pour milk for us, Grandmother, I'm almost ready with the rest of our breakfast." She placed glasses nearby and retrieved the pitcher from the icebox. The fragrant spicy sausage and the tantalizing coffee bubbling on the stove filled the air as Brigetta stood on the back porch and clanged the bell hanging on the post.

Bram bounded up the steps and Cornelis followed at a slower pace. The bounce in Bram's step and gleam in his eye increasingly irritated Cornelis. More than anyone else in either family, Cornelis was vigilant in his observations of the young couple. Losing none of its early charm, their love was growing deeper and stronger as the two learned to trust each other, discovered new intimacies, explored each other's secrets, and unearthed a level of sensual delights that both stunned and enchanted them.

Cornelis was clearly in a deep funk when Bram led the four of them in morning prayers and devotions. Cornelis' thoughts through it all were less than spiritually uplifting. Amazingly, Bram seemed to satisfy Brigetta completely, and it was equally evident she fulfilled Bram's every dream, as well. They were like salt and pepper, or a sail for a sailboat. But Cornelis heard the man-talk around the livery. He knew things about the ways of a man with a woman. He also knew Brigetta had lived a sheltered life. She probably didn't know what to expect from the marriage bed.

Brigetta, serving second-helpings of pancakes to both Bram and Cornelis, could hardly have realized the randy thoughts burning behind Cornelis' brooding gaze.

Bram caressed her bottom out of the others' view and sent the blood rushing to her face and forced a startled, "Oh!" from her parted lips. Cornelis looked up curiously, a forkful of pancake halfway to his mouth, and noted his brother's dancing eyes. Both then looked at Brigetta who attempted to explain her abrupt exclamation with a lame,

146   Rough Terrain

"I just wondered if anyone would like some more coffee?" She rushed to the stove to get the coffeepot.

Bram took pity on her and turned to Cornelis. "With the ground as soft as it is after the rain last night, today would be a good time to finish digging post holes in the north field." Cornelis nodded and Brigetta finished her breakfast with idle chitchat with Grandmother, all the while unobtrusively contemplating the two men.

Bram was by far the more handsome, but Cornelis would make a young woman happy, too, once he got the wanderlust out of his head and realized there was more to life than automobiles. He mentioned almost weekly how he looked forward to leaving Dutchville behind to find a job with automobile in the title. Nothing wrong with that, but thankfully Bram cared about something that would be around for a while: God's green earth.

Grandmother had helped dry the breakfast dishes, and then Brigetta settled the older woman in a comfortable chair out under an overhanging elm tree and tucked an afghan around her knees. "Are you sure you want to shell these peas? It's an awfully big bowl of them!"

"I want to help Rebecca and I know she hopes to put up peas tomorrow. If I tire, I'll just rest right here. You run along, dear child, and finish your housework. If I need anything, I'll ring the bell." She pulled the dinner bell closer to her chair and smiled at her granddaughter-in-law. "You seem to be doing a good job of keeping our Bram happy—I've never known that young man to smile so much as in the past year. I thought his face would split open this morning at the breakfast table!"

Pleased, Brigetta blushed and within minutes was hurrying along the foot-worn path between the two houses on the farm. She set up the ironing board, put several sadirons on the kitchen stove to heat, and mixed up a coffeecake to bake while she ironed. Baking would keep the stove hot for the irons and, without wasting firewood, she would also have a mid-morning treat for everyone.

She had just begun ironing a pillowcase when she heard Cornelis on the back porch. "I'm going in to town to pick up a piece for our plow from the blacksmith. Bram said you might want me to stop by the parsonage and pick up the dresser your mother is giving you."

"Wonderful! *Tante* Lena said last Sunday that it's ready. I'd go with you, but I can't leave Grandmother." Brigetta returned to her ironing, humming happily as she mentally planned how she would fill each drawer.

Soon, she heard the horse whinny. Setting the sadirons back on the stove and moving the cooling coffeecake to a rack, she hurried out to help Cornelis unload the dresser. She carried one large drawer as he hefted the familiar piece of furniture from her childhood bedroom that would now be part of her married life. Together, they returned to the wagon and brought in the remaining drawers.

When all was in place, Brigetta sighed, "Oh dear, the top drawer must still be at home. But don't worry about it. I can go to town this afternoon and get it—Grandmother can even go with me; she'd enjoy a buggy ride. We'll have afternoon coffee with Mama and *Tante* Lena. Thank you, Cornelis—you can see I needed the dresser by how full this shelf is!"

Cornelis followed Brigetta to the closet and nodded as he looked at the loaded shelf. "It wouldn't be hard to put an extra shelf in here, right above this one. Of course, you would have to use a stool to reach anything on it, but if you only used it for things you rarely need, it should help out."

"What a grand idea! I'll tell Bram."

Cornelis shook his head. "No, I never did give you a wedding present and it's high time—you've been married over a year! How would you like a closet shelf as a belated wedding present from your one-and-only brother-in-law?"

Her delight in this suggestion wrapped itself around his heart and made him feel as though he had bestowed jewels upon her—but it also twisted envy's sharp edge another turn in his chest. He stepped into the closet, pushing aside the clothing, to allow a look at the inside walls on either side of the door. "While I'm at it, I could put a couple of hooks right here, too, if you'd like."

"Where?" Brigetta stuck her head in, and Cornelis shifted slightly to allow her space beside him to observe the same bare walls.

Cornelis looked from the wall to Brigetta's face, her delicate features screwed up in serious contemplation of his suggestion. "Could you put two on each side of the door?"

"Sure. How high would you want them?"

She stretched her arm up and over to touch the wall at the very spot she imagined a hook should be, "Right here would be perfect for my side; you figure out how high to put the ones on Bram's side."

Cornelis scratched a mark on the wall with his fingernail right where Brigetta's finger was pressed. Just then, without warning, breezes lingering from the previous night's storm billowed the curtains at both windows and converged mid-room with enough strength to blow the closet door shut.

"That's quite a breeze this morning! Oh, no!" Brigetta exclaimed, and pushed against the door. It was wasted effort; the door was not only latched shut, but unyielding. She fumbled with the doorknob in the darkness. "Cornelis, help! The doorknob won't turn—we're trapped in here!"

"I'm sure it's just stuck. Could be warped. Here, let me try." His efforts also were in vain.

She pushed his hands away from the knob and tried again—jiggling, tugging and pushing without results. One firm twist accomplished something at last: a screw loosened and they heard the scraping sound of metal sliding, followed by the thump of the doorknob falling out of its moorings to land on the floor outside the door. Brigetta held the worthless knob in her hand.

With a startled whimper, she knelt to peer through the tiny opening out into the sunny room beyond the closet. She looked up at the shadow next to her that was Cornelis—the still form sharing the darkness with her. He extended a hand to help her back up in the crowded space.

"What do we do now, Cornelis?" she asked in a tremulous voice.

"Someone will find us. We just wait."

"But your grandmother is outside—what if she calls for help and there's no one to answer?"

"Then she'll just wait, too! Come here." Cornelis then made one of the worst decisions in his nineteen years.

"What are you doing, Cornelis?" Brigetta struggled in the firm full-body embrace that pulled her much closer to her brother-in-law than morals and propriety allowed.

Cornelis' lips imprisoned hers in a kiss that pressed against her mouth and nearly gagged her with its insistence, effectively cutting off her words. His hands pined her head in position to receive his intrusion into his brother's realm. Brigetta struggled futilely to escape. Instinctively, she kicked, connecting with Cornelis' ankle. Even though she felt him stiffen with pain, she realized she was no match for his virile, work-hardened body.

Her frenzied sobs startled Cornelis into loosening his grip. She pulled away and pounded on the door. A single shaft of light came through the quarter-sized doorknob hole and she frantically fumbled with the unfamiliar metalworkings of the broken fixture, attempting to jam the doorknob back into place and function. Nothing gave way. They were prisoners in the closet as surely as if guards kept watch outside the door.

Cornelis breathed heavily. "Since it seems we'll be in here for a while, we might as well make the best of it." He found her bosom in the darkness and his thumb began to trace a rhythmic pattern as his breathing became labored.

The clothing in the small space muffled Brigetta's scream. "Stop that, Cornelis, this is *zonde*! I'm married to your brother."

"Yes, but you deserve to be happier than I *know* Bram can ever make you." His left arm pinned her to him as his right hand continued its purposeful actions and roaming. "You see, Brigetta, I know all about my brother's, uh, inadequacies—he can't possibly please you like I could."

Despite her fears and anger, Brigetta was alarmed at how her body betrayed her. Sensations so like what she sought and reveled in with Bram erupted within her—yet, Cornelis' touch provided none of the utter bliss Bram's did. *How can this be?* Her breathing was choppy, mingling gasps and tears and protests. "Bram and I are happy. Stop this!"

In one quick motion, Cornelis clutched her buttocks and pulled Brigetta up against himself, thrusting and rubbing suggestively against her stiffened body, his hands branding every place they touched. She clamped her knees together in utter terror and shrieked again, "Help! Someone!"

"Who do you expect will come? Bram's is mending a fence on the farthest corner of the field—too far away to hear you inside a closet in your house, silly goose!" His fingers worked steadily in the darkness; his breath was steamy against her neck and face. "We might as well enjoy ourselves as long as we're stuck in here, Brigetta! Don't worry. It's me— Cornelis."

Even knowing Bram would eventually return to the house, Brigetta despaired. She had been married long enough to know Cornelis had invaded the sanctity of her marriage to his brother—and her private spaces. Bram loved her until their bed rocked like the San Francisco earthquake, but Cornelis was turning her body into a traitor against all she held sacred. Her limbs were weak, her hidden places throbbed with untold secrets, and her heart was heavy.

Brigetta burst into tears and Cornelis reached out to her. She flung his arms away and swung wildly, still holding the doorknob. Her hand connected with his face. Startled, he dropped back with a yelp of pain.

She quickly moved to the farthest corner of the closet and slid down the wall where she curled into a fetal ball. He dropped down beside her and murmured placatingly, "I'm sorry, Brigetta. I didn't mean to upset you. You didn't need to hit me. I'll probably have a shiner from that swing you took at me. I just thought…"

"No, Cornelis," she interrupted, "that's the problem. You didn't think. What you have done in this closet is wrong." Brigetta hiccupped and shrank back against the corner amidst Bram's clothes. She clutched a pants leg from his wedding suit against her cheek like a child seeks comfort from a familiar blanket.

Her sobs eventually stilled and she squinted in the darkness. Cornelis sat quietly, cross-legged, in the middle of the floor, just an arm's length away, her dresses thrust behind him and brushing his shoulders. "You should be ashamed, Cornelis. We're relatives now—and everything you have done to me in this closet is sinful. If this is how you treat the Dutchville girls, shame on you."

"I said I'm sorry." Cornelis said.

Silence.

"I didn't mean to scare you." Cornelis' thoughts were turning more rational and he was beginning to realize the past few minutes had been most unwise. Brigetta was far too upset to escape notice of their rescuer. He had sought for honey and angered the bees instead.

Gingerly, Cornelis touched his eye. His assessment of Brigetta's aim had been accurate; he could feel his left eye swelling shut. Once they were rescued, he was going to have to do some fast-talking to explain this mess. To accomplish that, he needed to get Brigetta past her fear before the door opened—and back to the spunky girl everyone knew and loved. *And it sure can't hurt to encourage her to forget this unfortunate episode.*

In silky tones, Cornelis attempted a speedy reconciliation. "Let me hold you, Brigetta. You're upset, I know. You really need to rest until someone comes to let us out. Come on, just sit next to me—you'll see I won't do anything wrong."

Brigetta pulled her knees even closer to her chest, tucking her skirts around her like a shroud. "No! If you ever come near me again, I not only will never forgive you, but I will tell your brother and your parents and my family and any girl you ever hope to marry *exactly* what you have done and how you refused to listen to my pleas to stop. You have brought shame and scorn upon yourself. Stay where you are and keep your hands where they belong." Her tone didn't bode well for *forgive and forget* any time soon.

Cornelis' heart sank, but he chided himself for giving up so easily. He still had time to reason with her. *I just need to analyze the situation and come up with something that will work.*

A voice sounded in the distance. "Brigetta? Hello!"

Brigetta stumbled to her feet with a cry of relief and pounded on the closet door as she cried out, "In here! Help!"

The two in the closet heard the front door open and close, floor-boards creak, and soon the all-too familiar voice once again called out, "Brigetta?"

Lena followed the responding muffled shouts and stopped in the doorway to stare curiously at the floor beside the closet in Bram and Brigetta's bedroom. In the middle of one of Lena's own rag rugs—the oval one she had braided from the heavy, durable material of Gustave's old trousers—was a doorknob. "Isn't *that* odd?" she mused aloud.

"*Tante* Lena? Help! Can you get the door open? The knob fell off and we're stuck in here!"

Even more startling than finding stray hardware on the floor was the sound of shuffling from within the closet and the sheer panic in her niece's voice. "Brigetta? What in heaven's name are you doing in the closet? And who is in there with you? I just waved at Bram out in the field."

There was the slightest pause before Brigetta's voice gave hints of her desperation. "*Please* get the door open, and hurry! It's…Cornelis in here with me." She didn't need to see a thing to know *Tante* Lena's lips pursed tightly at that revelation.

"Where does Bram keep his tools?" Lena asked in a chilly tone. Even Cornelis cringed at the sting of her words and all she left unsaid.

"Out in the buggy barn. No, wait! He was working on the pump—look there first." Brigetta fought against tears as she heard *Tante* Lena leave first the room, then the house.

Soon, Lena returned and worked to remove the hinge pins. From inside the closet, Cornelis caught the loosened door and stepped out ahead of Brigetta to lean it against the wall.

Brigetta froze in the closet doorway, staring into Lena's questioning stare. Those eyes missed little: Brigetta's hair was a flyaway mess of tangles; Cornelis' face was red and blotchy, and his left eye was turning colors. Brigetta's clothing was wrinkled in suggestive places, drawing Lena's eyes from her niece's bosom to her crotch and back up to her burning face. Cornelis attempted an attitude of cockiness that crumbled beneath Lena's penetrating gaze.

"What's going on here?" Lena demanded.

Brigetta looked at the floor and then quickly turned her head in Cornelis' direction as she spit out, "Cornelis was showing me where he could put in some extra hooks and another shelf, but I am quite sure I don't want any hooks in my closet. And the shelf we have is plenty," she said firmly, staring directly into her brother-in-law's face.

Cornelis flushed and bent to pick up the doorknob. "I don't believe this is broken. The screws just must have come loose. Why don't you ladies let me put the door back on its hinges and fix the doorknob?"

Brigetta suddenly gasped, "Grandmother! She is probably frantic with worry!" She fled the room.

Lena picked up the dresser drawer that had been her reason for coming out to the farm. "It's a good thing you left this behind or the two of you would still be in the closet when Bram comes in for lunch." She pushed the drawer firmly into the empty slot. Not one word she said actually warned or condemned or chastised, but Cornelis knew her intent did all three.

"Yes, Ma'am," he said respectfully. No outsider would have known his simple reply couched regret, fear, and respect, but Lena heard them all.

What worried her was she heard no true repentance. "I'll be watching. And don't you forget it." She turned on her heel, bringing a memory to Cornelis' mind of a time long ago when he had attempted to touch a hen's chick. The back of his legs still evidenced a scar from that mother's beak.

Lena approached the big house in time to see Brigetta helping Bram's grandmother along the path to the outhouse. Lena could tell the girl was rattled. *As well she ought to be.* Lena waited, heart pounding, pacing Rebecca's spotless kitchen. Brigetta's back was to the kitchen as she walked beside Grandmother down the hall to settle the older woman in her bed.

That completed, Brigetta skidded to a stop in the kitchen doorway, startled to see her *Tante* Lena waiting there. Lena pushed a chair away from the table with her foot and nodded curtly toward it. "Sit."

Brigetta hesitated only briefly. The two women sat in silence for an awkward moment, neither knowing what to say, what to ask. At last, Brigetta spoke. "The wind blew the door shut, and then the doorknob fell off when I tried to open it. That's what happened."

Lena frowned. "I hope so." Her tone was cold; she pushed away from the table, leaving the room without a backward glance.

Brigetta sagged in her chair. *Why did* Tante *Lena not even ask what we were doing in the closet—even though I know she wonders why we're both acting so guilty?* The minutes grew into a half-hour and still she sat. Finally, she tiptoed down the hall, waited outside the bedroom door until Grandmother's steady breathing guaranteed she was asleep, and then leaned against the wallpapered hallway. *If* Tante *Lena doubts my word—and she has known me since I was born—how can I expect Bram to believe me?*

She made a hasty trip home. Taking a basin of warm water into the bedroom, she pulled the curtains closed and scrubbed every part of her body Cornelis had touched. In addition to several spots on the skirt of her dress, she was horrified to find her undergarments similarly stained. She quickly buried all the clothing she had worn in the bottom of the dirty laundry. Redressing quickly, she gulped back a sob pushing itself to the surface—that must stop: it would soon be lunch and she must face Bram…and Cornelis. *Oh, God, how can I face them both in the same room?*

With heavy heart, she left home and headed off to start lunch in Rebecca's kitchen. The sun was high in the sky, drying up the puddles on the road. Food prepared, she rang the dinner bell once and a second time, but still saw no sign of Bram and Cornelis coming in from their work. At last she made a tray for Grandmother and took it to her room, settling her in the rocker beside a low table. Then, she packed up a basket with generous portions of meat and cheese, breads, sweets, and tea.

She spotted Bram working at the far corner of the field, but there was no sign of Cornelis. She meandered through the rows of waist-high corn and flourishing beans toward Bram. Her heart was heavy, but she was glad he was alone.

"Where's Cornelis?" Bram asked, annoyance evident in his tone. "He should have been back from town long ago. I've been waiting for him to help me dig new post holes."

"I thought he would be with you. I haven't seen him since mid-morning." Brigetta's voice trembled and she stiffened her shoulders as she warded off the impulse to fling herself into Bram's arms and sob her heart out. She felt dirty inside, but knew this was neither the time nor place for the conversation they needed to have.

"If he isn't working, he doesn't need to eat! Leave the basket with me and I'll save what's left for him." Bram's morning had been filled with hard work and his energy needed replenishment. Brigetta's morning was ruined by shame, and she could hardly lift one foot in front of the other on her way back to the big house.

Cornelis was on a short list for both of them, but while Bram's mental list was headed *People Who Had Better Show Up Quickly,* the heading on Brigetta's slate read *People I Never Want to See Again.*

Taking the long way across the field toward home, Brigetta shuddered as the horrors of the morning washed over her. All because of a door-slamming breeze, her life was shattered. Who knew if Cornelis would have attempted the same thing under different circumstances, but the point was he *had.* She stopped outside the bedroom window and peered into the room she shared with the man she loved. The closet door was back in place, leaving no sign of anything out of the ordinary. Except for the newly delivered dresser, the room looked the same as when Bram had left it that morning.

But Brigetta knew she would never see the room without seeing the struggle in the dark closet played out over and over again on the stage in her mind. *I fought against Cornelis, but how can I ever prove that? Only Cornelis heard when I spoke my mind, and he could say he was only doing what I allowed.* God was Brigetta's only witness, but she knew the places and the ways Cornelis had touched her and the unwilling responses her body had given—those were reserved for the marriage bed. *Can God forgive the sins of the morning?*

She stopped in her own kitchen long enough to collect her mending basket and retraced her steps to the big house. Grandmother had fallen asleep in her chair, the lunch tray set on the low table. Brigetta looked at the kind woman and envied her peacefulness. Fear that no one would believe her pushed rational thoughts from her mind.

Out in the field, Bram brushed the hair out of his eyes and swiveled his shoulders in their sockets to loosen the kinks from his labors. He noticed a spiral of smoke coming from behind the barn. *Cornelis is burning garbage instead of helping me? That fellow is about as wishy-washy as anyone I've ever met.*

Stomping off, frustration building with each furrow he crossed, Bram headed across the fields to his brother. He grudgingly admitted

Cornelis was doing a task that needed doing, and last night's heavy rain certainly meant fire danger was low, but to change tasks without so much as a howdy-do? That was inexcusable. *Maybe it's time for Cornelis to leave home and pursue his dream—his heart isn't here.*

"Hey!" Bram called angrily to his brother as he rounded the corner of the barn. "The last thing you said to me in the field this morning was that you'd go to town and then be back to help dig post holes. So, why are you burning garbage instead?"

Cornelis looked briefly over his right shoulder at his brother and kept on raking branches and rubbish toward the fire he monitored. "It seemed like a good day to burn," he responded sullenly.

"I don't deny that, but what happened to the plans we made at breakfast?"

"Plans change."

Bram sighed and shook his head, thoroughly disgusted with his younger brother. "Here's what's left of the lunch Brigetta made. Eat up."

Cornelis' back stiffened but he didn't turn. "You saw Brigetta?"

"I just said she brought out our lunch."

"What did she have to say?" Cornelis asked in a strained voice.

"Huh? Other than that she hadn't seen you since mid-morning, not much. Come on, Cornelis. Leave the pile to burn. You've got everything cleared around it, and the ground is soaked. It will be fine. Eat, and then come help me."

Bram looked up just as Cornelis turned slightly. "What happened to your eye? It's swollen shut!"

"Believe me, I know."

"Well? What happened?"

"I guess I got in the way of Brigetta's elbow when we unloaded the dresser. Don't worry about it."

"That looks more like some big guy swung at you and connected. Did Brigetta see the damage her dainty little elbow can do? You'd better go up to the house and have her put a beef steak on it."

"Yeah, she knows about it," Cornelis said insolently, "and she didn't seem too worried about it, so I'm not going to waste my time asking her for help."

"She's your sister-in-law, for crying out loud."

"I said *no*, okay? Just accept what I say, for once. And get that lunch out of here—I'm not hungry."

Bram stepped back a few paces and watched his brother kick a branch into the fire. "Okay. Suit yourself, but if it were my eye, I'd take care of it." He ignored Cornelis' muttering, picked up the lunch basket and walked away without a backward glance.

Brigetta's most recent conversation had been noticeably brief. Usually, she amused him, delighted and intrigued him—but a man would starve if he had to subsist on the scant offerings of Brigetta's words to him in the field this morning.

Cornelis' bruised eye speaks more of someone hauling off and hitting him than him running amuck Brigetta's elbow. He walked past the buggy and saw the welded piece of the plow still on the floorboard. *Something must have happened at the blacksmith's shop. Cornelis probably mouthed off about automobiles being better than horses. But why would he blame Brigetta for the damage to his face?*

Bram expelled air like an engine blowing off steam and moved along to his parents' house. He smelled apple pies baking before he even reached the back porch. He had been curt with Brigetta when his anger was really with Cornelis. He needed—wanted—to make things right with his wife.

"Mother will appreciate those—but surely only *one* is for her, and the other is for your loving husband!" Bram teased.

Suds flew in the air with Brigetta's flailing arms. "I didn't hear you come in!"

"So I gather! You must be miles away to not hear my *klompen* on the back steps!"

Brigetta flushed and reached for the lunch basket. "Good; you brought back the lunch basket. I'll wash up the tea bottle…oh, there's still food in here. Didn't Cornelis ever show up?"

"I found him—he's out at the burn pile behind the barn—but he didn't want to eat. That's quite a shiner you gave him!"

Brigetta's already flushed face reddened even more and she turned quickly back to the sink. A plate slipped out of her hands and thudded dully against the basin.

Bram stood silently, puzzled and increasingly annoyed. "What's going on? Neither of you will talk to me, and when I told Cornelis to come in and let you put a beef steak on his eye…"

"No! I'm not good with injuries. You take a steak to him. Out there."

"That," Bram drawled, "would be a wasted beef steak, wouldn't it? At least if he stays in the house and keeps the steak wrapped, we could have it for supper! Outside, the bugs will get it."

"I don't want to care for his eye. Please." The pleading in her voice would have melted a heart of stone.

"Brigetta, what's wrong? Talk to me. I know something's going on, but for the life of me, I can't figure out what. Are you worried I'll be upset just because your elbow did such gaudy damage to Cornelis' eye? Accidents happen!"

Brigetta spun around, wide-eyed. "That's what Cornelis said? My elbow hit him in the eye?"

"Something like that, as unbelievable as *that* seems, given the rainbow of colors he's showing now!"

"What do you mean, unbelievable?" she asked, her voice cracking.

"You can't possible do that much damage. You've poked me in the ribs at night all the time and all that happens is I wake up! Not a single black-and-blue mark after over a year of sleeping with you!"

"What else did he say?"

One black eyebrow arched. "Interesting. Cornelis just asked me what you had to say, and now *you* ask me what else *he* said. Brigetta, my dearest bride: tell me what's keeping you from looking me in the face."

Brigetta took a deep breath and swallowed hard. She looked up but quickly averted her gaze to his hairline. "I plan to, but first I need time to think. If I don't think before I speak, I, we—everyone—could regret it."

"I'm not leaving until I hear what you have to say. Take all the time you need, but when you're ready, I'll be right here." Bram opened the icebox and pulled out a jug of buttermilk. After pouring a tall glass, he sat down at his old place at the table and pulled out his pocketknife and a hunk of wood.

Brigetta's mind skittered back to the day when young Bram had faced up to her family and told his story with honesty. Each time she held the hard-carved skate Bram had given her that special day, she remembered her pride in his forthrightness, his humility, his honesty in the face of potential punishment. *As his wife, I owe him the same.*

"Let me check on Grandmother and be sure she's still sleeping. Then, I want you to come home with me so I can show you exactly what happened." She fled the room, leaving Bram to stare at the two apple pies cooling on the kitchen table and wonder what had transpired that morning to knock life in this northwest corner of Iowa so far off-kilter from the rest of the world.

Not one word was spoken on their short trip between the two houses. Bram reached for Brigetta's hand and was jarred by her clutching grasp on his—almost as if he were a lifeline thrown to a drowning sailor.

Once inside the cottage, Brigetta slowed. She led the way to their bedroom. Bram's quick gaze took in the dresser now in place in the corner. He turned curiously to his wife. "Yes?"

Brigetta's voice was so low it was difficult to hear her despite the stillness in the house. "Cornelis brought the dresser," she pointed needlessly, "and I told him now I wouldn't have such crowded closet shelves.

Then he offered to build us an extra closet shelf for a wedding present, and said he could put up hooks up, too. Somehow, when I was showing him where I wanted the hooks, the closet door blew shut."

Brigetta stared at the curtains blowing gently in the windows, hardly a breeze strong enough to do more than flutter organdy. Bram reviewed the jumble of words that had just spilled over Brigetta's lips. So far, the story was mildly interesting, but hardly worth a black eye.

Before Bram could formulate a question, Brigetta attempted to bridge the gaps, "We were both in the closet—looking at where the hooks could go when the door blew shut." Tears filled her eyes and tugged at Bram's heart, even though he was still clueless as to why they surfaced. "I tried to open the door, but the doorknob fell off and we were stuck in there."

"Brigetta, the doorknob looks fine."

"I know. It is now, because Cornelis fixed it. I'm not finished yet."

"Sorry. Go on, then."

Brigetta's chest heaved; each breath she took hurt, like knuckles bumping across a washboard. "It was dark and Cornelis grabbed me and touched me…in ways that are not right. Outside the marriage bed." The last words ended in a whisper. Brigetta swallowed hard and looked Bram squarely in the eye. Her eyes mirrored her tormented soul.

Realization struck him full-force. His fists clenched and his eyes narrowed. "Are you saying what I think you're saying?"

"Yes, no, I mean, I think so. I don't know. All I know is he…he kissed me in an awful way, and clutched at my…body in ways only you—but not like you, because you are always gentle and loving." Tears now cascaded down her face, unheeded. "Oh, Bram! I was so afraid. And angry. And helpless!"

"So your elbow *did* do the damage to his eye?"

"No. I had the inside part of the doorknob in my hand—when it broke, I kept hold of the knob when the rest of it fell out on the floor outside. As soon as I could get free from Cornelis, I swung at him to get away altogether, and I wasn't even thinking about how I was still holding the doorknob when I hit him in the face—in his eye. I was just trying to slap him."

Bram walked to the window and looked out toward the barn that blocked his brother from his view. "How did you get out of the closet?" he asked in a low, controlled voice.

"*Tante* Lena came. Cornelis had left one drawer at home—I mean, my old home—and she brought it out. She took the door off its hinges, and let us out. Then Cornelis fixed the doorknob and that's the last I saw of him. I ran over to the big house to check on Grandmother."

"Stay here," Bram ordered coldly. "I'll bring Grandmother back over here. I doubt Cornelis will bother you again."

Fifteen minutes later, Bram brought the buggy up beside the back steps and gently helped his grandmother into the living room. Only the set of his jaw told Brigetta of the turmoil in his soul.

He retrieved Brigetta's mending basket from the buggy and set it down close to the rocking chair his grandmother had chosen. "Grandmother is here to spend the afternoon in her old house. I will see you both later. Grandmother, how about if you eat supper with us? We'll take you home this evening in time for bed. Mother and Father will be home after dark."

Grandmother nodded, oblivious to the tension between the young couple standing behind her. Bram refused to meet Brigetta's eyes. She reached out for him and he moved toward the door, avoiding even her touch.

First Tante *Lena, and now Bram. What if no one believes me?*

It was a long, quiet afternoon in the small house. Brigetta listened to endless stories of the two brothers growing up, best friends—different as night and day, but always there for each other. "Rebecca and Hans are so proud of their boys. And so was their Grandfather de Boer." Brigetta felt sick to her stomach at the travesty the day had wrought in the family. *All because of hooks in a closet.*

Having settled his grandmother in with Brigetta, Bram sat in the buggy seat until the horse grew restless. He knew he had to do something—but what? *I want to believe Brigetta—but is love making me blind?* He was sick with hate for his brother. *My brother—the one who has looked to me as his playmate, his protector for our whole lives—why would he do this horrible thing? The whole time I've been married to Brigetta, has my own brother been lusting after her?*

Resolutely, Bram flicked the reins and began the short, familiar trip to the parsonage. *Tante* Lena would be sick with what she had witnessed—and she knew mercifully less than he did about all that had transpired. If nothing else, he needed to speak to her before she talked with anyone else. Just as he turned on to the street by the church, he saw Gustave and Hanna leaving the driveway in their own buggy, dressed for afternoon calls. *Good*—Tante *Lena will be home alone.*

He found Lena out in the garden, a half-full basket of peas beside her. "Bram!" She pushed herself up and looked into his expressionless face with something akin to trepidation filling her throat. "What brings you here? Where's Brigetta?"

"At home. I understand you brought a dresser drawer out to the house this morning."

"Yes, Cornelis had picked up the dresser, but we both missed the top drawer—I noticed after he was gone—so I took it out there because I knew Brigetta would want to fill the drawers right away." Her flushed face told Bram much more than she imagined.

"And then you had to remove the closet door? That can't have been an easy task."

Lena sighed. *He knows. But what does he know?* "There was no other way to get the two of them out. The doorknob was on the rug, in pieces."

"Did they say what happened?"

"Just that the wind blew the door shut and the doorknob broke. I don't know what they were doing in the closet in the first place." Mortification shaded her tone. "From the looks of them when that door came off, whatever went on in that closet wasn't good. She wasn't raised to act in such deplorable ways, Bram."

"Thank you for delivering the dresser drawer, *Tante* Lena. Brigetta really appreciates it. I won't keep you from your garden work any longer."

Lena stared down the road after Bram for a long time, her eyes following his retreat until he became just a silhouette. She hadn't had a moment's peace since her morning discovery, and sensed the episode was far from over. She despised gossip as much as she hated the *zonde* she feared had occurred in the closet, but she wondered if it was her responsibility to tell Brigetta's parents of the morning's disastrous event, or if the right thing to do was keep her own counsel. But she really knew little to tell—the marriage bed was murky territory to Lena. *What if I told them of sin, and it was only the appearance of evil?* Lena sighed and knelt beside her basket of peas, wishing desperately for wisdom greater than her experience.

Bram, riding along the puddled road, fought against anger and revenge, sorrow and despair. He now needed to talk to his brother, even though doing so allowed his sibling an unwarranted view into a most glorious and private sanctuary: his marriage. With each word of Brigetta's story of the closet, hatred had built upon increasing anger with such ominous power it frightened him. The recounting became a weapon of destruction, a weapon of hatred. Hatred for Cornelis, the brother he had known and loved since his birth.

Then, remembering *Tante* Lena had said *Brigetta wasn't raised to act in such deplorable ways,* he wondered if she doubted the story. The first niggling doubt about his wife's part in the sordid episode brushed across Bram's mind and insinuated itself into a tiny crack.

He found Cornelis behind the barn, leaning against the building watching the fire burn. Seeing Bram, Cornelis jumped to his feet, a look of surly fear clouding his usually jovial face. "Where did you go? I saw you take off in the buggy."

"To town. To see *Tante* Lena."

Cornelis' lip curled, but he said nothing.

Bram moved to within arm's length of Cornelis and took a fighter's stance though he struggled to keep his tone neutral. "Brigetta tells me you touched her in ways reserved by God for me, her husband. She also tells me your black eye is from when she hit you with a doorknob—in hopes of fending you off."

"And I suppose you believe her?" Cornelis shrugged insolently and scoffed, "Your little bride isn't the innocent lamb she would have you to believe. Sure, I touched her, but she liked it. We both know I'm more capable than you of making her truly happy."

Bram clenched and unclenched his fists, gritted his teeth, truly appalled by the crudeness of his brother's words. He rolled forward on the balls of his feet. "What do you mean by those crude remarks, Cornelis?"

"Oh, don't try that act with me—I overheard the conversation long ago between you and Mother and Father about how you're sterile. I can't believe Brigetta would marry you, if she knew—or does she know, huh? And tell me, how *do* you keep that pretty little thing happy in the bedroom?"

Fire burned in Bram's eyes, and his whole body stiffened. "This is not something I will discuss with you, or anyone else. What happens between me and Brigetta is sacred and private."

Cornelis laughed coarsely. "She sure responded to a *real* man, let me tell you. From my first touch, I could tell she was ready for loving! And wanting it, too, if she hadn't suddenly gotten all righteous and prissy on me."

With a roar like a caged animal let loose, Bram charged. The brothers grappled and fought like hellions, each knowing the other's weak spots and secret moves, and equally matched in strength and size. Every boyhood fight was replayed ten-fold. In their youth, there had been no predictable winner since each boy was brawny. But now, Bram had vengeance empowering him—his grip was firmer, his punch more terrifying, and his aim more sure. He was fighting for broken love, grieved hearts, wounded relationships, and shattered hopes. Bram fought a righteous fight.

Cornelis struck out in retaliation—never a winning move, even under better circumstances than this. The injury Brigetta inflicted had weakened him. Bram's attack caught him off-guard even though he had suspected it would come sometime. His conscience did battle against his spirit, sapping his strength, and the knowledge right will win—plus the realization he was fully in the wrong—did little to make him the victor. Cornelis fought a losing battle.

One last twist, one final punch, one more painful jab and Cornelis sank to his knees, bleeding, bruised, and holding a shoulder that was possibly dislocated. Blood spurted from his nose, his lower lip, and a gash on his chin. A section of his hair was considerably thinner than when he last combed it; strands of it were evident in one of Bram's wounds.

Panting, Bram leaned against the barn and gasped out the frightening words that capped his anger. "Get out of here. Don't go near my wife, or my house, until I get past my anger with you—and there's no telling how long that will take. You had better see Doc Draayer, because not one person on this farm will help you in any way today. You disgust me with your evil ways. I am ashamed to call you my brother."

Cornelis struggled to his feet and staggered toward a horse in the pasture next to the barn. Without saddling up, he limped beside the animal all the way to the big house, hanging on to the horse's mane for support. Bram watched the door until Cornelis stepped back outside, carrying a canvas bag. He mounted the horse—obviously a painful task—and urged it into a canter.

Bram watched until he could no longer see Cornelis and then hobbled to the pump to clean up. From the looks of things, Cornelis had packed up a few personal things—enough to be gone a few days. *Good. I don't know what I'll tell Mother and Father—even the briefest accounting of this day will break their hearts.*

His body ached from its unaccustomed battle and his heart was heavy with grief. *Is any of what Cornelis said true? Does Brigetta need more than I can give her?* He was just glad his parents weren't at home to see the brothers limping away from their private battleground. Rebecca did not believe in brother fighting against brother. *How can I ever tell Mother and Father about what led to the fight? And how will I explain Cornelis' absence?*

With water running in rivulets from his head, down his neck, stinging each open wound through the rips in his shirt, Bram stood on the back porch and listened to the drone of low voices. The cottage had been such a precious sanctuary for over a year; he wondered if that would ever be possible again. He heard his grandmother say, "They are both such good boys," and he closed his eyes and sagged against a pillar. He could hear the murmur of Brigetta's voice and visualized her ripe young body beneath his brother's hands. Bile rose in his throat and gagged him.

He clutched the pillar until his breathing stabilized, and forced himself to take several deep breaths. He rolled his shirt sleeves down to cover several deep scratches and one bite Cornelis had inflicted, and smoothed his wet hair with hands that throbbed from bruised knuckles and broken skin. One knee ached intensely, and his neck felt wrenched—but he had one consolation: he had given worse than he got. Once he had wondered why God hadn't let him go to war to fight the enemies of the United States; now he wondered why the enemy at hand had turned out to be his closest kin.

Bram let himself in the kitchen door and walked quietly down the hall toward the bedroom, hoping to change clothes before seeing anyone; a gasp behind him told him he failed. He spun on his heel and raised his finger to his lips, pointing at the parlor where his grandmother sat with quilt blocks all around. Pulling Brigetta into the bedroom behind him, he closed the door.

Instinctively, she reached to help him out of his shirt, crying out over his wounds, caressing his skin and hair. "Did Cornelis do this to you? What happened? Oh, Bram!" Her voice, though low, revealed her panic.

"I'll heal. Right now, I need to get cleaned up better than I could out by the pump."

"I'll bring in the wash tub and find the ointment. What a terrible day this has been."

"It's not totally lost—for the first time, I know what it's like to fight for the honor of someone I love. I have never loved you more than I do today."

Her lips trembled and her eyes misted. "So you believe me?"

He nodded, flinching with the motion. "I admit, I wondered at the whole story, but Cornelis' attitude said a lot. I know your love is strong enough that what he said could not possibly be true."

"I don't know what *he* said, but I want you to know when we were stuck in the closet," she pointed at the offending door with enough venom in her eye to paralyze a den of thieves, "I told him to never come near me again and if he ever did, I would tell everyone exactly what he did to me."

Bram's eyebrows shot up at the fervor of his wife's words. He still wasn't sure what had occurred in the closet, but he now knew Brigetta had not instigated it, nor had she enjoyed it. *Lust, ludeness, and lies—not a great day for Cornelis' reputation.*

Brigetta's ministrations to her husband soothed his wounds and calmed his spirit, even as he marveled at how she could do so with her own soul in such turmoil. With Grandmother settled in for a nap on the sofa, Brigetta followed Bram out to the back porch. All Bram's energy was sapped—there would be no more fieldwork today.

They passed the remainder of the afternoon sitting close together on the top step, hands clasped while they talked of sweet and private things—pulling a veil across all the hurt of the day for a brief respite— until it was time for evening chores.

After supper dishes were washed, Bram and Brigetta took Grandmother for a buggy ride before settling her in for the night. Cornelis had not reappeared on the farm but, as Bram listened to Hans' radio and Brigetta knitted, they heard his horse return about an hour after the evening train whistled. Grimly, Bram cared for the restless animal, wishing the beast could tell the tale of the ride that left Cornelis' dried blood on the mane.

The next morning, Hans knocked on their back door just as they were finishing breakfast. "Where's Cornelis?" he asked abruptly. "He wasn't around when we got home at midnight, and his bed wasn't slept in. Your mother's worried."

Brigetta spoke up quickly. "He's taken off for a few days—caught the train, didn't he, Bram?" Knowing these innocent-sounding words fell short of "...*the whole truth, and nothing but the truth...*" made her color rise. "Maybe he's off to find a job with automobiles."

Hans frowned. "If that isn't just like something he'd do—take off without a proper farewell to his mother, and waiting until we're gone to do so." He removed his cap and drove his fingers through his hair, a frown twisting his features grimly. "Wonder how long he's been planning this?" He shook his head, expecting no answer.

"I'll go see Mother this morning and try to ease her worries some," Brigetta offered.

Bram's eyebrows arched as he marveled at her resilience. "Thank you, Brigetta." He wasn't eager to see his mother until his bruises had healed a little more, and Brigetta had just helped him forestall the inevitable. *I can't believe Father hasn't noticed anything.*

"Let's go, Bram," Hans said. "If there's just the two of us, and the day's awasting. Now that I take a look at you, you're looking quite roughed up, there, son—what happened to you?"

"Oh, I just wasn't looking out for myself. I'll be fine, and so will we— Cornelis hasn't liked farming for a long time, Father. You'll notice we get as much done today as always. There have been three bodies working before, but only two of us had our hearts in it." Bram held open the screen door for his Father and they left the kitchen.

Brigetta spun a tale so convincing that Rebecca expressed only the expected regret at her son's disappearance without a proper goodbye, and so few clothes. "Did he take anything to eat, Brigetta?"

To get trapped in a lie by such a fine point seemed too awful to contemplate, so Brigetta hedged, "I'm sure he did. With his appetite, I imagine food was even more important than socks!"

Leaving Rebecca to resume her tasks after a day away, Brigetta returned to her own kitchen in search of a sense of equilibrium. She was determined to be the best wife possible to Bram—to banish every horrid thought and plaguing memory. They would never look back on this time and laugh but with God's help, at least they could move beyond it.

September 1919

◆

Three postcards throughout the summer—all from Chicago—assured the family Cornelis was safe. He made no mention of returning to the farm, and wrote of seeing a great variety of automobiles though being quite vague about the exact nature of his employment. Now with harvest upon them, and needing to hire an extra man to take Cornelis' place, his absence was heavy on everyone's minds.

Rebecca perched the cards along the windowsill. Her constant concern over her youngest son's well being intrigued Brigetta. *Does becoming a mother make one blind to a child's dark side?* Brigetta's relationship with her own mother gave her little to draw upon in understanding a mother's heart.

Were we wrong not to tell Hans and Rebecca the whole truth? Brigetta's sheltered life had not prepared her for a life of subterfuge any more than it had for Cornelis' attack in the closet. She kept her own counsel and worked beside Rebecca throughout harvest.

Bram rarely spoke his brother's name, something that somehow escaped Rebecca's notice but sounded a bugle's call in Brigetta's heart. Bram's outward wounds and bruises healed, but his heart remained damaged. His daytime thoughts returned often to the brother-against-brother confrontation behind the barn. Nighttimes, as he lay beside his sleeping wife, nagging thoughts of what had precipitated the fight chased sleep as effectively as any nightmare.

Their marriage took on a desperate struggle to regain and retain the wonder of its first year. Brigetta launched a full-scale effort to be all she had been, and more. She showered kisses on Bram's face and opened herself to his loving as if in welcoming the good, she could banish the bad.

The two of them savored each elusive, fragile moment of joy. At such times, Bram could almost believe none of it had ever happened. Almost. Sorrow clung to their joy like tar to a new pair of shoes, leaving reminders all around. It took all Bram's willpower to banish Cornelis' image from his mind each time he reached for Brigetta in the moonlit bed.

A random haunted look crossing Brigetta's face reminded Bram of the crushing memory she bore but could not speak of. At those times, he drew her near to him and loved her until her clouds dissipated. It was all he could do for her, and he, likewise, desperately needed those moments of closeness.

One dewy morning as Brigetta stood in Rebecca's back yard tossing scraps from the harvesters' breakfast to the chickens, she gulped back a wave of nausea erupting within her. She bent over just in time to prevent the torrent of her own breakfast from hitting her skirt. The chickens clucked wildly, delighted at this unexpected feast. Brigetta turned away, light-headed and nauseous.

She pumped a handful of water to rinse out her mouth, another to slosh on her face, and a third to cleanse her hands. Straightening up, she leaned against the pump and looked quickly at the kitchen window. *Good. No one saw anything. There really isn't a lady-like way to lose one's breakfast!*

Still feeling queasy, she returned to the kitchen and helped Rebecca begin preparations for the next meal. But several days later, the same thing happened. Only this time, the two women were crossing the field to take mid-morning drinks and sweets out to the crew. Brigetta threw up on a cornstalk and nearly bent it to the ground when she groped for balance. Rebecca exclaimed, "Brigetta! You're ill!"

Brigetta waved her back as another round spewed forth. "I don't know what's wrong, but I'm sure I'll be fine. Let's get the food out to the men, and then maybe I'll go home and lie down for a while."

Rebecca eyed her with concern and then shifted her own load to take some of what Brigetta carried and they continued on their way. "Please don't mention this to Bram," Brigetta pleaded. "He treats me like a child if he thinks I've even got a sniffle! I must have eaten something that didn't agree with me."

By the end of harvest, Brigetta knew something was seriously wrong. She was losing weight, unable to handle certain smells—all too aware of just how many smells were in abundance on a farm and in the kitchen. The timing of her symptoms could not have been worse: with the field harvest nearly complete, the garden was now in full production with fruits and vegetables ripening at a record speed. It was all she and Rebecca could do to keep up in the kitchen. Everyone fell into bed at night almost too weary to sleep.

One afternoon, Brigetta took the buggy to replenish their canning supplies at Vander Molen's store. On impulse, she turned a corner and parked the buggy under a tree in back of Doc Draayer's office. Soon, she was in his office explaining her strange and now frequent symptoms. "If you could prescribe a tonic, I would appreciate it."

"And you say this has been going on for how long?" Doc Draayer asked, conducting as discreet a physical examination as possible, given the acute discomfiture of his patient.

"Fully two weeks, but even before then somewhat; I've been feeling odd for over a month. Bloated, and what-not."

"When was your last monthly?"

Brigetta blushed furiously. "I don't know."

"Try to think back. What was growing in the garden then?" Doc asked patiently, rephrasing his question to help Brigetta corral her embarrassment.

"It was when tulips were in bloom. Oh, my, that would have been in May!"

Doc tugged on his moustache. When he met her eyes, his gaze was kind, but questioning. "Brigetta, you do know about Bram's possible condition, don't you?"

"Yes," she whispered. "He is most likely unable to father children. But we are happy together, nonetheless." Her cheeks reddened, but she met Gerrit Draayer's eyes directly.

The doctor nodded slowly. "I'm glad to hear that—though not surprised. Most likely Bram is sterile, which is why I am puzzled by what you are describing. If any other young bride were sitting in my office telling me symptoms such as you have described, I would say she is expecting a child."

Brigetta's hands flew to her lips and fear shaded her eyes. *The closet! Oh dear God in* hemel.

"Brigetta, let's wait a few more weeks. Then, if you still haven't had your monthly, come see me again. Meanwhile, take it easy—get as much rest as a busy farmer's wife can get this time of year, eat whatever tastes good to you to keep your strength up, and keep your husband as happy as he is each time I see him."

Brigetta smiled weakly. Blindly, she scrambled to tuck her clothing back in place and left the doctor's office in a rush.

Doc Draayer sat for several minutes, lost in troubled thoughts. If ever a situation deserved the tag "opening a can of worms," it was this one. *Happy young couple...the Dominie's daughter—the daughter of long-time friends, mind you. Could Brigetta be guilty of an adulterous relationship? Oh, it's a can of worms, all right.* He sighed and pulled out his pocket watch. The day was too short, the line of patients too long for him to just sit in his office in the dismal company of such pejorative thoughts.

That night when Bram reached for Brigetta in the darkness, she burst into tears and buried her head in her pillow. The act of comforting his wife replaced their acts of loving that night. Bram fell asleep none the wiser as to the cause of his wife's tears.

Over the next days that stretched into a week and beyond, Bram watched Brigetta unobtrusively. He had little experience with her silence and it made for long evenings, shortened meals around the table, and very little stimulating conversation. His soul felt as parched as a field in a drought.

Then, one morning he found her kneeling beside the slop bucket, one hand braced against the wall. "Brigetta! What's wrong?"

She looked up guiltily and wiped her mouth on the dishtowel she held. Pale, she staggered to her feet and brushed past him to the kitchen. Pulling a clean towel from the drawer beside the sink, she bent over the sink and splashed water from the basin on her face, dried herself and tucked the towel into her waistband. She then hurried to the stove as if alone in the room.

Bewildered, Bram watched her turn sausages and stir eggs and give her attention to bread toasting in the oven. Finally, he realized she had no intention of discussing what had just occurred. "Brigetta! You are ill—you should be in bed, not in the kitchen! Go lie down, and stay in bed until this passes."

Brigetta spun on her heel and grasped the back of a chair as she blurted out, "If I'm to stay in bed until this passes, I'll be there for several months because I'm pregnant."

Pregnant! The word whipped around the room, ricocheting off sideboard, icebox, stovepipe, windowpane, and hitting Bram in the chest with each pass. One simple word accomplished what even Cornelis' angry punches had not done: it knocked the wind out of him and rendered him useless. He pulled out a kitchen chair and stumbled, clutching the edge of the table, and he sank down.

"Brigetta, how can this be?" He dropped his head into his hands, elbows propped on the table. Seconds ticked away into minutes. "Oh, Brigetta. In the closet with Cornelis…"

"Bram, I..." She could not finish. There were neither Dutch nor English words to adequately express her pain.

"It's a good thing he stayed away, because I would surely...oh, God, help me." Bram raised tormented eyes to his wife—the woman defiled by his own brother. Hatred that had finally settled below the surface now festered again in his heart and spilled into his words. "Now what do we do, Brigetta?"

Slowly, Brigetta pulled a chair out from the opposite end of the table and fell onto it. "What do you mean, 'what do we do?' We're having a baby—we'll raise it."

A bee buzzed against the window screen. A bird swooped from branch to branch in a dogwood bush. All God's creatures in the vast world outside celebrated the life the Creator gave them with unabashed joy. But in this Iowa farm kitchen, Bram and Brigetta de Boer contemplated God's creation with sinking hearts; the two who should be the happiest felt nothing but shame and horror.

Bram inhaled and released the air cautiously as if he feared uncontrolled words would rush out. "We have a problem, Brigetta, don't you see?" He looked down the length of the table at his beloved wife and felt her anguished look pierce his soul.

"Yes," she whispered. "Your condition...this child..." Again, she could not finish. Never in her young life had words failed her as often as they had since the realization that her life was ruined. She could not even marshal coherent thoughts.

"Brigetta, I have never asked you to elaborate on what happened in the closet because I knew the pain recounting it caused you. It seemed cruel to keep that memory alive, but now I must know. Tell me exactly what happened."

She looked at Bram with potent pain, "He kissed me and rubbed my bosom," red streaks ripened her cheeks as she recalled her body's responsive tightening even to Cornelis' rough touch, "and then he pulled me so close I felt his manhood rising and he rubbed my private place with...himself."

Her words, suddenly no longer halting, tumbled out and filled Bram's ears like the roar of a storm. "I was so ashamed and afraid. When I changed clothes afterwards and I found stains that only have come when you and I have...Oh, Bram! I have prayed over and over, but apparently this child is God's punishment for such dreadfulness."

Tears suddenly streamed down her face. Bram was too lost in his own misery to reach out in comfort. Her face buried in her hands, she cried so violently that tears pushed out between her fingers and ran like a river down her wrists, dampening her sleeves.

"I have tried to be a good wife to you—even more so since this tragedy, but I will never understand why my body betrayed me when Cornelis touched me. I had thought such responses were sacred to marriage, but I must be a harlot!" She blew her nose noisily, but the words that followed were as soft as spring's rains. "I am so sorry, Bram."

Numbed by the tumult of revelations hitting him like a cross-line windstorm, Bram stared at the lingering scars on his hands. Had he known all these details the day he fought Cornelis behind the barn, there would have been a funeral following his parents' return—not just scars on an elder brother's body. There was a terrible question requiring an answer, one a husband hopes he never needs to ask his wife: "Did Cornelis put his manhood inside you, Brigetta?"

She locked eyes with him. "I don't know, Bram. At first I was certain he had, but we were both standing. You and I are always in bed, so I can't imagine how...but the stains on my clothing..." Her naiveté even after months of marriage clouded her knowledge of unseemly things. "It was hard to tell what was his hand and what was...not," she finished in a whisper.

"So it is possible Cornelis..."

"Please do not say those words again, Bram. The answer is yes, I believe so. But I do not know for certain. I know only what I felt like in my private place, and what I found on my clothes later."

"How do you know you're pregnant, Brigetta?"

"I have not had my monthly since May, and for the past six weeks, hardly a day has gone by I have not vomited. I must be several months along."

Bram moaned with utter anguish. Nothing could change the fact of his sterility. The honor of the role of father of this unborn child fell to his now-absent brother. Mumps had not affected Cornelis—a fact now evident in his ability to impregnate a frightened young wife in just a few stolen moments in a closet: something her loving husband had been unable to do in all the unions of their marriage. Nights of unimaginable ecstasy in each other's arms, nights of passion and exhilarating seduction without a resulting pregnancy.

As many times as we have joined together, Brigetta would have been pregnant long ago if I were whole. As if he required additional proof of his inadequacy, Brigetta's daily sickness hadn't begun until after the calamity in the closet. And now Brigetta would bear Cornelis' child.

Bram would be expected to feed and clothe, love and admire, play with and provide for his brother's offspring. He would be forced to see daily evidence of his brother's brazen virility. His own loving acts could never plant a seed within his own wife to provide a sibling for this child. A haunting cry burst from Bram's mouth as he pushed away from the table. His chair toppled and clattered against the floor, coming to rest on its side. He escaped to his life-long haven: the soil he loved and understood, the soil that never betrayed him.

Brigetta slumped in her chair. Bram had issued no pleading invitation for her to join him. No twinkling eyes today suggested frolics midst the rows of leafy vegetables. No tantalizing whiffs of intimate conversation as they weeded and hoed. Just the slamming door separating man and wife.

Brigetta looked up when she heard spatters on the stove. In a gesture that summed up her feelings, she dumped the kettles' contents into the slop pail along with the remnants of what had spewed forth from her stomach to change this day into a glimpse of hell.

The hours dragged by on leaden feet. Brigetta waved across the lawn at Rebecca, but did not go over to the big house. Bram worked in the garden alone, accomplishing much, but enjoying the work less than ever before in his experience.

With Bram obviously wanting to be alone, Brigetta sought for an occupation that offered her the same. She carefully pinned pattern pieces to a length of dotted Swiss. Just as she held her scissors in position for the first cut, she stood upright with a start, nearly swallowing a straight pin. *I'm making this dress, thinking I will wear it for the church supper. But by next month, I could need maternity clothes, not a frivolous cinched-waist frock.* Pretty things lost their appeal when viewed from that sobering perspective. She removed the pins and buried the material in the cedar chest.

Instead, she stitched a hem on a bed sheet. *Soon we will need to find room for a cradle or crib in the house. But where?* Hans had slept in the living room of this house years ago when he was a child. *That's why the big house was built: there is no room here once a baby begins to grow.* And there was little room in her heart for a baby, either. Fear, loathing, and anger—all these crowded the spots a mother's love should fill.

Half-heartedly, she made up a lunch plate and took it to Bram. He stopped working long enough to eat, but little conversation passed between them. Each stretched out, close but without touching, on a patch of grass beside the garden plot; their lunch was a quiet affair. *Food prepared, food eaten; sustenance without camaraderie. However will we survive the months ahead?*

At supper, Bram ate steadily, but without comment. Brigetta attempted several venues of conversation: "I thought the cabbages looked extra large. Surely some will be ready to sell this week. Are the potatoes doing well?" but she gave up hoping for more than scant replies from her taciturn husband. Though physically only three feet away, Bram was miles away in thought.

Bram's forehead creased as he blurted out. "Brigetta, I have done much thinking in the garden today."

She sighed with relief. "I, too, have been thinking all afternoon. I have felt so distant from you—if we are to survive the next months, we must not keep our thoughts from each other. It is important we talk, even though it is hard."

Bram's response attacked the weakened girders of their relationship as surely as any marauding army. "We cannot keep this child, Brigetta. To do so will destroy our marriage. I love you too much to allow that to happen."

A gasp burbled from Brigetta. "We cannot *keep* the child? Whatever will we do with it? A child is not like a stray kitten that can wander in the fields until someone takes it in."

"No, no, I didn't mean we would destroy the child. But we could put the child up for adoption. At first, I had thought we could secretly have the baby, and then leave it at an orphanage. But then I realized your pregnancy will soon become quite obvious, so that isn't the answer."

Brigetta retorted. "Of course it isn't—the child is not an orphan. You are talking nonsense, Bram."

"I cannot pretend to be its father. If we try to raise it, each time we look at it would bring back the horrible circumstances of how it was conceived. What if it looks like Cornelis?"

She felt numb. *While I have been worrying about my expanding waist-line and finding room for a crib, Bram has been trying to erase every-thing—out of sight, out of mind.*

He continued, "Each time I would see it running across the yard or sleeping in its bed, I would always be reminded of who its father is."

Brigetta closed her eyes and saw a boy with curly red hair tossing a ball in the air—and that same lad grown big enough to help his father in the fields, a father whose every glance told of his stony disinterest. She saw a little girl with soft russet eyelashes resting on chubby cheeks while she slept—and a grim-faced Bram turning away from that sight and ignoring her tiny proffered hand as they walked along together. She could not imagine growing up with a father so distant.

Bram's words penetrated her fog. "Your reputation will be tarnished with those who know of my condition. I surely do not want that, nor do you."

Brigetta gulped great chunks of air. *This must be what it is like to go under a giant ocean wave.* "Oh, Bram! I cannot believe what I'm hearing. Yes, we have a problem, but to give away a child? What will that solve? It will just be something else to shame us."

"If you are unwilling to give up this child, I do not see how we can be together."

A strangled cry ripped open Brigetta's soul. "You would make me choose between you and the baby? Where are these thoughts coming from? It as if suddenly I don't even know you!"

"I am asking you to choose *me*—the one you can see and hold and touch, the one you promised before God to love until death do us part—choose me rather than an unseen, unknown child who will sever our relationship as surely as the butcher's knife cuts marrow from the bone."

Brigetta's voice was but a whisper; "We made promises to God and each other, Bram."

Seeing her chalk-white face, he softened his tone. "I desperately want to preserve our marriage. I love you, Brigetta. No one in Dutchville would know if we were to put the baby up for adoption, as long as you are gone while you are…pregnant." The word stuck in his throat like a chunk of dry bread.

"Where would I go?" A cold hand closed around Brigetta's heart.

"If we move away from Dutchville for the rest of your pregnancy and gave up the child in another place, we could put this all behind us and rebuild our lives."

"Move?" Brigetta echoed the word that seared her heart. "How can this be a solution, Bram?" Her voice reached a fevered pitch.

"It's the only way to preserve *us*." He reached across the table and grasped her hand firmly. "I have known since I was young that I am a good farmer—I could get a job elsewhere quite easily."

"You would leave your farm?" Brigetta whispered in disbelief.

"Just for a year or two. There are institutions where women go to have babies they cannot keep. Couples who desperately want children come there to adopt a child."

"How do you even know of such things?" Brigetta's mind could barely function.

"The Jaans' oldest daughter was adopted from such a home in Des Moines because they could not bear children. She is a happy child, you must admit."

Brigetta admitted nothing; her world was whirling at a mad tilt, making her ill.

"If I stay in Dutchville, how would you explain being gone from home for an extended period of time? It would then look as if we had divorced. No, our home must be elsewhere for a while."

A wordless keening burst from a cavern within Brigetta. She pulled her hands out of Bram's grasp and pressed them against her chest. "But we have just begun our lives together! I cannot imagine being apart from you."

"Do you love me, Brigetta?"

The question reached Brigetta in her desolation. "You know I do! That's why hearing you say these horrible things is so hard! We would first be separated from each other for months—and then the baby forever." Her sobs and anguished cries punctuated each word.

"Do you realize how knowing the woman I love is pregnant by my brother is destroying me? I can hardly imagine what it is doing to you. We are struggling with something that is far beyond what we are able to deal with."

"We have been so happy and this awfulness is consuming all that pleasure; I can scarcely remember how good it was." She bit her lip until she tasted blood.

"Our being separated is really no different than if I had gone to war."

She shook her head firmly. "That would have been an honorable separation. The other wives would have been companions, friends with like problems to commiserate with me. No, this is a shameful separation."

"Think of how the rest of our lives will be if we don't do something like I have suggested. If you can think of another way to preserve our future, please tell me. I am not happy about my idea, either, but I can see no other way."

She sagged visibly. "So many tragedies, so many lies, all from the encounter with Cornelis in the closet."

"It will give great joy to another family, and it will be able to have a happy life. That would hardly be possible if it stayed with us."

"He, or she, Bram, not *it*."

Bram pulled back as if struck. *He or she—a human being.* He felt the blood drain out of his face.

Brigetta pushed back from the table and left the kitchen. Out on the porch, she stared unseeing at the backyard until her eyes lit upon her bicycle. Without a word to Bram, she hitched up her skirts and mounted the bicycle and turned it toward town.

After riding aimlessly for some time, she found herself on a familiar corner. A light in the buggy barn indicated Gustave was caring for the horse. Brigetta bypassed the parsonage and rode across the lawn. Tears brimmed at the sound of Gustave's whistle and she steeled herself as she leaned the bicycle against the building.

"Papa?"

Gustave started. "Brigetta! I didn't expect to see you tonight! Where's Bram?"

"He's at home. Can I talk to you?"

"Shall we go inside? Your Mama and *Tante* Lena are washing supper dishes."

"Let's talk out here."

Gustave wisely assessed his daughter's anxiety and continued to curry the horse, knowing that deepest thoughts find their best expression during normal activities.

Brigetta watched him work for several minutes, the silence broken only by Gustave's intermittent whistling and the horse's shuffling. "Papa, how do you know you love Mama?"

Gustave's hand stilled against the horse's broad back—the only sign her question caught him off-guard. "I've often wondered if anyone really knows *why* they love another person."

"Could you make a list, if you had to? A list of all the things you love about Mama?"

He tilted his head thoughtfully. "I imagine such a list would be unsatisfactory on two levels. First, it would tend to include visible things. I could say I love your Mama because she is beautiful, because of her angelic singing voice, because she grows stunning flowers. But would I stop loving her if her looks changed, or she lost her voice, or was unable to garden any longer? No, of course not."

"Why, Papa? Why would you?"

Gustave ached to pull up a bale of hay and say *Tell me what is wrong, Sweet Pea. Let me help* but knew the conversation would end abruptly, so he continued to brush. "That's where such a list fails on a second level. I would tend to include invisible things—things impossible to understand or explain."

Brigetta's forehead furrowed. "*I* don't understand."

Gustave smiled. "I could say, I love Hanna because of how I feel when I'm around her, or because she is good, or because she loves me."

"Those sound like good reasons to love someone."

"They are excellent reasons—in fact, without such invisible things, I doubt love can last. It's things I can't explain and can't deny that won't change or disappear. Sometimes the invisible brings great joy, but it can also bring the greatest pain. It's easy to *feel* like I love Hanna when I'm experiencing great joy, but the times I *know* I love Hanna are when I am experiencing the greatest pain and yet, in the depths of my heart, I cannot deny my love for her is still alive."

"If I tell you I don't think I could explain what you just said, but I understand in my heart, would that make sense?" Brigetta asked with a flash of the impish grin Gustave cherished.

"Absolutely. And if I told you I'm not sure I could repeat it, would that make you wonder if it's any less true?"

"Absolutely not! Oh, Papa—thank you from the bottom of my heart. I had better get home before dark." She stood and brushed hay off her skirt. Before she disappeared into the dusk, she leaned toward Gustave and dropped a kiss on the top of his head.

Gustave watched his daughter wend her way back down the road. Then, he put his tools away, spread hay for the horse, and blew his nose briskly. "I wish I knew what that was about," he told his well-curried horse.

Brigetta let herself back into her house and stopped short upon seeing Bram still at the table. "I needed to clear my head—I don't like the lies. I can't imagine telling our families about the incident with Cornelis in the closet, but…"

Bram's words came out in a rush. "I don't like the lies any more than you do, but keeping the child and passing him or her off as our own— *that* would be living a lie, Brigetta."

Brigetta nodded dismally. She twisted the ring signifying her vow to love, honor, and obey Bram. Vows that gave credence to the invisible reasons they loved each other. *Greatest joy, greatest pain.*

Her hands shifted to her locket, the words engraved upon her heart as surely as on its gold: *Yours for all time.* Bram wasn't leaving her, though he certainly could have. He was asking her to help preserve their marriage vows. But if she refused to give up the child, she could lose Bram—if not physically, then surely emotionally.

Her mind leaped to the past, remembering Hanna's years of depression. *Through it all—in spite of it all—Papa loves Mama.* There were few recollections of a happy Hanna within Brigetta's storehouse of childhood memories; could she ever wish such a life on a child of her own? There would be no *Tante* Lena to bridge the gaps for this child.

With the impending birth, Brigetta faced a tough decision: life as a mother without a husband—or life as a wife without a child. Each option carried a terrible secret. She knew her father had been thrust into a world incomprehensible to most husbands, of being both father and mother to a child bereft of a mother's devotion. Brigetta did not want to do that to Bram, if such a choice were hers to make. And it was.

Despite reliving it repeatedly, she wasn't certain about what had happened in the closet. The sheer revulsion of reality was devastating. *What if I, like Bram, find I am unable to love a child who reminds me of such a horrific event? The child would then have two parents unable to provide genuine love.*

She remembered her impassioned parlor speech to their parents about how a family of two was still a family. To stubbornly insist on keeping the baby would resound like empty words.

But the deciding factor was plain: She had made vows that mattered. She had made a promise to God—and Bram. *If I break those vows...*"Tell me exactly what you think we should do, Bram." Her voice trembled.

To his credit, Bram did not take his wife's capitulation lightly. He looked into Brigetta's red-rimmed eyes and swallowed hard, remembering the trust that used to shine out at him from their depths. The spark that was the essence of Brigetta was clouded by sorrow, and he was as much to blame as Cornelis for extinguishing it.

"I am a hard worker, a good farmer—my skills and natural abilities make me a desirable employee. If I am able to find work at the right place, I will learn much to help me be an even better farmer once we return home."

Brigetta sagged with shallow relief at hearing those final words. *Someday, we will be back to our home. Without a child, but still together.*

"It will not be easy for a long time—perhaps, never—but we must do the best for all concerned, Brigetta. We can build a life together that will be good again. And this is best for the child."

She nodded, and steeled herself against the threatening tears.

"I have thought about where we might go. The area surrounding Minneapolis, Minnesota, could offer many opportunities and would not be so far away we cannot easily return. I will go seek work for myself and learn about institutions for you."

Brigetta tried to blot out the mental image of a small baby being left behind as she walked away. "No. If you are going to Minneapolis, I must go with you. I meant it when I said we must go through this together. I cannot stay at home while you are out making decisions alone that affect both of us."

But good intentions aside, that night as they lay side-by-side, Bram and Brigetta fell asleep without holding each other close. The house creaked around them, sounds outside their bedroom window eerily filled the night, and not one word, not one touch passed between them in the darkness.

The next morning, Rebecca knocked on the screen door. Seeing Brigetta in the kitchen, she let herself in. "You certainly are lost in thought! You didn't even hear me knock! Bram says he has something to tell us, and he hinted broadly you both want to drop by tonight."

"Did he say what it was?"

188   R o u g h   T e r r a i n

"I think it was prompted by seeing sorghum cake cooling on the table! So, I have come by to personally invite you for supper tonight. We will have *wortel stamppot* with lots of *rookworst* along with the cake. Tell Bram I'll grate the carrots extra fine and mash the potatoes the way he likes them so my *stamppot* meets his high standards!"

Around his parents' supper table, Bram revealed their fledgling plans. "Father and Mother, lately I have realized there is much I do not know about farming. I want to learn more than I can just by trying new things on my own. Brigetta and I have been talking over an idea."

He reached for Brigetta's hand and smiled at her, squeezing her fingers in a hidden signal. Just a heartbeat too late, she smiled crookedly. "It's still sketchy."

"Since you are still young, Father," Bram continued, aware of the bewildered silence, "and there are plenty of families nearby with strong young sons in abundance who could take my place here, it is a perfect time for me to hire out to some place where I can learn a great deal and then return to our farm and do an even better job."

"Go someplace? Leave here? I had no idea, Bram, you had such plans in your head."

"I guess marrying Brigetta has expanded my view of life!"

Hans' brow furrowed. "No one from these parts has ever left home to learn more about farming. In fact, where would you go? I can't imagine another farmer around here who could teach you much. The earth itself is a mighty good teacher, Bram, and we've got one of the best farm sites around, thanks to your grandfather's foresight and good investment."

"I may have to go farther away than what you're thinking, Father. Perhaps north to the area around Minneapolis or..."

"Minneapolis!" Rebecca's lips formed a silent *O*.

A note of pride coated Hans' words. "I shouldn't be surprised— you've always had loftier ideas than anyone else. What do you think, 'Becca?"

Rebecca stirred cream into her coffee, weighing her answer carefully. "I always knew Cornelis would someday leave the farm in search of something better. But I never imagined Bram leaving." She looked at her eldest son with eyes spiked with pain. "Never."

Bram hastened to reassure her. "I would leave so I *can* return a better farmer. I would be like those who go off for further schooling and then come back home to use their learning." No one around the table could think of a single person who had done such a thing, but the example presented a new perspective.

"I suppose I could hire a few young fellows from larger farm families or even someone from town who helped us with harvest."

"I know the farm will someday be mine; that's why I want to do the best I can with it." Bram leaned back in his chair with an air of one who has the world by the tail. "I'm thinking I'll take most of my tulip bulbs with me to test them in other soils and keep on working with them. But, other than the tulips, the rest of what we do can go on without me for a while."

"You would dig up your tulips?" Rebecca asked, stunned. "How long will you be gone?"

"Not all of them, Mother, I know you and tulips! But since we could be gone for a few years, I don't want to lose all the work I've put into the bulbs so far." Bram helped himself to more *stamppot* to let all he had said settle.

Walking home soon after dinner, Brigetta asked, "When will we go to Minneapolis?"

"As soon as possible, given your condition." Bram replied. "Don't worry, Brigetta. It will all work out. We'll just take one step at a time."

"We're on the brink of telling many lies to many people."

Bram's own conscience reared up. "God knows our hearts, Brigetta. We did not bring this trouble on ourselves." They walked on in silence.

Brigetta had made only one fifty-mile trip in her life, from Dutchville to Sioux City. She could not imagine how far away Minneapolis must be. *How do we pack for a trip of that magnitude? What about food? Where will we sleep?* She felt bewildered by the rapid changes already upon her—and the thought of all yet to come made her dizzy.

The next evening found the young couple with their heavy hearts and deep secrets sitting on the porch with Gustave, Hanna, and *Tante* Lena—all five seeking a cool place in the shade after a hot, sticky day. The pitcher of buttermilk sweated along with them. "Your garden is doing well," Bram said, nodding out across the lawn.

Lena beamed. "I've got a lot of competition in the family now! I added an extra foot to the pole for the beans to climb to encourage them to grow taller than yours."

Brigetta took a deep breath, feeling like a swimmer with nose pinched shut, preparing to jump into the deepest part of the swimming hole. When she spoke, her words had a forced brightness. "Bram, you had better give *Tante* Lena fair warning that the gardening competition will soon be tougher!"

All eyes moved quickly to Bram who nodded and leaned back, setting the porch swing in gentle motion with his feet. "I need to learn more about farming than I can at home. I'm going to seek work elsewhere for a while and learn all I can, and then come back home and put it all to good use."

Three foreheads furrowed. The swing's chains grated against wood as Bram and Brigetta nervously waited.

Examining first Bram's face, then Brigetta's flushed cheeks, Gustave mentally replayed his buggy-barn conversation with his daughter, but limited his words to the facts at hand. "That's a startling announcement, but I'm sure you've given it a great deal of thought. What do your parents think, Bram?"

"They see it has good potential. A lot rides on me—what I am able to learn from a master farmer. I'd like to think of myself as an able learner."

Hanna said, "No one denies that, but this has come up quite fast, hasn't it? Will you wait until spring to go?"

"No, I'm going to start looking soon—within the next week, in fact. I don't want to lose any opportunities someone else could snatch up before next spring."

"So soon?" *Tante* Lena asked with a frown. "That's hardly time to plan."

"We won't be *moving* anywhere next week—just beginning to look," Bram hastened to assure her. But the word *moving* caught everyone by surprise, like a wrinkled rag rug one trips over in the dark. They sat quietly, recovering from the jolt six little letters can produce.

"Wouldn't it be good to get more settled in as a married couple and postpone—not give up, just put off—this idea for a year or so?" Gustave suggested sensibly.

Tante Lena added darkly, "I came to Dutchville many years ago and, despite my promises, I have never gone back home. Of course, Hanna is here, but still…" Her words trailed off. When she resumed, her gaze was penetrating. "Once you go far from home, it's hard to return. It makes me sad to think of you doing that, Brigetta—you are your parents' only child. Hanna and I at least left two brothers and another sister to care for our parents." She tipped her head in Bram's direction. "And Cornelis has taken off to *Chicago*," her tone said *North Pole*, "so Hans and Rebecca are to be left alone also?"

"Cornelis had wanted to leave the farm for some time. We're not really leaving like he did—we're going away with the intent of coming back with new skills and ideas."

Hanna brought the voice of reason to the discussion. "Gustave, you now sense what my parents felt when I came across the country to marry you. Dutchville is home for both Bram and Brigetta. They will be back. My parents didn't have that guarantee."

Gustave held his wife's forthright gaze. "You're right." He stared out across the back yard for a full minute before turning to Bram. "Son, you are to be commended for wanting to improve yourself. I wish you all the best in your search for a good place to work and learn. Just one thing: don't keep Brigetta away from us too long."

192   R o u g h   T e r r a i n

Lena frowned and rubbed her hands together absentmindedly. "You don't even have a satchel, Brigetta. The one I used when I came out to Iowa certainly isn't getting much use under my bed." She disappeared into the house, hoping no one noticed her blinking back tears.

"She's right—we can use a satchel," Bram agreed. "And we'll have to build some boxes to pack up our belongings once we know where we're going."

Brigetta's head jerked up. *Boxes? Packing? This begins as a short trip— but the end result is a move.* She spoke quickly to divert the threatening tears. "Papa, could we borrow the big boxes in the buggy barn—the ones from when you and Mama moved here?"

Gustave nodded. "I don't see why not. We'll have to drag them out in the sun and wash them well since they've been gathering dust in the barn for many years."

"I'll be happy to come over tomorrow," Bram said. "Thank you— there is much to do now with our plans rolling along."

The next morning, Bram and Brigetta returned to the parsonage and worked diligently with sturdy brushes and buckets of soapy water to clean the accumulated grime from the heavy wooden crates. After they positioned the boxes in the sun to dry, they headed to the railway depot.

The solemn stationmaster sold them two round-trip tickets to Minneapolis. "The train pulls in, loads up, and leaves quickly, so don't be late," he cautioned. "These tickets are good for one week. When are you planning to leave?"

Bram looked quickly at Brigetta. "In two days. We'd like the morning train." Brigetta swayed as a wordless sound escaped her lips. He pulled her close.

Back home, Bram headed for the field and Brigetta dragged the laundry tubs, washboards and wringer outside next to the pump. It wasn't the usual day for that task, but she wanted all their clothes clean.

By suppertime, much had been accomplished: the laundry was dry, several loaves of bread and a batch of cookies cooled on the table, and

Brigetta had cooked most of the day's garden pickings, saving some for their trip. She hard-boiled a dozen eggs in the same water with the supper potatoes, adding them to her growing list of foods for the trip. She wasn't taking chances on finding edible food in a strange city.

Bram talked with his parents about handling chores in his absence, and then cleaned out the horse stalls in the barn, replaced a few shingles on the roof of the chicken coop, and chopped up a dead tree for winter firewood. It was as if in keeping busy, they didn't need to think. Well past their normal bedtime, they fell into bed too exhausted for more than a kiss that was really merely a peck.

The next day began early and ended late as they accomplished an amazing amount of work. Brigetta cleaned with a vengeance. Even the front stoop didn't escape her water and brush. Ironing, handling more garden produce, and finishing the mending filled in the minutes not used to pack the satchel.

Bram and Hans worked together in the field all morning. Midafternoon, Bram saddled his horse and rode in to withdraw sufficient money from the Dutchville Bank for the trip, and then he and Brigetta cleaned the chicken coop.

As if she needed a poignant reminder for the reason behind the bustle and activity, Brigetta kept little food down all day. Dusk found her in the garden with Bram, picking vegetables and swatting mosquitoes. "So many tomatoes are ripe now. I know Mother will can them, but I'm going to take some with us."

"I'm sure they grow tomatoes in Minnesota, too. We will not starve!"

She sniffed disparagingly and kept on picking. Soon her basket was filled with tomatoes, cucumbers, peppers, carrots, radishes, and celery—a veritable rainbow of vegetables she carried into her kitchen.

Bram teased her throughout their late supper about trying to empty the icebox into his stomach as she piled his plate high with beets, sliced tomatoes, potatoes, squash, roast chicken, and rhubarb sauce for dessert.

"You grow such good vegetables, Bram. Our pantry will never be empty as long as you're in charge of our garden." The words hung between them as reality hit: their garden would soon be left behind.

They filled the brass tub with teakettles of hot water and buckets from the pump and bathed before climbing between sheets warmed by the sun. Brigetta's hair was still damp and smelled of lavender as it spread across her pillow beneath Bram's nose.

Exhausted, but unable to sleep, Brigetta mentally reviewed the clothes laid out atop the cedar chest: the dress she would wear was beginning to feel tight around the middle, but it was the roomiest one she owned; she reminded herself to pack a needle and thread in case a seam popped open on the trip.

When I return home, I must let out seams in other dresses. How odd to think of a child growing so large within me that soon my clothes will not fit. It was possible to cover a growing stomach under an apron for a while, but one could not wear an apron indefinitely—and certainly not to church. *Eventually, secrets show. Whatever will I do for clothes?* She rolled over, away from Bram who shifted slightly in his sleep and flung his arm across her body.

Both de Boers tossed restlessly through the night and woke early, glad to be beyond the reach of their troubling dreams. Hans took them to the train station, and waited until the train pulled out of the station.

Looking back from the top step to their car, Brigetta caught the look of great sadness lodged on Han's countenance; an echoing response reverberated within her. A trip of this magnitude usually held much excitement—planning, recounting of all events. This journey, however, was too weighted with secretive deceptions to host much gladness or spawn many tales for future retellings.

Once on board, Bram and Brigetta sat together on a rear-facing seat, with *Tante* Lena's satchel, containing their clothing, and a canvas bag stuffed with food positioned between them on the floor. Brigetta looked around the car with interest.

The train conductor walked the aisle, punching tickets that he wedged in the clip over each seat, answering passengers' questions, all the while holding on to the straps overhead when the train swayed around curves. When he reached Bram and Brigetta, he examined their tickets and said conversationally, "Final destination: Minneapolis. Off on an adventure, eh?"

Bram nodded and offered a weak smile. The conductor moved along and Brigetta settled in to examine the people around them. Surely, no one else was making a trip for such heart-wrenching purposes. The general levity of their fellow passengers depressed her even more.

The countryside unfolded outside the train, great puffs of smoke at times obliterating large chunks of scenery momentarily. Beyond the cars clattering along the rails, the world was just awakening; behind the soot-smudged window, Brigetta's world was expanding.

Across the aisle, a young boy woke and stirred. Scanning his surroundings quickly, his eyes rested briefly on Bram and Brigetta, then closed, and reopened to stare at them intently. Long, dusky lashes framed his dark curious eyes. Bram winked at him and he quickly shut his eyes again. Moments later, he peeked beneath fluttering eyelids and found Bram still watching him. This time, he stared back.

Bram pulled a coin from his pocket and examined it. The boy's eyes followed it as it rolled along Bram's palm, wove in and out between his thumb and fingers, and suddenly was lost. *Lost!* A gasp escaped the small red lips—echoed by Brigetta. Mesmerized, the audience of two watched as the coin reappeared—from behind Bram's ear! The boy looked at Bram, then at Brigetta, and suddenly a grin flashed across his face and disappeared just as quickly. He sucked his thumb and contemplated all he had seen.

Brigetta looked at Bram in astonishment. *Just when I think I know everything about him, he produces magic tricks that enchant children!* Sobering, suppressed thoughts quickly intruded. She allowed her hand to press against the child growing within the folds of her dress—a child who would never meet Bram, never clamor for *just one more* before bedtime. She turned away and let a veil of tears obliterate the world rushing past the window.

Brigetta dozed off and on, Bram studied a seed catalog he had stuck in his pocket, the woman in the seat opposite them crocheted an anti-macassar, and the train ate up the miles, spitting them out in puffs of smoke.

Lunchtime in the dining car was announced. Some left immediately; others like Bram and Brigetta brought out boxes and bags. The de Boers ate a silent lunch from the canvas bag. Then, Brigetta leaned against Bram's shoulder and dozed, lulled by the swaying train and the sound of Bram's voice making idle conversation with their seatmate.

"What takes you to Minneapolis?" Brigetta jolted awake at their seat-mate's innocent question.

"I'm investigating some business opportunities," Bram replied.

"It's good you can take a trip together before the baby comes."

"The baby?" Brigetta whispered, stunned.

"You're not showing much yet. I've had six children myself, and lost four. Seeing you is like looking at myself in the mirror. Couldn't help notice your food didn't sit quite right. You're lookin' a mite peaked, even with the little naps you've taken. Don't worry—it will pass as you get along."

Signs? Six? Lost four? Peaked? All the starch drained out of Brigetta, the effort of trying to forget—and hide—dribbled all the oomph out of her like the last drops of water from a pump. Bram put his arm around her, sharing her distress at discovery.

"Rochester, next stop!" the conductor bawled, heading through the car at a purposeful pace. "Fifteen-minute stop. Take your tickets if you leave your seats." His voice, repeating the news, rolled back, muffled when the doors between the cars closed behind him.

The train arrived noisily at the station, making further conversation impossible. They waited for the final jerk and whistle that signaled their arrival.

Within minutes, the train spilled its occupants out on to the boardwalk, with Bram and Brigetta in their number. They walked around the station, stretching their legs until they needed to reboard the train. As was apparent from the bits of conversation around her, many of their fellow travelers on the train planned to stay in Rochester to keep appointments with the Doctors Mayo.

The train taking them north on the final leg of their journey was full of people who had boarded in Rochester. Crutches, bandages, or canes were in evidence for some, but equally many were leaving their cares and worries behind in this town with the famous doctors who worked miracles.

As the train moved through verdant farmland outside Rochester, Brigetta knew she would hear the woman's words for a long time even though the seat opposite them now was occupied by an elderly couple.

How did she know I'm pregnant? If a total stranger could detect her terrible secret, it would not be long before everyone would know. *This trip has become increasingly urgent—Bram simply must find a place where he can work and a place where I can hide.* "Maybe it was riding backwards or the train lurching that made me nauseous this morning. I certainly hope my condition isn't as obvious as that woman made it seem."

"Sometimes it's easier for total strangers to see things those more familiar with us miss," Bram mused. "We must pray that God will help us find a way out…" His words faded. They looked at each other guiltily—both knew better than to think of God as anything less than a very present help in time of trouble.

Restless with such accusing thoughts ramming his conscience, Bram headed off to walk the length of the train. When he returned in a few minutes, he wore a jubilant smile.

198   Rough Terrain

"Look, Brigetta, a newspaper was left in the dining car! The porter said he would throw it away so he let me take it. It's a *Minneapolis Daily Tribune* from earlier this week. You'll find this interesting." He folded the paper open for her perusal. A boxed announcement read:

WANTED!
Diligent experienced farmer to work as Steward at the Rochester (Minnesota) State Hospital. Responsibilities: oversee large-scale farming activities, supervise patient workers, and expand crop production to support the increasing hospital population. Provide three references. Interested individuals interview with the Superintendent at...

"Oh, Bram! You could do this job!" Brigetta reread the advertisement once again, savoring every word. Since the paper was several days old, interviews scheduled in several Minnesota cities were already past. However, two dates remained for Minneapolis: the first, earlier that day, and the second, the following morning.

"They've probably had quite a few applicants. In fact, they may have already hired someone at one of the other places." In the few minutes since he had spotted the newspaper, he knew he wanted this job desperately and needed it even more but he was afraid to get his hopes up.

"I can't believe anyone there could teach you anything about farming."

"I know, but doesn't it sound like an interesting job?"

"It appears to be a good match for you. But I don't understand the part about 'will supervise patient workers.' If it's a hospital, why would patients have to work?"

"A good question; I'll ask the superintendent tomorrow, if I meet him."

"What about references?" Anyone in Dutchville asked to supply credentials for their own Bram de Boer would be shocked.

"I'm not sure. They probably are looking for someone to attest to my farming abilities." A frown creased his forehead. "I suspect all they need now is names of people who can assure them what I tell them is true."

Brigetta said staunchly, "If they think you're lying, they don't know Dutchmen very well." Like a shot fired without warning, her words stunned them. Lies had been in abundance lately, and there didn't appear to be a ceasing any time soon.

Brigetta tried to imagine more of the town called Rochester than the chaos she had observed at the train depot. *It is so different than home! I saw no one in Dutch clothing, and I heard no Dutch spoken.* She frowned. "But what about me? Where will I go? Is there a place in Rochester where…"

Bram turned ashen. He looked out the window until the evening dusk reflected his image in the windowpane. Finally, he leaned close to her. "Minneapolis and Saint Paul are large cities—hundreds of thousands of people, I've heard." The unsaid thoughts traveled a slick rail between them: *Surely, with so many people, there must be a place women go to have a baby they cannot keep.*

While they ate bread and cheese and drank from the jar of tea, Brigetta sighed. Bram said, "We'll come through this, somehow. We're crossing some rough terrain now, but it won't always be this way."

Brigetta nodded sadly and repacked the canvas bag. Bram leaned back and closed his eyes. In that unguarded moment, Brigetta saw the strain on his face and realized Bram was as battle-weary as she. *Where did all this come from—a relationship broken between brothers, a level of intimacy tainted, dishonesty with our families…and soon, an unwanted baby.*

Their fellow travelers moved up and down the aisle, bumping into their seat with the swaying train's movements. Finally, Bram spoke. "The first thing I will ask in Minneapolis is how to find where the interviews are being held. If I am able to interview, and it appears they are interested in hiring me, we will find a place for you. Then we should be able to go home tomorrow on the night train."

It was late in the day when they arrived in Minneapolis. The train station was noisy and littered from the day's crowds; passengers were irritable. Shouted greetings and rebukes mingled with announcements of train departures and arrivals until Brigetta believed she could actually *feel* the din. She held tightly to the canvas bag and checked several times to be sure Bram still had *Tante* Lena's satchel in his hand.

Bram navigated through the confusion of the teeming depot. He asked several people for directions to nearby lodging, and where to find an inexpensive hot meal. Finally, he found someone who knew the location of the building mentioned in the newspaper announcement. Soon, they were out in the unfamiliar city, looking for landmarks in the faint light of street lamps.

They found a diner and ordered a simple supper. Brigetta was entranced with being waited on and by the clamor of conversations all around them. The light, flavorful meal sat easy on her stomach and she cleaned up every drop in the bowl. The woman on the train had assessed correctly—it had been a long time since Brigetta and food were on friendly terms.

A young man at the YMCA counter welcomed them. "Only two rooms are still available on the floor for couples. You'll have to share the bath at the end of the hall with the others on your floor. It's fifty-cents a night, payable ahead."

Bram and Brigetta sighed with audible relief. They accepted the key, agreed to a list of rules and regulations, and climbed the stairs to the little room in the middle of the hall, facing the street.

The key turned hard, but the transomed door opened easily. The dangling overhead light that Bram flicked on with a switch by the door revealed an iron bed with a pile of linens at the foot, a dresser with glass knobs on its two drawers, a small table with two chairs, and a tiny closet with a gaggle of wooden coat hangers. A pair of muslin curtains barely met in the middle of a tall, thin window, but Brigetta was relieved to see the window shade between the fabric and the glass could provide a semblance of privacy from the outside world.

"Well!" Bram said with false heartiness. "This is nice, isn't it? Small, but we're used to living in tight quarters. Wait until our families hear our room had an electric light!" He had crossed to the window. "Come see the view! We can look out across the trees and see some of the city! That's something we can't do at home!"

Brigetta nodded morosely. Home seemed so distant it was like a world imagined from the stories on her childhood bookshelf. All that was familiar in this strange new world was contained in the bags they held and in the person who shared this room with her tonight.

I want life to be like it was before Cornelis and the closet. I just want to be home. Home in our cottage, cooking supper, washing dishes, talking over our day and plans for tomorrow. Plans that aren't about Bram getting a job that excludes me. Plans not about me going to a place where I must leave my baby.

My baby. She felt dizzy and grasped the back of a chair tucked beneath the table.

"Let's use the washroom and crawl into bed. We've had a long day, and tomorrow will be busy," Bram suggested, barely stifling a yawn. He held out his arms and she flew to him and nestled in, soaking up the comfort, the love, the familiar.

Whereas joy selects a fine-tipped quill to create beautiful swirls that tell its tale in sun-swept skies, trouble uses a thick brush to paint its subjects, leaving a wide swath of grimness on a dark canvas.

Odd noises in the night interrupted their slumber and they slept fitfully on the hard and lumpy bed. Even the morning seemed strange: the sun entered the room from the wrong direction.

The growls emanating from Bram's stomach as they ate from the canvas bag indicated his farmer-sized appetite was not satisfied. When Brigetta could not finish her portion, Bram accepted it with little coaxing.

"Perhaps we can find another diner and have some coffee on our way to the interview," he suggested. Within an hour, they had enjoyed coffee and buttered biscuits at a small café and were standing before a large building on a crowded corner. The sign on the door proclaimed: *RSH interviews.*

"This is it. The address is right, and RSH must stand for Rochester State Hospital" Bram's voice cracked with nervousness.

"Wait! I can't go in with you!" Panic rolled across Brigetta's face.

Bram's confidence visibly sagged. "I'd rather have you in the building with me than be worrying about you outside. There must be some place where you can wait."

With pounding hearts and sweaty palms, they pushed open the heavy door, stepped across the threshold and found themselves in a spacious entryway doubling as a reception area. A woman seated at a large oak desk looked up from her paperwork and smiled broadly. "Hello!"

Bram made a jerky start across the wooden floor, gaining confidence as he covered the space from the door to the desk. "Hello. I'm Bram de Boer. I'm hoping to interview for the position of Steward at the Rochester State Hospital."

The woman nodded and smiled. "Welcome! My name is Miss Margaret Milner. Everyone calls me Miss Peggy. As you can see, we're not flooded with applicants today!" She waved her hand at the vacant chairs along the wall. "In fact, we thought about canceling today's interviews, but it's a good thing we didn't, isn't it?"

"Yes, Miss Peggy," Bram answered respectfully. "I've come from Dutchville, Iowa, and am looking forward to an opportunity to meet with the Superintendent."

"Iowa! My goodness! Let me tell the Doctor you're here. Please have a seat."

Bram and Brigetta sat stiffly in two chairs, awkwardly clutching the two bags. Brigetta stole a glance at Bram. *He looks scared, and his trousers are terribly wrinkled, and my stomach is churning.* "You'll do fine, Bram," she whispered.

He jerked as if he had forgotten she were there; he nodded uncertainly. "We'll see. I wonder why no one else is applying if it's such a good job?"

Brigetta had no well of reassuring answers to that disturbing question, so she reached for his hand and held it firmly, gaining as much assurance as she gave.

A door across the room swung open and the receptionist returned, followed by a tall, thin man with a wild shock of curly black hair. His booming voice preceded him as he moved toward Bram with outstretched hands, "Hello, young man! I'm Doctor Randolph Gray."

Speechless himself, Bram stumbled to his feet and reached out to receive the firm handshake that threatened to topple him. "I'm Bram de Boer, Sir. And you are the Superintendent?"

The Superintendent 's laugh rumbled in his chest, "Yes, indeed. And who might this be?"

Brigetta sucked in her breath as Bram stepped aside, allowing Doctor Gray full view of her trembling form. "This is my wife, Brigetta."

The tall man bowed gracefully as he took her hand. "A pleasure to meet you, Mrs. de Boer." He straightened and smiled into her eyes before turning back to Bram. "Let's begin the interview."

Bram looked questioningly at Brigetta as he turned; she nodded quickly and sighed with relief. *This is a kind man—he will treat Bram with respect and consideration.* She looked at Miss Peggy who was shuffling papers and decided there was no reason she could not sit quietly right there. Certainly, no one else needed any of the dozen chairs circling the room.

Hand on the doorknob, Doctor Gray stopped abruptly. "Would you please join us, Mrs. de Boer? Miss Peggy tells me you're from Iowa, so this move could be quite a change for you. I'd like you to hear about what your husband could expect from the job since your support of his efforts will ensure his success."

Startled beyond words, Brigetta picked up their bags and trotted along behind them down a long and narrow hallway, around a corner to a room where a brisk fire crackled in a stone hearth. Four wingback chairs clustered around a coffee table made a most inviting scene. In one corner, a silver coffeepot sparkled in the light of a wall-mounted gas lamp.

Once they had settled into the comfortable chairs, Doctor Gray smiled. "May I offer either of you a hot drink? No? Well, then, I'd like to start with you telling me about yourself. What part of Iowa is home for you?"

"Dutchville is the town closest to my home. It's near Sioux City. I farm with my father."

"What interests you about the Steward's position at RSH?"

"I was intrigued about expanding crop production. I have attempted to improve crops and increase production on our farm with gratifying success. I have sold vegetables and flowers from our garden for many years—even though many of my customers already have their own plentiful gardens. They often turn to me for advice on how to improve their own produce."

"It sounds as if you have a good life, Bram. Why are you seeking to leave?"

Brigetta tensed; Bram sat a little straighter and met Doctor Gray's gaze. "I have always known I have a gift in working with the land—the soil responds to me in ways I cannot explain. But I have a yen to learn more than I can at home. I am looking for an opportunity to improve my skills. I was rejected from the Armed Services because of a minor medical problem. But a friend helped me see my abilities in farming are just as valuable as any soldier's skills. I want to be the best possible farmer."

Brigetta expelled a breath quietly. *What a marvelous answer!*

Doctor Gray nodded thoughtfully. "We've seen few applicants for this job because so many men have been called into service. Since you've already explained why you are at home, that answers my next question." Crossing his long legs at the ankles, the superintendent leaned back in his chair. "Let me tell you about the Rochester State Hospital and what we are looking for in our Steward; I'm sure you probably know little about our institution."

"That's correct. I learned about the position from a newspaper I found on the train coming up here. We had a brief stop-over in Rochester, so I know where the town is located."

"The institution sits just over a mile east of Rochester. We have about 1500 mentally ill patients. Despite the name 'hospital,' our patients do not have an illness as much as a condition that likely will never be cured or completely controlled or changed. For them, our facility is an asylum—a safe place where they are accepted and can make worthwhile contributions."

Bram and Brigetta were caught up in the cadence of Doctor Gray's voice and intoxicating fervor.

"We believe in creating a environment in which everyone is accepted as they are, protected from harm, and given a meaningful task to accomplish. Our treatment is simple: give a person a task to do and as perfect an environment as possible in which to live. Under such conditions, the mind is calmed and a person is less destructive. For many of our patients, the Rochester State Hospital is the first place they have felt important—outside, they are shunned. At RSH, they are expected to work, to contribute, to help their fellow patients as vital members of a larger group."

"Exactly what tasks do they do?" Bram asked.

"For many, there are the farms. They are large enough to support all the needs of the Hospital and supply some products, like turkeys, for instance, to several other state institutions. The patients are crucial to the farming activities. The Steward oversees the workers, makes decisions, sets the planting and harvesting schedule—but the farms are far too vast for him to run alone. He is dependent on the patients. He is not only the master farmer, he is the supervisors of those patients who work the farm."

Bram looked doubtful, "But 1500 patients? How can there be enough work for all to do?"

"I should finish my descriptive tour! We are truly a self-sufficient town, if you will, that offers a wide variety of jobs for our population. Since we are outside Rochester itself, we have our own water supply and many other necessities of a town. Some patients work in our dairy that boasts some of the finest Holsteins you'll see anywhere—in addition to hogs and sheep and chickens and all the animals one would expect on a working farm."

"It sounds like the state hospital is really multiple farms."

"Yes, indeed. Other patients love working in the grain fields that support our livestock. Still others are kept busy with the acres of gardens needed to supply food for the patients."

"But still…" Bram frowned, still mentally envisioning 1500 people he would supervise.

"Not everyone works on the farms or even in the gardens and greenhouses. Many help in the bakery and kitchen, or run our laundry that operates from sunrise to sunset, six days a week. Let's see, what am I forgetting? Oh, yes, the tailor shop, the shoe-and harness shops, and mattress and upholstery buildings; a cannery; a slaughterhouse and rendering room with a smokehouse nearby. We also have a kiln for making bricks. These are all staffed by patients and supervised by paid employees. The employees, like the Steward, provide the oversight of the various activities and projects."

Doctor Gray could tell the de Boers were overwhelmed by his recitation of facts. "I should also tell you the property includes not only rich farm land and all the buildings needed for the occupations I mentioned, but we have some of the prettiest woods and rolling hills and meadows in all of southern Minnesota. Several limestone caves provide chilled storage for fruits and vegetables we grow. A creek runs through the property beside a railroad spur devoted to our use. And the rock quarry on the property is large enough to provide the building materials for most of the hospital facilities."

Bram blinked and pursed his lips thoughtfully. "Do employees live on the property?"

"Yes, for the most part. We have several dwellings devoted to staff housing. The Steward's house is a large home on a hillside on the northwest corner of the property. It looks out over a field where cattle graze, and is near the rock quarry. It is a restful spot."

"So you are in charge of the patients' medical care, and the Steward is in charge of the farm?" asked Bram.

Doctor Gray nodded. "Even though the patients have satisfying work to do under ideal conditions, they require medical attention for their conditions—that's where I come in."

"Are any of the patients who work on the farm considered dangerous?" Bram's question mirrored Brigetta's silent concerns.

"Many patients are kept medicated. Depending on how well they respond to their treatment, they may or may not be able to work. Some are kept in restraints for their own protection and the safety of others. Occasionally, some patients lapse into deep depression that prevents them from working for a time," Doctor Gray replied honestly. "And, with the variety of patient activities, we see our fair share of broken bones and other such injuries and influenza and other diseases just like any village. For such patients, we are a hospital in the most common definition of the word."

"I had no idea how extensive the Rochester State Hospital is." Bram turned honest eyes to the Superintendent. "I wonder if I am qualified."

"Let me be the judge of that. Tell me more about your farm."

Bram reached into his deep trouser pocket and pulled out the well-worn notebook. For the next few minutes, he showed Doctor Gray the detailed records he had maintained over the years. He explained the notations about planting schedules, rainfall charts, and fertilization, and how he had adjusted his plans yearly. "As long as I have customers and our crops increase, I figure I'm doing something right."

"What is the secret for the high demand for your vegetables?"

"I constantly question things like why a certain type of seed? Why different kinds or strengths of fertilizer for different crops? What makes one field better than another for growing corn? When is rain good, and when is it harmful? Why did one field grow spectacular corn or oats last year, and only an average crop this year? When is the perfect time to pick suckers off a tomato plant?"

"Good questions. And how do you find the answers?"

Bram paused pensively for a few moments. "By experimenting. From weighing the answers others give against what I see happening in my own fields and garden. I have learned a lot from my father. He has years of experience to draw upon, and he learned farming from his father. But he also is willing to try new ideas, and has given me freedom to test my theories."

"All you've told me is certainly impressive. What else do I need to know about Bram de Boer?"

"I'm not sure it's important to you, but I do have a hobby—and being a Dutchman, it is really a special interest. I have worked extensively with tulips, both with bulbs and seeds, crossbreeding, testing my theories of forcing bulbs and developing new varieties. My mother believes tulips feed the soul!"

The superintendent ran his fingers through the mass of curls atop his head. When he removed his hand, they sprang back into place. "You might be surprised how helpful feeding the soul is for our patients." He looked thoughtfully into space for several moments, resting his chin on his hand. His eventual question was a surprise: "How tall is your corn?"

"Up to my shoulders."

Doctor Gray's eyebrows shot up. "Really? All of it?"

"Except for the field I fertilized twice—that's over my head!" Bram responded with a grin.

Doctor Gray's booming laughter filled the room. "I wish I could see it! In fact, I wish I could taste it!"

Brigetta's head jerked up. "Doctor Gray, excuse me?"

He turned toward Brigetta. "Yes, Mrs. de Boer?"

"Could I show you something?"

"Surely."

"Excuse me for one moment," Brigetta said, glancing around the room. She picked up the canvas bag and walked quickly to the small corner table. She removed one cup from its matching saucer and worked quickly with items from the canvas bag. Within minutes, she returned to waiting men.

Holding out a saucer with four quarters of a tomato, several slices of a cucumber, thin carrot strips, a bright-red radish, and a leafy stalk of celery all arranged prettily on the plate, she turned to Doctor Gray with a winning smile. "Please experience Bram de Boer's garden for yourself!"

He leaned forward and accepted the saucer. He stared at it with interest before selecting a tomato section. It was plump and firm, juicy and red all the way through; the look on his face was one of sheer pleasure as he savored every taste. He then polished off one of each of the other vegetables—crunching, biting, chewing, and relishing each and every one.

No further urging was required—he devoured the remaining segments of tomato, scooped up the cucumbers and radishes, and stared at the remaining carrots and celery in his hand with the first hint of discomposure. "I'm embarrassed to have eaten almost everything! My goodness, Bram—to think you grew all this delectable array I have demolished!"

"Something you may not realize, Doctor Gray, is Bram and I picked these vegetables two days ago! You cannot begin to imagine how good they are when they are first picked. You've just tasted why people line up to buy Bram's produce every Thursday morning, all summer long. Wouldn't you?"

"No doubt about it. I just wish I had saved one hunk of tomato to take home to my wife!"

Brigetta walked back over to the table and returned carrying two tomatoes, a cucumber, a fistful of radishes, and the rest of the celery. "Take this home to her. Tell her if Bram is hired as Steward at the Rochester State Hospital, I will personally see to it you have vegetables just like these—only they will be fresh-picked. I wish you could taste his strawberries."

Doctor Gray groaned. "So do I, Mrs. de Boer. My wife and I simply adore strawberries!" While Brigetta cleaned up, Bram asked and answered Doctor Gray's questions, offered several ideas for ways he would approach a few farming dilemmas facing the hospital, and thoughtfully considered two options for expanding the garden plots, recommending one on the basis of natural water flow, over the other with extensive sunlight.

"That is exactly what the former Steward said, but he would have planted corn where you suggest putting oats. However, your reasoning for oats is sound."

Doctor Gray unfurled his legs and smiled across the semi-circle of chairs. "You're a young fellow, Bram de Boer; I'm sure some would say too young and inexperienced, but I like your ideas, and you understand your strengths and weaknesses. You have a good head on your shoulders to help you make decisions. I'd like to offer you the job as Steward of the Rochester State Hospital. Will you accept it?"

Bram's jaw dropped and he turned to find a similar response from Brigetta. He recovered and swallowed hard. "Yes, Sir. That is, if my wife…"

"Yes! Oh, yes, yes, yes!"

"There you have it, Sir—you've hired me!"

"When can you start? You'll want to go home to settle your affairs and arrange for a move, but your house is waiting for you. The previous

Steward had to retire due to ill health and has moved back to Wisconsin to be near his wife's family. So it's all ready for the two of you to move in."

Bram turned slowly to look at Brigetta's stricken face. He moistened his lips and swallowed hard. "I will come alone, at first. My wife's, uh, grandmother is quite ill and not expected to live much longer. Brigetta is going to live with her and care for her for the next few months."

"I'm sorry to hear about your grandmother, Mrs. de Boer, but I fully understand your need to be with her for a while. Where does she live?"

Brigetta's throat constricted until she thought she would choke even on saliva. She couldn't meet the gentle eyes of the superintendent, and he mistook her discomfiture for sorrow. "I'm sorry—you must be close to her."

Her nod was the lie that gave him the answer he sought. Bram spoke a little too quickly, "She lives in Minneapolis near other relatives—but they have asked Brigetta to come and stay in her home. So that's one reason this job is so interesting to me. It allows us to be closer together than we'd dared to hope."

Brigetta walked over to the window, staring unseeing at the trees beyond the building. Bram and Doctor Gray spoke of salary, moving plans, the expected starting date, and other details. "Brigetta?" Bram called across the room, "Doctor Gray suggests we stop in Rochester on our way home to see where we will live. What do you think?"

Before she could respond, Doctor Gray asked with a quizzical look on his face, "So you're returning to Iowa, too, Mrs. de Boer, rather than staying in Minneapolis?"

"I need to go home to make arrangements for a longer visit than I had first planned." It all sounded weak and suspicious to her own ears, but Doctor Gray accepted Brigetta's fabrication as truth. She caught Bram's eye. *We are digging a deep hole.*

They shook hands with the superintendent and gathered up their bags, agreeing to meet him at the Rochester train station the next day. Doctor Gray walked with them back out to the reception area where the sound of clattering typewriter keys greeted them. "Miss Peggy, we have a new Steward!"

"Oh, I'm so glad, Doctor Gray! Something told me your search would be over. Congratulations, Mister de Boer."

"Are you part of the staff in Rochester, or do you work here?" Bram asked, looking around the room.

Doctor Gray responded, "Miss Peggy is my secretary. This is the office of a lawyer who is a family friend. He is in court for several days and agreed to let us use his office. It has worked out well. Miss Peggy has been able to keep up with correspondence while helping with scheduling interviews."

The woman smiled, "Tell me, Doctor Gray, what made you decide on Mister de Boer?"

The superintendent winked at Brigetta. "Do you have anything left in that bag to share?"

Brigetta reached across the desk. "May I?" she asked, removing the saucer from beneath Miss Peggy's coffee cup. She then opened the canvas bag and cut several slices from the remaining chunk of cucumber, arranging them in a semi-circle on the saucer. In the curve, she added thin slivers of radish and the last stalk of celery before she slid the plate across the desk. "Please, have a taste. I'm sorry you're only getting leftovers."

Miss Peggy stared at the saucer and looked up at Doctor Gray. He said, "Go ahead. The answer to your question lies on that plate."

Her eyes widened with the first taste. She needed no urging to take a second bite, this time creating a tantalizing combination of radish and cucumber. She purred with contentment. "I understand! Oh my, I don't usually eat radishes, but these aren't bitter, and the cucumbers have some substance—they're not all juice and seeds!" She took a satisfying bite of celery and licked her lips. "Even the celery is tasty!"

"Secrets of the soil, Miss Peggy," Bram responded with a twinkle in his eye.

After exchanging farewells, Bram and Brigetta crossed the same threshold, but with lighter hearts than just hours before. Hand-in-hand to maintain a sedate walk instead of frolicking with the total abandonment of propriety they longed to exhibit, Bram abruptly dropped the satchel and pulled Brigetta into a tender embrace. "Do you know how much I love you?"

"If it's not at least a bushel and a peck, I can't bear it!"

"Oh, far more. More than anything, anyone, any-any!"

"A lot, huh?" she said mischievously.

"Can I buy lunch for the best wife on the face of the earth?"

"If that's me, then you're going to have to because I just fed the rest of our food to the good Doctor Gray and Miss Peggy!"

"What an amazing idea you had, Brigetta! Who would think a job could be had for a taste of two-day-old vegetables?"

"He was looking for proof you could do what the Steward needs to do. That's what I gave him. I just wish he could see your garden and farmland, and I guess he will since you're the new Steward!"

Over lunch at a diner, some of their euphoria dissipated as they came back to reality and admitted they still had a major hurdle to overcome. It took a second cup of coffee before Brigetta had an idea. When the waitress brought their bill, Brigetta asked, "Do you have a minute to answer a question?"

"Sure, if I know the answer."

"We came to Minneapolis to visit our cousin, but lost the slip of paper that says where she's living for a few months. It's a place where," she paused and lowered her voice, "girls go who are in the family way without a husband."

The waitress nodded sagely. "That'd likely be Saint Simon's Home for Wayward Girls."

Brigetta blanched at the appellation but asked, "Does that sound familiar, Bram?"

Bram twirled his spoon silently until it clattered to the table. "Could be…is there another place?"

The young woman tucked her pencil behind her ear and then snapped her fingers. "There's a place run by a couple of do-gooders. Your cousin could be there, but she'd have had to agree to live by their rules and all. No nights on the town, no drinking and such."

"She's not a bad girl—just got in trouble this once, so maybe that's the place. What's it called?"

"No name; just goes by 'the Thompson House,' that's the do-gooders' name."

With directions to each place sketched out, Bram and Brigetta paid their bill and left the diner. "A good idea you had—but we need another one now when you're showing up at the place and not planning to stay just yet. How will we explain that?" Bram asked bleakly.

They found a bench beneath a tree by a trolley stop and gingerly sat on its splintery boards. "I could be your sister." A flood of tears roared in Brigetta's head. She brushed the back of her hand across both eyes and blinked quickly. Automatically, her fingers sought out the locket. *Yours for all time.*

Bram sat woodenly beside her, so lost in his own distress he had nothing left to give. "Oh, Brigetta, as interesting as it sounds to be the Steward at the Rochester State Hospital, I wish we could go home and grow tulips for the rest of our lives. No trouble with Cornelis. No baby. No lies."

"Not a day goes by that I don't wish Mama and *Tante* Lena hadn't offered the dresser. If only Cornelis had just gone to the blacksmith that morning." She burst into loud and blinding tears, gulping for air. Bram drew her close and the two of them clung to each other on a bustling street in Minneapolis and wept together over things that could not be.

When the second trolley-car driver pulled over and glared at them for making him stop, they picked up their bags and looked at the crumpled paper telling their future. "Bram, I don't think I could bear to be labeled a 'wayward girl' for the next six months,"

The tremor in her voice wrenched his heart even more than her tears. "Let's visit the Thompson's House and save the other for second choice."

Large sprawling trees and a wooden fence offered shade and privacy to the foreboding two-story house on the corner. Bram and Brigetta stared from across the street for several minutes. "Someone in the corner window on the second floor is looking at us, Bram."

"Then let's make our move before the neighbors report us as vagrants."

The doorknocker made Brigetta jump with its harshness. She clutched the canvas bag with perspiring hands and willed her knees to cease shaking.

A thin-lipped, long-nosed woman answered the door. Brigetta's instant impression was of a stork in utilitarian clothing. Several strands of mousy brown hair had dared to come loose from the knot high on her head. *They'll be sorry they were so wild—she'll probably cut them off to show them who's boss.* Brigetta reprimanded herself sternly for such harsh thoughts—but felt a lot less guilty when the woman finally spoke, having finished a thorough review of them. "It's not often both sinners show up at our door."

Bram's face flamed vivid red and Brigetta heard him suck in his breath. She sensed he was just seconds from turning on his heel and leaving the porch. *Wayward girls—that's the alternative.* "Mrs. Thompson? May we come in? I'm Brigetta de Boer and this is my brother, Bram."

One eyebrow arched above a cool gray eye. The left cheek twitched. The fingers on the right hand tapped a rhythmic beat on the back of the door. She stepped back enough to open the door and led them to a gloomy parlor. Motioning toward the settee, she seated herself in a horsehair chair and primly positioned her hands on the knees. "You don't appear to be far along."

"I am just into my third month."

216 Rough Terrain

" You will be put on a list and may return when we notify you of the next vacancy. But first, you must agree to our rules. Until their final confinement, all girls in our home must attend church services, twice on Sunday and once mid-week, and participate in daily devotionals and prayer meetings here in our home, and read the Bible every day, and show true repentance."

"Repentance?" Bram repeated in a cold voice. "What would Brigetta need to repent? She was attacked by an intruder in our home."

With scorn fringing her lofty tone, Mrs. Thompson replied, "You'd be amazed at how many girls are on our doorstep because of such 'attacks,' never willing to admit to sinning."

Brigetta felt the starch go out of her backbone. "When do you antici-pate an opening?" she asked politely. Bram's look was filled with caution and concern, rebuke, and disbelief. She could read his mind: *Brigetta, are you sure this is where you want to spend six months?*

Mrs. Thompson pursed her lips. "Two girls will give birth by the end of the month. The earliest you could come would be the first of October."

Both de Boers sighed with relief. *The first of October! Perfect!* "I had thought you meant a much longer wait. How much is the fee for staying here?"

"It's not a simple fee. Girls who come early work for their room and board as long as they are able. Those who come later, pay a set fee. Part of the agreement you must sign is that you relinquish all rights to your child to us. We then charge a fee to the adoptive parents."

"So," Bram said coldly, "you profit from the *sins* of the girls you house."

Mrs. Thompson answered him with a sanctimonious air. "It is our Christian duty to help the afflicted. We have not caused their condi-tions—we offer them a way out of disgrace. Perhaps you should make other arrangements."

The canvas bag Brigetta still clutched fell to the floor with a muffled thud. "Let me be sure I understand: I can live and work here up until I am ready to give birth. During my time here, I attend church services and follow other rules regarding Bible study and prayer. At the time I am confined, I pay you for the care I receive until after the birth. I sign a paper saying I agree to place the baby in your care to put up for adoption. Is there anything I have missed or misunderstood?"

"No, you have stated it correctly. But your brother has reservations."

Brigetta placed a gently hand on Bram's arm. "He is still so upset, having just learned of my condition, he is not himself. He realizes this is a good place for me, don't you, Bram?"

Had he been required to reply, Bram would have choked on the word *good*, but he nodded wordlessly.

"May I see the paper you will ask me to sign?" Brigetta asked sweetly.

Mrs. Thompson stood and walked to a desk across the room, returning with a single sheet of paper. Bram leaned over Brigetta's shoulder as they read it together. His finger pointed to *No male visitors* and the page wrinkled within her grip.

"There's one rule I want you to be sure you understand," Mrs. Thompson's voice jolted them. "Whenever you leave the house, you must always be accompanied by another girl. Any violation of these rules results in banishment from our home."

"You have said 'we' and 'our' several times," Bram noted. "Does your husband share your responsibilities?"

"Mister Thompson passed away fifteen years ago. My sister, Miss Beal, and I attend to the care of the girls up to and through their confinement, and the babies until they are adopted."

"If I sign this paper today, may I be assured of a place in October?" Brigetta asked in a low voice.

"Certainly. You will be able to work until February, at least. The fee is noted at the bottom of the paper. We would expect it to be paid by December."

"The fee will be paid," Bram clipped each syllable short.

Brigetta signed the paper and Mrs. Thompson filed it away in the desk. On their way to the door, a spine-tingling shriek erupted from an upper room and ricocheted down the curving staircase. Brigetta grabbed Bram's arm in fright.

Mrs. Thompson's face evidenced little concern, though she offered an explanation. "My sister was unable to join us because one of the girls is giving birth today. There is less enjoyment in the end results of sinful pleasures than in the fornication."

Bram stiffened and Brigetta tugged on his sleeve to caution him against speaking his mind. On the doorstep, she turned with great dignity. "Good day, Mrs. Thompson. I will see you on October first." She tugged Bram off the porch. Only when she was confident no prying eyes from the Thompson House could find them did she halt.

"Brigetta, I can hardly stand the thought of you being with that woman. If her sister is anything like her, you are in for six months of utter horror."

"Bram, it's either the Thompson House or the Home for Wayward Girls. Which would you prefer to write on the letters you send me?"

Bram stormed ahead, *Tante* Lena's satchel banging on his leg with each step. Brigetta hurried to keep pace, frightened by the chasm she felt between them once again. "Bram, wait! Please don't make me run!"

He skidded to a stop. "Brigetta, I thought the hatred in my heart for Cornelis these past weeks was the worst sin I could ever commit—but it has unleashed a capacity for even more hatred. I wanted to lash out at that self-righteous woman and tell her a thing or two about Christian duty and serving God."

"Bram, do you have a pencil?"

This rational question stopped his tirade. "A pencil? Whatever for?"

"I need to write down directions to the railway depot. Otherwise, I'll get lost when I return."

Bram pulled a pencil out of his pocket, found the ticket stub from the train, and took a calming breath. They walked slowly toward the railway station, stopping to note landmarks, street names, and directional turns. "We'll rewrite it so there will be no confusion," Bram promised.

They found a hotel close to the train depot and paid for a night's lodging. This time, they clung to each other throughout the night; there was so much to absorb, too much to understand. With strange night sounds all around—bells, voices calling across streets and down alleys—Brigetta lifted her head to peer into Bram's troubled eyes. "Will you sing to me?" With the familiar tune and comforting words of *Psalmen 23* gently nudging worry aside, Brigetta gradually fell asleep as secure in Bram's arms as sheep in the Shepherd's embrace.

*De Heere is mijn Herder, mij zal niets ontbreken…grazige weiden;…stille wateren…*Bram sang it several times, nearly choking on lumps in his throat, and then hummed until he knew Brigetta was safely asleep. In the darkness, his soul ached for cool waters, green pastures, safe places.

Bram lay awake for a long time, stroking his wife's smooth skin, breathing in the fragrance of her hair, capturing memories to last the lonely months ahead. Tears pooled in his eyes and spilled down, soaking the pillow beneath his head. *It is not a good decision I have made—but to purposely destroy the rest of our lives?*

The trip to Rochester passed quickly. When the train pulled in to the depot, they stepped out into the sunlight with a combination of excitement and anxious thoughts. As promised, Doctor Gray awaited them. "Welcome to Rochester, de Boers!"

The Superintendent led them through the crowd to the waiting buggy. The countryside was alive with birds and crops, picturesque beneath the autumn sun. About a mile out of town, they curved around a final bend in the road, Brigetta gasped, "What majestic buildings!"

"I never tire of seeing them. The most distinctive ones are built in Tudor style and are equally impressive to first-time guests and those, like myself, who see them on a daily basis."

Bram looked from buildings to fields, hillsides to barns, meadows to woods. "Such variety in one place!"

"Do you understand now how even just arriving in this scenic place begins the therapy for some patients? Especially those who come from the din and dirt of a city."

A tour around the hospital grounds, viewed from the buggy seat beside their new friend pushed their imaginations to the limit: receiving wards, silos, brooder house and hatchery, the nurses' homes, corral, staff residences, ice house, greenhouse, and more—it all became a blur. Doctor Gray said, "Let's head on up to what I know you really want to see, Mrs. de Boer—the Steward's home."

Turning the buggy around, they wound their way over a bridge across the creek and rode along beneath the interlocking branches that canopied a quiet road. "We often have picnics here," Doctor Gray pointed to a fire pit. "Staff and patients, alike, enjoy that." Within just a few hundred yards, he asked, "Do you feel the coolness? To your right and up this hill are the limestone caves I mentioned where we store vast quantities of fruits and vegetables to last us through the winter."

Their buggy burst from beneath the trees into full sunlight and moved along a meadow alive with birds and rabbits and squirrels. They rode in silence for several hundred yards before Superintendent Gray pointed to a vast grassy hillside. "This is our cemetery. Men are buried to the left, women to the right. It is a peaceful place to walk—not at all like many cemeteries, which seem to me to be quite grim."

"It seems almost restful," Bram agreed, watching birds swoop from the woods on either side across the wide-open space reserved for those whose lives on earth had ended. "It must be comforting for family members to visit."

Doctor Gray's lips tightened. "Unfortunately, those who are buried here have often been rejected by their families. The shame of having a relative with mental problems is often too much for a family to bear. It makes it all the more important we become their family, as I mentioned in our interview yesterday."

Oh God—where is the kindness now? Am I to show compassion to strangers when I know I am hurting the one most important in life to me? Bram's hands broke into a sweat.

Brigetta sighed deeply; sadness that was her daily attendant weighed even more heavily on her heart. *Perhaps growing up with Mama will help me understand, but I am so consumed with my own problems I have little left to give others.*

"Do you see the entrance to another cave at the far end of the cemetery? It is a makeshift morgue we use during the winter months when the ground is too frozen to dig graves. Again, I feel it is totally lacking in morbidity, just part of the landscape."

With an open field to the left, and sun-dappled woods to the right, they continued north. Abruptly, Doctor Gray halted the horse and both de Boers looked at him questioningly. He smiled broadly, "There's your house! What do you think?"

Bram and Brigetta looked around, at each other, and back at their guide. "Excuse me?" Bram said politely.

Pointing straight ahead, toward a thick grove of trees marching proudly up a knoll, Doctor Gray said, "Right through there!" He clicked a command to the horse. "From where we are, it is a case of not seeing the forest for the trees, or rather, not seeing the house for the trees!"

As the buggy moved up the long narrow well-traveled path, Bram and Brigetta caught glimpses of white stucco with wood batting—a towering home that dominated the impressive hillside. Doctor Gray slowed the buggy and turned to his passengers with a smile. "Let's go see your new home!"

Brigetta snapped her jaw shut. The two-story house loomed in full view. Walking up a winding path to reach the back door, she clutched Bram's hand and whispered, "Surely this can't be where we'll live?"

They hurried to keep pace with their enthusiastic host. "...it came in a boxcar on a train. It's a Sears' house—ordered right out of the catalog and built by a crew of carpenters from town with help from our patients. It was constructed in 1913 and you will be the second family to live in it—for what I hope is a long time. Let's by-pass the back door and enter the house properly through the front door."

So many windows! Such a big lawn! How many rooms are there, anyway? Where will we ever get enough furniture to fill this place? Brigetta's mind raced with the wonder of it all.

They climbed an impressive set of stairs to reach an inviting porch, complete with swing. Two large windows flanked the front door, and through them, Brigetta could see empty, sunlit rooms.

Using a key he carried on a massive ring attached to his belt, Doctor Gray swung open the door and held it for Brigetta, then Bram to enter before him. "One has a real sense of quiet privacy here."

Tall ceilings, flowered wallpaper, an east-facing piano window with exquisite leaded glass, an arched entrance from the parlor to the dining room, a door leading to a stubby hallway with a bathroom and two bedrooms. Moving from room to room, Brigetta's voice took on new levels of excitement. "Look, Bram! A bathroom!"

"No little house outside to find in the middle of the winter? How will we ever get over missing that?"

"If you mourn the loss too much, there's still an outhouse in the back yard! We left it there because when the patients are working nearby, we didn't want them to knock on your door and disturb you."

The kitchen had a door leading to a back porch the same size as the front porch. The view from both porches was magnificent—trees, trees, and more trees. To the west, a steep incline with a path running along its peak. Directly north, a narrow grassy field sloped gently to the east. Also to the east, a greenhouse. "Perfect for tulips, Bram! Both the greenhouse and the lawn beside it!" Brigetta pointed out to Bram. The back porch had another door leading to the full basement with sturdy walls and a packed dirt floor.

Feeling as if they were following a maze, Bram and Brigetta followed Doctor Gray to a second set of stairs leading to one vast open upper room. Though no walls divided the space into rooms, Bram looked around and exclaimed, "There is space for five or six rooms here!"

"I would think so. If a family with children ever lives here, they'll be motivated to finish off this upper level. But for couples like yourselves, the first floor and basement are probably space enough until you have a family." Nodding vaguely at Doctor Gray, Bram gripped Brigetta's hand.

The three of them gazed out each window in turn, looking across fields and woods. It was a most magnificent sight, and Bram and Brigetta's exclamations of awe were genuine. Bram pointed out a squirrel's nest directly at eye level, and they watched the antics of an entire family of red squirrels for several minutes.

"Over there is the slaughterhouse, and the greenhouse hotbeds, and the smoke house and other assorted buildings. Just beyond the buildings you see to the east, is a marvelous bog—you'll hear the crickets and frogs at night, I'm sure!"

"It is all so enormous! The house, the hospital property…"

"Yes, but before long, it will all become familiar—just like every corner of your farm in Iowa. Bram, would you like to see more of the fields and farm buildings? I realize we'll have plenty of time to talk over other details once you get here, but I know you'd probably like to have some things in your mind to ruminate over during the next few weeks."

"Yes, I'd like that. If you have time, I would welcome your company and your explanations of what I'm seeing."

Brigetta spoke up quickly. "Doctor Gray, may I stay here in the house?"

"That's a good idea. Here," he reached into his pocket and took out a tablet and pencil. "Use this to record things women always want to remember about a house! If you're like my wife, you'll probably count drawers in the kitchen, and make note of colors in the wallpaper, and draw yourself a floor plan to decide on what furniture goes where! We'll return in," he consulted his pocket watch, "an hour."

Brigetta stood on the front porch and watched the men disappear down the hill to the south, across the field, around the curve, and then out of sight just beyond the cemetery. Back inside, she wound her way through each room, touching woodwork, running her fingers over the flocked wallpaper in one room and the satiny finish of another. Despite her stern warnings to herself to pay attention to the task at hand, her mind wandered.

Leaning against the curved arch that separated parlor from dining room, she stretched up to touch the peak and remembered how Gustave had marked her yearly growth along a similar archway in the parsonage. *There will be no pencil marks for growing children on this wallpaper.*

She opened more cupboard doors in the kitchen than she could ever imagine filling, and stared at three closets, each with ample shelving for their clothes and linens.

Following stepping-stones around the entire perimeter of the house, she paced it off. "It is at least sixty feet by thirty feet and two stories high, and then the basement and attic, too! Whatever will we do with so much house?" she wondered aloud.

Moving more slowly, she walked again to the sun-dappled west side of the house, unseen birds in the wooded hillside filling her ears with their rapturous songs. She pulled branches of lilac bushes against her cheeks; they were no longer in bloom, but bore ghosts of abundant blossoms. *"Look for me when the lilacs bloom…I'll come back…with a heart that's fond and true."* She remembered the words, but felt no music in her soul.

She continued around to the east side, walking beneath lofty fir and spruce trees that whispered secrets of the hills. She returned to touch the waving branches of baby's breath and bridal wreath bushes flanking each side of the front steps, gravitating toward the welcoming porch swing. She closed her eyes, breathing deeply of the verdant meadow smells that wafted up the hillside.

Sadness anchored itself to the bits of joy she had dared to feel, tugging each delight, every thrill into the churning depths of despair. *This is a large and overwhelming place for just two people to call home. It needs a child's voice calling from room to room, the sound of pounding footsteps on the stairs, the sense of a child's presence in each room. Can just two make it feel like a home?*

Leaving the swing, she strode across the porch and let herself back in to the house. She moved purposefully, talking and making notes. "A nearly square parlor, very nice for conversation. Four windows in the dining room, good for morning sun and catching evening breezes. Several possible corners for my china cabinet. Nice, wide floor space in the kitchen—and ten cupboards, three shelves each. Six drawers."

She spoke loudly, as if noise alone would scare unwanted thoughts. "Cream-colored wallpaper with roses in the parlor. Rose-colored wallpaper with satiny strips in the dining room and hallway. Roses galore on the bedroom wallpaper. My, somebody surely liked roses!"

She pushed herself to write down something about each room, and when she heard the squeaking wheels of the returning buggy, met both men at the door with a smile pasted in place. "Did you have a good tour, Bram?" she asked with forced brightness.

Bram looked at her suspiciously as she flitted past him with sprightliness she had not shown for weeks. All the way to the depot, she chattered. Little missed her observing eye. Wildflowers, birds' songs, the horse's smooth strides, the buggy's new paint—all were fodder for discussion and when they reached the edge of town, Bram felt as exhausted by all her chatter as if he had run along behind the buggy the whole way. Doctor Gray seemed delighted with every word she spoke, but Bram knew his wife well enough to recognize something was amiss.

"Thank you, Doctor Gray, for taking so much of your time with us. Since Brigetta will be up in Minneapolis for an undetermined time, I am glad she was able to spend time in the house."

"My pleasure. If you were able to stay longer, you would be able to meet more people than we saw in our brief tour, Bram, but there will be ample time later."

Waiting with them until they boarded the train, Doctor Gray told them of all Rochester offered its citizens. Brigetta's head spun with the description of the Mayo doctors' medical care, and the recitation of stores and shops, churches, restaurants and hotels, recreational activities and businesses in abundance.

The past two days had exhausted Brigetta's capacity for new and exciting things. She craved something familiar, and felt like a horse heading for the barn as she waited impatiently for the train to take them home.

Once seated on the train with Rochester disappearing behind them, Bram turned to Brigetta and asked, "Did you like the house?"

It was a perfectly normal question, but Brigetta's response was anything but expected: she said, "I loved it," and promptly burst into tears. Totally bewildered, Bram held her close and let her cry. The mournful whistle blowing at crossings matched her mood perfectly and she appeared to have no end of tears.

Eventually, her sobs subsided and she relaxed against him, falling asleep without explaining her emotional outburst. Bram searched his mind for anything in his innocent question that could have prompted the tears. Stumped, he leaned his head against hers and they slept soundly.

When they finally awakened, stiff and dry-mouthed, dawn was teasing the sky. New people slept on the opposite seats, which was startling in itself, since they had been unaware of the train stopping to discharge and pick up passengers during the night.

Bram walked through the swaying cars to the dining car and returned with a breakfast tray. Few words passed between them despite their minds overflowing with all that was new.

Since no one knew the time of their return, no one met them at the train depot. The stationmaster offered his buggy and Bram gratefully accepted, promising to return it promptly. They neared their farm just as the roosters crowed, and Bram halted the buggy at the edge of the road. Brigetta understood perfectly: they were seeing the farm through new eyes today. The garden seemed to have grown with wild abandon during their absence, the trees seemed more vivid in their race to acquire fall colors. And their small house seemed small indeed.

Brigetta drove their buggy back to the depot behind Bram in the stationmaster's buggy. She soaked up the everyday scenes, wondering how she could ever have taken them for granted. All too soon the familiar would be only memories.

They stopped by the parsonage on their way home, catching Gustave, Hanna, and *Tante* Lena still at the breakfast table. Lena filled two extra plates, and while they ate, Bram and Brigetta told abridged stories of what they had seen and done. "It was amazing to find a newspaper on the train, and then be able to interview for such a perfect job," Bram said.

"It sounds like a good place to learn many things, but I'm surprised you must move so quickly," Gustave said.

"They are harvesting crops, as we are here, and the Steward supervises the patients who work in the fields and gardens, so there is much to do. I will need all winter to get to know the patients who will work with me and to become familiar with the equipment and make plans for spring planting, and there are animals to care for all year long."

"But where will you live?" asked Hanna.

Brigetta attempted a description of the majestic house on the hill, managing to capture her own amazement at its spaciousness and instill the same sense of wonder in her listeners. "It reminds me of a park! There are trees and hills and creeks and meadows—it's beautiful!"

"We'll let you get settled, and then we'll have to take the train up to see you," Lena said.

Bram's fork clanged against his teeth and Brigetta spilled coffee across the eggs on her plate. They locked eyes; Bram recovered first. "I know we will look forward to your visit, but maybe you should wait to make such a long trip until spring when the crops will be coming up."

"Yes," Brigetta said quickly, "nothing shows the special Bram de Boer touch yet. But wait until spring, and that will change!" *What if they were to come when I am at the Thompson House?*

The weight of lies was growing heavy. Bram and Brigetta sat like pillars of stone in the buggy, giving the horse free rein. They found Rebecca washing up breakfast dishes. "Oh good! You're home! We thought we heard you earlier, but didn't see any signs of life at your house. Let me ring the bell and get Hans in to hear everything!"

"We borrowed the station master's buggy to get home, and had to return it. So you did hear us earlier," Bram explained.

When Hans joined them, they repeated the stories told at the parsonage, each account covering some things and omitting others. The timing of their move most affected Hans, and Bram could tell he was concerned about handling the farm alone. "We'll talk with some young fellows, first thing," Bram promised. "If they can come out now to start while I'm still around, I can show them the ropes."

"I have thought perhaps I'd take over selling from your vegetable wagon until the garden produce is gone," Rebecca said. "That will give us some extra money to pay the hired help, and we surely don't need so much for ourselves."

"What do you want to do about your cottage? What if someone we hire wants to live in it?" Hans asked.

Brigetta's head jerked up. *Someone else living in our house?* She quickly looked at Bram; he scratched his head. "I'll let you know tomorrow."

Back home, they faced each other across the kitchen table. "Bram, we have to think this through. We have made a commitment to the Rochester State Hospital for you to become their Steward. It will be spring when the baby is born. You cannot leave them in the spring—you will have to stay there at least throughout an entire year."

"That's why I've said we plan to be gone several years. Even when I didn't know where we would be going, I wanted to be fair to the person who hired me."

"I know—but we haven't talked about things like what to do with the house. Your parents could let a hired hand live in it, but I don't want to leave our things here for someone else to use. And that's moving a lot more to Rochester than we had thought about. We hardly have enough furniture to fill one floor of that house, even if we took every piece we own!"

"We'll bring out the boxes from your parents' buggy barn, and build more to pack anything else we want to take. I'll need your help to dig up tulip bulbs and pack them carefully, and you'll need my help to pack and lift our belongings. It is a big job, but we'll do it together. I'll make a list."

"I'll need to pack separately what I take to the Thompson House. It's better to pack it here than try to find things once we arrive in Rochester," she said woodenly. Bram nodded, unable to trust himself to speak.

After several trips in the buggy, the boxes from the parsonage were at the farm. *Tante* Lena contributed several fruit crates, and Hanna added another canvas bag on the last trip. Brigetta leaned down from the seat, and drew Hanna into a tight hug, releasing her just as tears threatened.

At the end of each day, Bram and Brigetta sat at the table with list in hand and checked off what they had accomplished. But Bram always thought of something else to do, so new items were added at the bottom. Inside the little house, cupboards and drawers emptied at a steady pace and the rooms echoed and looked bare.

Brigetta packed *Tante* Lena's satchel for her time at the Thompson House. She had little to pack—she had no time to make larger dresses. Tucked in among toiletries and clothing, Brigetta added several favorite books, her Bible and *Psalter*, the carved wooden skate wrapped in a handkerchief, a carefully wrapped bottle of ink, and writing paper and envelopes placed between the books. She purchased enough stamps for weekly letters to Bram.

The Ter Hoorn crates filled quickly. Afternoons and early evenings, Gustave, Hans and Bram sawed and hammered planks of wood to make more boxes, filling them as soon as they were completed. The women tied bedding and rugs and rags around each piece of furniture before the men nailed tables and chairs, china hutch and pie saver, bed and cedar chest into crates. Even the ill-fated dresser was secured in a box, and two bicycles filled another.

It was almost festive, working with the combined families to pack up the young de Boers and send them off to worlds unknown to those in Dutchville. Under any other circumstances, Brigetta would have been wild with delight.

The last Sunday, Brigetta sat in the pews at the Dutchville Reformed Church and heard her Papa preach, she wept silently in the pew. Gustave spoke of the Patriarch, Abraham, and his faith in God during hard times. Brigetta looked at her own Bram. *Does his faith falter like mine as we face the future?*

Unable to sing the *Psalmen* without sobbing, Brigetta stood with her hands hidden in the folds of her dress and pressed against the new life she carried in secret shame. Bram's voice, usually so rich and full, sounded hollow beside her throughout the singing. She wondered if their marriage—that sacred union begun within the walls of this church—could survive the terribleness of their decision.

Their last night on the farm was a somber time. Just before sundown, Bram and Brigetta walked around the property, lingering in the garden. Fresh-dug mounds evidenced where tulip bulbs had flourished. Filling his hands with rich soil, Bram held them out for Brigetta to inhale the earthy fragrance. "What if I can't get good results from Minnesota farmland?"

"When you succeed with different conditions, you prove you are as gifted a farmer as I know you to be." Bram let the earth sift through his fingers. The one place they didn't walk was behind the barn. They didn't need to see that spot again: the painful memory of the dastardly battle between brothers would never dim.

At last, there was nothing left to do. Their beds and bedding were packed in the many crates and boxes now lining the platform at the railway station, and Brigetta had cleaned the empty house until every corner sparkled. They walked across the yard to spend the night in Bram's old bedroom. Bram held Brigetta tenderly as she cried silently against his chest in the room where he had carved a little skate so long ago.

As her sobs faded and she fell asleep, he listened to the familiar nights noises of the farm that had been his home for his whole life. The wind in the trees, the night noises of birds and crickets, the creaking of the house—so many sounds, so many memories.

Their final day was spent visiting with family and friends, stopping by the bank to close out their account, and packing food for the trip and their first days in Rochester. As dusk began to descend upon Dutchville, seven people in two buggies rode in funereal formation to the railway station and formed a subdued group along the wooden platform.

At least three times, *Tante* Lena reminded Brigetta to check the jar of honey throughout the trip to be sure it wasn't leaking.

Hans mentioned twice that Bram would need to make sure all their boxes arrived, or immediately file a complaint.

Rebecca whispered in Brigetta's ear, "Here's just a little something to use to buy something pretty for your new house," and thrust a folded bill into Brigetta's hand.

Hanna tucked a clean handkerchief into Brigetta's pocket two different times, and each time said the same ten words: "Just in case you need a hanky on the train."

It was almost a relief to have the train pull into the station, spouting great dark clouds of choking smoke. Hugs and kisses all around, quick embraces and handshakes repeated, and then only five remained on the platform to wave as the train took their children to places unknown.

When the train rounded a curve and disappeared from sight, Gustave and Hans pulled out handkerchiefs and blew their noses loudly. Lena and Hanna turned toward Rebecca and the three women merged into a triangle of sad murmurings. It already felt odd, and they could still hear the train's whistle in the distance.

As night cloaked the countryside, quietness descended inside the train. Voices lowered, movement slowed, and passengers settled. Bram whispered, "I will hate to see you go." The tears in his eyes unnerved Brigetta.

They secured drayage at the Rochester depot to deliver the crates and boxes to the house on the hill. Bram paid two of the men to help him pry open the crates and carry furniture up the hill. Brigetta first found the box Hanna had wisely marked as containing bucket, soap, and rags. After filling a bucket of water at the pump, she began to wipe each shelf and drawer before putting dishes and linens in place.

"Hello?"

Brigetta blew a strand of hair away from her eyes. The kitchen doorway framed a stately woman with pitch-black hair and dancing eyes. Instantly, Brigetta was conscious of her everyday Dutch dress with its dirt-stained hem and soap-spotted bodice—so unlike the woman's crisp burgundy linen dress with its stylish cut and trim lines. She had never felt less attractive than she did before this unknown and dignified visitor with a feathery veiled hat and snowy gloves.

Belatedly remembering her manners, Brigetta snapped her jaw shut and wiped her hands on her apr0n. "Hello."

"You must be Mrs. de Boer. I am the official RSH welcoming party! I'm Mrs. Randolph Gray. My husband told me so much about you!"

"Please, won't you come in, Mrs. Gray? Yes, I'm Mrs. de Boer. Brigetta."

"I don't mean to impose on moving day, but I wanted you to know I took the liberty of asking the iceman to deliver a load of ice. He should be here soon." Without ceremony, she placed a covered dish on the counter. "I'm glad to have a chance to meet you before you leave for Minneapolis. My husband says your grandmother is gravely ill."

Brigetta nodded, avoiding her visitor's eyes, and peeked into the dish. "Thank you for bringing us supper. And for thinking of the ice."

A musical laugh trilled. "I have an ulterior motive. I've heard about the strawberries you have promised us! You certainly made an impression on my husband with your presentation of such fine vegetables. He examines everything I put on his plate now and says, 'I wonder what Bram's potatoes taste like?' or 'I imagine all Bram's green beans are long and succulent!' It has become quite interesting to have my meals so carefully analyzed!"

Brigetta walked Mrs. Gray to the porch, and then returned to face the boxes once again. When the bed was in place, Brigetta shook out familiar bedding and soon the bedroom seemed more like home. She then unpacked Bram's clothes, lingering over shirts she would not wash for many months, trousers she had mended over the past year, and handkerchiefs she had ironed weekly. She fled the bedroom in search of less emotional tasks.

She restricted her efforts to the essentials—it was important to have dishes unpacked and the pantry shelves lined with canned goods, but hanging pictures on the walls could wait. She wanted to position the limited furniture they had brought to make the rooms look fuller, but it wasn't necessary to unpack all the books. Even with limited activities, there was still much to do.

Near the end of the day, Bram went in search of a buggy he could use in the morning to take Brigetta to the train. While he was gone, Brigetta soaked in the familiar copper tub and tried to ease her aching muscles. Her head lolled back against the rim, and she stared at the unfamiliar ceiling. When she climbed out, she noticed the reflection of her feet and ankles. On impulse, she knelt and dropped the towel beside her.

Reflected back at her in coppery hues, she saw the gentle curves of the growing baby within her. Instinctively, she cupped her hands beneath the strange and slight protrusion of her body shaping itself to shelter a new life, and shut her eyes against the stabbing pain of realization. *It is real. I have not imagined anything—there is a real child growing within me.*

"Brigetta?" Bram's voice in the distance startled her from her reverie into action.

"I'm taking a bath," she called and hurriedly finished drying herself. It was a relief to allow her gown to enshroud the truth.

It was only as she lay in bed listening to Bram's gentle breathing close to her ear that she faced the fact that in all the days since she had told Bram she was pregnant, he had not once looked on her body in the light. At first, he had avoided seeing her by falling asleep quickly—this made all the more painful by the memories of delight on his face during all the other months of their marriage when he watched her undress each night in the lamp light. Those intimate moments ended the day of Cornelis and the closet.

For weeks, Bram didn't reach for Brigetta. But then had come the nights—always in the darkest hours—when he loved her with such fierceness it was as if he were pounding his anger into her softness. But there had been no more morning loving, no times of feasting their eyes on each other's bodies, no sharing caressing gazes as potent as touch. And now on this last night before their long separation, they simply clung to each other.

"Bram, my letters to Dutchville won't a have a Rochester postmark."

"Send them to me; I'll add a note before I mail them."

Brigetta nodded, her head bumping against Bram's chin. "Promise me—once we are together again, no more lying. Ever. About anything."

"I promise." He pulled her so close she could scarcely breath. They drifted into a dreamless sleep that offered little more than rest for their tired bodies.

Early the next morning, Bram swung *Tante* Lena's satchel into the buggy and turned to Brigetta. She wore a pale grayness like a second skin as she took Bram's hand and slowly brought it to her lips. She kissed each fingertip before nestling her chin against his palm. She lifted smoky blue eyes to him. "Hug me hard enough to last six months."

Bram drew her into the shelter of his arms. He traced the outline of her face with his chin and followed the lines of her body as far as he could reach. She stood perfectly still, absorbing his touch like fresh clay receiving the imprint of an artist's hand. Bram's lips carried all the longing of a groom. Brigetta's response gave back all the earnestness of a bride. It was a kiss that would march shoulder-to-shoulder with the lingering embrace across the lonely nights of the months ahead.

The buggy ride from the house on the hill to the depot was all too swift. The crowded platform at the Rochester depot did not lend itself to tender farewells or lingering embraces.

"Take care of yourself, Brigetta."

That was what you promised Papa you were going to do when we married—take care of me.

"Be sure to write."

Six months—oh, God, what have I done?

With the sound of the train whistle fading behind him, Bram headed east to the hospital. The morning sun blinded his eyes, giving him a reason for his tears. The closer he got, the more he slowed the horse—he was in no hurry to begin his life without Brigetta.

Brigetta sat alone on a seat for two on the train. Parting from Bram drained all her hidden resources of strength and fortitude. Their marriage rested on unstable ground and leaned dangerously in the prevailing winds.

October 1919

◆

After only two wrong turns, with helpful Minneapolis citizens setting her straight, Brigetta viewed the Thompson House from the same corner where she and Bram had stood. It looked no less foreboding today than it had been then. In fact, knowing the personality of the woman who awaited her arrival, Brigetta approached the front steps with a churning stomach.

Just as she was about to lift the knocker a second time, the door opened and Brigetta was face-to-face with a most remarkable sight: a bright-red pompadour above two sparkling gray eyes wobbled right at the level of Brigetta's chin. Brigetta's eyes widened and she felt a smile— a genuine smile—push itself from beneath her sadness up through layers of gloom to its vacated place on her face.

"Aren't you a pretty one—so nice and tall! This is the first of October, so you must be Brigetta! My sister has told me about you, and I've been eagerly awaiting your arrival. I'm so sorry I wasn't able to meet you the day you and your brother stopped by, but I was delivering the most amazing fellow—of course, I say that about them all."

"You are Miss Beal?"

The most glorious laugh erupted from the tiny woman. "Miss Beal, it is!" she chortled, and then dropped her voice to a stage whisper. "My sister always likes to rub it in she married, and I am still single. Of course,"

236

she confided, "if all husbands are like the departed Mister Thompson, I'd say I got the better deal of the two of us, if you know what I mean!"

Brigetta nodded, having not the slightest clue what Miss Beal did mean, but wanting desperately to please this delightful person. "Oh, I'm sure." *Why on earth would any man choose crusty Mrs. Thompson over the refreshing Miss Beal?*

"Let's go into the parlor before I show you to your room, and you can tell me all about yourself."

Brigetta felt a dead weight settle on her shoulders as they entered the room. *All about myself? Will I ever tell the true story of Brigetta again?*

She need not have worried—Miss Beal's interest in her centered solely on what she enjoyed, what foods she craved, her favorite things from a world almost forgotten over the past two months. "Tulips! I love tulips! Your brother must be an amazing fellow—so many men think flowers are silly!"

When Brigetta mentioned several unfamiliar Dutch dishes, Miss Beal clapped her hands delightedly and exclaimed, "Won't we have fun in the kitchen? My sister says I always leave a mess, but I do enjoy experimenting with new things. One night next week let's fix, what did you call it? *Stamppot*—it sounds wonderful!"

On and on they talked. Without realizing it, Brigetta relaxed and asked questions, and gave answers, and through it all, the room lost its power to haunt her. Miss Beal reached out and clasped her hands. "Brigetta, we are going to be dandy friends! Now, let me tell you a little about the girl who shares your room."

Brigetta caught her breath. *A roommate instead of a husband.*

"Sometimes roommates become quite friendly, and sometimes the girls find friends amongst the others in the house. Either way, there's always someone around when you want to visit. We all eat together, and you are paired with a different girl each week for tasks around the house and yard, and for when you leave the house. I'm sure my sister told you all the house rules." Brigetta looked up just in time to see Miss Beal roll her eyes heavenward.

"Yes, she did." Brigetta smothered a grin behind a fake cough.

"Aren't they dreadful? But, just like we need laws to live by in our town, we need rules here to make our lives easier. The girls are from many different backgrounds, and so rules just make life fair."

Explained that way, Brigetta did not feel quite so much like a noose was tightening around her throat. "I wish I could have met you that first day," she said pensively as they climbed the stairs.

"You have shown you're made of good stuff—you met my sister and came back anyway!"

Amazed at Miss Beal's honesty, Brigetta had little time to give it much thought before Miss Beal knocked on a door near the end of a long hall. "Missy? I've brought your new roommate!" For the first time in her life, Brigetta looked into the guarded eyes of an ebony-skinned girl. Face-to-face with a fragile girl who also carried a child she would not keep, Brigetta felt an instant kinship.

Miss Beal gently guided Brigetta into the room. "Since Missy has chosen the bed closest to the closet, your bed is next to the window." She chatted merrily above the unnatural stillness in the room. Having performed these initial introductions many times, she knew no matter the combination, there were awkward moments at the beginning.

"Missy, before I let you show Brigetta around the house, let's introduce her to the rest of the girls." Brigetta caught herself staring at the long dark fingers with their lighter tips, and mentally comparing the rich undertones of Missy's tightly-kinked hair to her own wispy locks.

In the kitchen where supper was underway, two girls halted a cheerful conversation as Miss Beal announced their names: Dolly and Etta. Brigetta attempted to assign clues to their identity: a funny giggle, long braids. Tall and thin except for a startlingly protruding stomach—was it Jan or Jean?

Out in the backyard, three girls took clothes off the line: Mattie so large she could not bend to pick up a dropped clothespin, and Tracey who laughingly helped her out, and Muriel whose face was so battered and bruised, Brigetta cringed inwardly. The encounter was made less awkward by Miss Beal's chatter about the apple tree and a birdbath needing cleaning. Brigetta had now met all her fellow inhabitants of the Thompson House. It was a motley collection, the common denominator being an unfortunate sexual encounter.

"Why don't you unpack now?" Miss Beal suggested, once again knowing just how necessary direction was during those crucial first hours. "Missy, will you please show Brigetta which drawers and shelves are hers?"

The satchel was soon empty, the few books arranged on the shelf, and the pitifully few garments tucked away in a drawer before Missy asked her first question. "When are you due?" Her voice had an intriguing musical lilt.

Despite the whole point of her being in this strange place was because of a pregnancy, the question startled Brigetta. "Uh, March."

"I'm due in January. So you'll have another girl in this room for your last two months. I've been here a month and you're my second roommate."

"Oh." Not even used to Missy, Brigetta could hardly comprehend sharing a room with another stranger before she returned to Bram.

"Just last week, two girls left, and so Muriel and Dolly took their places," Missy rambled on and on, watching Brigetta's every move. "Where are you from?" she asked abruptly.

"Iowa."

"Why did you come all the way to Minnesota? Do you have family here?"

Brigetta offered the tested lie: "Yes, my grandmother." She felt around the bottom of the satchel, her hand finding the final object in the bag: the carved skate.

"What's that?" Missy asked curiously.

Brigetta fought against the tears that blinded her. "A carving."

"May I see it?" Missy shifted off her bed to stand beside Brigetta.

Slowly Brigetta opened her hand. "I love to skate; Bram—my brother—carved this for me many years ago. It was probably silly to bring it along."

"Why not put it on the shelf over your bed? No one will touch it there, and you'll be able to see it every day. I put my special things on the shelf over my bed. Come, I'll show you."

They curled up on Missy's bed and Brigetta admired a glass-bead necklace, a tiny red corduroy purse with a button clasp, and a Bible with the name *James Wilford Sattick* engraved on the cover. "A church donated a box of left-behind Bibles to the Thompson House and Mrs. Thompson says I can have this one—it's the first book I've ever owned, so I don't care whose name is on it."

"Your first book?" Brigetta could not restrain her astonishment.

"I barely know how to read," Missy admitted without embarrassment, "so I really don't need books, but I like having a Bible."

"I love to read, Missy. I'll be glad to help you learn. How old are you?"

"Almost sixteen. My birthday is next month." Brigetta felt a sadness wash over her that took her breath away. *When I was sixteen, I was falling madly in love with Bram, not having a baby.*

"I brought several of my favorite books along with me: *Hans Brinker or The Silver Skates*, and *The Five Little Peppers*, and *Little Women*." She crossed back to her side of the room and pulled a book off the shelf. "We can start with this one—the 'Little Women' in the title are four sisters, and I have loved it since I was a little girl."

Missy looked doubtful, "It's an awfully fat book. I would hate to start and not get it finished before I leave here."

"That's months away! We'll not only finish this one, we'll read another—trust me."

"If you help me with my reading, how do I repay you?"

Brigetta was on the verge of saying nothing was required, but a quick glance at the proud thrust of her roommate's chin let her know this wasn't appropriate. "You can be my friend—it's hard for me to make friends when I'm…" She touched her gently rounded belly.

Missy threw her arms around Brigetta in a sincere hug. "Like Miss Beal will tell you over and over, God still loves you—don't let the bad things that have happened to you make you forget that. And you've got goodness in your heart, I can tell."

"I like Miss Beal," Brigetta said fervently, "I really do."

Missy dissolved in laughter. "Of course you do—everybody likes Miss Beal! Mrs. Thompson—now, she's another thing altogether. But, we figure if Miss Beal has put up with her for her whole life, we can put up with her for a couple of months."

Around the supper table, Brigetta bowed her head in thankfulness for much more than the food. Considering how she had dreaded coming back to the Thompson House, it was turning out to be an interesting segment of her life. Seven girls with a common crisis surrounded her. And she had found a solid anchor in a stormy sea: the unsinkable Miss Beal with her overflowing love and humor.

At evening devotions, Mrs. Thompson looked up sternly. "Who is humming when I'm reading from the Holy Scriptures?"

Brigetta's cheeks flamed. "I am, Mrs. Thompson, I'm sorry."

"I should hope so. To hum during Scripture reading—I've never heard tell of such sacrilege."

Brigetta bravely spoke up. "I beg your pardon, but I wasn't singing *during* Scripture—I was *singing* the Scripture. We Dutch sing the Psalms."

Miss Beal interjected before her sister could speak a word, "Sing it aloud for all to hear."

"I'm not sure if the English words would match the tune."

"We'd like to hear it in Dutch, wouldn't we, girls?"

Seven girls, who would have cut off their right thumbs for Miss Beal, agreed instantly. Scripture reading with Mrs. Thompson in charge was more than enough to turn a young lady away from God's love; Miss Beal welcomed any opportunity to remedy the problem.

Brigetta began to sing. When she reached the final words of the song Bram had sung to her just last night, she could not contain the tears rolling down her cheeks. Even though they understood not a single word, her audience leaned forward, caught up in the beauty of her pure voice and the mesmerizing music:

*Gij richt de tafel toe voor mijn aangezicht, tegenover mijn tegenpartijders…*Utter silence reigned as the last note faded. On that first night in October 1919, eight girls found comfort in the timeless words of the twenty-third Psalm—promises, assurances, and hope.

Only Mrs. Thompson sat with tight lips. Her authority was undermined: she had lost control of the Scripture reading. Her only recourse was to pray even longer than usual tonight. But even that was snatched away from her when Miss Beal suggested sweetly, "Brigetta, would you offer our evening prayers in Dutch?"

In Dutch? Mrs. Thompson looked sternly at her sister.

Miss Beal continued sweetly, but firmly, "It is most fitting to offer thanks to God in the same language as that beautiful song. We can all pray along with Brigetta in our hearts."

Brigetta closed her eyes against Mrs. Thompson's icy glare. *Dear God in* hemel…It was almost as if she were sitting around the table in the Dutchville parsonage once again; her burdens lightened with each word. Mrs. Thompson was not sure what Brigetta covered, but she grew uncomfortable when she recognized her name. She would have been aghast to understand Brigetta's fervent petition for patience to live with her for the next six months.

Twenty-four hours after having fallen asleep in Bram's arms, Brigetta lay awake in the stillness of the Thompson House. Even though missing Bram was like a brick on her chest, she felt safe here. Miles away from

Hadley Hoover

the man she had promised to love forever, Brigetta fell asleep with her locket pressed against her lips.

*   *   *

In the big lonely Rochester house, Bram stretched out his foot in search of Brigetta as he had so many times since that blissful May 1918 wedding night. It was an automatic reflex, but one without the usual results: there was no Brigetta beside him in this bed. He had sent her away, banished her from his life until she could come back without the baggage of a child not his own.

Bram nearly choked on his gulping sobs. He had to sit up to breathe; he dropped his head into his hands. Releasing emotions he had harbored since the day he fought with Cornelis, he cried until he had no more tears, but still he felt no release from his sorrow.

The next evening, he pushed away a half-empty supper plate. He pulled a lantern closer to him on the table and whittled a pencil to a fine point. At last, he pulled a sheet of paper and an envelope from Brigetta's stationery box and stared into the lamplight. If the letter reached Brigetta unopened, he wanted to tell her things she would like to know. But he didn't want to make life any more miserable for Brigetta than necessary if Mrs. Thompson read it first.

He attempted the easy part first: addressing the envelope. He had no sooner written *Mrs.* than he realized even the seemingly easy part was fraught with problems. He tried to erase the word, but nearly rubbed a hole. Rather than waste an otherwise perfectly good envelope, he changed it to *Mister and Mrs. Hans de Boer* and returned the envelope to the stationery box. He was more careful the second time: *Brigetta de Boer, The Thompson House, East Lake Street, Minneapolis Minnesota.*

He propped this envelope up against the lamp and stared at it. If all letters to Brigetta took this long, he would get nothing else done on letter-writing night.

Dear Brigetta,

I hope this letter finds you well. Did you have any difficulty in finding the house? I hope your satchel wasn't too heavy for you to carry.

There is a birds' nest on a knee joist outside the kitchen window. I hear the birds' evening song as I write. I have the door open to the back porch. It's almost as if the birds are singing the opening bar to "Shine On, Harvest Moon."

This evening, I began planting tulip bulbs. There is a thick ridge of limestone about a foot beneath the soil, so I hope it has not infused the ground with anything harmful to tulips. I know little about limestone, so we will see next spring.

Your brother, B r a m.

It was the first letter Bram had ever written to Brigetta. Just like the card he had sent her long ago, he did not sign off with full disclosure. But this time he filled in the blanks.

*   *   *

After breakfast the next day, Missy took Brigetta to the attic; the other girls joined them, chattering as they climbed the stairs. Brigetta's keen sense of her surroundings was in full play as her new friends sorted through an array of dresses and undergarments to find better-fitting clothing for her to wear.

Wires stretched from pillar to post, sagging beneath the weight of coats and dresses and out-of-season clothing. Several large wardrobes bulged, sleeves and stockings peeking out of drawers and doors. At least a dozen shelves lined one wall under the eaves, filled with dozens of pairs of shoes and boots, hats and umbrellas in various states of repair.

"Where do these clothes come from?" Brigetta asked.

"Churches and rich people and such…Not everything is useful," explained the girls, their voices mingling as all added tidbits: "Some things we give to a mission…If something needs cleaning, put it in this laundry basket...We divide what we keep into sizes...Make a stack of what needs mending..."

Within the first week of Brigetta's arrival, a wagon pulled up to the back door. The driver unloaded a dozen bags and boxes. "Shopping day, girls!" Dolly sang out, bringing a thundering herd from all corners of the house.

Brigetta looked at Missy curiously. They were washing breakfast dishes together and Missy flung her dishrag into the soapy water with a squeal of delight. "Come on, Brigetta!"

Even Mattie, whose labor had begun early in the morning, trudged up the stairs. Shopping day was too good to miss, and since Mrs. Thompson insisted on exercise every day, this filled the bill for Mattie. Seven girls rushed to the back porch and each carried something up to the attic.

Squeals of laughter, long and drawn-out whistles, *ooohs* and *ahhhs* erupted regularly from the girls huddled over the newly arrived goods. Tracey snatched up a hat with a lacy veil and clapped it on Brigetta's head, startling her. "What a fine lady you are, Miss Brigetta!" she said with a broad accent.

"Isn't she, though?" Jean bowed dramatically as if before royalty, her hand brushing the floor. "Oooh, someone help me up! I'm about to faint!" Those closest by hoisted Jean back to a standing position, and fanned her with a petticoat someone grabbed from a box. "I'm fine now, thanks, luvs. A word of advice—don't bow too low when you're eight months along!"

They all worked to sort the newly arrived items into piles determined solely by the size around the waist, a factor of great importance to all who would wear them in the future. As the morning ended, Brigetta was amazed to realize she had actually enjoyed herself—the girls formed a cocoon around her and she willingly nestled into it.

Mattie's baby was born just before midnight. Brigetta's jumbled dreams were jarred by sounds unlike anything she had heard before.

246 Rough Terrain

Mattie's seemingly endless cries in the night told of pain and anguish not soon to be forgotten. "Missy?" Brigetta whispered.

"It's okay," Missy said with wisdom beyond her years. "Mattie's baby is coming tonight. Miss Beal and Mrs. Thompson are with her. Just put your pillow over your head and try to sleep."

"Where will the baby stay?"

"The baby is only here a short time. The new families come right away."

"But what if there's no one who wants to adopt a baby?"

"There's always someone." Missy had doubts on this topic, but this was not the time to mention such.

Brigetta pulled the pillow around her ears and held it in place with hands clenched into fists. She felt bruised by the thoughts colliding in her pounding head. Even with the pillow firmly in place, she heard Mattie's anguished voice, "My baby! Please let me just hold my baby!" A low rumble of Miss Beal's gentle voice mingled with the mournful sobbing in the darkness.

"Will they let her hold the baby?" Brigetta asked in a tremulous voice.

"No; Mrs. Thompson says if we see the baby, we'll have a harder time forgetting."

A long silence followed. *Forget the baby? Forget the baby I will carry for nine months, the baby I feel moving within me?*

Brigetta rolled over on her side and faced Missy's bed. In the moonlit room, she could see Missy's rounded belly and two dark-skinned hands caressing the white-sheeted mound. No sounds came from that bed, just the gentle motions of a young mother who would all-too-soon cry out in the darkness of another night.

The next morning, Miss Beal appeared at the breakfast table without Mrs. Thompson. While Mrs. Thompson prepared the baby for the new parents to pick up, filling out paper work, and meeting them in the parlor, Miss Beal lingered over breakfast with the other girls, helping them through the fresh realization of what was ahead for them. Only when the parlor door closed would the day pick up its normal routines.

Passing around a large bowl of oatmeal with raisins, she pressed brown sugar and cream—two additional treats for these particular mornings—on each girl. "Mattie gave birth to a little girl who is already making her new family happy."

Brigetta leaned back in her chair. In all that had flooded her mind, little had centered on what awaited her baby. She was realizing that when she left the Thompson House, so would her baby—it would become part of another family, a family she would never meet. She didn't trust herself to linger on these thoughts and forced her attention back to the conversation around the table, a conversation kept active by an experienced Miss Beal.

A letter arrived addressed to Brigetta. At lunch, Mrs. Thompson held the letter between her thumb and forefinger as if fearful it would bite her. "Brigetta, this letter appears to be written by a man's hand. Did you not understand the house rules?"

Brigetta swallowed hard and looked Mrs. Thompson directly in the eye. "I'm quite sure it is from my brother, Bram. You met him when we came to inquire about a place for me here."

"How unusual, since you have brought shame upon your family, for your brother to write a letter."

"He has just begun work on a farm near Rochester. I am quite sure he is writing to tell me of his new job, since I will be going to live with him when I leave here. If you would like to read it, you may."

A frown creased Mrs. Thompson's forehead. It was an unexpected offer, and quite tempting.

Brigetta decided to fling herself into the fray. "I expect he will write to me on a fairly regular basis, and I will write back. I have brought sufficient stamps and stationery."

"This is most irregular…" Mrs. Thompson began.

"…but not without precedence," Miss Beal interjected. "If girls have family members who wish to write to them, it is a good thing. The rules of our house simply say friendships with male acquaintances must be halted while a girl lives here. We say nothing of severing family ties."

Though she had won a victory, she knew she walked a thin line. It would not take much for Mrs. Thompson to withdraw permission for Brigetta to receive or disperse mail. Still, she must warn Bram to be careful in what he said and how he said it. Just because today's letter was unopened did not mean others would escape a prying eye.

She accepted the letter from Mrs. Thompson and tucked it away in her pocket to read privately. By nightfall, she knew it by heart. She pressed it against her cheek, inhaling the imagined fragrance of Bram's own hand, kissing the flap he had licked to seal the envelope.

Up in their bedroom, Brigetta wished Missy would read more quickly during the daily session with *Little Women*. She exhibited great patience when her pupil wanted to review yesterday's toughest words. At last, the reading lesson ended. She waited until Missy fell asleep, and then she pulled a book off the shelf above her bed and used it as a writing tray. In the dim light of a lantern, she wrote her first letter to her husband.

Dear Bram,

I received your letter today. So many things have happened already I scarcely know where to begin. My roommate is Missy, a sixteen-year-old colored girl. We read Little Women *together each night to help her learn to read better.*

There is a wide assortment of donated clothing in many sizes. That is a great relief to me since I hardly need to collect such clothes.

A baby girl was born last night. This morning the new parents came to pick up the baby, and Mattie will stay here until she is able to travel home.

Except for hanging clothes on the line and raking, there is not much outside work. We help with meals, mending, cleaning the house, etc. I am the oldest one here.

I am enclosing a letter for our parents. This is a short letter to you, but it is late at night and I must save time for the other letters before I go to sleep.

Your sister, Brigetta

The letters to the two sets of parents were nearly identical. It was difficult to write convincingly about Rochester when she knew so little to say. She retold Bram's story of the birds' singing, hoping he could find other things to include in the section he added.

She mentioned an afternoon shower had sent her scurrying to bring in laundry from the clothesline. She told of making a cake for supper, omitting the fact that, with ten people around the table, it had only lasted one meal. Then, she closed with profuse and sincere proclamations of her love for them.

Over the next few weeks, discussions ranged from playful to informative to honest discussions of life as the girls knew it. Brigetta learned brothers, fathers and stepfathers, uncles, neighbors—all supposedly trustworthy relationships—had fathered the babies growing within the girls.

Only Etta had an unknown attacker; she had been alone in the barn when a tramp surprised her, and the sheer terror in her eyes as she recounted the event left no one doubting her story was true. Brigetta vowed never to repeat her story of an intruder again—to do so would make light of Etta's real horrors.

Muriel's bruises began to heal, but her spirit was still wounded. It was her second time here—both times the result of a drunken father sneaking into her bed while her mother railed at the girl for enticing him to her bed. In fact, Muriel's mother had waged the injuries. Brigetta felt a chill descend over her.

Soon, Jean's confinement arrived, but this time the baby was born mid-day. That night, Brigetta was paralyzed by the sound of a baby crying, a sound soon muffled, but heard nonetheless. "We'll have popcorn tonight," Missy whispered across the room. "We always do when babies cry at night."

250   Rough Terrain

A light tap on the door followed within minutes. "Girls, let's have a popcorn party!" Miss Beal whispered conspiratorially. Seven girls in nightgowns slipped into the kitchen. Soon, bowls and napkins and water glasses were in place and the girls pulled chairs around the familiar table.

"Have I ever told you about the time my sister and I scared our cook?" Miss Beal asked, fully aware that with her established set of stories devoted to just such times as this, no one around the table could possibly know this one. The schedule was carefully planned for specific months of the year and never changed, thus no story was ever repeated during a girl's stay at the home.

January's story was about when Miss Beal slipped on the icy steps of the courthouse and pretended to have fainted because she was so embarrassed. February's lively tale was of a train trip to Chicago when Miss Beal's seat companion drooled on her collar. And so it went throughout the year, all tales carefully executed with the intent to entertain, to divert attention from the drama around them, to make a despairing time less potent.

Miss Beal's story tonight recounted an event from childhood. She told of the young Beal sisters climbing out their bedroom window to perch on the roof. "We inched ever so carefully on our bellies along the shingles until we could peer over the edge into the kitchen below."

"Weren't you afraid?"

"At first, but I always wanted to do the same things my sister did, so I pretended to be brave! She whispered a plan to me, and we started giggling so hard I remember fearing I would fall off the roof into the rain barrel below! We scared our cook half to death with our solemn voices!"

"Whatever did you say, Miss Beal?"

"We leaned towards the open window and said in deep voices, 'Birdie, this is the Lord speaking: you're a good cook. I am well-pleased with you!' My goodness, that woman jumped high! For days she told everyone she met that God had spoken to her right through the kitchen window! And how his voice sounded echo-y, like two voices—'real holy-like,' she always added!"

Around the kitchen table in the late hours of the night, the girls sat wide-eyed at the thought of Mrs. Thompson on a roof. Miss Beal's spontaneous laughter swept them all into the safe net of her love for them. It was difficult to imagine Mrs. Thompson *ever* doing something so sacrilegious as pretending to be God, but Miss Beal put a human face on her ominous sister, helping the girls gain the trust they would need at the crucial time ahead: Mrs. Thompson would be the one who took their babies away, just as she had Jean's tonight, without allowing even a glimpse.

One day, Brigetta spotted a young girl standing disconsolately on the corner, looking up at the Thompson House with fear visible in every fiber of her body. In a flash, Brigetta detoured past the cleaning closet and snagged a dust rag on her way to the parlor; she carefully closed the door behind her. The doorknocker soon sounded and Brigetta could hear Mrs. Thompson's footfall on the stairs. "Yes?" the chilly voice queried, as if surprised to see a frightened girl on her steps.

Brigetta could barely hear the girl's voice, but she knew first-hand the impression that was burning itself on the girl's fragile spirit as she stood on the threshold. At the first inkling of a hand on the parlor doorknob, Brigetta began a flurry of dusting; her crystal-clear voice sent the first song that came to mind across the carpeted room: "*Reuben, Reuben, I've been thinking, what a fine world…*" until a gasp from the doorway interrupted her impromptu solo.

Had a brass band marched out of the wallpaper, Mrs. Thompson could not have been more stunned. "Brigetta! While I'm sure the sentiments of the song are appropriate to a girl in your condition, please refrain from singing secular songs in this house. Whatever are you doing in here?"

Brigetta spun around. "Why, hello!" Her ear-to-ear grin included both the tight-lipped woman and the shaking girl beside her. "I was rather distracted when I dusted in here yesterday, and my conscience wouldn't let me rest until I did the job right."

Brigetta raced across the room and flung her arms around the woman's spindly body. "I'm sorry to have startled you. I'll leave you to talk with our guest." Her dazzling smile accomplished her goal: one friendly face had been noted.

Mrs. Thompson sank into a chair, stared at the doorway after Brigetta's departure until she remembered the girl still standing in the shadows. "My goodness. Please have a seat. I am Mrs. Thompson..." And so began an interview with another in the parade of desperate young women who found their way to the Thompson House.

But this young girl saw a different person than the one who had frightened girls through the years—the Mrs. Thompson she saw was a most flustered woman, the recipient of all the zest for living that had enchanted everyone who ever met Brigetta before the episode with Cornelis and the closet. Brigetta had dared to cross a line in that woman's heart that only Miss Beal knew was drawn in sand, not set in stone.

✶   ✶   ✶

Dear Brigetta,

This is a fine farming operation. Many patients are able to assist in farm and garden chores as part of their work program. They are good workers, though they have bad days and then must be restrained or otherwise kept inside the hospital. But for the most part, each person I have met enjoys working with the crops or animals.

I have learned much about this institution by looking over the inventory just completed. By my next letter, I will have copied parts of it to help you know what I do each day.

I spent a pleasant evening with Doctor and Mrs. Gray. She cooked a good meal even though it wasn't at all like Dutch food. I hope I didn't bore them with talking about you as much as I did.

Your brother, Bram

*   *   *

Dear Bram,

I am quite glum today. I found some books in the collection here I have not read before, but they are certainly not entertaining. In fact, they are quite boring. I was glad to find a copy of Little Folks' Gems *like we have at home. Reading about Peter Rabbit and Jack and the Beanstalk and Hansel and Gretel makes me wish I were a child again.*

Your sister, Brigetta

*   *   *

Dear Brigetta,

I am glad you have activities and the girls to keep you occupied. If you wish to have other books to read, I will send them. I filled the back page of the letters you sent for our parents and mailed them this morning.

As I mentioned in my last letter, the full inventory of RSH covers nearly 200 pages. A two-page summary lists the contents which include real estate; provisions and groceries; household supplies; clothing; fuel and light; hospital and medical supplies; postage and telephone; stationery; library; supplies for instruction and amusement; scientific apparatus; material for manufactures; building and plumbing materials and supplies—each section contains explicit details.

Two additional areas most affect me: farm supplies and live stock (includes both purchased and raised farm products, greenhouse stock and supplies, horses and mules, cattle, hogs, poultry, and all other livestock), and machinery and tools (includes engines, dynamos and steam pumps, engineers' and plumbers' tools, wood-working machinery and carpenters' tools, agricultural machinery and tools, vehicles, and all other machinery and tools).

Each line is subtotaled and totaled and the bottom line is a staggering $1,342.013.53. As you know, I pride myself on keeping detailed records. It pleases me such is important in this job. I submit regular reports to Doctor Gray, and will send a copy each time to you.

Your brother, Bram

Bram spent days harvesting wheat. A horse-drawn reaper cut the grain and laid it on a platform. Two men, long-time patients at the hospital, hand-tied it into bundles they then set up in shocks. Dry bundles from an earlier harvest were then hauled back to the barn on wagons and set in cone-shaped stacks.

Then, they began corn husking. Upon learning of the day's work, one patient said the first words Bram had heard him utter in all their days of working together: "Corn husking is a long, tedious task." Bram found no argument with that. They started early in the morning before sun-up; stars still visibly lit the charcoal sky. The men ripped open the husks with pegs attached to their thumbs. Bram worked along side them, noting with approval that they worked steadily, breaking the corn at the shank and tossing it into a wagon, one ear at a time. Long and tedious summed up the days devoted to husking corn quite well.

Dear Doctor:

We put up about 120 loads of Reed Canary Hay. We shredded and picked up about 3,800 bushels of corn of very good quality.

The State Corn Husking Contest will be held in one of our fields on the last Saturday in October. We are leaving sufficient acres unharvested for this event. It will be a social event for patients and employees alike as we welcome others from around the state to our institution.

The turkeys have been accredited and bonded.

Sincerely, Bram de Boer, Steward

*   *   *

Dear Doctor:

Nearly 100 acres are plowed and put into winter wheat and rye. We are now shredding corn. We have shredded and picked up from fields 4,400 bushels. We finished digging potatoes and got 7,019 bushels. The carrots, beets, squash are out and the cabbage is almost all cut.

Sincerely, Bram de Boer, Steward

*   *   *

Dear Doctor,

We shredded corn all month and have plowed as fast as the ground was cleared. Shredded a total 10,665 bushels of corn of very best quality.

Wagons have been cleaned and repaired. Brooder houses are banked with straw to serve as laying houses during the winter. All cattle are looking good, though one bull has cut his hindquarter. We are swabbing against infection.

All late summer vegetables are in the cellar, and storage bins in the caves are loaded with apples and root vegetables.

Sincerely, Bram de Boer, Steward

November 1919—February 1920

◆

Dear Brigetta,

There is so much to tell you about this place, I scarcely know where to begin. Everyday I learn a little more that makes me proud to be associated with such fine people. A carved wooden plaque hanging inside the Administration Building sums up the philosophy of patient care: Honesty, compassion, searching. I find those traits evident in practice, not just in theory.

There is another fine hospital in Rochester, Saint Marys Hospital; Catholic sisters run it. They work closely with the Doctors Mayo and their fellow physicians. Surgeries are performed here for all six state hospitals, and done by surgeons affiliated with the Mayos, as well as those doctors themselves.

I actually have little to do with the hospitalized patients. The patients I see help out on the 880 farm acres RSH owns and the 440 acres we rent.

All patients receive good care, good food, and what Doctor Gray calls physical hygiene—which is where I come in. It simply means meaningful work to do. The School of Nursing on the grounds supplies nurses to provide patient care. There is also a school for children. Since patients stay a long time, child residents are thus able to keep up with their classmates back home.

There are many things for patients to do in addition to the work program required of all who are able—a fine music program and there are many sporting events, such as softball games.

Your brother, Bram

P.S. I purchased several things at an auction. I will write about one in each letter until you know them all—except for one piece I will keep as a special surprise. Here is this letter's revelation: Mrs. Gray helped me bid on a large mirror I hung on the dining room wall to the right of your corner china hutch. It is quite handsome with its walnut frame.

*   *   *

Dear Bram,

An auction! The mirror sounds lovely. I can hardly wait to see the surprise!

Missy turned sixteen this week. Do you remember when I was sixteen? I decided to give her a birthday party. Miss Beal was quite willing, but Mrs. Thompson showed her usual disapproval of anything not according to normal procedures! When Missy and Dolly accompanied Mrs. Thompson to market, the rest of us baked a chocolate cake with brown-sugar frosting, and decorated the dining room with ribbons and feathers and other such finery from the donation boxes.

I have many happy birthday memories from my childhood, but several girls are still in their childhoods—with happy times few and far between, I fear. Missy was so surprised she burst into tears. She never had a birthday party before—can you imagine? She adores all our gifts: a pin-cushion to tie around her wrist, a button jar filled with buttons from donated clothing that is only good for rags, an autograph book, and a beaded headband. It was great fun and gave us all a lift.

I think of you often, and wait impatiently for the mail every Tuesday.

Your sister, Brigetta

P.S. The letters from our parents make me homesick, but I read them over and over.

*   *   *   **

Dear Brigetta,

Missy is to be envied for having you for her roommate. I am proud of you for reaching out to others when your heart is heavy. I have made some friends among the employees. Some are male nurses. The hospital is a fair employer for the nurses, paying from twelve to eighteen dollars per month, with room and laundry provided. Their working hours are from 5:30 am until 9:00 pm, with exception of two half-days off each month, two Sundays off each month, and two evenings off each week. I play checkers with the men, though my schedule, as is usual for farmers, is governed more by the weather than the clock.

I'm not sure what you recall about the buildings on the hospital property, but I find them intriguing. The Administration Building is the most ornate, with a columned porch out front and topped with a cupola. The wings of the building are where the inmates reside. These are so starkly different from the hub as to appear almost like separate buildings. They stick out from the center like several spokes of a wheel and have bare walls with windows running along their full length. The windows of the patients' rooms are spaced in regular and exact sequences, giving a repetitious appearance, floor after floor.

When I asked Doctor Gray the reason for the contrasts, he explained how the precise uniformity matches the philosophy of bringing steady discipline to the lives of the insane. He said even the housing is an important part of their treatment. Such careful planning truly defines this institution.

Your brother, Bram

P.S. I am writing in the light of a ruby-red 25-inch-high banquet lamp. Mrs. Gray said a similar one in the Sears catalog costs $5.90, but I paid not even half that price. While not an auction purchase, I have added something *else to the household—this addition has a name, even though he does not yet know it: I call him Chum.*

*   *   *

Dear Bram,

Oh, is Chum a dog? How I wish we had a dog here—often the girls are so sad, and to sit with a dog close at hand is one of life's great comforts! If Chum is not a dog, then I am sure he is something equally wonderful to earn that name.

I have been worrying so about the fee we must pay. I was glad to learn the Rochester State Hospital pays such good wages.

There are several new girls now. Miss Beal says I am a rare case, arriving so early in my pregnancy. Sometimes our secret is too much to bear, Bram—it would be so wonderful to be able to talk over all my troubles with someone (especially someone as kind as Miss Beal) but I keep it all inside. A girl named Louise has come in Tracey's place and she cries long into the night; sometimes there's just no comfort to be had.

I am relieved to tell you I am finally able to keep all my food down. In fact, I have a healthy appetite, and am getting quite plump. Hug Chum for me, if he is a dog.

Your sister, Brigetta

*   *   *

Dear Brigetta,

As you can see from the letter I enclose, Father and Mother are quite impressed with all I've told them, so I hope my letters don't bore you. I am learning much.

Not only is the patient care remarkable; the farming activities are equally impressive to a farm boy from Iowa. For instance, each day we collect 1500 quarts of milk from our own herd of nearly one hundred registered Holsteins and other milk cows.

The cook says kitchen workers prepare 45,000 gallons of vegetables each year, and even 7,000 pounds of rhubarb! While I was talking with her, I could smell bread baking; she said they bake 400 loaves daily! She cut the heels from a loaf just coming out of the oven, like we used to do; it was so hot I could hardly hold it. I miss you, Brigetta. Sometimes even happy memories make me morbid.

I also learned the laundry processes 7,300 pounds daily, and seamstresses make 24,000 items each year. I know you always hated the chicken coop with those birds flying in your face and pecking at your hands. There is a flock of 2,000 hens here: that means lots of eggs, and beaks pecking away! And then there are the turkeys—we raise enough to meet our needs, and also to ship off to the other state hospitals for their holiday dinners. Oh, I almost forgot: there are also five ducks and seven geese!

This week some employees will play for a dance for the patients. They asked me if I play an instrument, but I told them I only sing. They want me to sing at the Christmas concert, and said Mrs. Gray can accompany me. Do you recall which box contains sheet music? (There are still many boxes to unpack—I put them upstairs until you are home) Or can you suggest a song and I can ask Mrs. Gray if she has music for it? I wish you and I could sing a duet.

Your brother, Bram and his friend, Chum

P.S. Can you hear that creaking? Oh, I imagine it must be your new rocker! It has a tooled leather seat and fancy carving above the spindles.

*   *   *

Dear Bram and Chum,

Oh, Bram, I dearly love a rocker when I sit to read. All my sheet music is packed with the Christmas decorations. Promise me you'll decorate the house so you can tell our parents in your letters about how pretty it looks.

We cut out blocks for four single-bed quilts. We even have flannel to line them: we cut up dozens of pairs of child-sized red Union Suits (what a silly contribution!) and are sewing them together to make quilt linings. We have an Edgemere sewing machine that is quite fine. Mrs. Thompson says everyone can afford one now, but I couldn't tell her that doesn't include a Dominie's family!

As always, while we work, we chatter away. I have lived a very sheltered life, Bram. The stories from these girls break my heart—I have had just the one tragic experience; some of them live lives of utter horror, and find this place to be the best part of their lives thus far. Here, they get three meals a day, share a room with only one other person—and have a bed all to themselves—and for the time they are here, no man who is tormenting them to do wicked things.

Are you getting enough to eat? I am glad you have at least one meal a day at the hospital, but please be sure to get a good breakfast. I would hate to find you withered away—how ever would we explain that to our parents?

Your sister, Brigetta

*   *   *

Dear Brigetta,

Your idea about decorating the house is a good one—it is quite dismal around here without all your pretty touches. I have asked if a group of patients can come hang greenery as part of their activities. I will personally take responsibility, after they have been here, to hang a few of the decorations you made.

Fieldwork is at a standstill with winter setting in. I am learning about the property so when spring arrives I will have decided what to plant in which field. The farmland is split up, somewhat. On the northwest, there are nearly 160 acres, then another 70 acres to the west, and 32 acres to the south, and almost 300 acres to the northeast, with the largest portion: 400

262 Rough Terrain

acres, also to the northeast. The value of the land alone is $88,105! In addition to all this, we rent even more farmland, bringing the total under my care to 1240 acres.

Your brother, Bram.

*   *   *

Dear Bram,

You forgot to tell me about an auction purchase in your last letter. Your life is so busy—you and I are growing apart, despite our letters. Sometimes I have trouble remembering what your voice sounds like.

Last night I dreamed that I saw Papa and Mama walking in front of the house. When I called out to them, they looked up and saw my big belly and kept on walking.

Do you still pray, Bram?

Your sister, Brigetta

P.S. What does Chum eat?

*   *   *

Dear Brigetta,

Writing letters is most unsatisfying, though receiving them makes a day worthwhile. Yes, I pray—for you, for us.

I haven't told you much about the buildings. Many are known by their functions: the boiler house, machine shop, laundry, store rooms, east and west barns, blacksmith and carpenter shops, cold storage plant, fire hall, lumber shed, greenhouse and greenhouse frames, straw shed, east and west hog houses, slaughter house, soap house, paint shop, ice house, cow, sheep, and horse barns, granary, chicken and hen houses, wagon shed, silo, the scale and oil houses—and several others I have yet to determine.

To accomplish all the farm work, there are twenty-eight workhorses, with other horses as well: two dray horses, four mules, two driving horses, and several colts. As you can tell from the listing of buildings, other livestock abounds. We currently have nine bulls, twenty cows, ten heifers, and eight calves—all full-blooded. Plus, over one hundred head of cattle, twenty heifers, and two dozen calves at grade. The hog barns are full: nearly fifty brood sows, eighty-eight shoats, well over two hundred pigs and two boars.

I ripped a large hole in the sleeve of my work shirt today; it caught on a nail. I will ask the seamstresses to mend it. I wish you were here—and not only to keep my clothes in good repair.

Your brother, Bram

P.S. I am happy to announce our dining room table survived the trip home from the auction without a single scratch. It will seat ten people with all the leaves in. Chum? He eats whatever I give him.

*   *   *

Dear Bram,

Have you noticed one of your old shirts is missing? When I packed, I buried it in the bottom of my satchel like a silly schoolgirl. Just smelling it reminds me of you. I will use it as a pattern to make you several shirts from the dry goods I brought from home. I tell you only because I do not want you to purchase new shirts when I can make them—we must save our money.

How wonderful to have a new dining room table! Now we must find ten chairs and then invite ten people to sit in them and celebrate such a delightful surprise.

Missy has grown quite cumbersome. Lately, she has been crying a lot and when she finally told me why, it broke my heart. She is desperately afraid no one will want to adopt a colored baby. I didn't know what to tell her, so I talked to Miss Beal. She says if there are no adoptive families, the babies go to an orphanage.

I miss you dearly—oh, I already said that: it's true and worth repeating. I miss you dearly, I miss you dearly. I miss you dearly. I miss you dearly. (How brave I feel!)

Your sister (maybe not so brave after all), Brigetta

✶   ✶   ✶

Dear Brigetta,

I had wondered what happened to that shirt, but can think of no better place for it to be than with you—to use as a pattern, I mean. I am surrounded with reminders of you, and do not consider you silly. I will appreciate the new shirts. It is a bitterly cold night, so I will write you a long letter by the fire.

I am pleased with the equipment here: a threshing separator, a tractor, a corn harvester, a mowing machine, a silage cutter, at least two dozen plows of various types and a dozen harrows. For the potatoes alone, there is a potato planter, digger, and two sorters! For the corn, there are two planters and shellers.

One building is filled with tools and equipment to make a farmer's work easier: sprayers, seeders, scythes, swaths, rakes, hoes and spare handles, shovels, forks and rope for haying, three-tine forks, four-tine forks for manure spreading, axes, spades and spare handles, picks, wenches and chains and pulleys, several grind stones, and hand tools for the garden such as knives and sprayers.

An equally impressive amount of equipment is devoted to animal husbandry: dehorning saws, bull rings, ear punches and tags, neck yokes and rings, feed ropes, hoof nippers, branding irons, and sow clamps, harnesses for various needs—and bells, whips, sweat pads, bridle bits, snaps, curry combs, horse brushes, fly nets—all to keep the hard-working horses in good shape and performing well.

But we also have machinery (such as a Nilson tractor) that would gladden Cornelis' heart—and it requires gasoline, oil, transmission grease, and axel grease—again, a lengthy list all accounted for. I am practicing driving in the barns over the winter so I will be competent, come spring. I am not sure how hearing this will make you feel, but it is becoming easier for me to think of Cornelis without such anger as I have had until now. But I am still not able to forgive him.

According to the inventory, we have 3,000 wooden berry boxes that must be saved from year-to-year, and 150 crates—my berry patch seemed large until I saw these numbers! There are fruit trees in abundance, too, as evidenced by hundreds of apple boxes. Hopefully, the apple trees at the base of the hill in front of our house will produce enough to fill the fruit cellar. I miss Dutch cooking.

Someone each year must count gunnysacks—the total is 1,000—and grain sacks—a mere 250—and 1,000 vegetable crates (can you imagine filling that many at one time from the garden back home?) Even the blacksmith accounts for his aprons (two) and he is kept quite busy because there are numerous wagons and buggies, with wagon tongues, spokes, and wheels of several sizes, wagon rims and reaches appear on the inventory list, as well. You will be happy to know I've seen sleigh runners and shoes (seven sets of each) so we will be able to enjoy a sleigh ride together next winter.

Because the hospital is state-owned property, the inventory covers items others would not think worth counting: large and small pictures, towel racks, room-dividing screens, settees and benches, the barber's chair, large and small card tables, wardrobes, window shades, wastebaskets, clocks, curtains, dresser scarves, towels of all types, linen napkins and tablecloths, mirrors, plant pedestals, footstools, large and small rugs—all are tallied every year! It is overwhelming, especially when I come home to our big empty house.

Your brother, Bram

266   R o u g h   T e r r a i n

P.S. Well, not as empty as when you last saw it. The six chairs that came with the dining room table fill floor space in one room! With the four kitchen chairs, we have ten chairs.

✶   ✶   ✶

Dear Bram,

Missy and I finished Hans Brinker. Now she is worried we won't finish The Five Little Peppers! So each night, she reads one chapter aloud to me, and I read two to her. The race is on since Miss Beal expects Missy's baby will be born earlier than first thought.

I knew it! I guessed you had separated the news of the chairs from the news of the table. I'm just glad you didn't tell me about one chair at a time for the next six weeks!

Making presents for Missy's birthday motivated the others to make gifts for Christmas! I am using scraps from the shirts I am sewing for you to make sachets for everyone. I had cut mint and some late herb from the backyard here and kept it in my drawer because it smelled so pretty, but have plenty to share with the others.

A donation box had a pair of frilly curtains that Miss Beal said I could have, and she didn't ask why! I am making aprons for Miss Beal and Mrs. Thompson, our mothers and Tante Lena. I am quite sure no one will know their fancy aprons used to be frayed curtains! I wish I had embroidery thread to make them even prettier. Perhaps you can make something for our fathers. I will send the aprons for you to mail home in time for Christmas, even though we have missed Sinterklaas.

Last night I dreamed about us skating. I could even hear the musicians. When I woke up I was surprised not to be wearing my skating shoes.

Do you still feel like a Dutchman? I, also, miss Dutch food, but even more than that I miss the Dutch services at church. Do you go to church, Bram?

I am tired of being apart. I am tired of being pregnant and not able to see my feet. I am tired of talking only to girls. I am tired of writing lies to our parents. I am tired of the noisy city.

Your sister, Brigetta

*   *   *   **

Dear Doctor,

Finished shredding 13,035 bushels of corn that was very dry. Manure is all hauled out on the fields. We have cleaned up a large amount of the dead and down wood. Have cut about 21,000 willow cuttings for use around the property. Livestock are in good condition. Cows are coming up on their milk.

Sincerely, Bram de Boer, Steward

**   *   **

Dear Bram,

Thank you for the embroidery thread! It arrived the day before I sent the box. I stayed up very late embroidering three little flowers on the pockets. I have almost finished the aprons for Mrs. Thompson and Miss Beal.

Since I only had postage enough for one box, I also sent the shirts I made for you. I am sorry they are not wrapped; they are a belated Sinterklaas present from me to you. Your gift of bookends for our fathers was a marvelous idea. Your drawing helped me "see" them.

I saw my silhouette in a shop window this week and was quite startled. I had known I am getting quite large, since I have visited the attic several times to select bigger dresses, but it was still quite a shock. I can no longer sleep on my stomach, and now see my puffy ankles only when I sit down and stick my feet out.

I have been feeling quite glum lately. Even making the presents has not been able to cheer me up. Miss Beal says it is common for pregnancy to affect a woman's moods, and I shouldn't be worried. But there is much

268   Rough Terrain

more than the pregnancy lingering in my mind and haunting me in the night.

I wonder what we will be like when we are together again. So much has happened that we have not shared. Sometimes I feel as if your letters are coming from a stranger. I am more than lonesome and sad; I am troubled that God no longer hears my prayers.

I hope Chum brings you more Christmas joy than this letter from…
Your sister, Brigetta

            *   *   *

Dear Doctor,
We have put up 2,300 loads of ice hauled from Silver Lake. The manure is all hauled out and spread over the snow on the fields. We have hauled hay and have been sawing and picking up, the wood we cleared earlier. We have been shelling and grading seed corn, grinding feed for the dairy herd and feeders. The cattle are looking fine.

Sincerely, Bram de Boer, Steward

P.S. Brigetta, there are no more auction items. I am working long days getting the ice into the caves, so cannot stay awake to write more; even my report to Doctor Gray is short this week. Miss Beal's explanation of your moods fits why you feel the way you do. There is no Dutch Reformed Church here; I go to church, though not always the same one. I, too, miss Dutch services.

            *   *   *

Dear Bram,
Missy had a baby girl on New Year's Day. We didn't hear anyone come to the front door during lunch when Miss Beal sat with us around the table and we assumed Mrs. Thompson was meeting new parents. But soon, Mrs. Thompson came in the back door, stomping snow off her boots. She must have taken Missy's baby to the orphanage.

Missy is napping while I write this to you. I offered to read all three chapters to her, but she just turned away. She is acting much like Mama did—withdrawn, depressed, and more like a rag doll than a person. It is quite worrisome to me.

I cannot think of anything cheerful to tell you tonight, except let's hope for renewed happiness in 1920.

Your sister, Brigetta

         *   *   *

Dear Brigetta,

Today I shoveled snow off the roof since we had two heavy snowfalls and I was worried about the load, especially over the porches. I also attached a log to a chain and dragged it behind a wagon up and down the path several times to clear the way. It was hard going, even for two of the strongest horses, because of a layer of ice beneath the snow.

As you can see by the enclosed letters, all our gifts to our families were much appreciated. Thank you for the shirts; they fit well. I'm saving my gift to you for when you come home.

Your brother, Bram

         *   *   *

Dear Bram,

Since I had nothing newsy to tell you, I didn't write last week. There is not much more to tell this week, other than I have another roommate, Karen. The father of her child is her uncle, and she's not sure if her baby is due in March or April, since her uncle stayed with them for several months.

I cannot believe all that fills my mind living here. Stories like Karen's, thoughts of all that could happen to the babies we give birth to, worries about how things are changing between us, dread for seeing people after this is all over and wondering if they'll be able to tell I am not—nor can I ever be—the same person again. Try as I might, I cannot always remember your face. And your old shirt no longer carries your smells, even in my imagination.

Your sister, Brigetta

*   *   *

Dear Bram,

When I looked in the hallway mirror this morning, I hardly recognized myself—my face is puffy, my hair is lifeless, and I have grown quite large in my behind, as well as in front. When I sit too long, I have trouble breathing. It is as if the baby is pushing against my lungs, and often kicks me something fierce.

I am angry with Cornelis for everything he has done, and angry with you for why we must be apart, and angry with God for ignoring my prayers. But since this letter is to you and not Cornelis or God, I will tell you I feel you have been unnecessarily harsh in your decisions. If you are lonely, then I say, "Good." You have brought it on yourself. You have banished me to a far away place and I do not know how we can recover from this.

Before, I trusted you, and believed our vows were sacred. Now, I see you are a cruel person; I do not know if I can ever trust you again. You obviously did not view our vows in the same light as I did. From all the stories the other girls tell about men they know, you have many good traits, but sending me here did not demonstrate them.

Your sister (and even that is more than you deserve), Brigetta

*   *   *

Dear Bram,

Please forgive me. I was upset. I was on the staircase when I shouldn't have been, and saw a baby going out the door with the new parents. Please rip that letter to shreds and then burn each and every little piece. While it was how I felt at the time, I do not hate you or God.

This baby is the only one I will ever have, and I must give it up. I know it would always stand between us to have the child in our lives, and I want more than anything to return to you and rebuild our lives together. But, oh, sometimes I want this baby, too.

Repentantly, Brigetta

         *   *   *

Dear Brigetta,

Your words were honest and well deserved. You said nothing about me I have not felt about myself, over and over again. There are many things I would undo if I could, beginning with Cornelis and the closet, but mainly things I said, the way I didn't listen to you, how I didn't seek advice from others because I thought we needed to handle this ourselves—the list is endless and frightening. I pray for God to forgive me, but I, too, feel the doors of heaven are closed to my petitions.

Do not give up hope. We will be together soon.

Your brother, Bram

         *   *   *

Dear Bram,

I am sorry I have not written. I caught cold somehow and have been sick in bed for two weeks, getting up only as necessary. Two girls (Muriel and Karen) had their babies since I last wrote, and we have three new girls. Kathleen is my third roommate now, taking Karen's place. I'm sure you aren't able to keep track of all these girls, but they fill my life and there's not much else to tell you.

Miss Beal has made me chicken broth and milk toast while I've been sick. Nothing tastes good, but I force myself to eat, especially when she reminds me if I don't eat, the baby suffers, too.

To entertain me, the girls made up a visitation schedule. Each spends an hour every day with me. It makes the time pass more quickly, and I have had interesting conversations with the girls.

Everyone believes I am loaded with words of wisdom and advice for them, like a big sister. If they only realized how ill-prepared I am—most of them are much more worldly-wise than I am or ever want to be.

I am propped up against the headboard of my bed to write this and am feeling rather dizzy. I have not been up this long for quite a while. I will try not to miss a letter again.

Your sister, Brigetta

*

Dear Mister Bram de Boer:

I am writing to tell you your sister, Brigetta de Boer, had a baby boy born February 20. Brigetta is weak, and Miss Beal is worried, we can tell. Brigetta asked me to write to you (since I am her roommate and have good penmanship) to tell you she will be fine. (If she does go to a hospital, I will use my own stamp and write you. That's just me telling you that part, not Brigetta.)

Even though the baby was born early, Miss Beal says he was in good health. Miss Beal says the new family can afford good care for the baby. Mrs. Thompson will let Brigetta stay here until she is stronger. Brigetta says she will take the train to Rochester as soon as she is able, and you are not to worry. I will miss her because she is one of the nicest people I have ever met. (That's just me telling you that. Brigetta didn't tell me to say that part.)

Sincerely, Kathleen Agatha Williams

Age 14. Minneapolis, Minnesota

In the big house on the hill, the Steward of the Rochester State Hospital sat at the kitchen table clutching the letter from young Miss Williams in his hands and sobbed inconsolably.

March—May 1920

◆

"Sir?"

Doctor Gray turned in his chair to face the doorway to his office. "Hello, Bram! You look troubled—is there a problem?"

"I would like to request two days off to go to Minneapolis and bring my wife home. Her grandmother passed away this week and I got the letter today, too late to catch the train. If I may take tomorrow and the next day, I will be back by Friday. One of the men will take care of Chum."

"Let's make it Monday. You've been separated from your wife for quite a while. Besides, you've taken little time off since you've started— we'll just figure this time to count against all that you've accumulated. We'll count one day away for the funeral, and two days to reunite with the lovely Mrs. de Boer, and consider this your monthly weekend off."

Bram made short work of his thanks and fled the office, sickened by the deception and edgy from loss of sleep the previous night. Except for the lack of full disclosure on his part, Bram and Doctor Gray had grown to like and respect each other. *But this is it—the lies must end.*

In the morning, Bram leaned back against the seat in the train heading north and let his mind wander. In the six months since his first ride along these tracks, life had radically changed, some for the good, some for the bad. The good was definitely the opportunity to work as Steward at the Rochester State Hospital; the bad was just as decidedly the chips and cracks and gouges in his marriage, the stains on his character and his weakened relationship with God.

Bram de Boer, Steward, was a rip-snorting success. Bram de Boer, husband and man, was a dismal failure. Even though she had followed up her angry letter with an apology, Bram knew every accusation was justified. But he would set things right. Once he and Brigetta were together again, they would be like newlyweds.

By noon, Bram walked along the streets of Minneapolis toward the neighborhood that had been Brigetta's home all these months. When he reached the corner where he and Brigetta had stood that September day, he stared at the house and felt bile rise at the thought of self-righteous Mrs. Thompson.

When he rang the bell, he wondered if its strident tones reached up into Brigetta's room. Almost immediately, the door swung open, and he looked into a smiling face. "Miss Beal?"

The woman looked surprised, taking a closer look at this stranger who knew her by sight. "Yes?"

"I'm Bram de Boer, Brigetta's…brother."

Instantly, Miss Beal stepped aside, and ushered him in. "Hello! We're awaiting an adoptive family, and when I saw a man alone, it took me by surprise. My sister is completing paperwork in the parlor, or she would have gotten the door. Have you had lunch yet, Mister de Boer?"

"No, I haven't, but I don't want to take any more of your time than I must. I've come to take Brigetta home."

"A man has to eat and Brigetta is just finishing her tray now. So let's get you some lunch, too."

They reached the kitchen doorway; Bram was taken aback by what appeared to be a roomful of girls, all in various stages of pregnancy. Their lively conversations fizzled. "Girls, this is Mister Bram de Boer. He has come to take Brigetta home with him. Kathleen, is there any more soup in the pot?"

Bram looked with interest at the girl who had written him the letter. She nearly tripped over the leg of a chair on her way to the stove since she paid more attention to this mystery-laden stranger in the kitchen than to her steps.

Another girl pointed to an empty chair, "That's where Brigetta sits. You can sit there while you eat your soup. Would you like bread pudding, too?"

Bram nodded and bowed his head in prayer, fully aware of watchful eyes. He picked up the soupspoon. Never had the simple task of eating a bowl of soup been so difficult for him or interesting to the girls. All conversation ceased; the awkward silence was loaded with unvoiced questions.

"Please tell me your names," Bram said, hoping to divert some attention. A jumble of voices obscured each proffered name and everyone laughed. Kathleen appointed herself the leader since, as Brigetta's roommate, she had earned special privileges. Starting to her right, she rattled off the names, and Bram nodded to the girls in turn.

Miss Beal returned bearing a tray with little food eaten. It didn't bode well for a strong Brigetta if she regularly sent back that much food. "I told Brigetta you are here, and she was quite surprised, but she has asked for Kathleen to help her pack." Kathleen straightened her shoulders proudly and left with head held high.

The doorknocker sounded, and all the girls looked at Miss Beal expectantly. She dropped into another empty chair. "Mrs. Thompson will get that, and while Mister de Boer is waiting for Brigetta to get all packed up, I'll tell you the story I promised you of how I learned to ride a bicycle."

Only Bram thought it odd to introduce a story into the chain of events; the girls took it in stride, in fact seemed to expect it. Miss Beal's tale was entertaining, and she was a masterful storyteller. Soon, even Bram blocked out the sounds outside the kitchen.

When Miss Beal swung her chair around, each person in the room saw not a curved-back kitchen chair but rather a bicycle intent on undermining a young rider's best intentions. And when she clutched the chair's back and rocked it in demonstration of how she had wobbled down the street, each person felt their world tilt, too. And with her retelling of landing in a bramble bush, not once, but twice in the same day, Bram could have sworn he felt prickles digging into his arms and face.

She ended the hilarious account with her efforts to keep her ankles out of a nippy little dog's mouth while pedaling to escape him. Listening, Bram knew Brigetta had told the truth about this marvelous woman.

Miss Beal said, "And that's how I learned to ride a bicycle—isn't it a wonder I did? When warmer weather comes, you'll see I'm quite accomplished!"

Suddenly, the kitchen door swung open, held in place by Kathleen who not only supported Brigetta but also carried the familiar satchel. Outwardly, her companion was still Brigetta, though now pale, unsteady, and obviously weak. But her lifeless eyes made Bram's heart sink. *What has become of Brigetta?*

When he looked at his wife, it was as if someone had pushed the *her* out of the transparent skin and moved in—for it was a stranger staring back at him through Brigetta's eyes. And that stranger didn't appear to like him at all, let alone love him a-bushel-and-a-peck-a-hug-around-the-neck's worth.

"Hello, Brigetta. I've come to take you home." Bram swallowed hard as he noticed the baggy dress, a most unattractive brown much-worn cotton shift that formed a turtle-like shell around the skeletal form within it. Where were the bright Dutch dresses? Where was the sparkle in her eyes? Where was the *welcome-thank-goodness-you're-here-at-last* greeting?

She merely nodded; if there had been even a ghost of a smile, it had left no trail.

"I see Kathleen helped you pack your satchel." Not even a nod this time. He directed his attention to the young escort with an incongruous bulge mid-body. "Is there anything else up in her room?"

Hadley Hoover

"No, Sir," Kathleen replied, "it's all in the satchel."

"Where is your buggy, Mister de Boer?" Miss Beal inquired. Correctly assessing that Bram had brought no extra coat, she pulled a cape off a hook behind the door and draped it around Brigetta's shoulders, tucking the hood around her head.

Bram was instantly stricken with shame. *No coat, and I should have realized Brigetta couldn't walk to the depot.* His mind turned to mush until he couldn't even determine the first step toward securing a buggy in Minneapolis.

The kitchen was silent as a tomb. Bram felt his mouth go dry. Brigetta was visibly sagging in front of him, and he was worthless to help her in any way.

"Halt!" A man's voice sounded above the crack of a whip and everyone's attention shifted from Bram to the back porch.

"A delivery!" one girl cried and ran to the door, followed by several others in swift pursuit.

Through the opened door, Bram caught a glimpse of a man unloading boxes and baskets, and with the rush of cold air clearing his head, he knew he was looking at a solution to his problem. Though taken aback to see a man step across the threshold of the Thompson House, the driver kept his thoughts to himself.

Bram inquired from the doorway, "Sir, may I ask a favor of you? For a fee, would you be willing to take two passengers to the railway station?"

"The railway station? That's a bit out of my way."

"I will pay you."

The desperation in Bram's face tugged at the kindness that had brought the driver to the Thompson House that day. "Would you be ready to go now?"

Bram looked back into the kitchen at Brigetta who sat slumped on a chair. She nodded ever so slightly, and he was beside her in an instant. Kathleen picked up the satchel, and Bram swept Brigetta up in his arms, carrying her across the kitchen with the same dread in his heart as in the parsonage kitchen years before—dread that his precious cargo could die because of him. The knowledge that everything now rested on his shoulders made Bram tremble.

The girls took turns bidding fond farewells to Brigetta, several leaning over the sideboard to fling their arms around her and kiss her cheek. She smiled and spoke to each one, but Bram could see her strength ebbing away.

Bram turned to Miss Beal. "How much more do we owe you? I know Brigetta required extra care."

"If there was any extra owed, it has been paid in full, Mister de Boer. Brigetta has been worth her weight in gold around here. Your sister," she paused ever so slightly, "is a remarkable young lady. I wish you both the best of everything." Then, Miss Beal crossed the porch and leaned down to Brigetta and cupped her chin. "Take care of yourself, Brigetta. Remember, God loves you and so do we." Brigetta nodded and mouthed a soundless *thank you.*

"Yes, thank you, Miss Beal," Bram repeated, "and please thank Mrs. Thompson, as well." Bram climbed in beside Brigetta, signaled to the driver, and they bumped along the rough-frozen ground of the alley. "I bought your ticket before I came to the house. I had hoped to stay in a hotel tonight to let you rest before the train trip, but I will need to pay the driver that money, instead."

Brigetta nodded and said dully, "Let's just go home."

The driver turned a corner sharply, and Brigetta clutched Bram to regain her balance. He quickly slipped his arm around her shoulders. Neither moved again until the driver pulled up beneath the depot's portico. Before he stepped down, Bram reached into his pocket and extended the promised payment.

That man shook his head. "It wasn't all that far out of my way. Find a matron inside," he nodded toward the depot, "and ask her where the girl can lie down. There's cots you can use for a sum," he added gruffly.

Hadley Hoover   *279*

Bram reached for the man's work-roughened hand and shook it fervently, "Thank you. I came unprepared and you have been like the Good Samaritan to us."

Embarrassed by Bram's gratitude, the driver mumbled intelligibly and held the satchel until Bram had lifted Brigetta from the wagon and steadied her beside him on the boardwalk.

A quarter of an hour later, Brigetta sank gratefully beneath a blanket on a low cot that, as the driver had known, could be rented by the hour. Sliding the satchel and Brigetta's *klompen* beneath the cot, he smoothed Brigetta's hair back from her damp, warm forehead and settled in on a low bench to watch his wife sleep. *So feverish, so pale—God, help us.*

Bram never left Brigetta's side during the two hours their money had secured. He soaked up the sight of her, replenishing dim images of her hair, the delicate structure of her face, how her eyebrows darkened as they arched across her face—memories that had nearly faded into oblivion over the past five months.

All too soon the matron called time. Bram shook Brigetta's shoulder gently. "Brigetta, our train leaves shortly and we must give up the cot now."

Her eyelashes fluttered and when she looked at him, she jerked with surprise. "I almost thought I had dreamed you." She shut her eyes again.

"Brigetta?" *What if she cannot make the trip? Whatever will I do? She has no reserves of strength on which to draw, and we are miles from home.* He gently lifted the blanket and folded it back. "Can you sit up? I'll help you with your *klompen.*"

Soundlessly, she turned toward him and moved her legs beneath her skirts, seeking the floor with the tips of her toes. She leaned against him until her dizziness passed.

"Did you lose the baby, lass?" a pitying voice asked from behind them.

Brigetta looked up into Bram's eyes with a paralyzing fear matching that in his chest. A sob, a moan…Bram turned to the matron who had certainly meant no harm, but had pierced their lie until it fizzled at their feet. "Yes, Ma'am, she lost the baby." And with an answer more truth than fiction hounding them, he guided his distraught wife to the train.

The conductor took their measure instantly, and finagled a seat for them at the front of the car. Bram showed their tickets and settled in; Brigetta's head rested against his shoulder.

She slept all the way to Rochester, and Bram repeated two prayers for the whole trip: *Please let the hospital wagon meet us*, and *Please keep discerning women like the matron away.*

The hospital's wagon awaited their arrival and Bram breathed a silent prayer of thanksgiving. While the driver helped others into the seats and loaded their luggage, Bram quickly settled Brigetta. Bram flinched each time he saw pain flit across her face as the wagon bumped and jolted its way along the country road.

Upon arrival at the hospital, Bram waited until the other passengers climbed down and retrieved their luggage, and then excused the driver, telling him he would return the wagon within the hour. Bram wanted no one to see that his returning wife could barely stand on her own feet, let alone climb the hill to their house. Anyone could justifiably wonder what kind of care a woman in her condition would have been able to offer an ailing grandmother.

For the second time that day, Bram carried Brigetta, this time up the slope to their home. He moved across the back porch, into the kitchen, through the dining room to the stubby hallway leading to the bathroom and their bedroom.

After a worrisomely long time in the bathroom, Brigetta emerged to find Bram patiently leaning against the wall. "Are you hungry?" he asked.

"Just tired and sore." Brigetta moved like a sleepwalker into the bedroom, scanned the room briefly as she stepped out of her klompen, and sank on to the bed fully clothed. Before Bram could even draw the curtains and cover her with a quilt, she was asleep.

After bringing the satchel up to the house and checking on Brigetta who slept like someone drugged, Bram returned the buggy and brought Chum home.

Brigetta still slept, and looked as if she could do so for some time. Bram worked quietly in the kitchen, heating up stew, feeding Chum. While he ate his supper, he looked over seed catalogs and his own journal. The house was still and the only light was the lantern on the kitchen table. Except for letting Chum out once, and back in a few minutes later, Bram sat for several hours in silence, starting letters to their families, reading, listening for any noise at all from the bedroom.

Chum noticed her first. His head came up, his ears tilted, and he rose cautiously. Standing between Bram and the unknown, the furry sentry did his job well. Brigetta moved toward the light, her fingers running across the smooth surface of the dining room table, as she came to the kitchen doorway. "Bram?"

He stood instantly, his chair scrapping against the floor; he caught it just before it toppled. "Brigetta, I didn't hear you get up." A low rumble started in Chum's throat, and startled Brigetta. "It's okay, Chum, this is Brigetta—I've told you about her."

Brigetta's smile was spontaneous and sincere. She held out both hands and Chum moved slowly toward her. One touch, a wagging tail, and a soft voice, "Hello, Chum. I'm so glad to meet you, at last. You're certainly a pretty fellow."

Apparently, that small speech made them best friends, and Chum— with hardly a glance at the man who had fed and watered, walked and loved him all these months—fell instantly and completely in love with the lady of the house.

Tears rushed to Bram's eyes as he watched Brigetta sit down and bury her face in Chum's curly coat of black fur. He watched Chum lift a paw to touch Brigetta's arm when she shifted to sit on the floor. He saw the bond form between the woman who was the love of his life and the dog that had filled a vast chasm in his heart.

Bram felt like odd-man-out. Brigetta had greeted him with none of the outpouring of love Chum received for merely existing. Peevishly, Bram asked, "Are you hungry yet? There's stew."

"I'm not hungry, but I know I must eat." She moved to sit by the table. Bram raised his eyebrows at this unanticipated shift in roles. Chastised by his own thoughts, he lifted the cover off a kettle on the stove. Finding the stew still warm, he dished it, added a slice of bread, and took the plate to Brigetta.

Trying not to stare, but not knowing what else to do, Bram watched Brigetta force herself to eat. When the plate was half empty, she looked at Bram. "That's all I care for. I'm sorry."

"It's the end of it, and not enough to keep. Why not let Chum lick your plate?"

It was an act destined to anchor Brigetta firmly in Chum's affection, and she laughed as he finished off the stew and looked up at her expectantly. "I'm afraid I've just taught you a bad habit, Chum! We can't have you begging at the table, so you'll just have to forget this happened tonight."

She laughs for Chum, and not for me. Ashamed of such jealous thoughts, Bram said, "Come, Brigetta. Let me show you the auction finds."

And so they examined the lamps, the dining room table with its six fine chairs, the rocking chair—none elicited the excitement Bram had anticipated. Finally, the surprise. "A piano! What beautiful wood." Brigetta lifted the cover and let her fingers bump along the keys, a random D, or a lilting A echoing from the sounding board into the room.

"Play us a song."

Brigetta sat on the bench and fit her hands around a chord. The result was jarring. "Oh, it's sadly out of tune."

"Of course. I hadn't thought. I've played a note or two, but never thought to have a real musician play it. I'll check with Mrs. Gray for the name of a piano tuner."

Brigetta lowered the lid over the keys, the discordance lingering in their ears. "It's a lovely piano, Bram." She caressed the dark wood behind the single piece of sheet music Bram had placed there to welcome her home.

Somehow, the song propped on the piano's ledge seemed inappropriate now: *Look for the Silver Lining*. There was no silver lining to this homecoming. Except for Chum, Bram's surprises were not a booming success.

Standing beneath the arch between parlor and dining room, Brigetta looked at the two rooms. They didn't look a great deal different than how she had left them. Granted, there were the new table and chairs, and the rocker and piano—but it didn't have a lived-in-loved-in feeling to it. "Do you feel at home here, Bram?"

He looked sheepish. "I spend most of my time in the kitchen when I'm here. I didn't feel like unpacking boxes without you."

She nodded, half understanding, half disappointed. "We should go to bed. It's late, and I'm sure you must get up early."

"Actually, I do not need to go back to work until Monday. Doctor Gray has insisted I take a few days off to be with you. He assumes your grandmother died. I'm not sure how I'll explain being home tonight, since there would have been a funeral if there were any truth to our tale."

Unconsciously, Brigetta bent to stroke Chum's head and the dog leaned against her. "That's right. You said you'd planned to stay in a hotel tonight." She sighed. "I wanted to put the lies behind us, but I suppose we're destined to tell a few more."

Bram nodded, and thrust his hands through his hair. "We'll say the funeral was yesterday, and we were still able to catch the train." He sighed. "Let's go to bed."

The house on the hill darkened. Two people who had slept alone for many nights lay awake with ever-faithful Chum beside the bed. Bram reached for Brigetta's hand and they fell asleep, fingers laced together on this first night in many months when Brigetta's roommate was her husband, not another pregnant girl.

*   *   *

Dear Doctor,

We have finished cutting logs and have sawed wood salvaged from same. We have cut about 600 fence posts. All broken limbs and rubbish have been picked up and hauled.

Seed grain is all cleaned and treated. We have a number of plants started that are doing nicely. We have been sprouting seed potatoes in the west cave.

Have been hauling rubbish and cleaning up around the cow barn. Moved colony houses to new and clean ground. The livestock looks good and is doing well.

Sincerely, Bram de Boer, Steward

Two weeks passed. Thankfully, chilly weather required Brigetta to wear the cloak, giving her shapeless body opportunity to adjust. The de Boers shopped at the general store and Rommel's Grocery on Center Street, and visited the Rochester Public Library where Brigetta was pleased to find an assortment of over 16,000 volumes from which she made her first selections.

Before going home, Bram took Brigetta past the variety of churches the growing town had to offer: one organized in 1857 according to the cornerstone, another the following year. "Over 400 members at this church." He pointed to yet another on a nearby corner.

"So many churches in such a small area—but no Dutch Reformed church. I wonder where we will feel at home."

"We can worship God with Dutch in our hearts, if not our ears."

Over the next few weeks, Bram kept the world at bay, giving Brigetta time to rest, to unpack boxes, and to become familiar with the vast house that was their home. Each noon he came home, often finding her sitting with Chum nearby and no evidence of any morning activity other than preparing lunch for him. It worried him; Dutch women never sat idle, and young Dutch women relished their homes, and their kitchens. Few Dutch smells emanated from the house on the hill.

"When shall we have our party and use our ten chairs around the new table," Bram asked casually one night at supper.

Brigetta looked at him in alarm. "Certainly now yet. Haven't you noticed I can scarcely fit into my own clothes? I wear only this brown dress from the Thompson House and one other—they are all that fit me, even though it has been nearly four weeks since..." The sentence ended abruptly as she choked back tears and fled to the bathroom.

Chum gave Bram an accusing stare and left the kitchen to stand guard by the bathroom door. When Bram approached, Chum growled at him. "I meant no harm," Bram told the dog and returned to his half-eaten meal.

It was bound to happen eventually, but neither Bram nor Brigetta could have predicted when. It was a crystal-clear Saturday morning, and Bram commented at breakfast that the chaplain from the hospital had mentioned he would like to stop by that day to meet Brigetta. "And of course you said, 'No, I'm sorry, it won't work out.'" Brigetta swirled coffee in her cup.

"No, actually, I thought it was a good idea. You've met so few people here, and the chaplain is a nice sort of fellow."

"And why exactly, did you think it was a good idea? Because you feel it is time for us to confess our sins? Or because you want someone to come by and tell us we need to reach out to others more? Or because you hope he'll tell me I need to be a better wife to you? Is that it?"

Floundering in a sea of unknown currents, Bram said, "A better wife? No. However, I do think it is time for us to...I mean, maybe talking with someone will help us..."

With a screech the likes of which neither Bram nor Chum had ever heard before from her lips, Brigetta opened the floodgates. "Do you have any idea how much I hate living here? I am stuck with the man who forced me to give up the only baby I will ever have all because you could not handle what people would say."

"But…" Only one word, but even that word was sucked up into the vortex of Brigetta's tirade.

"You do not have any idea what my life was like in Minneapolis, and now that I'm back, you expect me to fit right into your life as your wife again. Let me tell you something: I got letters from my 'brother,' Bram for so long I have a hard time thinking of you as my husband anymore."

Wide-eyed and paralyzed by a nameless fear, Bram swallowed hard. "Surely you can't mean that. We are married—we took vows to love and cherish each other."

"Now's a fine time for you to remember—where were those lofty thoughts when you left me at the Thompson House? You never once visited me—even at Christmas." She hiccupped and choked, angrily swiping away her tears. "We're not *married*, Bram. A husband would never do to a wife he loves what you have done to me."

"I made the decision *because* I love you."

"No, no. You were thinking of yourself, not me, not us. You've started a new life that excludes me, and now you expect me to just forget all about the past nine months and pick up on loving you like my husband again? Well, *brother*, it isn't going to be that easy. I feel closer to Chum than I do to you. At least he doesn't disappoint me."

"But, I…" Bram rightly realized he had no defense. *Why didn't I go to see her? Why should she view me as anything but a brother, and not even a great brother?*

Before those thoughts burrowed too deeply into his soul, a flare of anger ignited Bram, too. *But she's not come back to me as a wife, either. That's right—she's failed me, too.* "I have bent over backwards to make your homecoming as smooth as possible. Every day someone asks me about you, and I'm forced to say, 'Oh, she's quite tired out from caring so long for her ailing grandmother,' and other such lame excuses. Come on, Brigetta—you sit up here in your sanctuary on the hill and I go down to the valley every day and tell lies to cover you. I gave up a lot, too, Brigetta. Granted, this job is good work and a good experience for me, but it's not my family farm—it's not my dream for my future."

A long silence ensued. "What shall I tell the chaplain about coming over?" Bram asked, at last.

"Tell him if he sets foot on the back porch, I'll sic Chum on him," Brigetta said darkly and turned her back on Bram. He sagged against his chair. *If the old Brigetta had said that, I'd laugh—but coming from the Brigetta I'm living with these days, I'm afraid she means it. And I'll bet Chum would do it for her, too.*

Like wooden clothespins struggling to hold sheets on a line in the wind, Bram and Brigetta lay in their bed that night, wondering if their besieged marriage could survive the current tempest.

The next morning, Bram rose early, dressed in the dark room, and ate a piece of toast standing over the sink—just like in the before-Brigetta-returned days. Hearing the door slam behind Bram, Brigetta dressed, fed Chum, and sat at the kitchen table with a single sheet of paper before her.

Dear Mama,

I would like to come home. Bram is a different person than when we lived in Dutchville. I will find work to pay you for my room and board. I have sufficient money for my ticket home. Please reply quickly.

Love, Brigetta

Brigetta made her way along the muddy path to the mailbox at the end of the hospital's road and put the envelope addressed to *Mrs. Hanna Ter Hoorn / Dutchville Iowa* inside the cold black box. The day had spring on its breath, but Brigetta's mind was trapped by the wintry thoughts frozen in her mind.

Hours later, she remembered that Bram brought their mail home each day—often having opened the letters from their families from force of habit. A knot formed in her stomach.

288   Rough Terrain

Conversations between Bram and Brigetta over the ensuing days were brief, utilitarian and stilted. Fully two anxious weeks passed before Bram walked up the hill after work and handed her an envelope addressed to *Mrs. Bram de Boer / Rochester State Hospital / Rochester Minnesota* in Mama's flowing script.

In the lower left-hand corner, the notation *Private* leaped off the paper. The seal was unbroken. Bram stared at Brigetta, noting her shaking hand as she held the envelope, unopened. It was obvious she had no intention of opening it in his presence. He picked up the slop bucket and headed out the door.

Brigetta flinched as the door slammed. She grabbed her cape and took the letter out to the front porch swing. Running her thumb beneath the seal, she forced herself to take a deep breath before extracting the letter. The envelope drifted to the floor, unnoticed.

Dearest Brigetta,

I received your letter several days ago and have devoted much thought and prayer to your request.

The answer, Sweet Pea, is no. You cannot return home, not without Bram. I know by your even asking such a question that you are experiencing trying times—grievous times, I have no doubt. But leaving Bram and returning home alone is not the answer.

No, child, you must make a home—build it from kindness and forgiveness, with prayer and laughter. Love is a decision—your father decided long ago that he loved me. Do you think our marriage would have lasted through the years if his feelings for me were based only on emotion?

Perhaps the first blush of your love is gone. Perhaps you have lost something in your move from the familiar to the unknown. But whatever the problem you face, you must face it together. Rebuild trust, and love will follow.

All my love, Mama

Brigetta read the letter, reread the letter, crumpled the letter in her hand, and then stuffed it into the deep pocket of her dress. *To be denied the home that raised me!* Tears blurred her vision until the trees in front of her melted into an evergreen porridge. *Perhaps I should have written to Papa...why did I not write to Papa? Or* Tante *Lena—she misses me, she says so in every letter.*

Slowly, she returned to the half-made supper and went through the motions of cooking. When Bram sat across the table from her, she was almost amazed that there was food to eat—she only vaguely remembered finishing the preparations. "Did your Mama send bad news?"

Brigetta's fork rattled against her teeth. "Just a letter."

"Was it in response to the letter you sent her several weeks ago?"

That same fork slipped from Brigetta's hand and clattered off the table to the floor. Chum shifted beside Brigetta, his sniffing and licking the fork the only sound in the kitchen. "You knew I sent a letter?"

Bram nodded, the sadness in his eyes so deep Brigetta caught her breath. "You forgot to put a stamp on it, and the mailman recognized the address from the many letters I have sent there, so he found me and I paid him for a stamp."

"Did you read it?" she whispered.

"No. If you had wanted me to read it, you would not have gone to such lengths to send it out secretly."

Brigetta's face burned and her stomach churned until she feared she would vomit.

"Brigetta, do you love me?"

She twisted her napkin into a tight knot. "Sometimes I love you so little that I feel lost—like I'm sinking into the hole that my love for you used to fill. Other times—and they are fewer and fewer since Christmas when you didn't even come see me—those times I love you so much that I cannot stand the pain of loving someone who has hurt me so deeply."

"The reason I didn't come was spelled out on Mrs. Thompson's form: no male visitors. I do love you, Brigetta. Or maybe I love the memory of you—the *you* I remember seems gone."

"The *me* you remember *is* gone, Bram. She died, bit by bit, over the days and weeks and months since Cornelis and the closet. Only shadows of her remain." Unaware of tears streaming down her cheeks, Brigetta pushed back her chair and left the kitchen.

She looked out the dining room window at the skeletal trees looming darkly in the moonlight. Her shoulders hunched as she wrapped her arms around her chest. Bram stood behind her. Even though his touch was gentle, she jumped. "Brigetta? May I hold you?"

Love is a decision. Love is a decision. In that moment, Brigetta knew her response to Bram's question would determine their future. In the old days, Brigetta would have leaped into Bram's arms—no, in the old days, Bram never would have needed to ask. These days, she recoiled from his touch. *Love is a decision, Brigetta—what will you decide?*

Bram didn't rush her. He looked over her shoulder at their hazy reflection in the window. "I overheard the chaplain talking to a patient's wife this week. She was angry because her husband is here, doing work he loves, while she faces overwhelming day-to-day responsibilities. The chaplain told her many of the heroes of the Bible were angry at God."

Brigetta sucked in her breath.

Bram's voice was soothing in the evening shadows. "He said Jeremiah and Job and even David often blamed God for their troubles. The chaplain said the worst thing we can do—much worse than getting angry at God—is to lose our faith because we believe God is uncaring."

The silence was not uncomfortable; their thoughts filled in the gaps.

"He sounds like a wise man. Like Papa."

"Like Papa."

Brigetta turned to Bram at the exact moment he reached out to her. They swayed in place, clinging to each other. "Come." Bram gently led Brigetta to the rocking chair. He drew her down to his lap, lifting her legs to curve around the arm of the chair. With her head resting against his shoulder, they rocked and rocked, the creaking chair setting the cadence for their thoughts.

For fully an hour, they said nothing. Chum fell asleep at their feet. Brigetta heard Bram's heartbeat beneath her ear; Bram breathed deeply, soaking up her essence. Eventually, her fingers smoothed his shirt and he smoothed her white-blonde ringlets. Their hands reached out and met, fingers lacing together, index fingers steepled above the others. *Here is the church, here is the steeple...* Bram felt her smile against his chest as they played out the child's game in silence.

"Brigetta? My legs are asleep." He felt her smile again.

She felt his responding smile against her hair. "That's not surprising. After dangling my feet for so long, I can't feel anything below my knees."

They fell asleep that night in each other's arms, a small step on a long journey home.

Over breakfast, Bram asked. "Can you love me again?"

Brigetta nodded slowly as she lifted tear-glazed eyes to him.

"For you to love me again like a husband, what would it take?"

"You could court me again. I don't want *things*—I want the realization that the most important thing in the world to you is me—nothing else." A thoughtful silence ensued. "For you to love me like a wife again, what will it take?" she asked softly.

"You can chase me until I catch you. If we begin to *have* fun again, eventually we will *be* fun."

"We need to *decide* to love each other—and learn to trust each other," Brigetta agreed, unconsciously making Hanna's penned words her own. "If we act as if we love each other, the feelings will follow."

"Do you think we can? Is it worth it to you?"

"We've invested a lot in each other so far. It would be a shame to walk away. If each day of our courtship and marriage were a penny, it would make a big pile. If I found that many coins along the road, I would stuff every one in my pockets."

"So, Mrs. de Boer. Are you ready to be courted?"

"I am, Mister de Boer. Are you ready to be chased?"

"Definitely. Would you like to close our meal with the prayer of thanksgiving?"

"I'd like nothing more than to sing the prayer with you."

For the first time, the kitchen in the house on the hill rang with two young voices raised in song. Halfway through the *Psalmen*, Chum lifted his head and joined in and the music joined healing laughter from two of God's Dutch children.

"Let's make a promise, Bram: this house hosts no more sad conversations. If we must discuss difficult things, let's go outside so our home can be a safe place."

When Bram came up the hill for lunch, the windows were open and curtains billowed out into the early spring air. He increased his pace. "Hello?" He stepped into the kitchen and sniffed the air. Nothing smelled like lunch. "Brigetta?"

He followed the familiar and wondrous sound of Brigetta's voice wrapped around a song until he found her, armed with scrub brush and bucket of sudsy water scrubbing the upstairs steps.

"Bram! What are you doing here?"

"I live here. Get used to me—you'll be seeing a lot of me!"

She giggled. "I know. I mean, what are you doing here now?"

"It's lunchtime."

Brigetta gaped at him, soapy water running down her arm as she held the brush mid-air. "Lunchtime?"

"You know, noon. The meal in the middle of the day. The one between breakfast and supper."

"I had no idea it was so late. Oh, dear!"

"You're certainly busy—no wonder you forgot. That's okay—I can always eat at the dining room at the hospital."

"And have them think I'm not taking good care of you? I didn't forget—I just wasn't aware of the time. Come, we'll have a lovely lunch." Ignoring Bram's grin, she blushed furiously. "Follow me, Mister, and I'll show you what a fine wife I am!" She marched down the steps, swept past him, and flounced her way to the kitchen. Bram pulled out a chair to watch.

With much pomp, she bustled about the kitchen, opening canned goods, slicing apples, moving dishes from cupboard to table in a frenzy of activity. When the kettle on the stove reached a boil, she sang out, "Ready!" and dished up their lunch: hot stewed apple chunks with raisins, cold cinnamon-laced applesauce, warm spiced apple rings, and generous pieces of fresh sliced apples. Bram stared at the table.

Brigetta slid into her seat, mopped her forehead with her apron hem, brushed back a stray lock of hair, and said sprightly, "Please help yourself."

Bram put apple rings on his plate, applesauce in the sauce dish, added chunky stewed apples to his plate, and then popped a slice of fresh apple into his mouth. "Do we have any apple cider?" he asked with wide-eyed innocence.

Brigetta's cheek twitched, and she pursed her lips several times. "I'm not quite sure. Perhaps in the fruit cellar," she said, at last.

They laughed until tears flowed. "You were right, Bram—I had nothing for lunch."

"No, you were right, Brigetta—you showed me what a fine wife you are!" And he proceeded to polish off his lunch.

Supper was a merry affair that began when Bram presented Brigetta with a wrapped jar. "Mrs. Gray sent this to you and says she's looking forward to visiting with you soon." Inside the wrapping was a jar of apple butter. Midst whoops of laughter, Brigetta sliced thick chunks of bread, and they enjoyed generous servings of the gift.

"I have a gift for you, as well. Let's go out to the swing," Bram said.

With Brigetta settled in, Bram knelt before her, reached into his pockets and extracted an intricately carved wooden skate. Brigetta flung her arms around Bram's neck and burst into tears.

"Many years ago, I promised you the matching skate. The first one was a gift when I feared I'd destroyed your body. This one is because I feared I've killed your spirit."

"In each case, yours fears were wrong. The first one I accepted from the boy I would grow to love. This one I accept from the man I'm learning to love again."

Each evening, Bram returned home to find a familiar Dutch meal prepared, something unpacked and in place within the house, and a wife who was regaining her physical vigor and zest for living. Each evening, Bram brought home stories from his day, greeted Brigetta with a lingering kiss, either washed or dried supper dishes, and marveled at all she had done during the day.

In April, Brigetta baked a double batch of gingerbread and found Bram in one of the greenhouses, working with several patients. While she was often introduced to men Bram worked with, this was her first face-to-face encounter with any women patients. They all stared at each other briefly, and then Brigetta smiled broadly and moved among them, insisting each worker take a piece of gingerbread.

When the plate was empty, she said softly to Bram, "Can I stay? I'd love to dig in the dirt with you for a while."

"Be my guest!" Within minutes, Brigetta had trowel in hand and was working next to Bram, just like the old days except this was a greenhouse as silent as the caves.

"Bram, let's sing," she whispered.

By the time they had sung *By the Light of the Silvery Moon* three times, Brigetta noticed several of the women swaying in time to the music. She broke into *Second-hand Rose* and gave it her all, tossing her head back on the high notes, and milking the low ones for all the melodrama she could find in them.

They noted a few questioning looks when they laughed all the way through *I'll Be With You in Apple Blossom Time*, especially when Bram changed the words on each verse to applesauce time, or apple jelly time.

When the women left the greenhouse, one mumbled to Brigetta, "I like your singing."

"Behold the charms of Brigetta! That woman has never said 'boo!' to me—but you walk in and she talks!"

The de Boer's renewed courtship flourished beyond its fragile beginnings. They took long walks as the days lengthened, Bram showing Brigetta many hidden spots on the fascinating hospital property. They climbed hills, marveled at the beauty of the limestone quarries, investigated the caves and woods, lingered in meadows coming alive with spring. Through it all, they spoke of things that lovers share as they slowly eased back into trust.

Brigetta and Bram finally hosted their first party. Bram popped bowls of popcorn to serve with Brigetta's Dutch cookies and sweets. The Grays, the chaplain, and three nurses were their first guests. The evening was a huge success. They played charades and twenty questions, and eventually gathered around the piano.

Brigetta and Mrs. Gray took turns accompanying the others. The only wobbly moment in the whole evening was when a nurse found the song *I'm Sorry I Made You Cry* in Brigetta's collection and the chaplain unwittingly said, "Our host and hostess have the perfect blend of voices for this one. Sing it for us, Bram and Brigetta!"

Even Doctor Gray wiped his eyes when the last refrain lingered in the air. Never had two more sincere voices sung the words, "*Won't you forget, won't you forgive, and don't let us say goodbye…*"

"That was beautiful!" Mrs. Gray exclaimed. "You simply must perform it at the next concert."

Emotionally drained from their heartfelt rendition of the contemporary song, Bram and Brigetta caught each other's eyes and froze. Abruptly, Brigetta launched into a foot-tapping rendition of *It's a Long, Long Way to Tipperary*, destined to shake off the poignancy of the moment.

✳   ✳   ✳

One morning in May, Bram took their cups of breakfast coffee out to the porch and set the swing in motion when Brigetta joined him. It was a glorious morning, and Bram was in no hurry to leave his wife. He suggested planting a tree each year on their anniversary. As they were discussing which kind of tree and where to plant the first one, he interrupted their idle chatter. "What do you know about that?" Grinning, he pulled Brigetta to her feet.

Within minutes, they were at the bottom of the hill and Brigetta gasped, "Oh, Bram! The tulips! Look—everywhere!" Scattered across the hillside in a riot of color, hundreds of stately stems burst through the carpet of green grass with vibrant blossoms.

"It's as if God spilled a rainbow across the grass overnight!"

Bram stared at the hillside thoughtfully. "I'm glad to see the limestone layer didn't change anything visibly. I'll want to harvest seeds from this first crop."

"That's hardly the romantic response to tulips, Bram!"

He looked at her with amusement. "You're right. They are beautiful—it will do these Minnesotans good to see some Dutch tulips!"

News of the tulips spread across the hospital grounds, from patients to employees and even to visitors to the hospital that day. At sundown, Doctor and Mrs. Gray walked over to see what the hubbub was all about. "Even in twilight, this hillside is like a vision! You truly have a gift, Bram," Doctor Gray commended his Steward. "I can hardly wait to see what you do with the crops!"

"Did you know that in just one day your house has earned a name? You now live in The House on Tulip Hill!" Mrs. Gray said.

"There will be even more—this is just the first of all Bram planted. He brought hundreds more bulbs and seeds from Iowa and planted them all last fall. You'll have to come by often. What tulip season lacks in length, it makes up for in sheer wonder."

Bram took out his pocketknife and bent to cut two perfect flowers. One, he presented with a gracious bow to Mrs. Gray. Then, he knelt before Brigetta and opened the palm of her hand, kissed it, placed the other tulip in her hand and closed her fingers around it. "The loveliest to the loveliest," he whispered and Brigetta closed her eyes and shivered. When Bram rose from his knees and Brigetta looked up, they were startled to see the Grays standing statue-still with misty eyes.

Doctor Gray cleared his throat. "You've created a thing of beauty." It was not entirely clear—nor was it important—whether he spoke of the flowers or the love evidenced between the Steward and his wife.

That night, Bram mysteriously disappeared into the bathroom after Brigetta climbed into bed. "Hey, Brigetta, happy early anniversary!"

She opened her eyes and focused on Bram in the bedroom doorway: Bram clothed only in a very short pair of long johns. She sat upright and stared and then flung herself back against the bed. Sputtering through her uncontrollable laughter, she said, "You saved them!"

"How could I ever toss out something you made special for me? Did you forget my promise to wear them every year on our anniversary?"

The two-month renewed courtship between Bram and Brigetta had evidenced that neither one wanted to rush in and ruin the fragile progress. But the night the tulips bloomed and the long johns appeared, they returned to an ecstasy not known for many months. Dawn painted the morning sky before they finally slept, satiated with love, satisfied with life.

Bram walked down the hill to work as tired as he could ever remember being, but he was undaunted by any task he undertook that day. He felt as strong as a driving rain, and powerful as the bulls in the pasture. And his grin seemed permanent.

Brigetta drifted dreamily through the day, sang along with the birds in the trees, made tea and forgot to drink it, took Chum for the same walk twice. And, in a gesture she knew Bram would understand, made a batch of doughnuts—that traditional Dutch New Year's breakfast symbolizing the circle of life—and served them with a pitcher of milk as the

298   R o u g h   T e r r a i n

sum total of their supper. It was a love feast for two—and they ended up back in the bedroom, long before the plate was empty.

             *   *   *

Dear Doctor,

We have planted about one and a half acres more strawberries, making a total of three and a half acres. The old strawberry patch seems to look very good although there is some winterkill. This patch will be plowed up and late cabbages put in as soon as it is through bearing.

About 5,500 tomato plants have been set out. Early cabbage looks very fine; we have about 12,000 plants. We have planted about 12 acres of potatoes in addition to 67 acres put in during April making a total of 79 acres so far.

Sincerely, Bram de Boer, Steward

"Bram! Hurry! You'll never guess what!" Brigetta's voice bounced in time with her *klompen* pounding along the path. Out of breath, she halted mid-way and clutched her side, panting.

He increased his pace, but not enough for Brigetta. She resumed her race toward him, flinging her arms around him as he lifted her off the ground and spun her around until her shoes flew through the air. Laughing, he rescued her wooden shoes and knelt to replace them.

"Our parents are coming! We need to get beds and I need to clean the house! Thank goodness we have enough chairs. What shall I feed them?"

"Whoa—slow down! When are they coming? How did you find out? No letter came today."

"No—they sent a telegram! It was delivered to the house—isn't that exciting? Here, read it!" She waved the yellow paper before Bram's face and he chuckled as he held her arm still long enough to grab it.

She step-brush-hopped a Dutch dance right in the meadow while Bram read aloud, "*Crops planted we five arrive evening train Tuesday leave Friday.*"

"That means your father's crops are planted, and the five—your parents, my parents, and it must include *Tante* Lena—will be at our house from Tuesday until Friday. Don't you agree that's what that means, Bram?"

Bram rubbed his chin. "Hmmm, yes, I'd say that's what it means—unless by the five, they mean Father's hired man is coming with four strangers," he teased.

"Oh, Bram! I'm so excited—tell me you're as excited as I am!"

"That's hardly possible, but it's mighty fine news! We'll have to have a party and invite everyone we've talked about in letters."

A shadow covered the sunshine of Brigetta's smile. "What if someone mentions my 'grandmother' and offers condolences?" Bram had no answer.

Except for underlying nagging thoughts of potential catastrophes, the intervening days flew by. Brigetta baked late into the night, repositioned the furniture several times, and inspected each corner with new purpose. She pedaled her bicycle into town where she loaded the basket until she wobbled riding home. She hired male patients to pick up winter debris on the hillside and trim bushes. Two women helped Brigetta until she was satisfied no house in Dutchville could rival the cleanliness of the House on Tulip Hill.

The workers finally finished their labors on Tulip Hill. "She sure hates dirt, that wife of yours," one woman informed Bram when she returned to the greenhouse for the more subdued activity of dividing strawberry plants.

"Thanks for helping—did she pay you yet?"

The woman nodded. "She paid us each day—and fed us, too. She hates dirt, and cooks good. It was never just coffee—always something to eat with a fork. She was always talking or singing. I've never met anyone like her before."

"That's Brigetta in a nutshell, all right," Bram agreed solemnly, surprised not only by such a long speech from a usually reticent woman, but how accurately she assessed his wife.

300   R o u g h   T e r r a i n

One morning, two strong and silent men diligently loaded five single beds and several other pieces of furniture onto the hospital wagon and delivered them to an eager Brigetta. She met them at the bottom of the hill—running along side the wagon and chattering the whole time—and then raced ahead of them to hold open the door. She directed the assembly of beds on one end of the upper level for Gustave and Hanna and one for *Tante* Lena behind a hospital screen at the opposite end, and the remaining two for Hans and Rebecca in the other main-floor bedroom.

"Bedding!" Brigetta cried out at lunch, so startling Bram that he bit his thumb instead of his bread. "The beds are bare, Bram. Bare!"

"If the hospital can loan us beds, they may also supply bedding," he said practically. "I'll ask the head housekeeper this afternoon."

"I'll come with you, and if they say yes, I'll bring it right home. And if they say no, I'll...they just can't say no, Bram! They just can't!" She burst into tears and Chum looked accusingly at Bram and moved to lean comfortingly against Brigetta.

"Please don't cry—Chum blames me," Bram protested mildly. "Why don't you finish what you're doing today, and let me do the asking first? If they say no, we'll sleep standing in the corner in our clothes and let our families have all the sheets and blankets and pillows in the house."

Brigetta burst out laughing, still crying, and flew off her chair to land in Bram's lap. "I just want everything to be perfect. This is such an important visit—they'll remember everything they see and go home and tell everyone about everything so I want to be sure it is perfect."

"They'll see how happy we are and forget every other thing, no matter how wonderful or imperfect it is."

Brigetta took his face in both her hands and turned his head until their eyes met. "We are, aren't we? We are happy again, aren't we, Bram?"

"Deliriously. Outrageously. Irrefutably."

"I love you so much, Bram. Do you know how much?"

"A bushel and a peck, a hug around the neck?"

"Exactly. You took the words right out of my mouth." Brigetta kissed him until linens were the last things on their minds. Bram raced down the hill to get back to the workers who awaited him.

Finally, the day arrived. Bram and Brigetta headed for town at least an hour before any train had been known to arrive. Brigetta could no longer wait at home, and Bram knew Reason was not a welcome guest in their home at that point. But he had to admit he, too, was eager to see their families.

"We'll have to remember to show them the greenhouse, the sewing machine, the piano and radio, and where you planted the tulips. Oh, I wish the tulips were still in bloom."

"It's asking a lot of tulips to bloom this long into June," Bram pulled Brigetta close in a bone-crushing hug to calm her and because his love for her was so intense it hurt.

"And Chum—oh, I hope they like Chum!"

"Who could not like Chum?"

"That's true—even the patients who don't talk to me like Chum."

"There are patients who don't talk to you?" Bram teased. "I find that hard to believe! I've seen you charm even the most sullen man in the fields into smiling at you!"

"I mean the ones I really have to pump to get to talk to me. They really aren't sullen. They're a lot like Mama used to be. They need a lot of love."

Bram's vision blurred. "No one like you has ever landed in Rochester, Brigetta."

At the depot, Brigetta literally bounced in place when a whistle blew in the distance. She clutched Bram's arm until he feared she would puncture his skin. The deafening noise of grinding brakes, the pungent odors unique to steam engines, the pushing and shoving as friends and relatives strained to get just closer to where people would spill out of the cars and across the platform—such was the adventure of meeting the train. But meeting relatives coming for their first visit was one notch beyond heaven for Brigetta.

Bram, with a flash of sadness, realized afresh how much Brigetta had given up. He wondered if those arriving would see secrets revealed in their eyes, shouted in all they could not say. The sight of his own mother banished introspection and Rebecca swept him into her arms, kissing him over and over, her characteristic Dutch restraint tossed to the four winds.

Just inches away, four arms caught Brigetta in a web of hugs as strong as any spider's snare. Tears streamed down Hanna and *Tante* Lena's faces as they alternately hugged her and held her at arm's length exclaiming, "You look so grown up! Such a lady! Look at you with your hair pulled up! Look, Gustave! Our Brigetta has become quite the married lady!"

Brigetta pulled away only to throw herself into Gustave's arms. "Oh, Papa—I'm not so grown up as all that! I'm still your little girl, but with my hair on top of my head instead of dangling around my neck. See?" With that, she yanked out the pins and shook her head. Her contagious laughter filled their hearts as her curls tumbled free.

The old Brigetta was back again—the child skating against the wind; the bride lifting her bride's basket high in the churchyard; the wife singing with her husband in the garden. While her voice blew life back into their memories, Bram ducked to pick up satchels, hoping to hide his tears.

It was a marvelous three days together. Seven voices sent *Psalmen* wafting through open windows, down Tulip Hill and across the meadows because Brigetta insisted each meal's closing prayer be sung. "You can't imagine how puny two voices sound, wrapped around the notes of songs that should lift the birds out of their nests! We simply *must* sing every single chance while you're here!" Every minute was filled with talk or singing, food, more talk, more songs, more food—and always the words, "You've just got to see…" followed by another trip down the hill, or up the stairs, or across the meadow or out into the yard.

Early in the morning on the second day of the visit, Brigetta sat up in bed with a start. "Bram, wake up! Let's take a breakfast picnic out to the quarry. Can you imagine how beautiful our voices will sound echoing back to us from the rocky cliffs?"

Bram rolled over and leaned on one elbow, blinking sleepily. "Huh?"

"We'll have hard-boiled eggs and biscuits with ham..." She was already out the door, her dressing gown flapping behind her. Bram flopped back on the bed, grinning. *It does sound like fun!*

Within an hour, the rest of the household had awakened. Bram and Brigetta remained secretive about everything except that they were having a breakfast picnic. "Just wait until you see where we're taking you!" Brigetta bubbled.

The trek roused appetites and curiosity. When they reached the turn leading to the first magnificent view of the white-gold limestone and time-carved cliffs, Bram paused to let them all gather as a group. The sun filtered through the leafy trees and reflected off the rocks in welcome. Brigetta's laugh echoed back at them while the five visitors gaped and gasped at the beauty before them. Without prompting, Gustave reverently began to sing *Psalmen 121*. Brigetta's eyes filled with happy tears as she added her clear voice to the others.

In the chicken house at the State Hospital, Marguerite thrust her hand beneath a hen just as the most amazing thing occurred. A choir of angels—through the woods from up in the quarry—burst into song. She understood not one word, but stood enthralled by the rich harmony wrapping itself around the words: *I will lift up my eyes to the hills—where does my help come from?*

Benjamin had just flung open the door to the hayloft, with his fellow worker, Anthony, behind him ready to send the first load of hay down to the cows waiting below. They were startled by the sounds of singing coming through the treetops straight at them. The two men looked at each other in amazement. "What do you suppose it is?" Benjamin whispered.

"A heavenly choir, most likely." Anthony swallowed hard.

In the sleeping quarters, patients still in their beds—having been watched through the night by the One who neither slumbers nor sleeps—awoke to majestic music.

Doctor Gray paused on his walk across the fields from his home. Unconsciously, he matched his stride to the strains he imagined he heard only in his mind, intrigued by what he could not translate: *The Lord watches over you.*

And those on the hillside finished off the words of the ancient Psalm with confident voices. While harmonies lingered in the sunlit morning, Gustave repeated the final verse reverently: *The Lord will keep you from harm—he will watch over your life; the Lord will watch over your coming and going both now and forevermore.*

On the rim of the quarry, Brigetta shook out blankets and spread the breakfast picnic before her family and their voices and laughter bounced back to them from the rocky cliffs while they ate.

On the second evening, having consumed prodigious quantities of food, Hanna said lazily, "I'm so stuffed I don't see how I could possibly move, but Brigetta—how about taking a walk with your Mama? Just the two of us."

Brigetta's heart pounded in her throat. She dared not look at Bram, knowing he sensed her fear, though not fully knowing the reason. "I'll get our shawls."

Mother and daughter walked almost as far as the cemetery in companionable silence before Hanna spoke. "So, Sweet Pea. How is it, being Mrs. Bram de Boer?"

Brigetta reached for Hanna's hand, entwining their fingers as they walked along. "It was horrid when I wrote you that letter, but you were right. To come home would not have solved anything."

"You seem quite happy. Are you play-acting while we're here, or is it real?"

"It's real—I must admit, the letter you wrote back was a great disappointment to me at first, but it was full of wisdom. You are so wise—love *is* a decision. I had to figure out what things I did back when I loved Bram and then begin to do them again as if I did love him. *That* felt like play-acting, but before I knew it, one day I realized I wasn't having to pretend anymore—I truly love him again."

"Do you know why you stopped loving him, Sweet Pea?"

"Oh, yes, I know." They walked, arm-in-arm, now. Hanna let silence reign while Brigetta sifted through her thoughts. "We had a shock—something Bram and I have agreed not to speak of. I cannot violate that, even for you, Mama."

"Nor would I want you to. I just want to be sure you are aware of what caused the problem so you can be alert if it were to return."

"It will not return, I assure you," Brigetta said fervently. "A problem of that nature is once in a lifetime."

Hanna's eyebrows arched at her daughter's passion, but she said nothing. *She's still our Brigetta—a sense of drama in every word!*

"Our love is renewed and even more precious."

"Your Papa and I love you and Bram from the bottom of our hearts—nothing can change that."

"I know, Mama," Brigetta whispered and led the way home.

*   *   *

February 20, 1921
Dearest Brigetta,
Please accept my invitation to the first annual "Moonlight Skate of Remembrance." We will begin a tradition tonight in tribute to hard times survived, and in anticipation of good times to be cherished. I want no partner but you.

With love, your Bram

May 1924—May 1927

◆

When tulips bloomed, Brigetta loved to meet Bram halfway home and soak up the sights of the riotous color overtaking their senses the closer they got to Tulip Hill. Tonight, with the sun sinking in the west just as the moon was rising, and the tulips picking up new hues in the fading light, they lingered for what Brigetta called *Ooooh and Ahhhh* time much longer than planned, stopping also to admire their newest anniversary tree. They picked up their pace across the meadow as they headed to the hospital for a play the patients were presenting.

"I know we can always borrow one, Bram, but do you ever wish we had brought our buggy from the farm?" Brigetta said wistfully as they walked along.

"Yes, I do. In fact, the last time I was in town, I stopped by the Willys-Overland Service Motor Company on Fourth Street."

"They have buggies?"

Bram smiled, "No, but let me show you something." He slowed and pulled a folded paper out of his pocket. "This is one of the automobiles Cornelis used to talk about." She leaned closer and stared at a Coles Phillips' advertisement for a 1916 Overland Roadster and gasped.

Brigetta read aloud with as much drama as the actors they would soon see: "*Exacting, appreciative, practical, hard-headed America has, as one unit, O.K.'d the small, light, economical, $615 Overland. They like its style; its good-looking lines; that smart, individual air of exclusiveness.*

306

They like its power and pep. It shoots up a hill like a streak of greased lightning. It gives, but seldom gets, the dust." She halted and looked up at Bram, wide-eyed.

"Keep reading. Mister Olson ripped this out of an old magazine when he saw it because he has one on the lot that belonged to a fellow who just bought a new one."

"*Give her a little gas and away she flies—free from vibration, rattle, stress or strain. Solid comfort. This car, unlike most of the smaller and popular priced makes, has none of that stiffness or rigidness about it. Deep, soft, divan upholstery and shock absorbing cantilever springs take all the stiffness out and put all the comfort in.*"

"Isn't that something? *Shoots up hills, soft upholstery!*"

"*Large tires (four-inch) also add materially to the riding qualities of the car. It's the little conveniences that seem to have the broadest appeal. The electric control buttons on the steering column, convenient foot pedals and shifting levers bring everything within everyone's reach—even the price.*"

"Can't you just see yourself sitting behind the wheel like the woman in the picture?"

"Me?" Brigetta stared at the carefree lady in a green brimmed hat reaching ever-so-easily to touch the *electric control buttons*, her high-top stylish white leather button boots resting ever-so-lightly on the *convenient foot pedal* and her scarf blowing in the breeze. She frowned. "I'd have to get a hat that wouldn't blow off."

Bram whooped with laughter. "Come on, Brigetta, we'll have to run now or we'll be late."

Sitting in the dark room during the first act of the play, Brigetta leaned over and whispered, "Who would teach us to drive?"

"I will. I know how to drive a tractor."

During the second act, Brigetta nudged Bram. "It's much more money than a buggy," she whispered sadly.

"We have more than enough for the car and your new hat." A smile twitched his lips.

During the intermission, Brigetta said, "Let me see that paper again." While others milled about, greeting friends and congratulating actors, she memorized details from an eight-year-old magazine about the car *O.K.'d by the Nation*.

Brigetta wiggled throughout the whole third act while Bram sat, fully aware of all that raced in his wife's pretty head. When the final applause began, she nudged him. "We could go look at it. Maybe sit in it, and you could drive it a little ways so at least you could say you've driven an automobile, and then we can forget about it."

Bram nodded solemnly. "Okay, tomorrow. We'll just look. Maybe drive up and down Fourth Street. And then we'll forget about it. Besides, someday it would need new tires, and that would be even more money."

"Someday I'll need new shoes, too," Brigetta snapped. "That's hardly a reason not to buy a fine automobile at a good price. You didn't decide not to marry me because I would require upkeep!"

"You're probably right. Especially since it is even cheaper than the advertisement says: it's nearly eight years old."

"Bram!" Brigetta squealed and stood with her hands on her hips, a picture of an indignant housewife. "How much less?"

"Oh, about half!"

It was Brigetta's turn to hoot with delight. She flung her arms around Bram and pulled him into a frenzied dance right there in the auditorium aisle. "We're going to have an automobile! Wouldn't Cornelis be surprised?"

"I almost wish I could tell him, don't you?"

"Yes, I do."

They walked home slowly in the moonlight, feasting on the stars, savoring the nearness of the one each loved best in the entire world. "I'm glad it's a 1916 model. That was a good year in our lives."

Brigetta smiled in the darkness and squeezed Bram's arm. "It's the year I bought your berries!"

"I'll never forget." Bram stopped in the path along side the woods and pulled his favorite berry customer into a breath-taking embrace and kiss that mined her soul.

The next morning, they caught a ride into town. After walking around the Roadster several times, they climbed in and grinned at each other, and then drove it up and down Fourth Street three times. Back at the lot, Brigetta caressed the shiny bonnet as Bram examined the headlights. "It would be a shame to not buy this, wouldn't it? I mean, it's quite stylish and a good price. Maybe this automobile could be part of our dreams."

"Perhaps. If you're sure you wouldn't rather have a buggy..." His words were muffled by a hug that shot him from the grassy automobile lot in Rochester right to the edge of heaven.

And so began the adventure of Bram teaching Brigetta how to drive. Before they returned home, she insisted on stopping by the milliner's to buy a hat exactly like the one pictured in the advertisement. "Now I'm ready to drive!" she announced.

Bram climbed behind the wheel of the de Boer's first automobile. "Watch what I do..." The ride home was Lesson One.

When Bram came home for lunch the next day, he was surprised to see the Roadster sitting in the middle of the tulips at the bottom of Tulip Hill. It was equally amazing to find a subdued and flushed Brigetta busily making their lunch, with her usual companion, Chum, nowhere in sight.

Lunch was accompanied by only the briefest of conversation until Bram ventured to say, "I noticed our automobile parked among the tulips."

Brigetta promptly burst into tears. "You might as well take it back and say we've changed our minds. I can drive a buggy just fine, and that's what I plan to do from now on."

Carefully, Bram weighed his words. "Did you have some problems?"

310   R o u g h   T e r r a i n

Sobbing, Brigetta admitted, "Chum won't even ride with me. He leaped from the seat beside me like I was a felon intent on killing him. I had to swerve to avoid running over him and that's when I destroyed hundreds of your prize tulips. I hate that Roadster! Return it and get our money back. All I ever wanted was a buggy like we have back home."

"Brigetta, my love, you've only had one lesson! It took me several weeks before I felt comfortable behind the wheel of a tractor. I'll bring the Roadster back up to the top of the hill, and tonight we'll have Lesson Two. And tomorrow, Lesson Three. If you just give it time, you'll be a fine driver; you'll see."

Brigetta's breath came out in uneven gulps. "I'm just afraid I'll kill someone. If you had been in my way when I was driving today? You'd be dead. Smashed as flat as the tulips."

"We'll have lessons, and you'll do fine," Bram promised. Brigetta pushed back her chair and came around to sit on his lap. Bram got back to work a bit late that afternoon because comforting a new driver can take some time.

*   *   *

It was a bright December day when Bram called from the back door, "Brigetta, put your coat on! There's something you simply must see!"

She came flying out of the bedroom. "What's wrong, Bram? It's not nearly lunch time and you're home?"

"I have a wonderful surprise for you!" Bram stood in the kitchen doorway, holding a gunnysack with strange bumps.

Donning full winter regalia, Brigetta stuck her hand in Bram's and skidded down the steep path beside him. "We're walking?"

"It's not far—just to the meadow across from the cemetery," Bram answered mysteriously.

All Brigetta could see was a wall of snow. Then, she noticed the wall of snow was in a huge circle. And finally, that the wall encircled a sheet of ice. "A skating rink! Bram, how simply glorious!"

Bram pulled their ice skates out of the gunnysack. Within minutes, the de Boers were lost in memories on the ice. They had skated for nearly half an hour before Brigetta asked, "How can this be? The creek isn't up here in the meadow!"

"It's a matter of weather cooperating with man's efforts to create a lake! I had a lot of help from the patients."

"You're an amazing man; we are going to skate every day until it melts!" Brigetta declared ardently.

Word spread, and patients joined Bram and Brigetta on the ice. Bram may have surprised his wife with a skating rink, but she matched him the day a patient who played fiddle provided skating music. After the first notes flew from beneath the man's fingers, Bram dropped to one knee. "Brigetta de Boer, will you skate with me?" It mattered little that no river sang beneath the ice—the moment banished all thoughts but those born along the Floyd River, years ago.

The ice rink was a popular place. Brigetta hurried through her household chores and raced across the snowy field to the skating rink. She taught some patients how to do figure-eights and others how to stand without toppling. It was Brigetta being Brigetta, enchanting everyone she met.

With the long winter evenings, the patients needed entertainment. Doctor Gray remembered two voices blending in perfect harmony around the notes of a poignant song. So began the singing, with patients and staff gathering around the piano on Monday evenings. There was a sign-up sheet for performers, with the only requirement being a willingness to sing—no spectators on Monday nights!

Whoever came formed duets, trios, quartets—finding songs to sing from the favorites of the day: *Ma—He's Making Eyes at Me* and *Toot, Toot, Tootsie, Goodbye!* and *Who's Sorry Now?* When requests came for

The Man I Love, Brigetta would slide across the piano bench, signal Mrs. Gray to take her place, and sing that song as a solo, with wild applause following each time.

Once over their shock of having someone as vivacious as Brigetta taking a personal interest in them, the patients loved music—singing, whistling, and humming, and many played musical instruments with great skill. Music, as the staff well knew, was good therapy. Brigetta worked hard to find songs to match voices and instruments, and invited those individuals up to the house to practice *My Rambler Rose* or *Three O'clock in the Morning* or *Yes! We have no bananas* or *What'll I do?* The results of all the Monday evenings around the piano needed an outlet. And so began the official We Sing Evenings, aptly named by the patients.

Granted, sometimes the scheduled performers failed to arrive, having been placed in restraints for their own and others' protection. Or they arrived, but denied ever having sung before in their lives, or insisted that a particular song—one practiced for days by another patient—was their particular property, or refusing to allow another patient to sing with them. It required quick wit and wisdom on the part of hospital staff to handle these problems and prevent violence from erupting, but Brigetta persevered to solve each patient's earth-shattering dilemma, sooth each wounded spirit, and put on a show that brought much enjoyment to all.

It was during a hurried supper on a We Sing Evening when Chum growled and his ears shot up. "What is it, Chum?" Bram asked idly. Usually, a deer coming down the hillside to feed brought out the guard-dog in Chum; they had learned to ignore many of his warnings.

But within seconds, a knock at the back door startled Bram and Brigetta and put Chum on full alert. "It must be someone Chum doesn't know," Brigetta whispered.

Bram pushed his chair back from the table and walked to the door, Chum instantly moving between his master and the unknown. Bram opened the door and the cool night air rushed in.

"Who is it, Bram?" Brigetta asked, worry mounting with Bram's unbroken silence.

"It's...Cornelis."

"Hello." The voice in the darkness sent an icy torrent rushing through Brigetta's veins. "I'm sorry to arrive unannounced, but..."

Brigetta crossed the room slowly. "Come in. Don't mind Chum; he'll come around once he knows you're..." She let her words fade, not sure *once he knows you're welcome here* was appropriate. But neither brother noticed the incomplete sentence as they stood, eyes boring into eyes.

Brigetta shut the door. "Have you eaten? We've plenty left. We're heading off soon to a musical performance if you'd like to join us."

"I don't mean to interrupt. I didn't give you any warning, but I wasn't sure if I'm welcome here."

"Have a bite to eat, and then come with us. You'll enjoy it. Won't he, Bram?" Brigetta's voice pulled Bram back to the present.

"Yes, come eat, and then we'll go. Every couple of weeks, the patients at the hospital put on a show Brigetta helps them organize. They're quite proficient at singing."

"I guess I'd like that. I just came in on the evening train, so your supper smells awfully good to me."

"It's just plain Dutch food, but will satisfy your appetite."

"How did you know where to find us?" Bram asked.

"I'm heading back home to Chicago from Dutchville. I wanted to see family once again. Mother and Father were also surprised to see me. They told me you moved here."

The air sizzled with unspoken words and thoughts.

"We came four years ago."

Cornelis laughed a little too loud. "I was surprised to hear you'd left the farm."

"Not *left*," Brigetta interjected, "just taking time off. Bram is learning so much here—when we go back home, he'll be the best farmer of northwest Iowa!"

"Father says you're getting quite an education here."

"It's a good place to work, but we'll go back to Dutchville some day."

"You haven't been back home? Mother says you left the same summer I did."

"No, we haven't been back. With the turmoil the country has endured, it has seemed best to save our money. Mother and Father, and Brigetta's parents and *Tante* Lena came to see us several years ago, though."

An awkward silence ensued. "You'll never guess what sits in our buggy barn, Cornelis—an Overland Roadster!" Brigetta said.

The brothers enjoyed a few moments of teasing and boasting about the qualities of that automobile until Brigetta gasped, "Oh, no! The program!" The Roadster definitely proved it could raise dust as they rushed off Tulip Hill and across the meadow, with Bram calling out landmarks they passed.

Bram and Cornelis sat side-by-side during the We Sing Evening. Bram sang one duet with Brigetta, and Brigetta sang one solo, but the rest of the program featured the patients and staff and was a delightful way to spend an evening that could have been most awkward. Cornelis praised Brigetta at its close, "I don't know when I've enjoyed an evening more! I'll have to tell my wife about it."

"You're married?" Bram asked, stunned. *What havoc one dreadful day levied that I wouldn't know such a thing.*

"Yes, and I have two children—two girls, one is just two, and the other born this autumn."

Bram and Brigetta's minds shouted: *You also have a four-year-old son, born February 20, 1920.*

The evening was at the stage where it should end. Brigetta bridged the gap. "Have you taken a room in Rochester, Cornelis?"

"No," he said sheepishly, "I came directly out to see you—I caught a ride with several others who were coming to the hospital. Will it be a problem to find a room at this late hour?"

Brigetta blocked out Bram's grim look. "Not at all—you can stay in our spare room."

And so it was two brothers who had been separated for years by shameful deeds and hateful thoughts slept once again beneath the same roof. Brigetta held Bram in her arms until he fell asleep, and then calmed him when he woke in the middle of the night in a sweat. She spent the night swamped by memories.

After breakfast—a fine Dutch breakfast straight out of Brigetta's *Tante Lena Book*—Cornelis said goodbye to Brigetta.

"Do you still hate me?" Cornelis asked as Bram drove him to the train depot.

"I have begun to forgive, as has Brigetta."

Cornelis watched the boardwalk fill with passengers awaiting the train to Chicago. "I am so sorry for that day. I have often wished it had never happened. Do you think of it, still?"

"Yes, with deep sorrow." *Every February 20.* "But we are rebuilding our lives. I hope you are, too."

"Yes, my wife knows nothing of that day, but I will tell her when I return home—it is important that she know the truth about why we have been estranged." In an awkward moment, the brothers stood and faced each other until Bram made the first move and stretched out his arms. No words were exchanged, but tears blurred their eyes as the two men rocked in place. The train rumbled into the station and within minutes, Cornelis was just a wave and a face in the window and Bram turned towards the Roadster.

In the House on Tulip Hill, Brigetta opened a box that contained dotted Swiss fabric with pattern pieces still folded within it, and sewed a new dress to symbolize her hope for the future. When Bram came home from the fields, Brigetta wore that dress and a subtle look of resolve: it was a new day, it was time to move completely beyond the past. Cornelis had reappeared in their lives and the brothers had not come to blows.

She had to believe somewhere in the world one special four-year-old boy lived a good life, filled with love.

*   *   *

Bram and Brigetta felt giddy as they watched Rochester disappear behind them: they were returning to Dutchville for a week-long visit. They would stay in Brigetta's old room in the parsonage since their small house was home to Hans' current hired man. "And I want to soak up absolutely everything Dutch about the town—we have become quite *unDutch*, Bram, and we must remedy that!"

He tweaked her nose. "Mrs. de Boer, I intend to purchase a new pair of *klompen*, and hope to eat only *vet and stroop* each morning for breakfast, and I will sing loudest of all for each and every *Psalmen*—can you beat those plans?"

"Hmmm, let's see. I plan to buy yards and yards of Dutch lace and two pairs of *klompen*, and will beg *Tante* Lena to fix anything with Dutch sausage in it since that's what I most dearly miss in Rochester. And I will not only sing louder than you in church, I will speak only Dutch once my foot hits Iowa soil!"

The first morning at breakfast, *Tante* Lena served rusk pancakes and sausage. Even though she had nothing but praise for the meal, Brigetta ate half of what was on her plate and fled from the table to the newly installed bathroom on the second floor. Gustave, Hanna, and *Tante* Lena looked quizzically at Bram. He shrugged. "She'll be fine when her stomach settles; it was a rough and dusty train ride." He grinned. "She's excited to be home!"

Brigetta and Bram visited friends, soaked up Dutch sounds from the old men who smoked pipes by the town square windmill, and admired the gardens under *Tante* Lena and Rebecca's care.

Mary Huitink, who was now Mrs. Mathijs van Steenwyk having married her stuffy old banker two years ago, invited them for an evening of visiting. Mathijs, Bram and Brigetta discovered, was not stuffy at all and only ten years older than his wife. Bram and Mathijs discovered a shared interest in woodcarving. Mary and Brigetta's conversation filled the evening until Mary served *Schoenlappers Taart.*

"This is marvelous, Mary!" Brigetta said dreamily. "Brown Betty is the best reason to allow a few pieces of bread to turn stale!"

"It hardly ever happened at home with all of us children. But with just the two of us, I find I can make a batch almost every week! We hope to have a family soon, so I tell Mathijs to enjoy *Schoenlappers Taart* while he can because with children to feed, there will be little bread left to get stale!" She asked casually, "Will you and Bram start a family soon, Brigetta? You've been married much longer than we have!"

"Only God knows," Brigetta hedged.

"Please forgive such a personal question—I know how I hate it when the old Dutch wives watch my belly to see if it is growing!"

"Nonsense, we're friends. And that's one thing that doesn't happen in Rochester—there are no Dutch wives around except for me!" she said, effectively diverting their conversation. "That's one thing I truly miss."

The next afternoon, Brigetta sprawled on her old bed, claiming she needed a nap after staying so late at Mary and Mathijs' home. She listened to the voices of her family and Bram in the parlor below and let the tears flow. She remembered lying in this very bed, sure then she was dying at the brink of womanhood. Today, she would give anything to discover those same bloodstains so frightening fourteen years before.

Truth thrust its head through the crust of her denial: she was pregnant. There would be no sitting on Papa's lap for comfort this time. There would be no consolation from *Tante* Lena. There would be no conversation with Mary about the wonders of a woman's body.

No, this was a road she had been down before with fearsome results. Together, she and Bram had worked hard to rebuild their marriage after the devastation of her first pregnancy. *Can our marriage survive a second onslaught?*

Suddenly, the most horrendous realization broke through the fog and she cried out in anguish. With Bram the certain father of this child, could he also have fathered the child left behind in Minneapolis? *To have given up a child on the basis of suppositions—can there be forgiveness for this?*

All the pain and loss of the past six years descended upon Brigetta until she could not move. Tears flowed and sobs wracked her body, sobs she buried in her pillow. She heard Bram's footfall on the stairs and his words, "I'll check to see if she's awake yet," and feigned sleep. She would have to face him and their families soon enough, but now she desired nothing more than solitude.

The remaining days of their visit required great skills on Brigetta's part to dodge questions. *It is almost as if I am in one of the patients' plays—acting the part of a woman pretending to have no cares. I know all the lines, I correctly interpret all the actions—and the audience is convinced.*

Once she saw Dutchville's fleeting landscape through the train window, she allowed her play-acting to end. "Remember our promise to keep our home free from sad conversations?"

"Yes, but certainly I'll understand how sad you must be after a visit with our families. Our intent with that promise was merely to avoid saying things that would haunt us long after they were said."

Brigetta nodded. "That's why we need to talk—on the train, before we reach Rochester. We have a problem, Bram."

"I know, and I understand. After seeing Dutchville again, you want to move back, am I right? We will, someday, Brigetta—I promise. Father agrees we should stay in Rochester for a few more years since it has been such a good experience and he is still able to farm."

She lifted grief-stricken eyes. "Remember when I was sick that first morning at breakfast? It wasn't from something I ate, Bram. I'm pregnant. As best I can tell, I'm over two months along."

Bram sucked in his breath. Fortunately, there was no one in the seat nearest them. The conductor collected tickets throughout the whole car before Bram spoke. "I'm not even going to ask you if you're sure."

"Do you realize what this means?" Brigetta asked with heated passion.

"I trust you fully, so I must be the father. It is such a shock to suddenly realize the problem Doc Draayer feared...oh, no," he whispered. "Oh please, God, no."

Brigetta gulped in a huge breath of air, like one drowning. "It is almost too horrific to contemplate, isn't it, Bram? What if we gave up a child of our love?" she whispered with a voice that shook and cracked.

Bram clenched and unclenched his hands. The ticket stubs over their seats seemed to mock him: Rochester. The place they had moved to on false suppositions. A sob rose and he choked it back.

For the next hour, Bram sat stone-faced, unmoving. His eyes were closed, and except for twitching muscles, Brigetta could have assumed he was asleep. But she knew better—Bram was experiencing the torment she had felt lying in her old bed in the parsonage. *What if? Why? What now?*

Brigetta touched Bram's hand. She craved comfort in the dark cave of recrimination, but found none in her husband. His hand was cold and unresponsive. He was lost in self-reproach and anguish.

Station after station was announced; people moved through the car in random fashion, laughing and talking, shifting luggage, finding and relinquishing seats. All such normal activities except for the couple who shared a most terrible fact: they were parents of a child they would never hold.

Bram wordlessly enclosed Brigetta in his arms. "I have wished ever since the day you left Rochester I had been man enough to bring you back home. Maybe God is giving us another chance in this child. We will love this child enough for both babies," he said, at last.

Back in Rochester, they went through the motions of a marriage: inquiring about each other's day, sharing tidbits of garden news, asking advice on plans for the evening, talking of shared friends. But it was all hollow and unsatisfying. Despite the fact this baby brought no shame with it, it was difficult to rejoice. Brigetta knew she should write letters to their families to share the news, but she had no desire even to address the envelopes.

Brigetta remembered Katie den Hartog—large with child—and how Antonie looked at her with such love that long-ago Christmas in Dutchville. Brigetta longed for that same love, but Bram was so fraught with hurt, anger, despair, and anguish that he had nothing left to give his wife.

Finally, Brigetta could bear it no longer. She knew Bram chastised himself endlessly for all that had transpired, but she feared it was something more keeping them from knowing some of the pleasure new parents should enjoy. "Bram, do you still love me?" she asked over lunch one day when scarcely ten words had passed between them.

His look wrenched her heart. "Yes. More than ever, realizing all you gave up because of my stubborn pride—and haven't turned against me. You are far more than I deserve, Brigetta, far more. Yes, I love you."

"A bushel and a peck, a hug around the neck?" she asked with enough poignancy shading their long-forgotten ritual to jerk him out of his despondency.

"That much and more," he responded and reached for her hand across the table.

"Please don't be distant from me, Bram. It reminds me too much of the first time. I need to start feeling happy about this baby or I am afraid I will become like Mama."

"I'm sorry—I am thinking too much of the first time myself. We must learn to celebrate the blessing of our new baby—a gift from God."

That night, Brigetta wrote of the anticipated April 1927 arrival of a grandchild for the recipients of the letters. Two households in Dutchville would resonate with rejoicing, and perhaps it would move back across the state border to infuse Bram and Brigetta.

One November evening, Bram told Brigetta, "I must go to Minneapolis on the morning train, but I will be back tomorrow night." He knew she assumed it was a business trip and said nothing to correct that notion.

Brigetta spent the day playing the piano, and then sat in her rocker and read poetry. With Chum at her feet, she made lists of names she carried in her pocket, standing on the back porch and calling out across the hillside, "Bartolomeus de Boer, suppertime!" *That has possibilities.* "Dirk de Boer! Come home!" *Sounds like I'm calling the poor child "dirt"!* She crossed that name off the list. "Maarta de Boer! Come in for supper!" *Would a little girl like the name Maarta, or is it only for old ladies?* She added a question mark beside it. "Sanna de Boer! Sanna! Time to eat!" *Sanna's such a happy-sounding name!*

As Brigetta called out names, Bram stood on another porch in Minneapolis—just as he had years ago with his scared and pregnant wife. He lifted the doorknocker. Mrs. Thompson appeared, looking no less intimidating. "Hello, I'm Bram de Boer. May I come in?"

The thin lips closed tightly, and the cold eyes narrowed as she recognized her visitor. "You're alone?"

"May I come in? I won't take more than five minutes of your time."

Curiosity tweaked, Mrs. Thompson allowed Bram entrance. Bram was ushered to the parlor, once again, and sat on the settee. "What brings you here?"

"In February 1920, Brigetta had a baby boy here. What became of the child?"

Mrs. Thompson straightened her bony shoulders. "Our records are sealed. We give no information to the adoptive parents, or the natural mother, or her *brother*." One graying eyebrow arched accusingly.

Bram flushed. "I was hoping to contact the adoptive parents."

"I have stated the rules. Will that be all?"

"If the adoptive family were unhappy with the boy, would they notify you?"

Mrs. Thompson gasped. "Unhappy with a healthy baby? Brigetta made the decision to give up a baby conceived in sin and if she now, as I infer from your questions, has changed her mind, she will find no help from me."

"I thank you for your time," Bram said through clenched teeth.

Bram was two blocks away when Mrs. Thompson huffed, "Of all the nerve!" Extracting a thick file from a locked desk drawer, she ran her finger down a list until she found *de Boer, Brigetta. Boy. February 20, 1920. Alfred and Mildred Wilson.* She stared at the words for a full minute, then replaced the file and relocked the drawer.

*   *   *

Two telegrams with identical messages arrived in Dutchville: *Beautiful healthy Sanna Brigetta born April 30. All well.*

June 1927—August 1940

◆

Dear Doctor,

With such a wet and cold spring, 10 to 15 acres could not be put in crop because of standing water. We will plant soybeans when it dries up so we can work the ground.

We planted about 124 acres of silage corn in June. We also planted 20 acres of sweet corn, ½ acre each of head lettuce, radishes, beets and dill, 20 acres soybeans, 1 acre each of rutabagas, carrots, eggplant, and peppers, 3 acres mid-season cabbage and, 2,500 more tomato plants.

The potatoes have been sprayed twice and are looking good. The corn, which we planted early, is looking fine. The grain looks healthy. We also hauled 92 loads of alfalfa hay into the cow barn and put up 29 loads of June grass, timothy and clover hay. The livestock look fine and we have plenty of pasture.

Sincerely, Bram de Boer, Steward

*   *   *

Dear Mama and Papa and Tante Lena,

Sanna grows like a weed! Bram says if we found her in our garden, we'd have to pull her out! They are such a joy to watch together—Sanna rides on Bram's shoulders and pulls his ears when we go for walks. I'm sure he'll tell you much more in his part of this letter.

We've wondered whether her first word would be Mama or Papa. Imagine how we laughed last night when she pointed an index finger at each of us and clearly said, "Chum!" If we hadn't been so delighted, I'm sure we would have been quite insulted!

Your loving children and grandchild, Brigetta, Bram, and Sanna

*   *   *

Dearest Brigetta,

Please be my partner tonight for our tenth annual "Moonlight Skate of Remembrance." Each February 20 reminds me that I want only you in my arms.

Your devoted Bram

*   *   *

Dear Mother and Father,

You'll soon be here! Don't forget to bring your Sinterklaas cape, Father! Sanna is worried that as the only Dutch child in Rochester, she'll set out her klompen in vain. She is the envy of her classmates, getting to celebrate for a full month.

I'm glad you'll be able to see her skate—Bram says she has the same grace on the ice his Grandfather de Boer had, and she certainly skates circles around me. No need to bring skates—we can borrow from the hospital. Skating is a favorite winter sport ever since Bram made the first rink years ago.

Bram is much beloved at the Rochester State Hospital. Even though we had planned to return to the farm long ago, this is a good place to be if we can't be with our own.

Your loving children and grandchild, Brigetta, Bram, and Sanna

P.S. Father, in one poorly producing field here, I planted buckwheat and then tilled it back into the soil and let the field stand fallow over the winter.

Production in that field increased the next season. You might try this with the east field next spring. Bram

*   *   *

Dear Doctor,
We plowed up an old alfalfa field that suffered winterkill and put in about 18 acres of late potatoes for a total of about 120 acres. All look good except the very first planting of about 25 acres that seems to be a poor stand.

We also put in about 15 acres into Sudan grass on the alfalfa field that was plowed up. This is for hay or pasture. It is very poor weather for making hay, as it seems to be impossible to get it dry. We have put up about 151 loads of alfalfa, 12 loads of sweet clover in the barn and about 20 ton in stacks.

Sincerely, Bram de Boer, Steward

*   *   *

Dear Mama and Papa and Tante Lena,
Thank you for the pretty Dutch dresses for Sanna's birthday. She would wear them all day if I let her. She is quite the little Dutch girl.

We are teaching her simple Dutch words and phrases, and she sings parts of the Psalmen with us at meals, but she will learn by leaps and bounds when she spends this summer in Dutchville! Please show her all the special places on the farm Bram loved when he was a child—she is fascinated with our early lives. I'll send money for the wooden shoemaker to fit her with new klompen.

I truly love my new Kalamazoo porcelain stove! Ask Bram's mother to show you her October 1934 issue of The Farmer's Wife *magazine. My stove is just like the one in the advertisement!*

Your loving children and grandchild, Brigetta, Bram, and Sanna

*   *   *

Dear Doctor,

We have picked 11,000 quarts of strawberries this year, and as soon as they are through bearing, they will be plowed up and late cabbages planted. We have in about 18,000 tomato plants that look very good. The total planting of sweet corn is about 24 acres. We have planted about 4½ acres of beans, 2 acres each of late peas and squash, 1½ acre each of lima beans, watermelons, and muskmelon, 3 acres of cucumbers, and 1/6 acre of celery.

Sincerely, Bram de Boer, Steward

*   *   *

Dear Grandfather and Grandmother Ter Hoorn and Tante Lena:

I love the books you sent that my Mama used to read. I will take good care of them like she did. I found a flower pressed in one of them that Mama says is from Grandmother's garden. Don't you think I am doing a good job with my cursive writing?

Love your granddaughter, Sanna Brigetta de Boer

*   *   *

Dear Doctor,

All the young cattle on pasture look very good. The dairy herd also looks fine. The sheep have been sheared and we have about 1,000 pounds of wool. One colt was born and is a very fine one.

The corn looks very good. There is some washout from heavy rains and it has been hard to keep cultivated on account of the weather. The small grain looks good, heavy in some places.

Sincerely, Bram de Boer, Steward

*   *   *

February 20, 1939
Dearest Brigetta,
Please accept my invitation to our "Moonlight Skate of Remembrance"
tonight. Just knowing you'll be in the circle of my arms throughout our
lives is God's best gift.
With love, your Bram

*   *   *

Dear Grandparents,
Today, in honor of Mama and Papa's wedding anniversary, we planted
another tree on the hillside. The first ones that they planted the years
before I was born have grown over my head! I helped dig the hole to plant
this year's tree and Mama says it will soon outgrow me.
The Bram de Boer family will perform "My Blue Heaven" for the hospi-
tal's summer concert. Chum howls when we practice, but I wish you could
hear us!
Love, your granddaughter, Sanna

*   *   *

Dear Mama and Papa and Tante Lena,
Sanna asked today whom she could possibly marry with no Dutchmen
in Rochester. I said long before she needs to worry about that, we'll be back
home and Dutch boys will follow her all over town. Bram said he'll chase
them off with sticks!
Sanna is such help with picking vegetables each evening, watering every
morning, and canning the surplus. She is such a sweet girl—almost a
young lady! She came home from her summer in Dutchville full of stories
of Tante Lena. I grew misty-eyed remembering how I, too, loved her as a
child—and still do!

Our fruit cellar is filled with raspberries, tomatoes and beans. And soon the apples will be ready, so we will be set for the winter.

Lovingly, Brigetta, Bram and Sanna

∗ ∗ ∗

Dear Doctor,

We planted about nine acres of sweet corn in three different plantings and it is coming up. We have about 270 acres of field corn planted. Some of this is coming up and looks good.

Early carrots, beets, onions, radishes, peas and spinach are coming good. We also have a good supply of radishes and spinach. Some of the beans are coming up. We have planted about 15 pounds of asparagus seed to start a new planting next year. We have planted about two acres of peas for canning. Late carrots and beets are planted.

The livestock looks fine. The young stock is all on pasture.

Sincerely, Bram de Boer, Steward

∗ ∗ ∗

Dear Grandparents,

It was wonderful to see you all again! Thank you for the wonderful summer. Every time I come I think it is the best time I've ever spent in Dutchville, and this year is the same—it was wonderful, and not just because I met Derek VanHousen! Papa frowned when I told him I have a boyfriend, but Mama reminded him it's not much different than when she rode her bicycle out to the farm to work in the garden with him.

Mama was surprised at how proficient I have become in Dutch. Derek doesn't realize how lucky he is to live in Dutchville all the time—if I lived there, I would make a point of learning to speak fluent Dutch. He thinks I'm the lucky one to live here. Mama says it's a matter of the grass being greener on the other side of the fence.

Love, your granddaughter, Sanna

*   *   ⋆   *

February 20, 1940
Dearest Brigetta,
You've never said no to my invitation to the traditional "Moonlight Skate of Remembrance," but I know you won't want to miss tonight. It will be a night we'll long remember, I'm promise, because I have a very important question to ask you.
All my love, Bram

*   *   *

February 21, 1940
Dear Doctor Gray,
It is with mixed feelings that I write this letter. I hereby submit notice of my resignation, effective July 1940. My records will provide my replacement with a smooth transition. I have worked as Steward at the Rochester State Hospital for many more years than I originally anticipated and have greatly enjoyed each one.
My wife and daughter join me in saying we will cherish the friendships made here. It is only for family reasons that I make this decision. Thank you for the many kindnesses you and Mrs. Gray have extended to us over the years.
Sincerely, Bram de Boer, Steward

*   *   *

Dear Mother and Father,
It is gracious of you to move to "our" small house and allow us to live in the big house. Sanna is already dreaming of how she plans to arrange her bedroom—she loves the fact it was once her Papa's room!

Bram has met with Doctor Gray several times about his replacement. Since Doctor Gray knows Bram is from Iowa, he plans to run ads in Iowa newspapers and "find a fellow just like you!" he says. Doctor Gray will soon retire, so the perfect replacement for Bram is one of his final goals. He says wonderful things about Bram's work, which makes me proud and helps us both feel the time spent here has been valuable. But soon we will be home, after twenty years away!

Your loving children, Bram, Brigetta, and Sanna

*　　　　　　　　*　　　　　　　　*

August 1940

Doctor Gray's tall body was stooped, but he carried himself with dignity as he crossed the room to meet the next applicant. Something about the young man intrigued him, and he found renewed vigor after a grueling day of interviews.

After a satisfying hour, he said, "I'm sorry to say our time is almost up. I admit, I wondered if we were wasting time when I saw how young you are, but I'm glad I met with you. You are young, given the high level of responsibility accompanying the Steward's position, but certainly not inexperienced. You have proven yourself as a man capable beyond his years—these glowing references attest to that. I'm sorry Mister de Boer couldn't meet with you to answer some of your more technical questions, but as I alluded to earlier, he and his family have already moved back to Dutchville, Iowa, so that his daughter can begin her school year there."

"I can certainly understand that."

Doctor Gray stretched out his long legs and contemplated his shoes in silence. "I'm offering you the position, young man—are you still interested after all you've learned about the Rochester State Hospital?"

"Yes, Sir! I accept with humble gratitude. Thank you, Doctor Gray— I won't let you down. Farming has never been just a hobby for me. Because of my father's handicap, our family's livelihood has rested on my shoulders for years. Even though we have lost our farm in northern Minnesota in order to pay medical bills, my securing this job will assure Father he has taught me well. The house you described sounds wonderful—my parents gave me a home years ago, and now I can return the favor."

"What do you mean?

"My parents were unable to have children, and adopted me as an infant."

"How interesting! Did they know your natural parents?"

"No, we only have one link to my natural mother—a note she insisted be given to whomever adopted me. In it, she begged that at least one of my names be Gustave. So, out of my parents' gratitude to that unknown woman, my name is Alfred Gustave Wilson."

"You have mighty big shoes to fill as you replace Bram de Boer—who also came to us as a young man—but I have a good feeling about you. Twenty years after the first such success—my interview trip to Minneapolis once again reaps a good harvest. Welcome to the staff of the Rochester State Hospital, Mister Wilson!"

Afterword

◆

Combining the histories of two places I have lived and loved has been both a challenge and a delight. In researching the history of our home, that former Rochester State Hospital Steward's house formed the model for The House on Tulip Hill in my mind. I then reconstructed the delightful town of Orange City Iowa into Dutchville and offer this book as my salute to the wonderful Dutchmen who shaped my adolescence.

The Rochester State Hospital is a vital part of Rochester Minnesota's history, though now viewed only on the pages of history and memories. There were both a Steward and a Superintendent at RSH during the time depicted in this novel, but the characters of Bram de Boer and Doctor Gray in *Uncharted Territory* are purely fictional.

I owe much to the employees at both the Minnesota Historical Society and the Olmsted County History Center who assisted me in dusting off the past. While working on this book, I met wonderful people, many of whom are former employees at the Rochester State Hospital. The same kindness they showed to the patients under their care was extended to me with my many questions. Thank you, one and all.

Hadley Hoover

About the Author

◆

Hadley Hoover holds two Masters degrees and works as editor for a national certification board for physicians. She enjoys old houses, train travel, and reading mysteries. Her website at www.hadleyhoover.com keeps readers up-to-date on her past and future titles.